DARK DREAM
SLEEP, MY LOVE

Robert Martin

Introduction by
Gary Warren Niebuhr

Stark House Press • Eureka California

DARK DREAM / SLEEP, MY LOVE

Published by Stark House Press
1315 H Street
Eureka, CA 95501, USA
griffinskye3@sbcglobal.net
www.starkhousepress.com

DARK DREAM
Originally published by Dodd, Mead & Company, Inc., New York, and copyright © 1951 by Robert Martin. Reprinted in paperback by Pocket Books, Inc., New York, 1952.

SLEEP, MY LOVE
Originally published by Dodd, Mead & Company, Inc., New York, and copyright © 1953 by Robert Martin. Reprinted in paperback by Dell Books, Inc., New York, 1954.

This edition copyright © 2024 by Stark House Press. All rights reserved under International and Pan-American Copyright Conventions.

"Jim Bennett, Private Investigator: A Case File" by Gary Warren Niebuhr copyright © 2004 and originally published by *Mystery*File*, issue #43, April 2004; reprinted by permission of the author.

ISBN: 979-8-88601-104-3

Cover design by Jeff Vorzimmer, ¡caliente!design, Austin, Texas
Text design by Mark Shepard, shepgraphics.com
Proofreading by Bill Kelly

PUBLISHER'S NOTE:
This is a work of fiction. Names, characters, places and incidents are either the products of the author's imagination or used fictionally, and any resemblance to actual persons, living or dead, events or locales, is entirely coincidental.
Without limiting the rights under copyright reserved above, no part of this publication may be reproduced, stored, or introduced into a retrieval system or transmitted in any form or by any means (electronic, mechanical, photocopying, recording or otherwise) without the prior written permission of both the copyright owner and the above publisher of the book.

First Stark House Press Edition: October 2024

DARK DREAM

Agency detective Jim Bennett is sent to Wheatville at the request of lawyer Sam Algood. Someone is taking potshots at Allgood on the golf course and he'd like to know who it is. While Bennett is investigating the golfing situation, he is also hired by Pete Donati, owner of Armand's Beauty Salon. Someone is sabotaging his curling process and burning his customer's heads. Between the two cases—and in spite of Allgood's flirtatious wife—Bennett figures to have an easy week of it, wrapping things up in no time. Then he meets the beautiful but scarred Marianne, Donati's wife and the real power behind Armand's. A man might very well murder for her. And in no time at all, someone does.

SLEEP, MY LOVE

Detective Jim Bennett is saddened to hear about his best friends' divorce. He'd grown up with Dan and Kay. On the rebound, Dan marries a goldigger named Louette. It's not a happy marriage. In fact, Dan confesses that he came home early and caught her with another man, and roughed him up. But when he and Dan go back to his apartment, they find Louette with a knife in her chest. And Dan becomes the only suspect. Then Bennett finds himself entangled in another crime when he receives a desperate plea for help from Dan's womanizing boss, Roger Quinn, whose lover is murdered in their hotel room. Both men claim innocence. But the odds are against at least one of them.

Robert Martin Bibliography
(1908-1976)

NOVELS

Jim Bennett series:
Dark Dream (Dodd Mead, 1951; Pocket, 1952).
Sleep, My Love (Dodd Mead, 1953; Dell, 1953)
Tears for the Bride (Dodd Mead, 1954; Bantam, 1955)
The Widow and the Web (Dodd Mead, 1954; Bantam, 1955)
Just a Corpse at Twilight (Dodd Mead, 1955)
Catch a Killer (Dodd Mead, 1956; abridged in
  Mercury Mystery Book Magazine)
Hand-Picked for Murder (Dodd Mead, 1957)
Killer Among Us (Dodd Mead, 1958; Detective Book Club, 1959)
A Key to the Morgue (Dodd Mead, 1959; Detective Book Club, 1959;
  Ace, 1960)
To Have and To Kill (Dodd Mead, 1960; Ace, 1961, abridged)
She, Me and Murder (Hale UK, 1962; Curtis, 1971)
A Coffin for Two (Hale UK, 1962; Curtis, 1972)
Bargain for Death (Hale UK, 1964, Curtis, 1972)

Standalone Mystery:
The Echoing Shore (Dodd Mead, 1955; Bantam, 1957,
  as *The Tough Die Hard*)

As by Lee Roberts

Little Sister (Gold Medal, 1952)
The Pale Door (Dodd Mead, 1955; Detective Book Club, 1955;
  Bantam, 1956)
Judas Journey (Dodd Mead, 1956; Popular Library, 1957)
The Case of the Missing Lovers (Dodd Mead, 1957)

Dr. Clinton Shannon series:
Once a Widow (Dodd Mead, 1957; Detective Book Club, 1957; Dell, 1959)
If the Shoe Fits (Dodd Mead, 1959; Crest, 1960)
Death of a Ladies' Man (Gold Medal, 1960)
Suspicion (Hale UK, 1964; Curtis, 1971)

7
Jim Bennett,
Private Investigator:
A Case File
by Gary Warren Niebuhr

17
Dark Dream
By Robert Martin

175
Sleep, My Love
By Robert Martin

JIM BENNETT, PRIVATE INVESTIGATOR: A CASE FILE
by Gary Warren Niebuhr

Robert Martin was born on October 16, 1908, in Chula, Virginia, to Joseph and Harriet (Repasz) Martin. Martin graduated from Columbian High School in 1927 located in Tiffin, Ohio. It is not clear if he had any other formal education. My sources say no, but according to Jim Felton, Martin's neighbor and a fellow enthusiast, he graduated from college in 1930. Martin was a bank teller for the First National Bank of Tiffin from 1928 until 1934. He became a stock clerk at the Sterling Grinding Wheel Company in Tiffin in 1934. Martin was their stock department manager from 1936 to 1941, and an assistant in the personnel department from 1941 to 1945. He married Alverta Mae Smith in 1942, and they eventually had two daughters and one son. Martin became the assistant personnel manager from 1945 to 1950 and then the personnel manager. He enjoyed shooting, fishing and golfing. He died in Tiffin on February 1, 1976.

Jim Bennett, the creation of writer Robert Martin, is a direct descendent of the ops created by Hammett and Chandler. Like these ops, Bennett carries himself with a stoic coolness. Despite being hit on the head numerous times or being shot more than once, it takes a lot to rile up Bennett. However, when angered, he can be a violent man. Yet in a quiet sort of way he empathizes with many of the characters he meets. He claims throughout the series to be "almost forty," and once he establishes a romantic relationship with his secretary Sandy Hollis, they never consummate their relationship or actually marry despite a long courtship. However, this does not keep him from kissing any woman he feels like.

Martin makes an attempt to create real puzzles for his detective to solve. Some of his novels appear to be modeled on the classic detective novels that originated during the Golden Age. Oddly, he manages to create dark and dangerous places for his detective to solve crimes in, yet he rarely uses the Cleveland area that is Jim's hometown. Instead, we get a small town noir series in the thirteen books, often set in an industrial setting perfect for noirish, hard-boiled tales. The industrial settings may ring so true because Martin worked in an industrial setting and evidently wrote what he knew.

James "Jim" Tobias Bennett was born in a small town in approximately 1913. He spent the last two years of his high school career in Cleveland where he attended school with Helen Connors, Kay Starr and Don Canfield, characters from *Sleep, My Love*. He played high school football. He served in World War II and had the rank of second lieutenant. He once worked as an auto mechanic.

Sixteen years prior to *Dark Dream* (approximately 1935), Jim had dropped out of college after studying law for two years. In later books, Jim refers to being "just out of law school" and claims in *To Have and to Kill* to be a lawyer and a member of the state bar association. In the last book in the series, *Bargain for Death*, he tells us he practiced law in Youngstown after he graduated from the Ohio State School of Law and that he worked for one year for a law firm in New York.

Jim then joined the National Detective Agency. For some unknown reason, in *Hand-Picked for Murder* it is called the American Detective Agency. By the time of *A Key to the Morgue*, the name of the agency is American-International. The National Detective Agency is a firm often referred to as being the private equivalent of the FBI. His boss in New York is always referred to as the old man. The old man owns 65% of the stock in the company and rules from afar with a reputation for being greedy. Jim went to the National Detective Agency's training school. He worked out of the New York office just after his training. By *Dark Dream*, Jim is the chief district agent for the Cleveland branch and owns some stock in the company. The sixth-floor office has a private backdoor entrance that allows Jim to enter without being seen by his clients.

Jim's secretary at the Cleveland branch is Sandy Hollis. Sandy is a long-legged woman with brown hair (later she has copper colored hair) and brown eyes. In *Tears for the Bride*, she has been with the agency for two years. She is waiting for a boyfriend who is a test pilot missing on a flight over the Pacific, but Jim kisses Sandy for the first time on this case. In *Killer Among Us*, Jim proposes to Sandy while they are staying in a motel in Maple Hill, Ohio. By a *Coffin for Two*, Sandy has a diamond engagement ring. For most of the books in the series, Jim is waiting for Sandy to pick a date for their wedding. However, this does not keep him from kissing other women with great regularity, and he almost sleeps with another woman in the last book in the series.

Alec Hammond is Jim's full-time assistant in the Cleveland branch. He is tall, lean man with red hair, freckled face and greenish eyes. In *The Widow and the Web*, Alec becomes the acting manager of the Cleveland branch when the big boss in New York transfers Jim to other work. Red Drake is a part time operative for the Cleveland branch. In *Sleep, My Love*, Jim also uses an op named Homer Shippen. In *Just a Corpse at Twilight*, Jim also has a part time op named George. In *Tears for the Bride*, there is an unnamed part time office girl on the staff. In *Bargain for Death*, he mentions having three full time helpers besides Sandy, Alec and Red. Jim's police contact in Cleveland is Detective Sergeant Dennis Rockingham, who later is promoted to Lieutenant.

Jim has black hair parted on the side and it always needs to be trimmed. He has blue eyes and weighs 190 lbs. He has a scar on his chin from when a man tried to kill him in Youngstown, Ohio, prior to the start of the series. Jim is a constant drinker, but seldom seems drunk. Jim is a smoker. Jim plays golf and is a trout fisherman. He reads westerns. Jim lives in Apartment D on the fourth floor in a building in Cleveland. His neighbor across the hall is Oswald McKinney, an investigator for the IRS Jim has a friend named Skip Gordon who is a Cleveland sports writer.

In *Sleep, My Love*, he describes himself as "pushing 40" (actually he is 40). In *Hand-Picked for Murder*, he is "almost 40" (actually he is 44) as he is in *Killer Among Us* (actually he is 45). By a *Key to the Morgue*, he would be 46, but still says he is "almost 40."

Two months prior to *Dark Dream*, Jim solved the murder of Alvin T. Bayne, a Cleveland businessman in a case we only hear about. Jim carries a Smith & Wesson .38 as his favorite piece and he also has a .32 automatic. Jim drives a coupé. He claims to be a card-carrying member of the Beaver Lodge of Cleveland. In *Dark Dream*, Jim's agency fee is $50 per day plus expenses (he accepts $100 a day plus expenses in *She, Me and Murder*). Jim kills a man on the *Dark Dream* case. He will kill again.

DARK DREAM (Dodd, 1951) begins out on the golf course at the Wheatville, Ohio, Country Club, where someone has been taking pot shots at lawyer Sam Allgood. He hires Jim to find out why. Jim discovers that Margaret Roark is challenging Sam's wife Katherine for the County Club female golf championship. Margaret is the daughter of Red Roark, a small-time professional golfer who died one year prior on the same day Red supposedly threw a golf match against the legendary Alabama Kid.

Margaret works at Armand's Beauty Salon whose owner, Pete Donati, wants to hire Bennett to discover who has been tampering with his equipment and harming his customers, a case which gets complicated quickly by murder. Meanwhile, Sam is having an affair with Lily Winters, wife of his law partner Jeff. Sam also connects to one of the major players in the beauty shop murder case, and Jim tries to work both cases simultaneously.

A great deal of the book contrasts the sordid affairs of some of Wheatville's residents with Jim's romantic love for a former beauty now scarred horribly after an auto accident. Definitely in the Hammett-Chandler school of writing, this tale manages to pull it all off in a neat little package at the end. The somber, stoic Jim Bennett makes an interesting character to follow.

In SLEEP, MY LOVE (Dodd, 1953), Jim is the witness to the slow descent of his high school pal Don Canfield. First, Don does not get the promotion he wanted at Connor Electric in Cleveland. Don's wife Kay divorces him, separating Don from his daughter Annie. Then, his boss Roger Quinn introduces Don to a floozy named Louette and a quick marriage follows.

But one day after Don catches Louette with another man, Jim and Don discover Louette's dead body in the couple's apartment. Before Jim can offer much help to his friend Don, he gets a panicky call from Roger Quinn. In a ratty hotel in East Grange, Ohio, lies the dead body of Melissa, one of Roger's many extramarital affairs. Consequences for these crimes fall on one character, and there are tragic results.

Martin makes us care about these characters because he is adept at creating their little worlds. He makes each one fallible, yet fully aware of their defects to the point where some accept the reasons for their eventual downfall. Although Jim may be a bit stoic, cold and hard to get close to—"I'm nobody's lover"—Jim is not afraid to accuse anyone, even someone he develops some feelings for.

In TEARS FOR THE BRIDE (Dodd, 1954), Jim is invited to a farm near Ridge City, Ohio, where his secretary Sandy Hollis's family is gathering. Sandy's brother Ralph is engaged to Eileen Fortune after Ralph dumped Judy Kirkland. Besides Judy sulking around Ralph, Earl Seltzman is wreaking ill will because he loves the now spoken-for Eileen. While part of a hunting party, Ralph is accidentally shot by Judy.

With everyone carrying a gun and bad attitudes, it is surprising when the first actual dead body is the kindly caretaker of the family farm, Rex Bishop. Bennett has to take the investigation personally when someone shoots at him, but also because he kisses his secretary Sandy for the first time. Although attractive to women, he maintains his distance from people, as when his reaction to leaving a sexually desperate widow alone is "it was men like me who were responsible for women like Daisy Browns."

There is an economy to this novel best summed up by Bennett himself when he states "people got shot at and women made passes and the liquor flowed and nothing added up." There is an economy in the explanation as well, making this rural crime story highly recommended.

On a routine assignment to verify the facts in the case of George Shannon, who fell from a ladder at the Ferris Abrasives plant in Steel City, Jim receives an anonymous note claiming Shannon's death was murder. In THE WIDOW AND THE WEB (Dodd, 1954), Jim finds himself yanked "back again in the world where people deliberately hurt other people, in one way or another, and I hated it."

Jim presses on when everyone else tells him to give the investigation up until one key witness is murdered. As always in these Martin novels, there are a number of fully developed female characters all of whom are damaged seriously by the consequences of their lives or the loss of someone important. While Jim may occasionally kiss one of the women, he still remains a cold lover who understands his own shortcomings. After thinking poorly of one of the women, Jim thinks "maybe she wasn't so bad, after all. Maybe it was me."

When it comes to stopping a criminal, however, he has deductive skills worthy of any detective. There is a melancholy acceptance of the irony of crime here when Jim says, "people did the things they had to do, because of one desperate compulsion or another, and that was the way it went into the record." Although the plot in this book would fill a short story, Martin executes it with characters that reverberate with honesty.

The *Widow And The Web* takes place in April, 1954, six months after *Tears For The Bride*. Jim has been transferred from Cleveland by the old man in New York. He is now working for the Industrial Welfare Commission's Department of Investigations, in a mid-southern state, on a trial basis for three months doing industrial safety and accident investigations. He is living in the Blue Ridge Hotel in Steel City which is four hundred miles from Cleveland. While working for the Commission he picks up a partner in Al Purdy. Al has a wife named Annabelle and two kids.

JUST A CORPSE AT TWILIGHT (Dodd, 1955) takes place in June, 1955. Jim says he has been working for the Commission for nine months (but by my count it would be 14). Jim mentions his annual salary is $8,300. He is in Beach Tree investigating the death of Frank Osborn. Frank had a serious case of silicosis, a lung disease, but the cause of his death was ruled a heart attack by attending physician and coroner Dr. Dick Jarrett.

When Frank's widow Alice is shot to stop the autopsy that Jim wants done on Frank's body, Jim discovers two prominent Beech Tree citizens were wooing the widow before her death. The battle settles down to contest between Jim and the local sheriff Abner Cornwallis. The central question becomes: why does everyone in this small town opposes the exhumation of Frank's body?

Martin attempts to make this struggle epic, but ultimately it lacks power and remains slightly undramatic and unemotional in the telling.

CATCH A KILLER (Dodd, 1956) begins with Martin reprising the opening of Raymond Chandler's *The Big Sleep* by having Jim visit the widow Lavina Hopkins in her Cleveland sunroom on a hot August day. There he hears of Francine, Lavina's young daughter, who years earlier had run off with trumpeter Johnny Wingate. When Jim tracks Francine down in Columbus, it is just as she is about to be reunited after a two year split with the trumpeter who is now a national sensation.

With a marriage planned, Francine is breaking the hearts of three different Columbus residents. Francine is also not interested in her mother's will that requires her to return to Cleveland in order to inherit. When Johnny is murdered during a break in a concert held in Columbus, Jim finds himself aiding the local police in a murder investigation.

While Martin will never be mistaken for Agatha Christie, he has developed a play-fair style that does a good job of creating suspects in his mysteries. Here, as always, his characters are well drawn but the plot becomes pretty obvious as it develops.

HAND-PICKED FOR MURDER (Dodd, 1957) takes place in August. Jim is shot in the shoulder on this case. It begins with a creaky old plot device: Hugo Howell's son Wayne will inherit $200,000 if he is married by the age of twenty-five. Otherwise, Wayne must split the money with his father. Hired by Hugo to break up the relationship between Wayne and Sandra Osterman, Jim finds he does not trust Hugo because he so desperate for the money. He also discovers Wayne and Sandra are already married. End of creaky plot device.

Hugo, being an alcoholic and cut off from any money, begins to irritate everyone in the small resort town of Lakeport. Eventually, someone tries to kill Hugo with an ice pick, only to stab the wrong man.

Hugo is one of the more maniacal characters created by Martin, and he is extremely well drawn. The story is set in a well-developed small town setting (including the resort area of Catawba Island), and the resolution is wonderfully done in a Golden Age sort of style.

For seventy-five years, Buckeye Abrasives has manufactured quality grinding wheels for Ohio industries from its plant in Maple Hill. But recently, a series of faulty parts have failed, and finally one broke during operations at the Portage Foundry in Toledo. A man is dead because of it in KILLER AMONG US (Dodd, 1958).

Jim is hired to come into the Buckeye plant as an undercover op, and he is on the spot when a wheel explodes and injures Howard Ackerman, a Buckeye plant executive. Sorting through a multitude of potential suspects, each with a definitive and well-defined reason for committing industrial espionage, Jim discovers a series of clues that eventually are able to provide a play-fair conclusion for the reader who likes details in their mysteries.

As a reader, I am more interested in the big swatches and this book has them. What better setting for the hard-boiled detective than a blue-collar environment like an abrasives plant. The men who dwell there and the women affected by it are well drawn, especially in regards the effects of their wayward affections, the dangerous work they do, and their desire for money and advancement. Jim kills a man but he is also grazed by a bullet in his side. The painful and evocative bittersweet final pages of this novel only helped me in regarding this as a classic in the P. I. field.

Alvin Bayne came into money through the produce business but his blue-collar background makes him uncomfortable at the Cleveland country club where he plays golf with Jim. He is also made uncomfortable by his wife, the former dancer Arlene Aragon. Then, he is made dead, shot in his own home while he was shaving in A KEY TO THE MORGUE (Dodd, 1959). Jim is incensed by Alvin's death, and his anger grows when two hoods molest Sandy while trying to get to him.

Jim knows that Alvin was about to change his will (gasp—not that old ploy!) so he hooks up with Alvin's lawyer Orville Hewing to launch a private and personal investigation. Then a shocking revelation about Alvin's post-divorce plans rock Jim's perceptions, yet he plunges on.

This is by far the darkest, most violent of all the cases so far. Risking his license and his reputation, Jim rolls from one killing to the next trying to clear his friend's name and eventually his own. Hard-boiled to the maximum, this cold and bleak tale is highly recommended.

In A Key To The Morgue (Dodd, 1958), Jim claims to be a member of a Cleveland area country club. It is September and he is driving a two-year-old Mercury that belongs to the agency. Jim now claims to have in his arsenal a 12 gauge shotgun, a Springfield 30-06 rifle and a Harrington & Richardson nine shot .22 revolver. He kills two men on this case, and at the end of it the "old man" in New York offers him the opportunity to succeed to the head when the old man retires. Jim's cop pal Rockingham has received a promotion to Lieutenant.

Maxwell Daney manages to run a soda pop industry, but he cannot manage his own love life in TO HAVE AND TO KILL (Dodd, 1960). On a July weekend, he has asked Jim and Sandy to be in his wedding party when he marries Laura Reynolds. That same weekend, Dixie McQueen invades his Lake Erie shoreline mansion. Dixie is from Chicago and has arrived under the impression that she is to meet

Max's mother Augusta and possibly qualify to be Max's intended.

With two women vying for the same man, a jealous Mom in the house, and one of the women's jilted lover on the scene, it should surprise no one that Jim finds a dead woman on the beach one night.

This one is structured like the Golden Age house party novels, with everyone isolated at the mansion making just enough suspects for a clue driven puzzler. There are clues here, and they work for the benefit of the plot, but the plot itself is too messed up with the inclusion of two deaf mutes and their bizarre story.

Yet, it was satisfactory in a traditional mystery sort of way, with less of the hard-boiled sensibilities evident in the last two novels in this series. Recommended mostly for its puzzle format.

A COFFIN FOR TWO (Hale [UK], 1962; Curtis [US], 1972) opens with a big coincidence. On a June summer night, Jim accompanies his reporter friend Jake Camp to a Beech Fork cemetery to visit the newly discovered family vault of the Keeting family. Jake had discovered the long forgotten vault while hunting for arrowheads, but both men are at the vault when distant relative Nancy Keeting arrives with the intent to move her relatives from this discarded vault into the real cemetery that lies a few short yards away.

But that is not the big coincidence. Jim then returns to Cleveland only to be hired by Emily DeWitt to find her missing husband, First Union National bank president Earl DeWitt. Earl was last seen in Beech Fork at a cemetery association meeting with cemetery custodian Sam Green. Coincidence? You bet!

However, eventually the oddity fades away in an amalgam of suspicion and misbehavior in the small town of Beech Fork, including a sheriff who could get a job in Raymond Chandler's Bay City if he needed one. Here is another book by Martin full of flawed characters in a small town noirish setting.

It is November, and Atlantis Productions in Los Angeles is going to make a film about the old man who is boss of American-International in SHE, ME AND MURDER (Hale [UK], 1962; Curtis [US], 1971). All of the PI offices are to send copies of their files to the film studio for the writers to produce the script. This worries former theatrical agent Enos Weber because he had asked Jim to investigate Enos' wife for a divorce proceeding.

Jim had refused the case, and handed it off to Cleveland PI Jake

Doan. Doan had copied Jim with the file, and now Enos wants it. The divorce was called off when Enos was able to use Doan's evidence to blackmail Atlantis president Hiram Wyndham and land a cushy job with Atlantis in Hollywood. Now Enos' sweet deal is threatened if the files are opened.

Meanwhile, the actress Tracy Kent, with whom Enos had an affair of his own, is in Cleveland and causing trouble. She is sleeping with the young actor Peter Ordway while being stalked by her sugar daddy, Harold McPherson. Then Ordway is dead, Sandy is kidnapped, and Jim goes into a rampage of hard-boiled action.

As the case evolves, the sordid motivations of the major players are revealed and no one comes out looking very good. The strength of the characters created by Martin carries this novel, set in seedy bars, roadside eateries and lonely-hearts hotels.

The final case in the series, BARGAIN FOR DEATH (Hale [UK], 1964; Curtis [US], 1972), takes place in July. Walter Larkin has big union negotiations upcoming at his plant in Central City when his wife Meg forces him to hire her wayward brother Peter Clovis as a plant negotiator. Jim is an old family friend, and Walter has hired him because of two problems at the plant. Jim manages to solve both of Maxim Products problems only to hand them an even bigger one when he belts the union negotiator during the talks. The plant goes on strike, and someone takes a shot at Jim.

Unfortunately, on top of being dumb enough to lose his temper and hit someone, Jim leaves the scene of the shooting without talking to the cops. His renegade style in this novel is not helped by some continuity problems within the plot. Characters, normally a strong suit for Martin, act like fools here, and the novel reads with a regrettable sense of confusion and disbelief, which is too bad for a series that has had few stumbles.

[this revised version originally appeared
in *Mystery*File* 43, April 2004]

DARK DREAM
Robert Martin

FOR VERTI

CHAPTER ONE

Sam Allgood's law office was above the Wheatville National Bank. I nosed the right front wheel of my coupé against a parking meter along the curb, stepped out to the sidewalk and put a nickel in the slot. I climbed the wooden stairway and walked down a hallway. A door lettered *Allgood and Winters, Attorneys-at-Law* was standing open and I went in. It was furnished with a few wooden chairs and a long table littered with dull-looking government bulletins. On a wall hung a big faded map of Wheatville and two framed diplomas from a Midwestern law school.

A thin, gray-haired woman in a black dress was sitting before a typewriter. She had a sharp beak of a nose, and, as she glanced up at me through thick-lensed glasses, she reminded me of some species of bird. I took off my hat.

"Is Mr. Allgood in?"

"Not at present," she said crisply. "He's having lunch at the lodge hall."

"What lodge?" I asked her.

"The Beavers," she said, and added proudly, "Mr. Allgood is Supreme Celestial Commander this year."

"Ah," I said, "a brother." I took out my billfold, flipped it open and showed her my paid-up dues card in the Cleveland chapter of Beavers. "Where's the lodge?"

"Around the corner," she said. "A big red brick building with white pillars."

"Thanks," I said, and went out.

I found the headquarters of the Wheatville chapter of Beavers without any trouble. From the looks of the building and grounds, the Wheatville brothers paid their dues promptly. I pressed a button beside an ornate doorway and in a couple of minutes a big man in a white bar apron opened the door.

"I'd like to see Sam Allgood," I told him, and I flashed my membership card on him.

He leaned forward and peered intently at my card, his lips moving silently. Then he snapped to attention, crossed the palms of both hands over his forehead, his elbows protruding, and focused his eyes on my necktie. "Give the password," he barked.

I took off my hat and placed my right hand over my heart. "True blue," I said.

He relaxed and held out a big red hand. "Welcome, brother."

I followed him down a cool dusky corridor. We emerged into a long room with a bar along one wall and a row of slot machines along the other. Through an alcove I saw a larger room filled with round tables. Most of the tables were empty, but at several of them men were playing cards. I glanced at my wristwatch. It was a quarter of two in the afternoon.

The big man poked his head into the card room and shouted, "Sam! A brother here to see you."

I heard a voice say, "Deal me out, boys," and a man walked into the bar. He was about six-foot-one, with a puffy white face which had once been handsome. He had thick black brows, rather small blue eyes and heavy black hair which he wore parted on the side. He was beginning to get fat, and his big frame was draped in a pale gray gabardine suit. He wore a white shirt, a red-speckled bow tie and tan-and-white shoes. I guessed him to be about thirty-five.

"Hello, there," he said, smiling. "Been looking for you." We shook hands.

"The lady in your office told me I'd find you here," I said.

He nodded and turned to the bar. "What'll you drink?" he asked over his shoulder.

"Ginger ale, plain."

"Oh, come now," Allgood said.

"It's a little early in the day for me."

He shrugged his big shoulders and said to the bartender, "The same, John—and a plain ginger ale."

The bartender poured and Allgood drummed his fingers on the bar. A thin stick of sunlight reflected light from his manicured nails. The bartender put two glasses on the bar. Allgood picked them up and jerked his head at me. I followed him through a door into a big room filled with deep leather chairs. There was a thick dark red carpet on the floor, a long table covered with magazines and a combination radio-phonograph-television outfit a little smaller than a grand piano. Allgood led me to where two chairs stood by the windows and handed me my drink. I sat down and gazed out at the sweep of green lawn.

Allgood said, "Your name's Bennett, isn't it?"

I nodded.

"When I called your office yesterday," he said, "I asked them to send you. We met at a party in Lakewood a year ago. Remember?"

I nodded again. "It was after the Midwest Open golf tournament. At the Erie Isles Country Club. Red Roark died that night. Wasn't he your professional here?"

"Yes," he replied, "for many years. Red was too old to enter that tournament—and he had a bad heart. He collapsed in the clubhouse afterwards, and he died in the hospital a couple of hours later."

I gazed out of the window, remembering that day in Cleveland a year ago. The Midwest Open, with the big money on a lanky kid from Alabama. And then Red Roark, an unknown small-time professional, had come up from behind to enter the final playoff. He led the Alabama Kid right up to the seventeenth hole, and then he missed an easy two-foot putt. He lost the match by one stroke. Somehow the word got around that Roark had taken a pile of money to throw the match to the Kid. They never proved it, but it didn't make any difference to Roark. He died that night.

I said, "Red was deadly with the irons."

Allgood took a swallow of his drink and gave me a wry smile. "I didn't call you down here to talk about Red Roark. I've got a job for you."

"All right," I said.

He shifted his big body in the chair. "In the first place," he said, "you're to pose as a visiting friend of mine from Cleveland. It's important that the fact that you are a private detective be kept secret while you are in town. Do you understand?"

"Sure. What's the job?"

He looked at me over his glass and frowned slightly. "We've got to play this thing carefully," he said in a low voice. "It's got me worried. I know your agency is reliable and I want you to use discretion. This is my first experience of this sort. I know what your fee is and how I pay it. But how do you work—what do you have to know?"

"Everything," I said. The build-up irritated me. "What is it—a woman?"

His handsome face flushed. He took another swallow of his drink and gazed out the window. "Why do you ask that?" he said in a tight voice.

I shrugged and sipped some ginger ale. I wished now that I had some whisky in it. "That's what a long-winded build-up usually ends with," I told him. "Why don't you tell me what you want?"

"All right," he said abruptly. "Somebody's been shooting at me on the golf course. I want to find out who it is, and I want it stopped."

I thought about that for a second, and then I said, "All right. What else?"

"Nothing, Bennett," he said in a level voice. "That's enough. It's a hell of a thing to be teeing off—and have a bullet zing past your ear."

"I can imagine. When did it happen?"

"It's happened three times—twice last week and again last Monday. Late in the afternoon each time."

"This is Wednesday," I said. "Why wait. Why didn't you call the police?"

He made an impatient gesture. "You don't understand. Get this, Bennett—the police are not to be dragged into this. That's what I'm paying you for—I don't want any publicity. The police and the sheriff's office would just mess things up—and they'd jump at a chance to get something on us."

"Us?"

"The Wheatville Country Club. Some of the people in town don't like us—you know how small towns are."

"Exclusive?" I asked him. "The club, I mean?"

"Our membership is restricted—naturally," he said coldly.

"I see. You bury your own dead. What goes on at the club is none of the town's business?"

"If you want to put it that way."

"Do you have the slugs?" I asked.

"What?"

"The bullets which were fired at you?"

"Oh," he said. "Yes." He took two flattened lead pellets from his coat pocket and handed them to me. "They were imbedded in the shelter house behind a tee."

I examined the bullets. They were small and I guessed them to be .22 long rifles. "Mind if I keep them?"

He shook his head, and I dropped the little chunks of lead into my coat pocket.

"Anybody playing with you when it happened?" I asked.

"No. Each time I was playing alone—practicing. There weren't many people on the course."

"Any ideas?"

He shook his head. "No."

"Any enemies?"

His big shoulders moved beneath the gray gabardine. "No more than any attorney has."

"Anyone else know about it?"

"No. I didn't tell anyone."

"You got shot at three times—and you didn't tell anyone about it?"

"Why should I?" he said. He hesitated and looked down at the glass in his hand. "Maybe I'd be telling the person who did the shooting."

"You think maybe it's a fellow club member?"

He shrugged again, his face expressionless. "It could be—I don't know." He finished his drink in one swallow and the ice clinked in the bottom of his glass.

I stood up. "All right. Let's go out to the club. I want to see where it happened."

He glanced at a gold wristwatch. "I can't. I have an appointment at three-thirty. But you go ahead. It happened on number six tee—each time. I'll call the club and fix it for you. You'll stay at my house while you're here. It'll look better that way. Do you need anything?"

"Well," I said, "at least I ought to have a golf club in my hand."

He took a ring of keys from his pocket, detached a small flat key and handed it to me. "Help yourself to anything in my locker."

"Where is the club?"

"Turn left at the Courthouse," he said. "The club is a mile and a half out. I'll meet you there around five-thirty for dinner. And remember, you're just a guest of mine from Cleveland."

We left the Wheatville lodge of Beavers and Sam Allgood walked with me to my car. He went up the steps to his office. I walked to a corner drugstore, found a telephone booth and called my office in Cleveland.

The pleasant voice of Sandy Hollis, my secretary, came over the wire.

"National Detective Agency."

"This is Jim," I said. "Down in the wilds of Wheatville."

"Hi, Jim. I'm glad you called in. I was just wondering how to locate you down there."

"Trouble?" I asked her.

"No. More business. You're supposed to contact a Mr. Donati, of Armand's Beauty Salon—right there in Wheatville. Isn't that nice, Jim?"

"No," I said. "One job at a time is enough. Why don't you send Alec?"

"They want you—personally. The call came in about an hour ago."
"All right," I said wearily. "I'll try and work it in. Now, listen. You can contact me here at the home of Sam Allgood. Got that?"

"Yes, sir," she said.

We talked a little more and then I hung up. I went out and sat behind the wheel of my coupé. So I had two jobs in Wheatville. I decided that Mr. Donati, of Armand's Beauty Salon, would have to wait. I drove to the Courthouse and turned left.

CHAPTER TWO

Sam Allgood had called Wheatville a small town, but I had been born in a really small town and it wasn't anything like Wheatville. My small town had consisted of a block-long Main Street, with a scattering of houses on the fringes of fields. The general store, on a corner across from a combination gas station and garage, had been the social center. We had a movie which operated on Friday, Saturday and Sunday nights; two churches, three groceries, a dinky railroad station, one bus stop and six bars. On the edge of the town were two establishments of dubious and exciting reputation known as "roadhouses." When I was in high school, a furtive visit to one of the roadhouses was the very peak of daring and sophistication. I hadn't been back to the town for a long time, but I supposed that the roadhouses were now called taverns, complete with gaudy neon signs and jukeboxes.

My town would be called a village now, because it hadn't grown and sprawled into a pseudo-city like Wheatville, Ohio, a community with a small-town background and tradition, but bigger and brighter, on the surface, at least, and with a big-city glitter and hustle. The population, I'd been told, was in excess of 30,000 and was still growing. This was due to the fact that it was located on a national coast-to-coast highway and was the central terminal of a great railroad whose tracks rolled east to the Hudson, seven hundred miles away, and west to the mountains of Nevada and beyond.

Wheatville was a mixture of the cracker barrel and the supermarkets, the town pump and the cocktail lounges. The big old homes were owned by the descendants of Indian fighters and thrifty pioneers. The spark, the hustle, was supplied by an ever-increasing horde of ambitious junior executives eager to make their mark in the community, constantly pushing and fighting to head committees concerned with various civic advancement campaigns. These young men, I knew, came mostly from the two branch factories of vast industrial concerns which had located in Wheatville because of the town's central geographical location and its railroad facilities. Maybe in twenty or thirty years Wheatville would be a real city; just now it was neither a small town nor a city, but a combination of both, with the old-line residents resenting the brash and commercial newcomers, and the newcomers scrambling and clawing for places in the business and social sun.

There are hundreds of towns like Wheatville in America, with the old fighting the new, but with the new and its golden clink of progress and profit slowly but surely settling the dust of tradition and ultraconservatism. Wheatville had an airport, I'd been told, and there was talk of building new modern schools to replace the ancient brick and wooden fire traps built in the dawn of the town's self-conscious awakening to its responsibilities as an American community which had long outgrown its log cabin and mud road era.

As I drove along the wide pleasant street I saw bright modern houses built beside weather-beaten frame structures which had been old at the turn of the century. Big gleaming stores crowded out small shops with dusty windows, and in the distance tall smokestacks towered against the summer sky. And then abruptly the town was behind me and I was driving between rolling green fields. It was a little disconcerting. I had lived and worked so long in the deep city jungle that here I felt out of place, foreign and uninitiated.

Presently, across the fields and at the top of a gentle hill, I saw a collection of low white buildings dominated by a larger building with a slanting red roof. I decided I was nearing my destination and I began to watch for a turnoff road approaching it. When I found it, I drove for maybe a quarter of a mile between rolling fairways and velvety greens, and I guessed that it was a nine-hole layout. Then the road swung abruptly right, and I found myself at the Wheatville Country Club. I parked my coupé beside a sign which said *Members Only* and walked along flat stones laid in a smooth lawn to a wide screened porch. The porch was deserted, but inside the clubhouse I heard the shrill babble of many female voices. Through a pair of French windows I saw about fifty women, all dressed to the teeth, jabbering away at card tables. I opened a screen door and followed a sign reading *Locker Rooms*.

A man in a white jacket stepped out from a swinging door and looked at me. He gave me a quick, cold smile and stood still. He was a young man, pudgy, with fat cheeks and thick yellow hair cut long like a radio crooner's. He glanced at my ready-made blue suit and at my dusty shoes which I can never remember to get shined. I felt that maybe I should have gone around to the service entrance.

"Whom did you wish to see, sir?" he asked politely.

"Nobody, sonny. My name's Bennett. Sam Allgood sent me out."

He stepped aside. "Yes, sir," he said quickly. "If you need anything, call me. My name's Rogan."

A man came through the doorway from the locker rooms. His spiked shoes made a clattering sound on the pitted hardwood floor. He was a tall man with a long sunburned face and a narrow yellow mustache. He had a thin hooked nose and a thin wide mouth. His eyes were gray and set far apart. He was wearing a white terry cloth pullover and gray flannel slacks, and was carrying about fifteen glittering golf clubs in a hundred-dollar leather bag slung over his shoulder. He stopped and hooked a thumb beneath the strap of the golf bag.

"Did I hear you mention Sam Allgood?" he asked. His gray eyes were friendly.

The white-coated Rogan said quickly, "This is Mr. Bennett, Mr. Winters. Mr. Allgood telephoned about him."

The tall man held out a hand to me. "I'm Jeff Winters, Sam's partner."

We shook hands. Rogan disappeared into the locker room.

Winters said, "Like to play with us, Mr. Bennett? I've got a foursome but we'll break the rules and make it a fivesome."

"Thanks," I said. "I'm just going to dub around a little—and I'm meeting Sam after a while."

He nodded. "I'll see you later." He clattered out the screen door.

I located Sam Allgood's locker. His name was on a white card inserted into a slot on the door. I opened the door with the key he had given me and took three irons from his golf bag—a number five, a number seven and a putter. I unzipped the ball pouch and pocketed three balls, and hung up my coat, hat and necktie. There was a bright red baseball player's cap with a long bill hanging on a hook in the locker. I tried it on. It fitted. Allgood's spiked shoes were a little tight but they would do. There were also three bottles of whisky in the locker, one of them Scotch, but I resisted the temptation and closed and locked the metal door. Then I went out.

A tall girl with a flat black hat the size of a bicycle wheel came out of the babble of the card-playing room and headed for the porch door. She was carrying a highball glass and she was walking fast. Her hair was black and it curled around her shoulders. She had a thin hollow-cheeked face, a thin straight nose, a red-painted full-lipped mouth and wide brown eyes beneath arched black brows. Her plain black dress and stubby-toed, three-inch-soled shoes had cost some man a lot of money. She stared straight ahead and walked for the door with a free, long-legged stride.

I kept moving. Unless one of us slowed down we were bound to collide. At the last instant I slowed down, but it was too late. We came together, hip to hip. Her drink splattered to the floor and we both jumped away from each other. The surprise in her eyes was as faked as my apology.

"Sorry," I mumbled.

She dazzled me with a flash of white teeth. "My fault," she said. "I wasn't looking. I just couldn't stand it in there anymore." She tossed her head at the sound of female chattering.

I didn't say anything.

"All right," she said, laughing. "I'll admit I met Jeff on the porch. He told me about you. I'm Katherine Allgood—Sam's wife. Of course, I could have gotten Jeff to introduce us, but this way is more interesting."

"Definitely," I said. "But I'm sorry you spilled your drink."

"You can buy me another," she said.

I looked at my watch. Three-thirty. Plenty of time.

"Of course," she said, "if I'm detaining you …"

"Not at all," I told her. "Where's the bar?"

She laughed and moved through an archway. I followed her out to a screened porch overlooking the ninth green, and furnished with tables, chairs and wicker porch furniture. We sat down at one of the tables. Rogan came out of a side door and stood quietly attentive.

"Scotch and soda," Katherine Allgood said to him.

I nodded, "The same," and Rogan went away.

"So you're a friend of Sam's," she said. "It's strange that he never mentioned you to me."

I squirmed a little in my chair. "Lawyers know a lot of funny people," I said.

Rogan came in with the drinks and she waited until he had put them on the table and left. Then she said softly, "I don't think you're funny. I think you're nice."

I couldn't think of an answer to that, so I held up my glass and grinned at her.

"Going to be in town long?" she asked.

"A couple of days maybe."

"You'll have dinner with us tonight?"

"I'm staying at your house," I said.

"Really? How nice."

A stout gray-haired woman in a purple dress and an imitation orchid for a hat came out onto the porch. "Katherine, dear," she said, peering at me intently, "we need you."

Katherine Allgood said, "In a minute, Myrtle."

"But, dear, we're waiting," the stout woman said.

Katherine Allgood sighed and finished her drink in two long swallows. "See you later," she said, winking at me, and she followed the woman into the clubhouse.

I drained my glass, left some money on the table and walked out to the first tee. There was nobody on number one fairway, but I could see a sprinkling of players scattered over the rolling course. I saw by the white-painted arrows sticking in the turf at the edges of the tee that it was a three-hundred-and-twenty-yard par four hole. I like golf but I don't have much time to play.

I teed up a ball and smacked it out with a number five iron. I got about a hundred and fifty yards and landed in a bunker. I walked down the fairway to the bunker, lifted the ball with a seven iron and landed thirty yards short of the green. I used the seven again and pitched up to within three feet of the cup. I holed the putt for a par and walked to the number two tee, feeling pleased with myself.

There was a foursome ahead of me, and I figured it was Jeff Winters and his crowd. I stayed behind them. When I approached the number six tee where Sam Allgood had said the shooting occurred I began to look over the lie of the land. There were lots of trees; number six fairway was bounded on one side by a row of poplars and on the other by a cornfield protected by a wire fence. Nailed to the fence at intervals were big black-and-white signs: *Out of Bounds. Do Not Enter*.

Number six hole was a hundred and seventy yards, par three. The cornfield ended just beyond the green. Opposite number seven tee, and just back of the field, stood a group of farm buildings and a green-painted house. As I stepped up to the tee, I saw that Jeff Winters and his party had holed out and disappeared beyond the poplars. I stuck a little wooden tee into the ground, placed a ball on it and looked around. Behind me in a clump of fir trees was a small three-sided shelter house, with a ball washer anchored in the ground beside it.

I turned back to my ball, dug in the spikes of Allgood's shoes and started my backswing. Something zinged past my nose and smacked into the shelter house behind me, and the wind carried a faint clear crack to my ears. I jumped back to the shelter house and stooped low.

I waited maybe a minute, but I couldn't hear anything but the birds and the bees and the distant mooing of a cow. I looked around at the walls of the shelter house. Just above my head was a splintered hole, and about two feet to the right of it were three similar holes. A bullet was imbedded in the wood and I pried it out with my pocket knife. It was a small caliber, probably a .22. A foot to the left were three shallow depressions, with the wood splintered a little around them. I took the slugs which Allgood had given me and laid them in the depressions. They fitted.

I heard the metallic rattle of steel golf clubs in a bag and I stepped outside. A pocket-sized girl was walking up from number five green, her head down. A small canvas bag of clubs was slung over her shoulder, and the sun glinted on her copper-colored hair.

"Hello," I said.

She looked up suddenly and stood still. She was a pretty little girl, in a tanned boyish way, with a short freckled nose and a small round chin. Her eyes were big and brown and her bronze hair was braided, each braid tied with a red ribbon. She was wearing a plain blue dress, short white socks and brown spiked moccasins. "Hi," she said, and she gave me a friendly smile.

I nodded at the green ahead. "This is my first time around the course. What club do you advise on this hole?"

She stepped up to the tee beside me, laid the bag on the grass and withdrew a junior-sized steel-shafter brassie. "It's a short hole," she said. "I use a number two wood." She added seriously, "But you can probably carry the green with a spoon." She nodded at my ball perched on the tee. "Put it on the green."

"I don't have a spoon," I told her, and I glanced nervously about for signs of a sharpshooter with a rifle. I didn't see anything unusual, and so I stepped up and hit the ball with the five iron. It sliced into the poplars at the right of the fairway. "Just a duffer," I said.

She laughed and teed up her own ball. She had a slow, easy swing, and the click of her club against the ball was a sweet, satisfying sound. The ball arched into the air and landed on the edge of the green.

"Nice shot," I told her as we picked up our clubs and walked down the fairway together.

"Thank you," she said seriously, "but I need more practice. I'm playing in a tournament on Friday."

"Is the competition stiff?"

"Pretty stiff," she said, trudging along beside me, a small trim figure in a blue dress. "I've got to beat Mrs. Allgood. We tied in the tournament last week, so we're playing eighteen holes to decide the winner."

"Mrs. Sam Allgood?"

She nodded. "She's plenty good."

"Who's the favorite?"

"Mrs. Allgood, of course," she said. I glanced down at her. There was a faint bitter twist to her small red mouth. "She's the club's woman champion—has been for three years. But now the tournament is narrowed down to just us two. She said I was getting too big for my pants."

"Now, now," I said. "Little girls shouldn't talk like that."

"Well, panties, then," she pouted. "Anyhow, that's what she said about me when I defeated Mrs. Nusbaum last Saturday. She was the leading contender for the championship."

"And now you are?"

"Yes. You see, Mr.—"

"Bennett," I said.

She grinned up at me. "Howdy, Mr. Bennett. You see, Mrs. Allgood was pretty peeved about my beating Mrs. Nusbaum. She knows that she can beat Mrs. Nusbaum, but she isn't sure about me. She's the champion, you see, and she wants to keep on being champion. Mrs. Allgood is a leader in everything. She's always giving luncheons and bridge teas and parties, and I'm just a working girl. I only belong to the club for one reason and that's to play golf. My father used to be the pro here. I guess golf comes naturally to me."

"What's your name?" I smiled down at her.

"Margaret Roark. Everybody calls me Peggy. Are you new in town,

Mr. Bennett?"

"Just visiting a couple of days," I said. "So you're Red Roark's daughter?"

She looked up at me quickly. "Did you know my father?"

"I saw him play once," I said. "A year ago, in the Midwest Open."

She averted her gaze. "Then—then you know what they—they said about him?" she asked in a low voice.

"Yes—but I didn't believe it."

She smiled up at me. There was a hint of tears in her eyes. "Thanks, Mr. Bennett. You look like the kind of a person who wouldn't believe a story like that." She lifted her small chin. "Red didn't throw that match. He was sick. He—he died right afterward, you know."

"Yes, I know. Do you live in Wheatville?"

She nodded. "Yes. I work at Armand's Beauty Salon—I do shampoos and manicures. This is my day off, and they said if I worked some late appointments tonight, I can have Friday off to play in the tournament."

"I see," I said slowly, remembering that I was supposed to make contact with Armand's Beauty Salon while I was in Wheatville.

We were approaching the green, and I moved over to the poplars where my ball was lying in the tall grass. I hacked at it with the seven iron. It moved two feet.

"Too bad," Peggy Roark said sympathetically.

I swung again and succeeded in lobbing the ball a yard from the green.

Peggy Roark laughed. "That's better. Maybe you can sink it from there."

"Not me," I said. I was looking over at the green house and the group of farm buildings across the fence. I glanced back up the fairway, and realized that anyone with a gun would have a clear shot at the sixth tee from almost anywhere in this immediate area. And either the farm buildings or the trees around the seventh tee would provide plenty of cover.

Peggy Roark dropped a long putt for a birdie two. I pitched up with the five iron and holed my putt for a shaky five. We crossed the rustic bridge over a little brook and climbed a gentle hill to the seventh tee. As we topped the hill, I saw a man leaning on a wire fence, watching us. He was wearing overalls and a sweat-stained felt hat. His face was red from the sun and he needed a shave. His eyes were a pale gray, set close beside a long nose, and they stood out sharply against his dark face. He was a young man, around thirty, with heavy shoulders and work-toughened hands.

"Howdy," I said, as we came abreast of him. "Your corn looks good."

He spat out a piece of straw he had been chewing. "That's right," he said. "And I aim to keep it that way."

"We could use some rain," I said.

"It ain't rain that worries me," he said, peering at me intently.

"Corn borers, brother?" I asked.

"Corn tramplers," he said. "They ruined half my crop last year, looking for lost balls. I aim to keep 'em out this year. You're a stranger hereabouts, ain't you?" His eyes were on my red cap.

"That's right."

He grunted. "Thought so. I know 'em all by sight. Silly game, ain't it?"

"Kind of," I said.

"Grown men," he sneered, and I saw that his two front teeth were missing, "chasing a little ball around a pasture." He spat contemptuously.

I grinned at him. Peggy laughed, and we moved on up to the seventh tee. While Peggy was driving, I looked over at the buildings of the farm across the fence. I spotted the shutters of a tiny window high up in the peak of a big barn. The shutters were hanging open. I glanced back at the farmer. He was still watching us.

As we walked side by side down the green fairway, I noticed that Peggy Roark was suddenly quiet. I said, "Did you hear a shot a while ago—just before I met you on the sixth tee?"

"No," she said, "but it could have been some kids down by the creek, shooting turtles. I used to do it myself—with a little .22 single shot rifle Red gave me. I was practically raised out here, you know."

"How long was your dad pro here?"

"About twelve years—until he died."

"Why did they say he threw that match?" I asked.

She tilted her small face up at me, and there was an angry glint in her eyes. "Why do you ask that?"

"Just wondered."

She bit at her lower lip, and looked down at the grass. "They lied about him—and he didn't have a chance to fight back. It—it killed him."

"Who do you mean by 'they'?"

"I—I don't want to talk about it," she said in a choked voice.

We reached her ball. "Sorry, Peggy," I said gently. "Lay it on the green."

She swung, but her stroke was ragged and too fast. She topped the ball, and it bounded over the grass and into a bunker fifty yards away. I kept tactfully quiet and she didn't say anything. Then she dubbed her bunker shot and three-putted the green. She tried to laugh, but it was a strained attempt. "I guess I can't concentrate," she said, "when I think about Red. He was such a—a swell guy."

"Sure," I said. "I won't mention him again."

By the time we started number nine, she was laughing and gay again. But she was six over par when we holed out on the ninth green by the clubhouse.

"Don't worry," I assured her. "You've got the bad shots out of your system. Friday you'll burn up the fairways."

She gave me a quick smile. "Sure I will."

I headed for the clubhouse.

"So long, Mr. Bennett," she said.

I turned. "Aren't you coming over to the club?"

She shook her head. "No, thanks. Mother will be waiting supper."

"All right. Good luck in the tournament."

"Thanks." She walked across the stone drive and tossed her clubs into a small faded blue convertible with battered fenders.

I crossed to the clubhouse and went up the steps to the screened porch. Four people were sitting there, all with drinks in their hands. Sam Allgood was there with his partner, Jeff Winters, and Katherine Allgood. Sitting beside Winters was a slender girl with long tawny hair, high cheekbones, like an Indian's, a pointed chin, dark blue eyes and a wide red mouth. She was wearing a thin tight green sweater, green gabardine slacks and white rubber-soled sneakers.

Sam Allgood got to his feet. "Hello, Jim. We've been waiting for you." He sounded a little self-conscious. "I understand you've met my wife and Jeff. This is Jeff's wife." He nodded at the slender blonde. "Lily, meet my friend, Jim Bennett, from Cleveland."

The blonde held up her glass and smiled. "Howdy, Jim."

I nodded and bowed in my best company manner, and Allgood handed me a tall tinkling glass. There was the roar of a car motor and the crunch of gravel. A blue convertible went along the drive and white stone dust drifted over the porch.

Katherine Allgood said, "I see you've met our little golfer. We watched you come up number nine."

I nodded. "You mean Peggy? She tells me that she's playing you for the championship on Friday."

"Kate's got a job on her hands," Jeff Winters said. "Peggy's good."

The blond Lily said, "You bet. She trains for her matches. Why don't you train, Kate?"

"I'm in training now," Katherine Allgood said. "How about another drink, Sam?"

Everybody laughed.

Allgood took a bottle from a table and poured whisky into all of our glasses. The sun was touching the tops of the trees across the fairways, and the porch was in shadow. I suddenly realized that I was tired. I sank into a wicker chair and tried to look attentive.

The blonde said, "I'm glad I'm not playing in that silly tournament. Let's eat."

Allgood winked at me. "Lily's always hungry," he said, and he added, "Or thirsty."

"Golf is a silly game," Lily Winters said, "but if you people want to make a little bet on the clay pigeons, or how many bull's-eyes I can make in fifty shots ..."

"We call her Annie Oakley Winters," Jeff Winters said to me. "She's deadly with a gun—any kind of a gun."

I felt that I should say something. "Which do you prefer, Mrs. Winters?" I asked the blonde. "A notch or a peep sight?"

"That depends upon what I'm shooting," she said. "Call me Lily."

Jeff Winters got up and moved his lanky form to the door. "Rogan," he shouted.

The lights had been turned on inside, and through the French windows I could see people eating in the room which had housed the afternoon bridge party. The white-coated attendant appeared in the doorway. "It'll be about five minutes, Mr. Winters. Shall I serve it out here?"

"No," Winters said. "We'll eat on the rear porch."

"Yes, sir." Rogan went away.

Jeff Winters turned to the rest of us. "Come on. We can have a drink at the table." He turned and entered the clubhouse.

Katherine Allgood took my arm and led me after him. Sam Allgood and Lily Winters didn't follow. They were talking in low tones, and I heard the blonde laugh softly.

The three of us had a drink at the table on the rear porch. I held a match for Katherine Allgood, and our eyes met over the flame. "Mr.

Bennett-from-Cleveland," she said, "what do you do? Sam wouldn't tell me."

"Why?" I asked, smiling at her. She was still dressed as I had seen her in the afternoon, except that she had discarded the bicycle-wheel hat. Her black hair was smooth and shining, and parted in the middle. She moved closer to me, and I could tell by her eyes that the liquor was getting to her.

"Why, Mr. Bennett-from-Cleveland?" she said. "Because I want to know, that's why. You don't look like the men around here. You look like someone out of a book. You don't talk much, and yet you say the right things at the right times. And there is a kind of watchfulness about you, and a cold alert look behind your eyes. Why is that? You're big, and yet you move about like a—like an Indian. How did you get that lovely scar on your chin?"

"Shaving," I said.

She laughed, a little too shrilly. "It looks like a rapier wound to me, or a cut from a bolo knife or a lance. You're a knight in glossy armor."

Over her head, across the table, Jeff Winters winked at me. I felt a little embarrassed, and I remembered that I was still wearing Sam Allgood's spiked golf shoes. "Pardon me," I said to Katherine Allgood. "The knight forgot to take off his spurs." I stood up and started for the locker room.

Jeff Winters called after me, "Tell Sam and Lily to come out here."

I got my shoes from Sam Allgood's locker and put them on. Then I entered the shower room, washed, combed my hair, put on my necktie and coat and moved toward the front porch.

In my college days it had always been a point of pride with me, along with my classmates of that era, to wear leather heels with a small steel triangle wedged into the outer edges. None of us would have been caught dead wearing rubber heels. The more noise our heels made in cloistered halls, the better. But when I grew older and began to work for the National Detective Agency, I changed to rubber heels. They don't make much noise on a wooden floor, and I was standing on the porch in the early evening dusk, unobserved by Lily Winters and Sam Allgood.

It was just as well, because he had her in his arms and was kissing her as though it was his death hunger.

I backed up silently. I didn't make any more noise than a cat tiptoeing on a White House rug. When I was well inside the clubhouse I began to whistle "Jingle Bells," and I started once more for the porch. When I got there, they were standing apart, and Lily Winters was lighting a cigarette. The glow of the match threw dark shadows beneath her cheekbones. She looked at me and laughed.

"That tune," she said. "Christmas in July."

Sam Allgood said, too casually, "Dinner ready?"

"I guess so. Jeff said I should call you two."

Lily Winters moved to the door. "Come on, Sam. Whatever Jeff says—we must do." There was a faint bitterness in her voice. She entered the clubhouse.

Allgood came up to me and asked in a low voice, "Have you found out anything yet?"

"A little. I want to talk to you later."

He nodded and moved to the doorway. The light fell across his face, and I touched his arm. "You'd better wipe that lipstick off your chin," I said.

He paused, took a handkerchief from his breast pocket and dabbed at his face. "Thanks," he muttered without turning around. I followed him out to the rear porch.

The dinner wasn't very good. Everybody drank too much, including me, and I was glad when it was over. Katherine Allgood hugged my arm and announced that she was riding into town with Mr. Bennett-from-Cleveland. Jeff Winters said he would lead the way in his car. I disengaged Katherine Allgood's arm and went to bring my coupé up to the front porch steps.

It was a dark night, but as I approached my car I saw a sudden furtive movement in the shadows. I stepped to the grass beside the drive and moved swiftly and silently. As I came abreast of the coupé I could see the faint glow of a flashlight, and the dark form of a man leaning in the open door. The light was shining on my open bag lying on the seat, and the man was pawing through the contents. I stepped up behind him and grabbed him by one shoulder.

The light went out and he swung violently around. The flashlight smacked me across my cheek, and I cocked a fist and jabbed fast against the unseen face. I heard a grunt and swung again. I missed, and he ducked low, twisted loose from my grasp and flopped to the ground. I made a dive for him, but I wasn't fast enough. He scrambled to his feet and scooted through a hedge, and I heard the thud of running feet on the turf.

I turned to my car, switched on the dash light and looked through my bag. My socks, underwear, handkerchiefs and extra shirts, plus a full bottle of Bourbon, were all there, but my Smith and Wesson .38 revolver was gone. I was sorry about that, because I'd carried that particular gun for a long time. I closed the bag, tossed it back upon the deck behind the seat and drove up to the clubhouse.

Jeff Winters and his wife, Lily, were just getting into a big black sedan. Katherine Allgood was standing on the steps. I opened the door of my coupé, and she came down and got in beside me. I waited for the sedan ahead to get moving.

Katherine Allgood said, "I need a drink." Her voice was a little thick.

I had part of a pint of rye in the dash compartment, but I didn't mention it. I didn't have to. She found it, unscrewed the cap and took a long swallow. Silently she handed the bottle to me, and I pretended to take a drink. I'd had enough to drink for one night. I put the bottle back in the dash compartment, but she got it out again. She held it in her lap, and said in a complaining voice, "What're we waiting for?"

"Sam, I guess."

Ahead of us, Jeff Winters did a shave-and-a-haircut routine on the horn of his sedan just as Sam Allgood came out of the clubhouse and descended the steps. As Allgood got into the sedan, I heard Lily Winters yell, "Where you been, honey?"

"In the john," Allgood said, and Lily Winters laughed shrilly.

The sedan moved down the drive, and I followed. When we hit the main highway, I had to hold my coupé at sixty-five to keep Winters' car in sight.

Katherine Allgood said, "You didn't answer my question."

"What question?"

"About what you do."

"I'm in the earthworm business," I told her. "I raise worms. Did you know that it takes nature five hundred years to make one square inch of top soil, but that one earthworm will produce the same amount in one year?"

"All right," she said. "Don't tell me." She moved on the seat until she was close beside me. "I still think you're nice," she murmured.

I was trying to keep Winters' taillight in view. "Sure," I said. "I'm nice."

Suddenly she reached out and flicked off the ignition switch. The motor died. I put on the brakes and pulled over to the side of the road. The instant the car stopped rolling she had her arms around my neck and was pulling me down to her. It was suddenly very quiet, and I could hear the crickets singing in the fields around us.

The motor ticked a little, like motors do when they are cooling, and Katherine Allgood's lips were on my face. She twisted her body toward me, and I could see a smooth expanse of nylon-clad legs. I kissed her. Her lips were hot and soft and I liked it, but I was thinking of Sam Allgood.

She clung to me. Her fingernails dug into the back of my neck and her breath was on my cheek. "That was good," she whispered. "Kiss me again."

I reached my hand for the ignition switch.

"No," she breathed. "No." Her voice was desperate, pleading.

I pressed the starter button. I felt like a fool, but there was nothing else I could do. Sam Allgood was paying me to solve his troubles—not get mixed up in them. He was my client and I was supposed to do him a job—but not this kind. I pulled the coupé back onto the highway and headed for town.

Katherine Allgood sat up straight and slapped me hard across the face. It made me blink and she slapped me again. I didn't say anything and I didn't blame her—but I wasn't going to make a play for her just because she was burning up with jealousy over her husband.

She huddled in the far corner of the seat and began to sob. When we reached the outskirts of Wheatville, she sat up and began to do things to her face with the aid of a handkerchief and a silver compact.

"Turn right at the next street," she said coldly. "Third house on the left."

The black sedan was parked in the drive, and I pulled up behind it. The white house was long and low and rambling. There were soft lights in a big living room and through the windows I got a glimpse of an oil painting and the top of a white porcelain fireplace. Katherine Allgood got out of the coupé without speaking and walked to the door ahead of me. But we entered together. Jeff Winters and his wife were sitting side by side on a white English lounge, drinking highballs. Sam Allgood was leafing through a record album beside a mahogany console at the far end of the room. The muted strains of a Strauss waltz floated through the house.

Jeff Winters held up his glass and smiled. Sam Allgood turned and looked at his wife. She walked straight across the room and disappeared through an alcove beyond the fireplace.

"Good night, darling," Allgood called after her in mincing tones, and he winked at me. He didn't get an answer.

"Kate's tight," Lily Winters said. She had a cigarette in her mouth and was trying to hit the end of it with flame from a silver lighter.

Jeff Winters steadied her hand. "So are you, my pet," he said, smiling.

She giggled and swayed toward him, her long yellow hair falling over her face. She flung the hair back from her eyes, reached out a red-tipped thumb and forefinger and undid Winters' neat polka-dot bow tie. Winters grinned at Allgood and me, reached down and pulled his wife to her feet, put an arm around her and led her to the door. "We better go home," he said, "before she falls on her face." He nodded at me. "Glad to have met you, Bennett. Be seeing you."

They went out.

Sam Allgood poured whisky from a bottle on a table, added a squirt of soda and handed me a glass. "Swell people," he said. "Jeff and I went to school together."

I nodded in agreement. Then I said, "Is Mrs. Winters really good with a rifle?"

He gave me a quick sidelong glance. Then he carried his glass to a chair and sat down. "She's good with anything—rifle, pistol or shotgun. She's won a lot of marksmanship medals. Why?" His eyes were a little foggy, but he seemed sober enough.

I shrugged. "Just wondered."

Suddenly he threw back his handsome head and laughed. "My God, Bennett, you don't think that Lily's the one who has been taking pot shots at me?"

"I don't know," I said. "You're paying me to find out. Across the fence from the sixth hole there's a farmer with a mean look in his eye on account of his corn. Have you been trampling around in his field?"

"You mean Lem Fassler," he said. "He's a crackpot. He won't sell his land to the club, and he won't let us on his property to look for lost balls. We put up an out-of-bounds sign, but some of the boys still climb the fence."

"Do you?"

He laughed again. "Bennett, I've got a terrible hook. When I drive a golf ball it usually takes a terrific curve to the left—I can't seem to correct it. Red Roark had me cured once, but he's dead now. Sure, I've been in Fassler's field hunting balls—but he wouldn't shoot me for it."

"He might try to scare you," I said. "A guy like that. Somebody took a shot at me this afternoon."

He stared at me in surprise. "No kidding?"

"I was wearing that red cap of yours. Maybe he thought it was you."

"Oh," Allgood said. He looked disappointed. He paused and then he said, "If you're so damn sure it's Fassler ..."

"It seems to me," I broke in, "that you could have figured that out for yourself."

He looked down at his glass. "I thought of Fassler right away," he said. "I even asked him about it. But I still don't think he'd do a damn fool thing like that."

"He had a reason," I pointed out. "You've been trespassing on his land."

"Not when I got shot at," Allgood said stubbornly. "I was on the golf course."

"All right," I sighed. "You'd better tell me the rest of it."

He got up and poured more whisky into his glass. "That's all, damn it."

"What about Mrs. Winters?" I asked.

He turned on me so sharply that some of his drink spilled to the rug. "That's none of your damn business," he snapped. "We've been close friends for years—Jeff and Lily and Kate and me. Jeff's my partner. What if I did kiss Lily? You're a grown man. You ought to understand about those things."

"Maybe I'm old-fashioned," I said, "but does Jeff understand—and your wife?"

He sneered at me. "Don't be naive, Bennett."

I shrugged. "I'm just a private dick trying to do you a job. By the way, I met little Peggy Roark on the course today. Do you think that her dad really threw that match to the Alabama Kid a year ago?"

He nodded. "It sure as hell looked like it. I saw the match and it was pretty obvious. Red Roark never missed a two-foot putt in his life, but he missed one on the seventeenth in Cleveland—deliberately.... But what's that got to do with it?"

"Nothing, I guess," I said. "Peggy Roark told me that she's matched against your wife in the tournament playoff on Friday."

"That's right," Allgood said. "And I'm afraid she'll beat the pants off Kate, too." He laughed shortly. "And Kate won't like it. She can't bear to lose at anything."

I said, "Want me to keep on working for you?"

"Of course," he said impatiently. "You haven't found out anything for sure yet."

I yawned and he told me where I was to sleep. I went out to my car and got my bag. When I came in, I saw that Allgood had poured himself a fresh drink. He had taken off his coat and tie, and was thumbing through the record album again.

"How about a nightcap?" he asked me. "It's early yet."

"No, thanks. See you in the morning." I walked down a thick-carpeted hall with mirrors on the walls and gilt tables and brocade chairs beneath them. My room was the second one on my left. The door to the first room was standing open, and there was a light inside. I peeked in as I passed. Katherine Allgood, fully dressed, was lying very still, face down, on the silken cover of the bed.

I entered the room beyond, closed the door and sat down in a chair by a window. From the living room I could hear the faint lilting strains of *Tales from the Vienna Woods*. Apparently, Sam Allgood liked the music of Strauss the elder. After a while the music stopped. I waited. Then, faintly, through the walls, I heard a woman's voice and Sam Allgood's laugh. The woman spoke again, shrilly, and I thought I heard sobbing. Sam Allgood's voice rose harshly, but muffled, and a door slammed violently. Then the house was quiet.

For a while I sat by the window, gazing out at the night. From far down on the square of this town called Wheatville the Courthouse clock bonged twelve times. Another twenty-four hours was beginning, and my work was still before me. I sighed, undressed slowly and crawled into bed.

Sleep came quickly.

CHAPTER THREE

The sun on my face awoke me, but I turned over and closed my eyes again. The house was very still, and I lay more asleep than awake, thinking drowsily of why I was in Sam Allgood's house and of what I was doing in the town of Wheatville. The happenings of the previous day crawled slowly across my brain, and I remembered with pleasure the feel of Katherine Allgood's lips on mine—and I also remembered the sting of her fingers as she slapped me.

I thought of the bullet sighing past my ear as I stood on the sixth tee of the golf course, and of the cold, vacant gray eyes of a farmer named Lem Fassler. I remembered Lily Winters' lipstick on Sam Allgood's face, and I felt a faint pity for Jeff Winters, a grave, friendly man with a cheating wife.

I thought of many things, and maybe I dozed a little. The sudden sound of a car starting close by aroused me, and I got out of bed quickly and moved to the window. Sam Allgood was backing a new red sedan out of the drive. I watched him as he drove away in the direction of the business area of town. Then I yawned, took off my pajamas, and in an adjoining bathroom I slowly shaved, showered and dressed.

As I stepped into the hall, I saw that the door to Katherine Allgood's room was closed tightly. I moved past on the thick rug into the big living room, where a bar of morning sunlight glinted on the porcelain fireplace. A colored woman in a bright print dress was gathering up empty glasses and full ashtrays.

"Good morning," I said.

She turned listlessly, and said in a tired voice, "You Mr. Bennett?"

I nodded.

"Mr. Allgood, he said for you to tell me what you want for breakfast. We got ham and eggs an—"

"Never mind," I broke in, grinning at her. "I'll get something downtown."

She nodded in approval. "Mr. Allgood, he usually does, too. Guess he don't like to eat alone. Mrs. Allgood, she's hardly ever up early." She paused, and sighed. "But I suppose you'll be having lunch here?"

I shook my head. "I think not ... What's your name?"

"Jennifer. Mr. Allgood, he calls me Jenny."

"All right, Jenny. Give Mrs. Allgood my compliments, and tell her I'll see her later."

She nodded gloomily.

I picked up my hat from the table, went out and walked across the lawn to where I'd parked my car at the curb. As I drove along the wide pleasant streets toward the center of town, I thought that the more I saw of Wheatville the better I liked it—as a town. It was close to the metropolitan area, and yet in the country, and I decided that if I lived long enough to retire I'd pick a place like Wheatville. All the advantages of the city, without the jamming crowds and traffic. A person could get quickly to where he wanted to go, no matter if his destination was a night club, a department store, a golf course or a trout stream.

As I turned into the street which circled the square, I spotted Armand's Beauty Salon on a corner opposite the Courthouse. The place had a fancy chrome-and-blue-tinted-glass front, with a small bright marquee over the sidewalk. I drove slowly past it, nosed into a parking space at the curb and dropped a nickel in the inevitable parking meter. Three doors from Armand's was a small restaurant. I went in, sat at a counter and ordered orange juice, toast and coffee. The place was filled with well-dressed men and women. Everyone was gay and cheerful, talking to one another. It was ten minutes before nine o'clock.

A young fellow in a gray tweed coat and flannel slacks sitting next to me said, "Hey, mister, will you please slide the sugar down here?"

I slid the sugar down to him.

"Thanks," he said. "Nice day, isn't it?"

"Very nice," I agreed.

He poured a liberal quantity of sugar into his coffee, and said, "I sure hope the weather holds up for the big tournament tomorrow."

"What tournament?"

He looked at me in surprise. He had a crew haircut and friendly blue eyes. "You must be a stranger in town."

I smiled. "That's right."

"Well, I'll tell you. This is a sport-crazy town. Everybody goes to the high school football games in the fall, the basketball games in the winter and baseball in summer. We've turned out some good teams—the high school won the Northern State Football Championship last year. But I'm talking about the golf tournament tomorrow. Little girl named Peggy Roark is playing off the country club championship with Mrs. Sam Allgood. They tied last week, and this'll be eighteen holes, match play. Peggy is good—her dad used to be pro at the club when I was a caddy—but Mrs. Allgood is good, too. The whole town is making bets on the winner."

"Who are you betting on?" I asked him.

He grinned. "Me? I'm putting my dough on Peggy Roark. She's cute." He paused and added hastily, "Mrs. Allgood is nice, too, but, oh, you know—she's older."

"I see. This Peggy Roark—her dad wouldn't be Red Roark?"

He nodded vigorously. "That's right. Best pro the club ever had."

I said thoughtfully, "Seems to me I heard something about him ..."

The young fellow broke in hotly, "It's not true. Red didn't throw the

Midwest Open—even if it looked like he did. Red was a right guy."

"Sure." I drank my orange juice and started on my toast.

The young fellow stood up. "Well, I gotta get over to the store—I work at Eddie's Auto Supply. We got a big sale on seat covers and batteries today." He placed a hand on my shoulder. "If you're in town tomorrow, come out and watch Peggy win."

"I'll do that."

At nine o'clock the crowd in the restaurant thinned out. I drank my second cup of coffee and moved to the cashier's desk at the end of the counter. With my change, a snub-nosed brunette gave me a friendly smile. "Thank you, sir. Come again."

"I will," I promised, and I went out onto the sidewalk. Friendly was the word for Wheatville, I thought. A dream of a town, I told myself fondly, just bursting with good will and neighborliness. Of course, there was a little matter of deadly bullets whizzing across a golf course, but nobody had been hurt. It was just a playful warning to golfers to keep out of a cornfield. Nobody could blame a man for not wanting his nice young corn trampled. I reminded myself to see Lem Fassler, the farmer, and ask him, in a friendly, neighborly way, to please refrain from alarming the country club members. That would take care of Sam Allgood's problem, and then I would see what trifling worry was annoying Mr. Donati, of Armand's Beauty Salon. But why would a beauty shop need a private detective? Suddenly I decided to find out—before I had my friendly man-to-man talk with Lem Fassler.

I lit a cigarette and smoked it while I loitered in the pleasant morning sunshine. Then I walked down the street to Armand's Beauty Salon, pushed open a heavy glass door and stepped into air-conditioned quiet. I moved over a soft midnight-blue rug to a small lacquered maple desk. A girl sat behind it. She gazed up at me coolly with eyes that almost matched the rug.

"Yes?" she said crisply.

I said politely, "I'd like to see Mr. Donati."

She pressed the tip of a gold pencil to her plump lower lip and gazed at me thoughtfully. Then she tapped the pencil on the glossy cover of a calfskin book embossed in gold. "Do you have an appointment?"

I took off my battered gray felt hat. "Just tell him that Mr. Bennett from Cleveland is here."

She frowned, opened the book and ran the tip of her pencil down the pages. I looked her over. When I entered I had seen her legs beneath the desk, and I knew they were all right. The part of her above the desk was all right, too. A rather narrow face, a straight nose with a little flare at the nostrils, a generous red mouth, long black lashes, neatly plucked eyebrows. Her hair was sleek and black and glossy, gathered low at the back of her neck. She was wearing a pale blue suit, tailored to a razor's edge, with a white starched collar peeking over the severe neckline. A little bronze plaque on a corner of the desk read MISS JUSTIN.

Her gaze lifted to the third button of my vest, passed blankly over my blue knit tie and came to a stop on my straight black hair. I suddenly remembered that I needed a haircut. She closed her book with a snapping sound. "I have no record of an appointment for you, Mr. Bennett. Armand is booked solid for the next week. If you'll leave your telephone number ..."

I said, "Do you mean to tell me that men come here?"

"Certainly."

"What for?"

"Manicures, waves," she said coldly. "And facials. Why not?"

I leaned forward and put my hands on the desk. "Look, honey, I don't want a hairdo. Just—" I stopped.

Behind Miss Justin a mirrored door opened and a man stepped out. He was a big man with wide heavy shoulders. I guessed him to be about six-foot-two, and around two-ten on the hoof. His thick tawny hair, lovingly rippled into mathematical waves, was long over his ears and at the back of his neck. He had a wide face, with a thick short nose above a heavy-lipped mouth, a firm chin cut by a deep cleft and thick yellow eyebrows over small, pale brown eyes. He reminded me of a male lion. He was wearing a knee-length, pale blue smock, belted snugly at his narrow waist and buttoned smoothly over one side of his big chest to a close-fitting standup collar. Below the smock were sharply creased gray-striped trousers and pointed black shoes.

The girl said hastily, "Mr. Donati, this gentleman—"

"Bennett's the name," I said.

The big man moved around the desk with a quick smooth stride and held out his hand. His grasp was firm, but his fingers felt damp and oily. "Ah, yes," he said in a deep pleasant voice. "Meester *Ben-ay*. This way, please." He stepped back to the mirrored door and held it open.

As I moved around the desk I winked at the girl. She turned quickly away and began to flip the pages of her book. I walked past the big man and stood still. He closed the door, bowed slightly, crossed quickly to another mirrored door and opened it. "*Allons*," he said, smiling. He had big white teeth.

I moved past him into a big room with a deep blue rug. Pale blue leather chairs were scattered about. Apparently, blue was the motif of the Armand Beauty Salon. Donati motioned me to a chair and sat down behind a massive blue leather and chrome desk. I sat down also and the deep chair gave out with a pleasant swishing sound. I dropped my hat to the rug and stretched out my legs. Donati leaned forward and folded his bare arms on the desk. His arms and wrists were thick and powerful-looking, and covered with golden hair. He smiled at me, showing his big white teeth. "Thank you for coming, Meester *Ben-ay*," he said.

"Bennett's the name," I told him, "and *allons* isn't the right word, exactly. You can drop the window dressing with me."

He frowned—for just an instant. Then he threw back his big lionlike head and laughed. He took a cigarette from a silver box on his desk and offered the box to me. I shook my head and extracted a cigarette from my own crumpled pack. He flicked a heavy silver lighter into flame and held it for me.

"*Merci, Monsieur*," I said, grinning at him. "You call this fancy establishment Armand's Beauty Salon. What's your real name and what's on your mind?"

He turned to flick ashes into a massive bronze tray. Light glinted on his carefully waved hair. When he turned toward me again, his smile was gone.

"My name is Pete Donati," he said harshly. "I used to be a cosmetic salesman—Detroit territory. Now I'm in this racket, and I need a job done. That's why I called you. You'll get your money, and I want the job done fast." He leaned forward, his big jaw set. One strand of his waved hair came loose from its allotted place and dangled over his broad forehead.

I held up a soothing palm. "All right, Pete. Don't get in an uproar. Tell me the job."

"Hair," he said abruptly. "High-priced hair—blond, black, red, gray and dyed. Some of the ritzy dames who come in here are losing it—under my dryers, in the permanent wave machines, all over the place. Their scalps are burned, and some of my best customers are going bald. They're all set to sue me—they would sue me in a minute—but what woman wants to admit in court that she's bald-headed?"

"Go on," I said.

"It's ruining me fast. Twenty-five bucks a treatment is a lot of dough, and a lot of those dames come here plenty often. I want to keep them coming. I've got to keep them coming—so that I can get the hell out of these sissy clothes and stop talking a cheap imitation of a French accent and get my damned hair cut and start living like a human being again." He paused and scowled at me.

I nodded sympathetically, and he went on: "Do you think I like going around with my hair curled like a chorus boy's, and saying, 'Meester' and 'Mah-dam' and 'Oui, oui'? And wearing these corny clothes? My wife got me into it. She made me go to beauty school, and she was right—we've made a lot of money. In a couple of years we can sell the joint and get the hell out. That's all I'm living for, all I dream about. My wife said, 'Call yourself Pierre or Antoine or Armand. Let your hair grow long and wave it, flirt with 'em a little, talk Frenchy—and sock 'em plenty for a treatment. They'll love it. We'll pick a town not too big, not too small, and we'll clean up.' Marianne said that and I'll give her credit." He waved a hand in a half circle. "This is all ours—all paid for. We're out of the red. In another couple of years I counted on cutting my hair, selling out and enjoying life. I've sure as hell earned it. And now we got clients with scorched scalps. It'll ruin us, all we've built up." He jabbed his cigarette viciously into the ashtray.

"Does your wife work in the shop, too?" I asked him.

He shook his big head. "Not anymore. She did at first—until she had an accident. But she worked in beauty shops for ten years before she met me, and she knew all the angles."

"Does she know you have hired me?"

"Sure. I got no secrets from her. It was mostly the dough she'd saved that put us in business."

"But you are the big drawing card?"

He frowned. "Yeah. Something like that."

"How many people work for you?"

He spread the fingers of one big hand. "Five. A receptionist, three operators and a bookkeeper."

"And that's the personnel of Armand's Beauty Salon?"

He nodded. "All except me." Suddenly he grinned. "And I don't work. I'm a hair stylist."

"Pardon me, but what's a hair stylist?"

He laughed shortly, got up and moved around beside my chair. He clicked his heels smartly, leaned over me, showed his teeth, raised both hands level with his arms and spread his fingers, thumbs and forefingers touching. "Mah-dam," he said in a mincing voice, "for your een-dividual personalitee Armand suggest zee part on zee left, just so, bangs over zee right eye, up-swirl in zee back. Zat coiffure, Mah-dam, Armand create for you alone." He straightened up and swore bitterly. "Don't laugh, Bennett. I get twenty-five bucks for that." He moved to his desk. "How about a drink?" he asked abruptly.

"It's a little early in the day," I murmured, "but if you insist ..."

He opened a lower drawer of the big desk and took out a tall slim bottle of brandy and two short glasses. He filled the glasses and handed me one. It was good brandy, smooth and hot. As I sipped at it, Donati sat down behind the desk and tossed off his drink in two swallows. Then he filled his glass again and scowled at me. "Well?" he said.

"It's a new kind of job for me," I told him, "but I'll snoop around a little. It'll cost you fifty dollars a day, plus expenses—and I like my hair the way it is. Which one of the five people working here would want to ruin your business?"

He moved his big shoulders impatiently beneath the sky-blue smock. "They've all been with me a long time, and I pay 'em good—for Wheatville. I've had a chemist check all my stock of lotions, oils, shampoos, permanent wave solutions, hair dyes, tints, soaps, lacquers—the works. He didn't find anything harmful in any of it. It's got me nuts."

"Where do you suggest I start?"

He took a swallow of his drink. "How the hell do I know? You're a private dick. I've read in books about the smart things you guys do—let's see you deliver." He drank again and sneered, "But I suppose you gotta have a murder before you can get going? You couldn't maybe clear up a simple little thing like this without publicity and cut throats and blood up to your ankles, could you?"

From outside the door a woman began to scream. "Take it off! Take it off! It burns, it burns!"

I started to get out of my chair, but Pete Donati gazed at me calmly. "There it goes again," he said wearily. "You take a look. I'm sick of it."

I went out of his office and moved swiftly down a mirror-lined corridor to a large room with skylights and big windows. It reminded me of an artist's studio, except that there were rows of bottles, funnel-shaped hair dryers, high leather-and-chrome chairs, more mirrors, manicure tables, the gadgets and weird machinery of the beauty doctor's profession.

At one end of the long room a blond woman was running around in circles, clawing at her head. Three girls in sky-blue smocks were chasing her. All three of the girls were snatching at the woman's head in futile attempts to jerk loose a series of small metal clips from her tightly curled hair. When this happened the woman would yell louder. I watched the scene, fascinated.

Miss Justin came running down the hall and over to the woman. "Hold her," she snapped at the three girls. The girls ran the woman into a corner and held her still, while Miss Justin quickly and deftly removed the clips from the woman's hair. When the last one was pulled free, the woman covered her face with her hands and began to sob. The three girls put their arms around her and led her through an archway at the end of the room. It was then I recognized one of them as little Peggy Roark, the girl I had met on the golf course. Miss Justin also disappeared through the archway. I walked back to Pete Donati's office.

He was talking on the telephone. I sat down and lit a cigarette.

"*Au contraire*, Mah-dam," Donati was saying. "Armand shall be dee-light to break deer othaire appointment so zat he can serve you. Ee-leven o'clock ... *Oui, oui*, Mah-dam!" He slammed the phone into its cradle with a vicious snap of his wrist. "They know that phony accent is a lot of hogwash," he said to me, "but still they go for it. Women!" He poured brandy into his glass, drank deeply, and gazed at me with brooding eyes. "Who got burned this time?" he asked sullenly.

"Some woman with blond hair."

He glanced at his wristwatch. "That would be Mrs. Osterman. Hair used to be gray—we changed it to blond for her. She's been good for at least fifty a month—her husband owns half the business blocks in town." He sighed. "All down the drain now. She'll probably switch to Bertha."

"What are those metal things you use on their hair?" I asked.

"Cold wave clamps."

I looked dumb.

"A fairly recent invention for permanent waves," he explained. "The most important improvement since the old-time marcel, and in common use now. We used to give all waves with electric machines—baked the waves in the hair. We still do some permanents that way—a few clients prefer 'em. The cold wave, or machineless method, doesn't require heat—merely a chemical solution on a pad held in place by a small clamp to hold the curls in position. Some shops don't use the clamps, but we find them more efficient."

"What's in the solution?"

He shrugged. "I don't know—some chemical to break down the structure of the hair so that it can be waved. We buy the complete outfits in individual kits. Each kit contains enough pads and lotion for one permanent wave. We had a chemist check the solution in all the kits in our last shipment. Nothing harmful in it. Just an alkali solution; nothing to cause a burn."

"And the operator soaks the pads in the solution and then applies them to the hair?"

He nodded gloomily.

"All right," I said. "I'll want the pads used on Mrs. Osterman's hair. Miss Justin just took them off."

"Okay. But you won't find anything."

"Something causes those women to get burned."

"Sure," he said harshly. "But what? It's driving me nuts."

"Do you have records of all your employees?"

He nodded his big head. "Hector has."

"Who's Hector?"

"Hector Griffith. He's a kind of combination bookkeeper, stock clerk, janitor and general handy man." He added with a faint sneer, "My wife hired him." He pressed a button beneath the edge of his desk.

I could have maybe said, "Seven-come-eleven," before the door opened and a tall slender man walked in. I guessed his age to be somewhere in the early forties. His hair was brown, cut rather short, parted on the side and graying a little over the temples. He had a thin face, deep-set intelligent brown eyes behind tortoise-shell-rimmed glasses and a thin well-shaped mouth.

He was wearing the uniform of Armand's Beauty Salon—a knee-length sky-blue smock. If the smock had been white, he would have resembled a doctor in a cigarette ad. He did, anyhow. All he needed was a stethoscope hanging around his neck.

Donati introduced us and we shook hands. Hector Griffith smiled in a quiet dignified manner. I figured he was wasting his time keeping books for Armand's Beauty Salon, and I thought of products he might sell his modeling service to—whisky, for example. I decided that he would look wonderful dressed in a tweed coat and standing before a shelf of books with a highball in his hand.

Donati gave me a quick wink and said, "Hector, Mr. Bennett is from the National Beauty Council. He's making a survey for us to see if there is any way in which we can improve our service—and get more money for it."

Griffith nodded seriously. "A fine idea."

"Mr. Bennett would like to look over the records of our employees," Donati said. "Will you get them for him?"

"Certainly," Griffith said quietly. He turned and went out. A blond girl poked her head in the door. "Mr. Donati, it happened to Mrs. Osterman. She says she's going to sue—"

Donati pointed a thick forefinger at her. "I know it, Millie," he snapped. "Isn't it time for Mrs. Dickson's manicure?"

"Yes, sir," the girl said breathlessly. She disappeared. Donati cursed under his breath and poured more brandy.

The telephone on his desk tinkled politely. He swooped it up, and his broad face was one big scowl. "Yes?"

I finished my brandy and lit another cigarette.

"Yes, yes, Hector," Donati said. "Everybody. Me, you, the girls, all of us." He slammed the telephone back into its cradle.

The door opened and a woman stepped inside.

I don't know how old she was. She could have been thirty—or fifty. She was wearing a white silk summer dress, very tight and very expensive, and white ankle-strap shoes with two-inch platform soles. Nice legs, bare, expertly tinted with leg make-up. Pale yellow hair fell around her shoulders in soft folds, framing her face.

When I got to her face, I stared. I didn't want to, but I couldn't help it. I knew I would remember that face for a long time, especially on dark nights when it was raining and clouds bunched behind the tops of tall trees. It was an ugly scarred face, pitted and lumpy—cheeks, nose, lips and chin—all horribly disfigured. Her skin was heavily coated with powder in a pitiful attempt to hide the ugliness, and the puckered scarred lips were painted a vivid red.

It made me want to swear. No woman should look like that. And yet, as I stared, I had a feeling of elusive beauty behind the horrible features.

Donati stood up and smiled at her. "Hello, honey. This is Mr. Bennett, the man I told you about. Mr. Bennett, meet my wife, Marianne."

I aroused myself as from a stupor. I stood up, mumbled something and bowed slightly. She smiled, and I saw that she had white even teeth—too perfect for the rest of her features. She spoke. I don't recall what she said, but her voice was low and rich and lovely, and it made my spine tingle. It was like champagne bubbling from a fountain.

She turned away from me, and spoke to her husband. "Darling, I'm so glad Mr. Bennett is here. I met Mrs. Osterman outside. She's—"

Donati held up a hand. "Yes, yes. I know," he said grimly. There was a gentle knock on the door.

Donati yelled, "Come in!"

Hector Griffith entered and stood just inside the door. His dark-rimmed glasses glittered in the yellow light as his gaze hovered upon Mrs. Donati for an instant and then swung to her husband. He held some small white cards in his hand.

"Give the cards to Mr. Bennett," Donati said curtly.

Mrs. Donati said, "Hello, Hector."

Hector Griffith turned and nodded gravely, "Good morning, Marianne." Then he turned and handed me the cards.

I placed them in my coat pocket, picked up my hat and moved to the door. "I'll be back," I said to Donati.

He nodded gloomily. Mrs. Donati smiled at me. I knew it was a smile, because I could see it in her eyes. The movement of her scarred lips was more like a snarl. I looked away quickly.

Hector Griffith gave me a polite little bow as I went out.

In the hallway I bumped against the receptionist, Miss Justin. She had been standing just outside the door. She let out a little startled gasp and backed away from me. Her gold-embossed leather book was tucked under her arm.

I jerked a thumb at Donati's door. "Just go right on in," I invited her. "You can hear better then."

She tilted her pretty nose in the air and stepped past me into the office.

CHAPTER FOUR

The big clock in the tower of the Courthouse told me that it was ten minutes before eleven. I crossed the square and entered Wheatville's biggest drugstore. It was almost exactly opposite Armand's Beauty Salon and I saw that it was one of a big national chain. A sign in the window said *Bring Your Prescriptions Here-24-hour Service—Open Day and Night.* There was a long soda and lunch counter, a vast array of bright shelves overflowing with every conceivable pharmaceutical commodity and counters stacked with an infinite display of objects, ranging from radios to Teddy bears. In the rear were two telephone booths.

I entered one of the booths and thumbed a worn directory until I came to BEAUTY SHOPS. Wheatville boasted no less than eight of them. I was not surprised, because I knew that many wealthy people lived in and around the town, and that some even commuted the sixty miles to Cleveland every day. Besides Armand's, there were three other shops with addresses close to the business district. The rest were scattered in outlying sections of town, small neighborhood shops, I guessed, perhaps worthy of my scrutiny later on. The town shops were *Gertrude's Beauty Shoppe*, and *The Moderne Hairdressers, Inc.*, and a place called *Bertha's Beauty Bar, the House of Thrilling Personalized Beauty Service*.

I had a glass of ginger ale at the soda counter. It blended very well with Pete Donati's brandy. Then I took a stroll around the square. I found Gertrude's Beauty Shoppe first. It was a dark hole in the wall between a beer joint and an electrical appliance shop. Dusty windows were filled with sun-faded cardboard boxes, presumably containing bottles of shampoos and lotions. I passed it up. If Gertrude's business was bad, the reason was obvious.

Bertha's Beauty Bar, a half block away, was different. It was almost as elegant as Armand's, with much chrome and indirect lighting. I went in.

There was a reception room like a doctor's office but fancier, with a green linoleum floor, red leather chairs, mirrors and tables covered with magazines. A man sat in one of the chairs, reading a gaudy-covered magazine called *Passionate Love*. He lowered the magazine slightly and stared at me silently over the top.

"Where's Bertha?" I asked him.

Carefully he closed the magazine, marking his place by turning the corner of a page, and laid it on a table beside his chair. Then he stood up. He was a tall man, over six feet, with narrow sloping shoulders and a puffy stomach bulging around a fancy plastic belt. His hair was too black to be natural, but it was thick and neatly waved. It covered the tops of his ears and flowed out in the back like a southern senator's. He had a smooth tanned skin, a high bony forehead and a wide thin-lipped mouth. His eyes were gray, with tiny bloody spiderwebs in them. A thin black mustache penciled his upper lip to the drooping corners of his mouth. He was wearing a lavender silk sport shirt buttoned at the collar, white whipcord slacks and white sandals over yellow socks.

He caressed his mustache with a long forefinger. "I'm Bertha," he said.

"Of the House of Thrilling Personalized Beauty Service?" I asked politely.

"I don't want any," he said.

"You don't want any what?"

"Whatever you're selling, my friend," he said.

"I've got a good line of shampoos," I said. "At a good price."

"No."

"How about wave pads?"

He turned away and picked up his magazine. "No. Nothing today."

"Kind of slow, huh?" I said. "I just came from Armand's. He gave me a nice order."

He turned slowly to stare at me thoughtfully. "Armand's." There was a flicker of interest in his eyes.

I nodded. "I been selling to Pete for a long time."

"Don't give me that guff," he sneered. "I happen to know that he buys all his stuff from Northern Ohio Beauty Supply."

"Not his shampoo," I said. "Or his cuticle nippers. He buys that stuff from me. It's a good account, too."

"So you know his real name, eh?" he said.

"Of course," I said, and I held up two fingers close together. "Pete and me are just like that. I'm the one who told him to change his name to Armand. 'Pete,' I said to him, 'you won't get any place in the beauty business with a name like Pete.' So he changed his name to Armand and now he packs them in."

"Him and his fake Frenchy talk," the black-haired man sneered.

"It makes me sick. I had the beauty business in this town all sewed up—until he muscled in on me. And now, like today, I'm just sitting around waiting for appointment calls. Had to send the girls home. It used to be a nice racket—until phonies like him began to spoil the public."

"Maybe," I said, "but they sure eat up that French stuff."

"Nuts," he snapped. "Now, take me. My name's Bert. I figure they won't go for that, so I call my place Bertha's Beauty Bar. Three *B's*, see? And 'Bertha' gives it the feminine touch."

"That's very good," I admitted, "but you can't beat that French angle. How about calling your place Bertholde's Beauty Bar? Or Pierre's? That's what the dames pay big money for. They like a romantic atmosphere with their hair-curling."

"Yeah?"

"Sure." I glanced quickly around the room. There was a sky-blue smock hanging over a chair on the opposite side of the room. "How many girls you got?" I asked.

"Three." He paused, and added gloomily, "Anyhow, I had three, but I never know if they're all gonna show up for work or not."

"Pete's got a clever stunt," I said. "Everybody in his place wears blue."

"I know it," he said. "But I make my girls wear white. It looks cleaner—like they was nurses."

"Too common," I said. "A color is better. More distinctive."

"Yeah?"

"Well," I said, "see you next trip." I moved to the door.

"Just a minute," he said. "What are you getting a gallon for shampoo?"

I turned slowly. I didn't know if shampoo was ten dollars or ten cents a gallon. "What're you paying now?" I asked him.

"A dollar-eighty-nine."

I took his word for it, and said briskly, "I can let you have it for one-seventy-six. For six gallons or more maybe I could shave it a little—one-seventy-two."

"That's a good price," he admitted. "What outfit you with?" I thought fast. "Marvello Cosmetics—out of Chicago."

"Never heard of 'em. How long has Armand been buying from you?"

"Oh, a long time—ever since they gave me the Ohio territory."

"How come you never called on me before?"

"Uh—well, the policy of the company has been to sell only one shop in a community. But recently they broadened the policy to include one or two other selected shops."

"Now that's big-hearted," he sneered.

"You don't want anything?"

"No."

I gave him a bright smile, said, "That's your privilege, sir." Once more I turned to the door.

Again his voice stopped me. "Could you make that shampoo a dollar-seventy even?"

I hesitated, moved my lips silently as if I were calculating my diminishing margin of profit, and then I said, "Well, if you took a dozen gallons ..."

"All right," he said quickly, and a secret smile of satisfaction at his bargain flickered around his lips.

I took an old envelope from my inside coat pocket and carefully wrote *Hickory, Dickory, Dock*. Then I glanced up, and asked politely, "COD?"

"My credit's as good as Pete's," he snapped.

I raised my eyebrows. "Charge? Certainly." I scribbled again, replaced the envelope in my pocket. "Thanks, Bertha."

"Bert," he said shortly. "Bert Horner."

I grinned at him. "Thanks for the order, Bert." I went out.

It was still too early for lunch, and since, by accepting Pete Donati's brandy, I'd already broken a rather flexible rule against drinking in the morning, I found a small bar close to the square and ordered a dry martini. Then I got out the cards Hector Griffith had given me and looked them over. They were all neatly typed, and I studied the ones which interested me.

ROARK, Margaret, 22, single, operator, machineless and machine permanent waves. Manicures. Salary, $30.00 per week, plus comm. and tips.

DONATI, Peter, 38, half-owner, married, one dependent, hair stylist. Salary, $200.00 per week, plus profits.

GRIFFITH, Hector, 44, bookkeeper, general office acc'ting, divorced, no dependents. Salary, $75.00 per week.

JUSTIN, Joyce, 27, single, receptionist, telephone operator, no dependents. Salary, $100.00 per week, plus bonus. (See Mr. Donati.)

I glanced briefly at the two remaining cards bearing the employment record of two girls who apparently specialized in simple hair washing, hair setting and manicures. Their salaries were listed at $40.00 per week, plus tips and commissions.

I drank the martini down to the olive, ate the olive, decided I was hungry and moved out to the street. It lacked ten minutes until twelve noon. The sidewalks were filled with noon-hour pedestrians, and a thick stream of cars passed in the street and jammed up at the traffic lights. I walked around the square to the big drugstore and called Sam Allgood's office.

A female answered, and from her prim dry tones I guessed that it was the bird-woman in Allgood's outer office. "Who is calling, please?"

I told her and she said, "Just a moment."

I waited maybe two minutes before Allgood's voice said, "What's the matter, Bennett?"

"Nothing. I just wanted to ask you to have lunch with me."

"Sorry—I'm tied up. Do you have anything to report?"

"Uh—nothing new, but I expect to have something definite soon."

"I hope so, Bennett," he said coldly. "I'll expect you for dinner this evening—about six-thirty. It'll look better to my wife. And remember, you're supposed to be a business friend from Cleveland. I don't want to worry her."

"I see," I said. "What kind of business?"

"That's your worry," he said sharply. "Think of something. And I expect you to wind up this work for me as soon as possible. What have you been doing all morning, anyhow?"

"Investigating," I said. "It looks like it's just a matter of pinning the shooting on the farmer, and—"

"I prefer not to discuss it on the telephone," he broke in sharply.

I laughed and hung up on him. To hell with Sam Allgood. He was a client, sure, but there was something queer about his hiring me to find out who was shooting at him—when it was obvious that it was the farmer, Lem Fassler. I hadn't decided yet what I was going to do, but I knew that I wasn't going to put on a red cap and stand on number six tee and wait for another bullet to come my way. I'd have to figure out another method of cornering Lem Fassler. In the meantime, I was in the unique position of having a choice of work. I could start snooping around for Pete Donati in an attempt to learn who was singeing his customers' hair and scalps, or I could set a trap for Lem Fassler.

The last idea intrigued me. Maybe I could hire some unsuspecting jerk to put on a red cap and stand on number six tee with a golf club in his hand, while I skulked in the bushes near Fassler's barn, ready to jump out and grab the farmer with a hot rifle in his hand. Then it would be a simple matter to compare the rifle with the slugs found in the shelter house, and Fassler's goose would be cooked.

I toyed with this notion for a while, but the big drawback was finding a stooge to serve as bait for the trap. Sam Allgood himself would be perfect, but I doubted that I could persuade him to help. Sam Allgood was scared of something or someone, and I wasn't at all sure that it was of Lem Fassler and his rifle. At least, I felt that Pete Donati was being honest with me. He had a problem, pure and simple. It was a problem that was affecting his income, his livelihood, and he sincerely wanted help. I hoped I could give it to him.

I had lunch at the restaurant where I'd eaten breakfast. As I paid my check, the snub-nosed brunette behind the cash register recognized me and smiled. "Glad to see you again, sir."

I bought a package of cigarettes and asked her if she could recommend a hotel to me. Since I was working for Pete Donati and not exclusively for Sam Allgood, I decided I needed a base of operations other than Allgood's house.

The brunette said, "The Hotel Seneca is the biggest and newest."

"What else?"

"Well, there's the Wheatville Inn. It's smaller and older, but it's quiet."

"That's for me. Where is it?"

She told me, and as I turned to leave, she said, "We're having braised veal for dinner this evening, with peach shortcake."

I smiled at her. "Sounds good, but I can't make it tonight."

"I'm sorry. Will we be seeing you again?" There was an Invitation, a something in her eyes, and I quickly noted the absence of any entangling engagement or wedding ring on her finger.

I hesitated, knowing that it was my move. She lowered her lashes and pretended to count quarters in the cash register drawer. And then I told myself firmly, *Business first, Bennett*, and I said, "Sure, honey, I'll be back." I went out quickly.

The Wheatville Inn was on a side street, away from the bustle and noise of the square. It was an old white frame structure, rambling and long with a wide veranda and much shrubbery, and many trees on the wide lawn. A friendly old pappy in a white linen suit and a black string tie greeted me and declined my offer to pay in advance—because my bag was at Sam Allgood's house. He tossed me a key and said, "You got an honest face, young feller."

A husky kid in a white T-shirt emblazoned with the words *Wheatville High School* took me up a wide stairway to my room on the second floor, opened the windows and turned on the lights. I tossed him a quarter and said, "Thanks, sonny. What's your name?"

"Gregory."

I pointed at his chest. "You play on the team?"

"Second string tackle," he said proudly. "I'm working here this summer."

"Fine, Gregory. If I need anything, I'll ask for you."

"Thanks, mister." He went out.

It was a nice room, spacious and furnished simply, with a big old-fashioned bathroom. From the window I could see the wide quiet street, and in the distance, beyond the town, the fields and trees were green in the afternoon sun. I took off my coat and shoes, and lay down on the massive feather bed. I thought guiltily that I was supposed to be working for two clients, but the bed was soft and the room was cool and quiet, and I drifted pleasantly into sleep.

It was three o'clock in the afternoon when I awoke. Hastily I rolled off the bed, washed my face in cold water, put on my shoes and coat and went down the stairs. The old pappy was still on the desk. He waved a friendly hand at me, and said, "Afternoon."

I waved back at him and stepped through the screen door to the wide veranda. Two elderly ladies were slowly rocking at the far end, and the surrounding grounds were cool and shaded. I followed a gravel drive to the street and headed for the square. Back here on the side streets the whole town seemed wrapped in a summer afternoon drowsiness, but when I reached the square I saw that many persons were on the streets and going briskly about their business. I stood on a corner and tried to make up my mind. Should I start working for Sam Allgood or Pete Donati?

Across the square my idle gaze fell on the chrome and blue glass of Armand's Beauty Salon. Almost automatically I headed in that direction. Sam Allgood would have to wait. Plenty of time to corner Lem Fassler. I pushed open the heavy glass door and stepped into the air-conditioned hush. From behind her desk, Miss Justin glanced up. When she saw me she looked annoyed and bit at her plump lower lip.

I said, "Is Mr. Donati in?"

"I'll see," she said coolly. "He came back after lunch, but he may have left again." She picked up her telephone and pressed a button on the edge of her desk. Presently she hung up with a decisive click. "He doesn't answer," she said crisply.

"How about Mrs. Donati?"

"She is rarely in the shop. She isn't here now."

I moved around her desk toward the mirrored door. "I'll just mosey on back," I told her.

She started to get out of her chair, the beginning of a protest on her lips, but I opened the door quickly, stepped inside and closed it behind me. I stood in the mirror-lined hallway and listened to the hum of the hair dryers and the faint babble of female voices. I crossed the hall and knocked on the door of Donati's office. I didn't get any response, so I knocked again, louder.

While I waited, a door opened behind me and I turned. Miss Justin stood at the end of the hall, silently watching me. I grinned at her, swung once more to Donati's door and turned the knob. The door was unlocked, and I pushed it open slowly and stepped inside.

I stared straight at the back of a small head of bright copperish hair with two braids hanging over small blue-clad shoulders. The shoulders were quivering. I saw a slender little waist and the back of a pair of straight sturdy legs. The top of the girl's head came to about where I would hang a watch chain, if I had a watch chain. She didn't turn around, but stood there trembling silently.

I looked beyond her and I saw Pete Donati. He was sitting in his chair behind the big desk. His head was thrown back and the front of his blue smock was soaked darkly from the shoulders down. I don't know what kept his head up, because his throat was cut from ear to ear.

I kicked the door shut. The girl before me began to sway and her knees buckled. I jumped forward and caught her before she fell. She weighed about ninety pounds. It wasn't until I'd dumped her in one of Donati's big chairs that I saw it was Peggy Roark, the little golfer. I left her and moved over to the desk. It was a mess. Blood had spurted to its glass top and dripped to the thick blue carpet. I had never seen so much blood from one killing. Of all the ways to kill a man, I thought, a cut throat is the worst.

There was a faint moaning sound behind me. I turned. Peggy Roark was stirring in the chair. She opened her eyes, and she saw Donati again. She squeezed her eyes shut and sat rigidly. Then her small body began to quiver. I moved over, grasped her by the shoulders and shook her gently. She opened her eyes and stared at me dumbly.

The freckles on her small round face looked as big as pennies.

"Tell me about it," I said.

The paint on her lips was like blood against the pallor of her skin. Her mouth worked soundlessly. Then she began to speak, her gaze fixed on my necktie.

"I—I came in—just now. I was going to tell him I'm quitting. I—I can't stand it here anymore. I knocked—and I came in—and I saw him ..." She covered her face with her hands and began to sob, the tears trickling between her fingers.

Somebody knocked on the door. I crossed to it and opened it about three inches. Miss Justin stood outside. "Is Mr. Donati there?" she asked curtly.

"Yes," I said.

She tried to jerk open the door. "I want to see him."

"I'm afraid you wouldn't," I said.

She bit at her lower lip in annoyance. "It's important," she snapped. I moved aside. "All right. There he is."

She stepped briskly past me into the office. Then she stopped abruptly, and she didn't fool around. She screamed long and loud. It made my ears jump. Hastily I closed and locked the door. She stopped screaming and began looking for a place to fall. I guided her to a chair and she flopped into it.

There was a babble of voices in the hall outside and somebody pounded on the door. "Go away!" I shouted loudly. The pounding stopped.

I moved over the thick rug and reached across Donati's desk for the telephone. But my hand stopped. The instrument was dripping with blood. I took a clean handkerchief from my pocket, draped it over the receiver and picked it up. The handkerchief didn't help much, and I held the receiver gingerly with a thumb and forefinger.

When I was connected with the police, I said, "Murder. Armand's Beauty Salon."

The cop on the desk stuttered a couple of seconds and then he blurted, "W-who?"

"Armand. You'd better bring the clean-up boys. His throat's cut."

The cop stuttered some more. "Who—who's calling?"

"Never mind that. He's dead, all right. I'll stick around." I hung up. My handkerchief was soaked. I left it draped soggily over the telephone.

I turned and regarded the two girls. Peggy Roark sat huddled in the big chair. Miss Justin watched me silently, her eyes glassy with shock. She carefully avoided looking at what was behind the desk.

I said, "Girls, this is kind of tough to take, but it can't be helped now."

Neither of them moved or said anything.

I said to Miss Justin, "He's been dead for maybe a half hour—or less. Who's been in here with him?"

She shook her head slowly. "I—I don't know. I've been out in front …" Her voice broke and she began to tremble.

Peggy Roark stared at me with big eyes. I asked her, "How many customers out there?"

"Four," she said quietly.

"How many entrances to the shop?"

Before Peggy could answer, Miss Justin said quickly, "Two—the front door and a door opening on an alley in the rear." Her voice was stronger, and I could see that she was steeling herself to resume the role of the efficient secretary. She didn't look at Peggy Roark.

"All right," I said to her. "Lock the back door—now. And bring me the key."

She hesitated for a split second. Then she said, "Yes, sir." She stood up and moved to the office door.

Peggy Roark stood up, too. I unlocked the door and the three of us stepped into the hall. The sound of the hair dryers had stopped, and a little group of people stood silently at the end of the hall, watching us.

"The back door," I reminded Miss Justin in a low voice. "I'll wait here."

She moved briskly down the hall, ignoring the silent group. In thirty seconds she came back and handed me a key.

"Thanks," I said, and nodded toward the group at the end of the hall. "Tell them about Donati—they may as well know. I'll go out front and wait for the police."

She turned slowly to stare at me. Her eyes were cold. "I think perhaps all of us had better wait for the police right here, Mr. Bennett," she said evenly.

It surprised me, and yet I admitted to myself that she had a point. I grinned at her and said, "I'm not going to run away."

She flushed and bit at her lower lip. "I think it best that we all stay here," she said.

"Don't worry," I said. "I'll be back." I turned away and entered the outer reception room without looking back. I went to the front door and peered out. A police cruiser was just pulling up at the curb beside a fire hydrant and a NO PARKING sign. Three cops boiled out and crossed the sidewalk. I let them in and locked the door. I handed the key to the fattest cop.

"The back door's locked, too, Chief," I said. "He's in his office—straight through that door on your left."

"You the guy who called?"

I nodded and showed him my agency identification card. He peered at it. Then he said, "Bennett, huh? Outta Cleveland, I see."

"That's right, Chief."

He held out a fat hand. "Heard a lot about you, Bennett. Do you know Lieutenant Rockingham on Homicide?"

"Sure," I said, "but—"

His eyes narrowed. "What're you doing in town?"

"Working," I said. "I'll tell you all about it. Right now, there's a corpse back there."

He nodded briskly. "Come on, boys."

I followed them back to Donati's office. As I unlocked the door, I saw that Hector Griffith had joined the little knot of people. Peggy Roark and Miss Justin were standing where I had left them. I said to Miss Justin, "Stop worrying, honey. I didn't skip." I opened the door, and the Chief and I entered. The two cops took up guard posts outside.

The Chief's mouth fell open. "Gawdamighty!" he breathed.

I followed him over to the desk. It was then that I noticed something that I had missed before—a small safe behind the desk, with the heavy door standing open.

The Chief saw it, too. "Robbery, by God," he said. "There's your motive."

CHAPTER FIVE

An hour and a half later I sat in Pete Donati's office, drinking his brandy. The interminable questioning was over. The cops had gone, Donati was gone, and, except for a big brown stain on the rug by his desk, the place was cleaned up. The coroner had been there, the flashbulb boys, a reporter from the local newspaper and all the rest. It was five o'clock in the afternoon, and Armand's Beauty Salon was hushed; the afternoon sunlight glinted through the venetian blinds on Marianne Donati's yellow hair.

She was sitting opposite me, her back to the window. Her long legs were crossed, her hands folded quietly in her lap. Her face was in shadow, and from where I sat she did not appear as ugly as she had earlier in the day. The feeling I'd had of beauty beneath her grotesquely scarred face was stronger, but still illusive and haunting, like a remembered dream. I stirred restlessly in my chair. Maybe it was the brandy or the subdued yellow light or her legs, or the quiet way she sat there, but I felt uneasy. I took a swallow of the brandy.

"He'll never get his hair cut now," she said softly, and her voice seemed to caress me. "He hated it so ... the long hair, the clothes he had to wear, the awful fake of it all ... and I made him do it. He did it for me ..." Her voice broke a little. "Poor, poor Pete ..."

I waited.

"I wanted him to be somebody," she went on in her dreamlike voice. "I wanted us both to have money, to do the things we wanted to do. I thought I was right. He was a cosmetics salesman and not doing very well at it, and I was working long hours in beauty shops for ten-cent tips. I—I guess Pete was happy, but I made him go to beauty school, and I planned the whole thing. He hated it, but he did it for me—for us. And now ..."

The words died out and the office was very quiet. Outside in the street a car horn sounded far away. I aroused myself as from a stupor. Her voice had a gentle, lulling quality and I wanted to sit and listen to it go on and on.

"What'll you do now?" I asked her. "Keep on with the shop?"

She shook her head slowly and sadly. "Not alone ... Not without Pete. I'll close up, sell out—go away. I'll get along. Pete had insurance ..."

A tiny devil prodded my brain and made me ask, "How much?"

"Fifty thousand. A retirement policy—for both of us."

I finished my brandy and forced myself to stand up. "Mrs. Donati," I said, and my voice sounded harsh in my ears, "do you have any idea ..."

She shook her head slowly. "Pete had no enemies."

"You think it was robbery, pure and simple?"

"I—I suppose so. Pete was careless about leaving the safe open. And he only banked once a week."

"How much did he keep in the safe?"

She lifted her shoulders a little. "I don't know. I haven't paid much attention lately. Maybe a thousand or two. Since the trouble started, business has fallen off."

I took a deep breath. "Did you and Pete—get along?" I asked her.

She looked up at me. "I was afraid you'd ask that," she said quietly. "But you're a detective and I suppose you must. Yes, we got along, as you say, until … until …" She lowered her head and stared at her twisted fingers.

"Until what?" A cold feeling started to crawl up the back of my neck.

"Until the accident—a year ago. We were driving home from Cleveland. Pete had—had been drinking. We hit the railing of a bridge. I—I went through the windshield."

Suddenly she tilted her face upward, and the light fell fully on it. "It left me like this, like you see me now. Pretty, aren't I, Mr. Bennett? Tiny pieces of bone are still working to the surface. They can't do anything about it—not for a long time. But I'm still Marianne, the Marianne that Pete once loved. The rest of me is the same … It was just—my face. See?"

She jumped suddenly to her feet, and turned with a swift graceful movement until her back was toward me. She tilted her face to the ceiling, and her long yellow hair fell in shining waves over her shoulders. I stared at her straight back and her slender waist, and at the backs of her long straight legs. The white silk dress fitted smoothly over her hips. She looked marvelous.

I reached for the brandy bottle with an unsteady hand and poured the amber fluid into my glass. The bottle neck rattled against the rim of the glass. I drank fast and the brandy burned my throat. The sweet haunting fragrance of Marianne Donati filled the room, and I forgot about the blood of her husband staining the carpet.

"Then what?" I asked in ragged voice.

She turned slowly. "Nothing, Mr. Bennett," she said quietly. "Nothing on the surface. Pete was still kind and considerate, as always. But I knew him too well. He was never very clever, but I loved him, and I knew there was another woman—maybe several other women … I could see it in his eyes. But I don't blame him, I really don't. I know I'm ugly; my face is ugly …"

Her voice died out. Suddenly the room seemed too dark, too quiet. I turned quickly and switched on a lamp beside the desk. She averted her face.

"Please," she said.

I turned off the lamp.

"I want you to stay, Mr. Bennett," she said. "I want you to find Pete's murderer—you, or the police. Just so he is found—or she ..."

"I'll stay," I said. I wanted to stay, even if she never paid me, even if I never found Donati's killer; and yet I didn't want to stay. One part of me told me to get out of Wheatville fast, and forget about a woman with a figure of a goddess and an ugly scarred face, but with the hint of great beauty beneath. There was nothing I could do for Pete Donati and I was sorry about that. He had hired me to help him, and once again I heard his jeering voice: *I've read in books about the smart things you guys do—let's see you deliver. But I suppose you gotta have a murder before you can get going? You couldn't maybe clear up a simple little thing like this without publicity and cut throats and blood up to your ankles, could you?*

Yeah, I was smart, all right. Smart as hell. Smart enough to let a client get his throat cut wide open almost under my nose. But Donati's problem had been singed hair and the ill will of rich women who worshiped at the beauty doctor's shrine. Donati hadn't been worrying about murder—his murder—but about the loss of patrons' revenue. Murder was my worry now, and Marianne Donati was paying me to worry about it.

Sam Allgood's problem now seemed petty in comparison. Sam Allgood and his sneaking affair with his partner's wife, and his guilt-complex worry over who was taking casual pot shots at him on the golf course. To hell with Sam Allgood, I thought, and to hell with his whole crowd. And yet, he too was paying money into the coffers of the National Detective Agency, and I remembered the words of the big boss, that stern, shrewd old man enthroned in his paneled office in New York: *As long as a client is paying us, do him a job.*

Marianne Donati was paying, and so was Sam Allgood. I had two jobs to do, and time was running out.

"I'll stay," I repeated.

"Thank you," Marianne Donati said quietly, and she moved to the door.

"I'll take you home," I said.

"You are very kind," she murmured, with her face averted, "but I have my car outside."

"You'll be alone," I said, trying to keep my voice steady.

She shrugged her slim shoulders. "I'm always alone, Mr. Bennett."

"No folks or anyone?"

"No—not anymore."

I stepped to the door and opened it for her. Together we walked through the silent shop and out to the sunlit street. I locked the door and handed her the key.

"You keep it," she said. "I have my own."

She crossed the sidewalk to a long pale gray convertible. I stepped up behind her as she started to get in and touched her elbow. She turned to gaze at me, surprise and faint amusement in her eyes. I felt like a fool and I stepped back. She slid behind the wheel and pressed a starter button. The convertible's motor was a bare whisper.

"Where are you staying?" she asked me. "At the Seneca?"

"No—the Wheatville Inn."

"Goodbye," she said softly.

I waved a hand and watched her car move away from the curb. She circled the square slowly, and I saw her slow down. On a sudden impulse I walked swiftly along the sidewalk, hugging the storefronts. When I came to the corner, I stopped, lit a cigarette and watched the gray convertible over the match. It stopped in front of the drugstore. A man stepped out and crossed the sidewalk. It was Sam Allgood. He got quickly in beside Marianne Donati, and the convertible drove swiftly away.

I walked slowly around the square and entered the drugstore. Hector Griffith stood just inside the door. He had a newspaper under his arm and was smoking a pipe. He smiled gravely at me. "Hello, Mr. Bennett."

"Hi, Hector. Did you see who got into Mrs. Donati's car just now?"

He nodded slowly, puffing on his pipe. "Yes. It was Sam Allgood. He is Marianne's attorney."

I raised my eyebrows. "At five-thirty in the afternoon? I thought lawyers closed up shop and went home at five o'clock."

He smiled faintly. "No doubt she is anxious for legal advice in order to wind up her affairs here. She told me a while ago that she intends to sell the shop and leave town—as soon as possible."

"Isn't that kind of rushing things? Her husband isn't buried yet."

He shrugged. "She can't do anything for Pete anymore. I don't blame her—I'd want to get away, too."

I said abruptly, "What do you know about Sam Allgood?"

He removed the pipe from his mouth and gazed at me with his clear grave eyes. "You're not from the National Beauty Council, are you?" he said, smiling faintly. "You're a private investigator hired by Pete Donati to solve the case of the scorched scalps, aren't you?"

I grinned. "How did you figure that out, Hector?"

He laughed softly. "Well, for one thing, your hair isn't long enough and curly enough for you to be a member of the Council. And for another thing, I happened to walk into Pete's office yesterday when he was calling your office in Cleveland. I knew that he was getting desperate about the trouble, and I also knew that it was the kind of thing he wouldn't want to put in the hands of the local police."

He paused, and then went on, "Also, I have a good memory. I saw your name in a Cleveland paper about two months ago in connection with the murder of a prominent Cleveland business man named Alvin T. Bayne. The story mentioned that James T. Bennett, district agent for The National Detective Agency, working in cooperation with the police, had secured evidence—"

"All right," I broke in. "I asked you about Sam Allgood."

He gave me a crooked smile. "Why?" he asked quietly.

"Look," I said impatiently. "I may as well tell you that Mrs. Donati has hired me to catch the murderer of her husband—if I can. I'm working in the only way I know how, and I asked you a question. What do you know about Sam Allgood?"

"Shall I speak frankly?"

"By all means."

He sighed, puffed on his pipe and stared out at the busy street filled with late afternoon traffic. People were hurrying in and out of the drugstore, and there was a crowd at the lunch counter. Hector said, "Sam Allgood is a clever lawyer. He has an attractive wife named Katherine who is quite prominent in Wheatville social circles. Sam drinks hard and he plays hard—and he isn't particular with whom he plays. His business partner is Jeff Winters, a man who is respected and liked by most citizens. Jeff also has an attractive wife. Her name is Lily. She's much younger than Sam Allgood's wife, younger than Jeff. She likes guns, and I understand she is a crack shot." He paused, and gave me a crooked smile. "I'm probably a cad for mentioning it, but you told me to be frank. It's rumored on the Rialto that Lily Winters is carrying a flaming torch, as the gossip columnists term it, for Sam—and right under her husband's nose."

"I see," I said. "And what about Sam? Is the attraction mutual?"

He nodded. "So I hear—at least, for the present. But the town wits have been so crude as to say that Sam picks 'em young, works fast and leaves 'em where he loves 'em."

"A charming practice," I said, and added curiously, "How do you know so many interesting details?"

He smiled. "Don't let the hustle and bustle of Wheatville fool you. It's just a small town, down beneath the crowds and the glitter. And I can see you aren't familiar with the more unsavory features of a small town. In a place like Wheatville, a beauty shop is a gold mine of juicy and scandalous information. There's something about the intimate lulling drone of a hair dryer that makes women talk." He sighed and added, "But don't take me too seriously. For all I know personally, Sam Allgood may be a model of husbandly faithfulness."

"Where there's smoke," I said, thinking of Lily Winters' lipstick on Sam Allgood's face.

Hector asked curiously, "But why are you so interested in Sam Allgood?"

I hesitated and thought fast. And then I decided that since Hector had already guessed my reason for being in Wheatville, and my identity, I might as well tell him the rest. Besides, I figured that if I was going to do any good for Sam Allgood or Marianne Donati, I would need help from someone who was familiar with the inside workings of the Wheatville social structure. So I told Hector about Sam Allgood hiring me to find out who was shooting at him on the golf course, and I confirmed his guess that Pete Donati had also engaged me to ferret out the reason for his clients' burned scalps.

Hector listened gravely. When I had finished, he said, "I can see why the shooting would worry Sam. Have you found out anything?"

"It is probably a dimwit farmer named Lem Fassler," I said, and I told him about the cornfield adjoining the golf course. "I hope to find out for sure and wind the thing up."

"If I can be of any help," he said, "let me know." He knocked the ashes from his pipe. "How about having dinner with me?"

"Sorry. I'm invited to dinner at Sam Allgood's." I moved out of the drugstore to the sidewalk. Hector followed me.

He gazed across the square at Armand's Beauty Salon and sighed. "I've got to work at the shop tonight. If Marianne is going to sell out right away, I want the books in shape."

"Is it all right with the cops?" I asked him. "About your going into the shop tonight?"

"Yes. I asked Chief Swartz, and he said it would be all right."

I said, "Are you going out to the club tomorrow to watch the big golf match between Peggy Roark and Katherine Allgood?"

He smiled. "I wouldn't miss it. Peggy's a nice little girl—I hope she wins." He lifted a hand and walked away.

The clock in the Courthouse tower told me that it was twenty minutes past six o'clock. I walked to where my car was parked near the Wheatville Inn and drove across town to Sam Allgood's house. As I parked by the curb in front, I didn't see anything of Allgood's red sedan. Jenny, the colored maid, let me in. She had changed the print dress for a black one, and she now wore a tiny white apron and cap. She said, "Mrs. Allgood, she'll be down pretty soon. Mr. Allgood, he ain't home yet."

I moved over the thick rug of the big pleasant living room. At one end a portable bar had been rolled in, stocked with ice, soda syphon, gin, whisky and vermouth, both sweet and dry. I stirred myself a double martini and poured it into a tall highball glass, skipped the olive, and moved to the big combination radio-phonograph-television console. *Tales from the Vienna Woods* was still on the turntable from the night before. I flicked the starting knob, turned the volume down low and sat down in a deep chair. The soft lilting music filled the room and caressed the ends of my nerves. I had finished my martini when the record ended, and I got up and mixed another. The record began again, and I leaned back and closed my eyes.

Presently a voice said, "Do you like Strauss, Mr. Bennett?"

I opened my eyes. Katherine Allgood stood before me. She was wearing a plain black linen dress with an off-the-shoulder neckline, and her smooth bare shoulders gleamed in the light. Her rather thin face looked a little pale and drawn, I thought, but her red lips were smiling and her expression was friendly. In one hand she held an empty cocktail glass.

I started to get up, but she placed a hand on my shoulder. "Please—sit still. You look tired."

I leaned back and smiled up at her. "Yes, I like Strauss—the elder. And I'm not tired."

"So do I," she said. "I mean about Strauss. Even the "Blue Danube." But I enjoy the more serious things, too, like—"

"Who wants to be serious?" I broke in, and I nodded at her empty glass. "Can I make a drink for you? I pride myself upon my ability to mix martinis."

"Ugh," she said in distaste. "Martinis. Sam likes them, too—that is, before dinner. After dinner he'll drink anything—Scotch, rye, Bourbon, beer. But who injected my husband into this?"

"You did."

"I'm sorry," she said. "I started out to tell you that I like Manhattans. I had one while I was dressing, and now I think I'll have another." She turned and moved to the bar.

I watched her as she poured whisky over ice, added sweet vermouth and Angostura, and stirred slowly with a long silver spoon. Over her shoulder she said to me, "Stir them gently, that's the secret. Don't bruise them. Isn't that correct, Mr. Bennett?"

"That is correct," I assured her, and I thought, *You've had more than one Manhattan, baby, while you were dressing.*

She turned toward me and a little of her drink spilled to the thick rug. She moved to the console, abruptly lifted the needle from *Tales from the Vienna Woods,* changed the record and said over her shoulder, "You'll like this—now, listen."

I sipped at my martini and listened. The slow, throbbing, almost inaudible strains of Ravel's *Boléro* crept through the room. The music grew louder, more insistent, with the haunting melody repeating itself over and over against the background of drums. Katherine Allgood turned to me and said brightly, "Do you know the story behind this? I mean, what Ravel was trying to say when he wrote it?"

"No."

She took a quick sip of her drink, and it seemed to me that her eyes were brighter, and that a little color had come into her pale face. "It's supposed to tell the story of a woman's awakening to love," she said. "Of her increasing awareness of joy, until—" She paused and gazed down at me thoughtfully. "Why didn't you want to kiss me last night?"

"You're making it up," I said, ignoring her question. "I mean, about the *Boléro.*"

Behind Katherine Allgood the drums beat louder, and the music swirled in the room. She gave me a slow smile. "You didn't answer my question."

I grinned at her. "Tell me more about the *Boléro.*"

"It's wonderful," she breathed, "if you know the story. At first it's quiet, serene, lovely—like a first caress. And then the drums began to throb, very faintly, and love stirs and the drums grow subtly louder …" She paused and drank.

I glanced uneasily at my wristwatch. Ten minutes until seven.

Where in the hell was Sam Allgood? Still with Marianne Donati? I felt a faint unreasoning anger. Where were they now? Parked on a dark country road in her car? At Allgood's office? At her house or apartment or hotel room, or wherever she lived?

Katherine Allgood said mockingly, "Don't you like my interpretation of the *Boléro?*"

"I like it fine—but I still think you made it up."

She smiled. "Does it matter?"

I said carefully, "I wonder what's happened to Sam?"

"Let's not worry about Sam. Let's have another drink ..."

"Sure." I stood up and moved past her to the bar. She stopped me with a hand on my arm. "I—I must apologize for Sam. He called me at noon to tell me that you'd be here for dinner. But he's frequently late—when he shows up at all." Her lips twisted in a faint bitterness.

"It's early," I told her. "He'll be along."

"Oh, don't," she said sharply. "Don't try to defend Sam. I know him. I know my dear husband well. He won't be home—I know."

I smiled at her, feeling a kind of pity for her. She was crazy in love with her husband and consumed with jealousy. Love and jealousy are a wicked combination. I said, "He's probably at the Beavers', having an extra drink with the boys." But even as I spoke, a picture formed in my brain of Sam Allgood and Marianne Donati, together, and I began to feel a sort of kinship with Katherine Allgood.

A small gleam of hope showed in her eyes, and she said quickly, "Perhaps you are right. I'll call the lodge." She moved away.

"No," I said, "you don't want to do that."

She stood still and averted her gaze. "No, I—I guess I don't."

The colored woman appeared in a doorway. "How soon you want to eat, Ma'am?"

"Mr. Allgood has been detained," Katherine Allgood said crisply. "Is everything ready?"

"Yes, Ma'am. The roast, it's clear done. It'll need some water if I don't take it out of the oven pretty soon."

"All right, Jenny. I'll serve dinner. You may go home."

The maid's eyes widened. "But the dishes, who'll do them?"

"You can clean up tomorrow," Katherine Allgood said impatiently. "Please go."

"Yes, Ma'am." The maid disappeared.

Katherine Allgood turned to me. "Well, what now?" she asked brightly.

From the rear of the house a door slammed, marking the departure of Jenny. "We might eat," I suggested.

Katherine Allgood arched her fine black brows, and held out her empty glass. "Have you forgotten?"

I took the glass and moved to the bar. She stood close beside me while I mixed the drinks—Manhattan for her, martini for me. As she took her glass, she said, "Shall we forget about Sam—and just think of us?"

"Sure." I lifted my glass. "To us."

She laughed gaily and drank. I drank, too, but sparingly. Two highball-sized martinis on top of Pete Donati's brandy were just about enough for me—before dinner, anyhow. She linked her arm in mine and led me to the big divan. We sat side by side and lighted cigarettes. She inhaled deeply and said, "I think this is fun. Don't you?"

"Sure," I said, but I was thinking of Pete Donati, with his throat cut wide open, and of Sam Allgood getting into Marianne Donati's car.

The gilt clock on the mantel chimed seven o'clock.

"You might act as if it's fun," Katherine Allgood pouted. She glanced sideways at me, and the invitation in her eyes was unmistakable.

I looked at her. She was mature, attractive and desirable, and more than a little drunk. And burning with jealousy. She wanted to strike back at her husband in the only way she could. And I was handy, as I'd been handy the night before. I sighed and thought, *Some other night, honey, some other time—maybe. But not tonight, not as long as I'm working for your husband. Maybe—just maybe—when your husband has paid me off, and Pete Donati's killer is off my mind, and when his lovely, hideous wife is off my mind, maybe then. I'm not noble, honey, not me, but this isn't the time or the place, and to hell with it.*

I stirred restlessly. Close beside me Katherine Allgood laughed deep in her throat. She leaned across me to crush out her cigarette in an ashtray on the low table, and her arm rested for a moment on my knee. Her glossy black hair was close to my face, and the clean scent of her was all around me. She took a long time with her cigarette, and I sat stiffly, my ears tuned for a step at the door, heralding the arrival of her wayward husband.

But no step came, and except for the throbbing of the *Boléro*, almost all drums now, frankly insistent, the big house was hushed and remote against the summer twilight. Over Katherine Allgood's head, through the big window, I saw the streetlights come on and shine yellowly through the trees. She finished with her cigarette at last, and slowly she sat up straight, her shoulder against my arm, her face averted. Almost automatically I put my arm around her and pulled her to me. She began to tremble, and the *Boléro* ended abruptly on a wild strident note. Her arms slid upward and around my neck, and I reached blindly for the table with my glass. And then her mouth was against mine and she clung to me.

It was a swell time for Sam Allgood to walk in. But he didn't.

A faint acrid odor drifted in from the kitchen. I pushed Katherine Allgood gently away. "The roast is burning," I said.

She laughed a little breathlessly, and brushed a hand over her eyes, like a woman in a daze. "R-roast?" she whispered.

"It's burning," I said. I left her, hurried through the house to the kitchen, spotted the gleaming white stove. I turned it off and opened the oven door. The roast was indeed burning. I left it smoking and returned to the living room.

Katherine Allgood was lighting a cigarette with a hand that trembled a little. She didn't look at me. The *Boléro* was starting over again, with a whispering beat of drums and almost the echo of a melody. It occurred to me that modern automatic music-playing devices were the nearest thing to perpetual motion yet discovered, and I wondered how many hours or days the *Boléro* would play, over and over, if the machine were allowed to run. I went over and shut it off.

In the sudden quiet the jangle of a telephone made me jump, and I decided that my nerves were a little frazzled. Still avoiding my gaze, Katherine Allgood stood up and walked into a small alcove where a telephone rested on a lacquered stand. Her end of the conversation went like this:

"Oh, hello, Sam ... Yes, we're waiting for you." Her voice was cool and controlled. "Of course, Sam, I understand ... Will you be very late? ... Oh, I see ..." There was a long pause, and then she said in a voice edged with bitterness, "Of course, dear. Business first." She turned and held out the telephone to me. "He wants to speak with you."

I took the instrument from her. "Yes?" I said. From the corner of my eye I saw Katherine Allgood move to the wide window and stand staring out at the night.

Sam Allgood's voice was thick. "Sorry, Bennett. Tied up with a client."

"That's all right."

"One of those things," he said. "You know."

"Sure, I know."

"You found out anything yet?"

"About what?" I asked innocently.

"About what I'm paying you for," he said harshly. "Remember?"

"Oh, that. Nothing definite yet."

"Look, Bennett, I don't like being a sucker. Are you working for me, or aren't you?"

"Sure."

"And how many other people?" he sneered. "I know what's going on. I'm not paying you fifty bucks a day while you dilly-dally around for somebody else."

"Who?"

"You know damn well who. Mrs. Donati is a client of mine, and she told me about you working for her. That's a nasty mess, Bennett, and you'd better keep your nose out. The police will handle it."

"Sure," I said. I couldn't tell him to go to hell, not with Katherine Allgood listening. "We'll talk about it later."

"You're damn right we'll talk about it. You lay off that Donati business."

"Goodbye, Sam," I said cheerfully, and I hung up on him.

I spotted my hat on a table in the hall, and picked it up on my way out. At the door I paused and said to Katherine Allgood, "I guess I'd better go."

"I guess you'd better." She spoke without turning around.

"Goodbye."

"Goodbye, Mr. Bennett."

I went out quietly and closed the door.

On my way down town I stopped at a sandwich drive-in and had two hamburgers and a glass of milk. Then I drove down to the square and parked on a dark street two blocks from Bertha's Beauty Bar. From the dash compartment of my car I took a small flashlight and a short, flat strip of steel with a slightly curved end. Then I walked through alleys until I emerged on the street close to Bertha's.

Except for a dim light inside, the place was dark. I moved down a narrow alley, turned a corner and paused in the darkness behind the shop. My flash made a yellow circle on a rear door. I turned off the light and went to work. It was easy to spring the lock with my curved strip of steel. The door swung open and I entered silently.

I went through the place with the flashlight. The blue smock was gone from the chair in the reception room, but I found it hanging in a closet. I turned the light on it. Written in indelible ink on the inside of the neckband was a name. The name was M. Roark.

I stuffed the smock under my coat and went out the way I had entered. I walked around the square to Armand's Beauty Shop. There was a light in the front of the place, and in my mind's eye I pictured Hector Griffith working over his books. I walked past the shop until I came to an alley. I turned down the alley, and cut back to a court which I calculated was directly behind the shop. I found the rear door which I had instructed Miss Justin to lock. It was still locked. I flashed the light around on the uneven bricks of the court. I didn't see anything—just dirty bricks, soggy cigarette stubs and chewing gum wrappers. I put the flashlight in my pocket and started back for the street.

I heard a faint scraping sound behind me, like feet moving fast over the bricks. I turned, but not soon enough. Something smacked me on the back of my head, and the bricks slanted up and hit me in the face. I wiggled and tried to get up. I heard a voice swear softly and a foot slammed me in the ribs—twice.

I gasped for breath and I tried to roll away. Somebody jumped on my back then with both feet, and a heavy solid object banged away on my head. My teeth bit into the bricks and I couldn't move. It was all I could do to keep sucking air into my lungs.

A voice close to my ear muttered, "Just a sample, my friend. Get out of town—fast."

The feet stepped off my back and I breathed a little easier. But not for long. A million lights exploded in my brain and I went all the way out. I was glad. It was a lot like going to sleep....

CHAPTER SIX

Pete Donati's blood was still on the rug beneath his desk. The office was going around in a slow circle, with the dry, brown smear of blood as its axis. I shut my eyes and opened them again. I lifted a hand to the back of my head. Beneath my hair, the scalp felt damp and pulpy. My back ached, and I was sure that the ends of my ribs were sticking through my shirt.

A man moved into my line of vision. I squinted up at him. It was Hector Griffith. He held a tall thin glass in his hand. "Have some brandy, Mr. Bennett," I heard him say. "It'll make you feel better."

I took the brandy—Pete Donati's brandy. It was the third time I'd had it, and I thought fleetingly, *What the hell? He can't drink it anymore.* I tried to sip at it, but my hand shook. I held the glass with both hands, but still it sloshed around. I tried to gulp it fast, and I damn near strangled. But in a couple of minutes I felt better and my hands steadied a little.

"Thanks," I croaked.

Hector Griffith gently took the glass from me. I peered up at him. He was in his shirt sleeves, and his collar and tie were loosened. His dark-rimmed glasses glinted in the light, and his lean, distinguished features were serious.

"You've had a rough time, Mr. Bennett," he said quietly. "Just relax for a little while."

"Hell with 'Mister,'" I mumbled. "Call me Jim."

"All right, Jim."

His gentle voice seemed to be coming to me from far away. I stared at him with dazed eyes, and I shook my head, trying to remember. Then the dark alley and the bricks and the feet on my back came back to me. I squeezed my eyes shut and tried to concentrate.

Hector's quiet voice seemed to drift out of nowhere. "... I was working in here, trying to finish things up ... Heard a commotion in back ... Ran out ... Found you lying in the alley ... carried you inside...."

"A guy slugged me," I heard myself say. "He beat me up. He's got big feet."

I took a deep breath. The brandy was a warm glow inside of me. I opened my eyes. Hector was in focus, and the room was undulating only a little. I saw the concern in Hector's eyes, and I tried to grin at him.

"Maybe I'd better call the police," Hector suggested.

I shook my head. "Hell, no." I felt in my coat. The blue smock belonging to Peggy Roark which I had taken from Bertha's Beauty Bar was gone.

I peered up at Hector. "See anything of a blue smock lying around—out in the alley?"

He looked puzzled. "A blue smock? We all wear them around here."

He placed cool firm fingers on my forehead. "Are you sure you feel all right?"

"I feel terrible," I said. "But thanks for lugging me in here."

He poured more brandy into my glass.

I drank, and I began to feel better by the second. I said, "Do you think it was somebody from outside who came in here tonight and killed Donati?"

He shrugged.

"Do you think it was somebody who worked for him—here?"

He shrugged again. "I don't know, Jim," he said. "I don't know anything."

I stretched out my legs and sipped at the brandy. "Never mind," I said. "What will you do—if Mrs. Donati sells the shop?"

He turned away. "Get another job, I suppose," he said bitterly. "Another two-bit job—bookkeeper, janitor, handy man. Pete Donati was right. He used to tell me that men like me were dime a dozen."

"Must you be a bookkeeper?" I asked him.

He turned to face me and there was a bleak look in his eyes. "A bookkeeper, or a soda jerk or a ditch-digger. That's all I can do now."

"Now?"

He nodded slowly. "I'll tell you something, Jim, and then you can forget it. You've been frank with me and I'll tell you about myself, and then to hell with it. Nobody in Wheatville knows, except Marianne Donati. Two years ago, in another town, far away, I was a doctor—a surgeon. I operated on a man and he died. They said I was drunk."

"Were you?"

"Yes—drunk as hell. It was an emergency, and I was the only surgeon available. It was my night off, and I had just come from a party when they called me. I refused, but they insisted—and I operated. I wasn't too drunk. My hands were steady and my brain was keen. I did a good job, as good as anyone could do, but the man was in bad shape. He died. His heart didn't stand it. He would have died anyway. But his wife sued me for malpractice, and she won. There was nothing I could do about it. They took away my license."

He lifted his glass and swallowed long.

"Then what?"

He smiled coldly. "The old story. I left the town where I'd practiced medicine for ten years. I hit the bottle, of course, and my wife divorced me. I didn't blame her. I had a little money and I just drifted. My money ran out, and I found myself in a bar here in Wheatville, spending my last dollar on whisky. And then Marianne came in—alone. She had a veil over her poor scarred face. The scars aroused my professional curiosity and I began to talk to her. We talked, and we drank, and I became drunk enough to tell her my sordid story." He paused, and spread his hands. "That was it. Before she left she gave me a job, and here I am." He finished his brandy, and said mockingly, "Touching, isn't it?"

I didn't answer. Hector's words had conjured into my fuzzy brain a vision of Marianne Donati, and I tortured myself by trying to visualize how she had looked before the night she had crashed through the windshield of her husband's car. The illusion of great beauty was there, but I couldn't quite grasp it and I stirred restlessly in my chair.

Hector sighed, and put on his coat. "Well, water over the dam.... Feeling better now?"

"I'll be all right." I sat relaxed in the chair and I didn't want to move.

"I looked you over pretty carefully," Hector said. "I'm sure there are no broken bones and no concussion. But you'll be pretty stiff tomorrow."

"Hell, I'm stiff now," I said, grinning up at him. "Thanks, Doc."

His shoulders straightened a little as he moved to the door. With his hand on the knob, he said quietly, "It's been a long time since anyone has called me 'Doc.' If you need me, call me. My number is Seneca 137." He paused and then added wryly, "Unless, of course, you would prefer to call a—a real doctor."

"You're good enough for me," I told him, and I pushed myself stiffly from the chair.

"Thank you," he said, and I saw a gleam of dignity, of pride, in his eyes.

We went out to the street together, and as we walked slowly to the corner, Hector said, "Good luck on your—your assignments. If I can help you in any way, let me know."

"All right. I'll probably see you tomorrow—at least, at the golf match."

He waved a hand and hurried away. I watched his tall erect figure moving beneath the street lights, and then I walked across the square to where I'd left my car. Cars were moving up the street, and people crowded the sidewalks. The clock in the Courthouse tower bonged the hour of nine in the evening.

From a directory in a phone booth in an outlying gas station I found the address of Peggy Roark. It was the only Roark in the book, and was listed under the name of Mrs. Christina Roark. The gas station attendant gave me directions, and I found the address without any trouble. It was a small white frame house close to the edge of town, on the road leading to the Wheatville Country Club. In the moonlight I could see a small yard, a garage in the rear, and a chicken coop in the middle of a wire enclosure. The rear of Peggy's old blue convertible protruded from the garage. Except for a light upstairs, the house was dark. I went up onto the porch and pounded on the screen door. I didn't get any response, and I pounded louder. A light came downstairs, and Peggy Roark opened the door.

She was wearing a pale blue flannel robe. It was open, revealing white pajamas covered with red prints of rabbits. Her copperish hair was still braided, and she was wearing white furry slippers. As she stared at me in surprise, her eyes big and dark in her small face, she looked about fourteen years old.

I said, "In bed?"

"Just reading. Mother has gone to a movie with a neighbor."

"Getting in shape for the big golf game tomorrow, huh?"

She smiled. "I'll need all the rest I can get. I've got to win."

"You'll win," I assured her. "Can I talk to you for a minute?"

She hesitated, her eyes puzzled. Then she unhooked the screen, and opened it. "Of course, Mr. Bennett," she said quietly. "Come in."

I stepped into a small parlor. It was very neat and clean and attractively furnished. On a table in a silver frame stood an enlarged snapshot of a laughing man with a golf club slung under his arm.

I said, "Peggy, I'm sort of helping the police investigate the death of Mr. Donati, and maybe you can help me. I—"

"Are you a policeman, Mr. Bennett?" she asked quickly.

I shook my head. "No—just a friend of Mrs. Donati's. She has asked me to help her."

"I see," she said, but I could tell by her puzzled expression that she didn't.

I said, "Did you lose a smock—like the one you wear at the shop?"

She looked startled. Then she said, "Why, yes, I did. I have four, and I've only been able to find three. But, why—"

"I found one with your name on it at Bertha's Beauty Bar," I said.

She flushed and glanced down at her clasped hands. "I—I remember now. I left it there." She looked up at me with big eyes. "You see, it's like this, Mr. Bennett. I went into Mr. Donati's office this afternoon to tell him I was quitting. I—I couldn't work there anymore. Bertha—I mean Mr. Homer—offered me a job in his shop, and I worked there the other day—to try out. He hired me, and I'm starting there on Monday."

"Why did you want to quit Donati? For more money?"

She nodded seriously. "Yes, that was part of the reason. Mother isn't very well, and we need so many things. Mr. Donati just didn't pay enough, and ..." She paused, and lowered her eyes. "But—but that wasn't the only reason I wanted to quit."

I waited. She raised her eyes. Her small face was pink. "Mr. Donati, he—he was always touching me, and trying to get me in his office alone with him, and he wanted me to go out with him. I—I just couldn't stand it anymore ..."

"I see," I said, "and is that why he didn't pay you as much as he paid the other girls? Because you wouldn't—uh—cooperate?"

"I hadn't thought about it like that," she said, "but I wondered why he didn't pay me more. I asked him about it once, and he just laughed, and said, 'Get smart, baby.'"

I said a bad word to myself.

To the girl I said, "And when I found you in his office this afternoon, you had just gone in to tell him you were leaving?"

She nodded quickly. "Yes, that is why I was there. And when I saw him at his desk, like that ..." She shivered a little.

"All right," I said, and I opened the door. "Go on back to bed." I smiled at her. "Good luck in the match tomorrow."

"Thank you, Mr. Bennett."

As I stepped to the porch, she hooked the screen door, said, "Good night," softly. Then the light went out, and I stood on the porch a minute, staring out at the moonlight on the grass.

I started across the yard to my car. From somewhere behind me a gun let loose with a sharp report, and a bullet whined past my head. I dropped to the grass and began to roll. I rolled head over appetite for my car, and slid beneath it on my stomach. The unseen gun barked again, and a slug tore at the collar of my coat. My neck burned, and I felt the spreading warmth of blood inside my shirt. I hugged the ground and waited. From somewhere close a car motor roared, and I heard the tortured whine of gears as it sped away. Then silence.

All up and down the street, lights were coming on in houses. I crawled quickly out from under the car, climbed in and drove away from there.

Ten minutes later I parked once more on the square in the center of the town of Wheatville, trying to decide what to do next. I was mad and I wanted to hit somebody with my fist. I wanted to feel a gun in my hand, and my finger on the trigger. But I didn't have a gun anymore, and I brooded about that. I wanted somebody to get sassy and knock a chip off my shoulder. I was spoiling for a fight, and I was sore all over. My neck burned where the slug had creased me, and my head ached and I needed a shave and a bath. And I was tired and felt like hell.

Finally, I made up my mind. I started the coupé and drove to the Wheatville Inn. Gregory, the high school bellhop, was sitting in a chair by the stairs, reading a comic book. The courtly old pappy on the desk had been replaced by a stout lady with gray hair and clip-on glasses. She smiled at me and I nodded. Gregory looked up and said, "Good evening, sir."

"Good evening, Gregory. Do you suppose you could bring me some ice and soda?"

He jumped to his feet. "Yes, sir."

I climbed the stairs to my room, took off my coat and shirt, and in the bathroom mirror inspected the shallow red groove over my collar bone. It was little more than a nasty scratch, but I shivered when I thought of what it might have been. I washed it with cold water, applied iodine from a kit in my bag and stuck a loose bandage of gauze and tape over it. Gregory came in with the ice and soda, and his eyes grew big at the sight of the bandage.

"Hurt yourself, sir?"

"Just a scratch, Gregory, just a scratch." I tossed him a half dollar.

He caught it deftly, said, "Thanks," and went out.

I made myself a stiff highball from the Bourbon in my bag. Then I propped myself on the bed, sipped at the drink and thought things over. I had finished the highball and was working on another when I heard a gentle rap on my door. I got off the bed, crossed to the door and jerked it open. I stared straight into the big blue eyes of Miss Justin. She had changed her severely tailored suit for a soft pale green linen dress and a big white straw hat.

I was feeling the whisky a little. "Come in, come in," I invited. "Nothing like a visit from a pretty gal. Will you have a drink?"

She stepped inside, closed the door and tossed her hat on the bed.

"What have you got?" she asked.

"Bourbon—but I'll order champagne, if you like."

She smiled at me. "I'll take Bourbon."

I got a glass from the bathroom and made her a highball. She began to drink, gazing at me thoughtfully over the rim of the glass.

"You're a private detective, aren't you, Mr. Bennett?"

"Who said?"

"Nobody said. But I placed the call for you for Mr. Donati. He hired you to find out the cause of the burned hair, and now Mrs. Donati has hired you to find the murderer of her husband. Isn't that right?"

"You're telling it."

She placed her glass on a table and lit a cigarette with a silver lighter. Then she sat on the bed and crossed her legs. She had nice legs, long, with slim ankles. She knew she had nice legs, and she let her dress stay where it was, well above her knees. I sat down in a chair opposite her and looked up at the ceiling.

"Let's see—Justin, Joyce, Receptionist. Twenty-seven, single, no dependents. Salary, one hundred dollars a week, plus bonus ... That's quite a lot of money, Miss Justin."

She lifted her slim shoulders. "You know a lot," she said, "but Pete Donati didn't give anything away. He must have thought I was worth it."

"No doubt."

She stared at me sullenly. "You're hard to get along with, aren't you?"

"I'm easy to get along with."

Suddenly she smiled.

"You might put on a shirt when a lady calls on you."

"Sorry. Too tired."

She pointed a slim finger with a red-painted nail at the bandage on my neck.

"What did you do?"

"I cut myself shaving."

"What do you shave with—a butcher knife?"

"What's on your mind?" I asked her.

She said mockingly, "Getting right down to business, huh?"

I nodded. "It's getting late and I have other fish to fry."

"When do you sleep?"

"Hah!" I said.

"You want to know what's on my mind," she said. "What's it worth to you?"

"Another drink."

She laughed and handed me her glass. "It's a deal."

I got up and refilled her glass. When she took it, her fingers purposely touched mine. I was too tired to do anything about it. Anyhow, one little playful interlude, like the one I'd had with Katherine Allgood, was enough.

She held the glass with both hands and lowered her lashes. "I wanted to talk to you," she said. "I've been thinking about poor Pete, and how he—he died. I tried the Seneca Hotel first and then came here, and, well, here I am." She looked up at me, and said in a level voice, "This is what I wanted to tell you—a short time before Pete was found dead, Mrs. Donati was in his office."

"So was I," I told her, "and so were several other people. So were you, maybe."

She flushed faintly and then said, "But Mrs. Donati was the last one with him. I saw her leave about twenty minutes before you went in and found him."

I leaned toward her and said in a low voice, "Was she carrying a bloody razor?"

She stood up and slammed her glass to the table. The glass didn't break, but an ice cube flopped out onto the rug. I stood up, too. I felt mean. I reached out, placed a hand on her shoulder and pushed. She hit the bed, not very gently. But she stayed there, staring at me silently. I sat down again.

Suddenly she smiled.

"I think I like you, Mr. Bennett."

"Swell," I said. "Is that what you came here for—to tell me that you like me and that Mrs. Donati probably killed her husband?"

"I want to help," she said. "Maybe I'd better tell the police."

"Go ahead.... What do you know about this Bertha—the fancy pants who runs The Beauty Bar?"

She leaned over and picked up her glass. "Bertha?" she asked casually. "Bert Horner?"

"Him."

"He's all right, I guess. A little swishy, maybe."

"I've talked to him," I said. "He didn't like Donati."

"Of course not. The whole town knows that. Bertha had the beauty business here sewed up—until Pete came to town." She paused and said, jeeringly, "I suppose Bertha cut Pete's throat—to get rid of the competition?"

I shrugged. "People have killed other people for a hell of a lot less reason.... Do you have anything else interesting to tell me?"

She looked down at the toes of her stubby brown-and-white high-heeled shoes.

"No. Pete was—was pretty decent to me, and I wanted to do what I could." She looked up and smiled. "I used to be a Girl Scout, you know."

"What about this hair burning business?"

"I don't know—really. It was ruining Pete's business. A faulty wave formula, I suppose—something like that." She sighed. "Just one of those things."

"You were pretty friendly with Donati, weren't you?" I asked suddenly.

Her black lashes flicked upward. "Why, Mr. Bennett," she said mockingly.

"Were you?"

She looked away from me. "Certainly I was friendly with him," she said. "He was friendly with all of us who'd let him. And if you were smart, you let him. But he didn't mean anything by it, really."

"Of course not," I said. "Just a big brother."

She laughed a little uncertainly. "Well, that's the way he was. You just had to know how to handle him. After his wife had her accident—well, you couldn't blame him too much."

I stirred uneasily in my chair, remembering Marianne Donati and the way she had stood before me that afternoon. "Was she a beautiful woman?" I asked.

Joyce Justin shrugged. "Yes—if you like blondes."

I sighed and got stiffly to my feet. "Well, it's been nice."

"Brushing me off, Mr. Bennett?" Her voice held a hard edge.

"I'm tired. You've peddled your story. Goodbye."

She slid off the bed and slowly moved toward me. There was a quirk to her red lips and a bright glitter in her eyes. When she was two feet away, she suddenly flung back her arm. I grabbed her wrist before she could slap me. She struggled viciously. I pulled her up against me, twisting her wrist behind her. Our faces were about six inches apart and I grinned at her.

Slowly she relaxed and pressed her teeth against her lower lip. With her lashes lowered, she leaned against me. I released her wrist then, and stepped back. She rubbed her wrist with her fingers and smiled faintly, as if at some secret joke.

"You affect me oddly, Mr. Bennett," she murmured. "It seems that I either want to slap you—or kiss you." She paused, still rubbing her wrist. "Right now I want to kiss you." She took a slow step toward me. "Do you mind?"

Joyce Justin was an attractive chunk of female, but I shook my head and grinned at her. "Not tonight, honey. Some other time." I moved to the door and opened it for her.

As she sauntered past me, she tapped a finger against my bare chest. Without raising her gaze above my chin, she said softly, "Just name the time, my friend." She went out and down the hall, her neat hips swaying a little.

I locked the door and took a hot shower. It made my sore back feel better, but my head still ached wickedly. I dried myself slowly and thought of Joyce Justin. It was very obvious that she had come to my room to throw suspicion upon Marianne Donati for the murder of Donati. But why had Joyce Justin bothered? Because of loyalty to Donati or because of jealousy of Donati's wife? Or because she really had seen Marianne Donati leaving Donati's office shortly before I found him?

I thought of all the angles as I shaved, but I didn't come up with anything. Pete Donati was as dead as he would ever be, and I was hired to find his killer. My little junket to Wheatville had developed into a twenty-four-hour-a-day job, what with the murder of Donati and Sam Allgood's problems. It looked like a busy night, and I was supposed to sleep at Allgood's house and wake up in the morning champing at the bit to corner the dastard who was shooting at him on the golf course.

I dressed quickly, and went down the stairs to the lobby.

The stout woman was still behind the desk. I went over to her and asked, "Who's the county coroner?"

She looked up from a crossword puzzle. "Old Doc Hendricks," she said, and she smiled. "That is, when he's sober."

"Thanks." I went across the lobby to a phone booth and looked in the directory. Hendricks, C.R., M.D. I called his number. He answered right away.

"Is it time, Maude?" he asked.

"Time for what?"

"Aw, hell," he said. "I thought it was Maude Simpson." He had a deep gruff voice. "She's expecting. Called me two hours ago. Said the pains was five minutes apart. I been sitting here keeping a bottle company, and waiting for her to let me know when she's really ready. You can't tell about Maude—sometimes she pops 'em right away, and then maybe she'll go eight-ten hours. Who the hell are you?"

"My name's Bennett. I was in Pete Donati's office this afternoon when you were there, but I guess the chief was too busy to introduce us. This may sound silly, but I'd like your official verdict on the cause of Pete's death."

"My God, man!" he said. "You saw him, didn't you?"

"Sure. His throat was cut wide open. Was that all?"

"That's enough, brother. He had a blow on the head, but that didn't kill him—just knocked him out. It's homicide, pure and simple, by a person or persons unknown." He chuckled. "Pete sure as hell didn't do it himself. An ear-to-ear incision with a thin sharp instrument. Severed the external jugular veins on both sides, the internal jugular veins and the carotid artery."

"Thanks, Doc," I said, and I hung up. I didn't know any more than I'd known before.

CHAPTER SEVEN

I left the Wheatville Inn, walked to the square and down the street to Bertha's Beauty Bar. There was a dim light inside, the same as before. My tinkering on the back door earlier in the evening made it a simple matter to enter. I stepped inside to a dark corridor and stood still. From somewhere close there came a low murmur of voices. A thin line of light streamed from under a door at the end of the corridor, and I moved toward it.

There wasn't any point in pussy-footing around. I opened the door and stepped into a dimly lit room. Joyce Justin and the big man called Bertha were sitting cozily at a tiny black enameled table bearing a bottle and two glasses. The man and the girl jerked their heads at me, like a vaudeville team. They stared silently for maybe ten seconds.

Then Joyce Justin smiled. "Hello, my friend. Have a drink?"

Bertha pushed back his chair and stood up. His long black hair was looped over his forehead, and he swayed a little on his feet. His eyes were small and mean, and his jaw stuck out. He began to move slowly toward me.

"Now, now, Bertha," Joyce Justin said, winking at me. "Mr. Bennett's a friend of mine. Make him a little drink." Her eyes held a hot, reckless light, and I wondered how much whisky she had consumed since she'd left my room at the Wheatville Inn.

"Like hell," Bertha grunted, and he kept coming.

I said to him, "How much you been paying your girlfriend here to ruin Donati's business?"

He didn't stop or say anything or slow his movement toward me. I stepped aside and balanced myself on my feet. At the same time I tried to keep an eye on Joyce Justin.

"Bertha!" she said sharply. "Don't be a fool."

He stopped and swung his head slowly toward her. "You told him, you cheating, double-crossing—"

She attempted a gay laugh. "I didn't tell him anything. You're drunk, darling. Sit down and be sociable."

Bertha swung his gaze back to me. "He knows," he said in a dead voice.

I saw fear in Joyce Justin's eyes then. She picked up the bottle and moved over to Bertha. "Here," she said nervously. "Have—"

Bertha lunged for me. I lifted my foot and kicked him in his stomach. He grunted loudly and doubled up. I swung for the girl, remembering the bottle in her hand. She swung the bottle at me, and I ducked, but I was a little slow. The bottle glanced off the side of my head and my knees wobbled. Through a haze of pain I had a glimpse of Bertha tugging at something in his hip pocket, and I tried to keep an eye on him and on the girl, too. Then Bertha leaped for me, and I swung to meet his charge. In the same instant the bottle hit me once more.

There was the crashing sound of breaking glass all around me, and I felt the sudden warmth of blood trickling over my right ear and down my neck. I went to my knees, and the green linoleum on the floor heaved up and down like the deck of a ship in an offshore squall. The figure of Bertha was a huge blur, like an image in a distorted mirror. I tried to stand up straight. I tried until the sweat ran into my eyes, but I couldn't make it. I fell on my face and my arms and legs felt as heavy as railroad ties, and there was a roaring and gurgling in my ears. I rolled my eyes upward.

The looming figure of Bertha was suddenly as clear as a Technicolor movie. He was standing over me, and I saw the white gleam of his teeth beneath the narrow black mustache. In his hand he held a small black bottle, and he was unscrewing the cap with frantic fingers.

From somewhere above me I heard Joyce Justin's cry of horror.

"No, Bertha, no!"

Things faded out. All I knew or felt was the cool linoleum beneath me. I wanted to sleep, and I remembered only a little. From a long way off I heard Bertha's laugh, a high, shrill, crazy laugh, and his echoing voice came to me as if from a long black tunnel....

"It's perfect! Perfect! They'll think it's suicide...."

I squirmed feebly on the floor. I heard Joyce Justin's desperate voice. "No, Bertha, no! You're crazy! Don't do it, don't do it, don't do ..."

Something smacked me on the head again, and I didn't hear anything, or know anything.

My fingernails clawed at my lips and I tasted blood. My throat was on fire. I rolled over on my stomach and coughed and gagged. My lips and my tongue burned, and it seemed as though a red-hot wire was rammed down my throat and tickling my heels. I struggled to my knees, and the room swam in a red haze before my eyes. I realized that I was clutching something in my hand and I held my hand close to my eyes.

It was a bottle. A small black bottle with a narrow square of paper pasted on it. There was writing on the paper. I spelled it out loud, and my voice was a croak in the stillness. "H_2SO_4—5% Sol." I looked dully at the little printed symbols, not caring much.

And then suddenly I flung the bottle away from me and stared wildly around the room. The telephone was on a table against a wall. I scuttled toward it like a crab; I reached up and, grabbing the cord, pulled the phone to the floor. I rolled over on my back and croaked into the mouthpiece, "Seneca, 137." I don't know how I remembered Hector Griffith's number.

He answered almost immediately.

I had to fight to get the words out. "Doc ... this is Bennett ... Swallowed sulphuric acid ... Bertha's ... Beauty Bar ..."

"Stay there!" I heard him yell and the wire went dead.

I rolled over on my stomach and dug at my burning lips and tongue with my fingers. My legs doubled up in pain and I vomited, and I didn't care whether school kept or not.

After what seemed like a long time I heard a crash and the tinkle of breaking glass, and Hector Griffith ran into the room. In one hand he held a quart of milk and in the other was a small black bag. My face was against the floor, but I rolled my eyes up at him.

I mumbled something. He knelt beside me, rolled me over and cradled my head on his knee. He held the bottle of milk to my lips and I gulped it down. It tasted wonderful, cold and sweet. But I couldn't keep it down. He tried again, and I drank like a man dying of thirst.

It stayed down. Hector opened his bag, took out a hypo needle, ripped open my shirt and jabbed the needle into my shoulder. Then he placed one cool dry hand on my forehead, and with the other he felt the pulse in my wrist.

"Doc—" I gasped.

He said, "Shhh!" as if to a child, and I saw his lips move silently as he counted my heartbeats. His lean face was grim, and the light glittered on his glasses. "A little slow," he said, as if talking to himself, "but not bad."

He reached into his black bag, and I got a glimpse of a double row of small bottles and shining instruments. He took out a pint bottle of whisky, unscrewed the cap and the neck of the bottle jarred against my teeth. "Sip it," he said. "Take it easy."

I sipped it and took it easy. The whisky burned like molten steel over my raw tongue. But he kept feeding it to me, a few drops at a time. After a while, I began to feel better, but my tongue, lips and throat still burned, and I ran my tongue over my blistered lips.

Hector took a small jar from his bag, and with his fingertips he applied a cool cream to my lips. He was like a nurse who loved her work, or like a mother with a sick child. I closed my eyes, and I felt him lower me gently to the floor. Maybe I slept a little.

When I opened my eyes, Hector was standing in the middle of the room, looking at a small black bottle. He gazed down at me and smiled. "You're lucky, Jim," he said. "It's only a five per cent solution—but still strong enough to kill you if you let it go. It eats the stomach right out of a person."

I sat up and Hector helped me to my feet. I leaned on a table and waited for the room to stop going around. Presently I raised a hand to my head above my right ear and felt a neat bandage held down by tape. My lips and tongue felt blistered but the burning had let up a little. I sat down in a chair by the table and began to talk in a hoarse croak of a voice. I told Hector all about Joyce Justin and Bertha, and what had happened since I'd left him.

He nodded his head gravely. "I'm sorry to hear it. I always liked Joyce—but I wondered."

"She was pretty friendly with Donati?"

He nodded slowly. "Receptionists in a town like Wheatville don't get a hundred a week for just—receptioning." He sighed and shook his head. "It's a hell of a world, isn't it?"

"Yeah," I agreed, "but guys like me would starve if people were what they should be. She was working with Bertha, trying to ruin Donati's business—and swing the trade to Bertha. It's my guess she worked it this way: she opened a few of the permanent wave kits, applied a small quantity of sulphuric acid to each pad, and closed the kit up again. Then, when the operator soaked the pads in the wave solution and applied them to the women's hair the sulphuric acid began to work and caused the burns. Donati's business would have soon been on the rocks. Women don't come back for a second sulphuric acid treatment."

Hector said, "Bertha was smart enough to make it weak. It would cause a bad external burn, but that's all. And it was easy to dispose of the acid-treated pads afterwards. Joyce Justin saw to that."

I nodded, remembering that Joyce Justin had been the one who had removed the pads from the blond woman's hair at the shop that morning. "This Bertha," I said. "Would he go further to stop Donati—say, cut his throat?"

"Feeling better now?" Hector asked.

"Sure. It takes a lot to kill me. Would he?"

He smiled faintly. "Bertha's a little queer, but I don't think he'd do murder. Not Bertha."

"Hell," I said, "he tried to kill me—and planted a bottle of acid in my hand to make it look like suicide. He had plenty of reason to kill Donati. Donati was hogging all the beauty business, and on top of that he had the inside track with Joyce Justin. Or at least he had enough money to pay for the inside track. If Bertha didn't kill Donati, who did? Somebody who needed money, somebody from the outside who knew about the money in Donati's safe, and who slipped in and slugged him—and then cut his throat to make sure, because maybe Donati recognized him? Somebody like that?"

Hector lifted his square shoulders. "It could be—I don't know." He gave a crooked smile. "It could even be me, you know. Naturally, I think a lot of Marianne, and I hated Donati—I don't mind your knowing it."

"What would you gain by killing him?" I asked curiously.

He sighed. "Nothing, I guess—except maybe some personal

satisfaction. Without Marianne, Donati would have been nothing. But he strutted and shouted orders in his phony French accent. I hated him for the way he talked, for the way he took all women for granted. I hated him for the shabby way he treated Marianne, a truly lovely and loyal person. I—"

"All right," I broke in, and grinned at him. "He was no pal of mine, either. But I'm working for his wife, and in my business you can't let a lot of personal feelings interfere with what you've got to do. Right now I'm interested in this Bertha and his double-crossing stooge, Joyce Justin."

"Tomorrow," he said gently. "You need rest."

"Tomorrow, hell. Time's a-wasting. Let's go." I stood up and moved a little unsteadily to the door through which I had entered.

"I kicked in the glass of the front door," Hector said dubiously. "Maybe I better tell the police."

"To hell with it," I said, and I placed my hand on the doorknob.

"Wait," Hector said sharply.

I turned to stare at him.

"Look, Jim," he said in his quiet, grave voice. "You're playing with dynamite. You know that Bertha isn't fooling, and whoever beat you up in the alley behind Donati's shop wasn't fooling, either ... Do you have a gun?"

"No," I said. "I had one when I came down here, but somebody swiped it."

He gave me his crooked grin. "A private detective without a gun? Heavens!" He opened his black bag, reached in and handed me a small flat .32 automatic. "I'll loan it to you—for the duration," he said. "I used to carry it when I was interning in Cleveland and made sick calls on the waterfront."

I took the gun, pulled out the clip and saw that it was full of bright brass cartridges. I dropped it into my pocket. "Thanks," I said.

"I still advise some sleep for you," Hector said.

"Not tonight, Doc," I said, grinning. "I'm still on the night shift. Come sunup, I'll be on the day shift for Sam Allgood."

He sighed, and stepped up to the door. "Lead on," he said. "You'll probably need another hypo before this night is done."

I opened the door and peered out into the dark court. Hector edged past me and stepped outside before I could stop him. Instantly the court rocked with gunfire, and I saw the quick flashes of burning gunpowder reflected on the brick walls. Hector pitched forward into the darkness.

I jumped back, flattened myself against the wall, jerked out the gun Hector had given me and peeked around the edge of the door. Something moved furtively at the end of the court. I took a chance in the darkness and squeezed the trigger of the .32—twice. Before the reverberation of the shots had died away I heard a thudding sound on the bricks, and I saw a blurred blob of movement. There was silence for maybe a second. And then there was the sound of light, quick footsteps, the rapid click of high heels running over the bricks.

I jumped out of the door and ran to the end of the court. In the alley against the street light beyond, I saw the form of a girl. A girl in a big hat. I aimed low and fired. She stumbled forward and fell to her knees. I ran to her and grabbed her arm. Joyce Justin twisted her face up at me.

"Damn you!" she gasped in fear and pain. "Damn you!"

I let go of her arm and she sank to the bricks, moaning. I hurried back to the small court in the rear of the shop. It was almost dawn now, and a gray light was displacing the shadows. I saw the still form of a man along the wall, but I moved on. I found Hector Griffith in a sitting position, with his back against the wall beside the door to the shop. I knelt beside him. "Where did he get you?" I asked.

I could see him better now. His face was pale in the gray light. He gave me a twisted smile. "I—I guess I'm more scared than hurt," he said. "Just nicked my side—I—I think."

I opened his coat, and I saw the red stain on his right side just above his belt. "I better call Doc Hendricks," I told him.

He brushed my hand away and probed his side with practiced fingers.

"No," he said. "It's all right. I can take care of it myself."

"That slug was intended for me," I said. "Bertha was hanging around here—just in case."

"So it was Bertha, then?" he asked wearily.

"Yeah," I said. "I'll be back."

I moved across the court to the still form of the man lying against the wall. I struck a match and leaned over him. It was Bertha, all right. Both of my bullets had caught him in the face—one under his left eye, and one at the corner of his mouth. He wasn't pretty. I shivered and threw the match away.

I turned and walked down the alley to the form of Joyce Justin. She was sobbing quietly, her face resting on an out-flung arm. I knelt beside her, and I felt cold and calm and sick at heart.

"Where does it hurt?" I asked her.

"My knee," she moaned. "I can't move my leg."

"All right," I said. "Take it easy. We'll look after that shortly. But first, I've got to know a few things. You were playing it both ways, weren't you? A little out-of-office-hours affair with Donati, for which he was paying you. In a nice way, of course, in the form of a salary, and you didn't object to a little mild blackmail. But that wasn't enough for you. You made a deal with Bertha to ruin Donati. Bertha gave you a solution of sulphuric acid to put on Donati's permanent wave pads. Bertha figured that ought to scare the customers away, even if Donati did have a French accent and wavy hair. But you got suspicious of me after Donati was killed, and you came to me at the Wheatville Inn and tried to throw me off the trail. It didn't work, and you knew it didn't. So you went back to Bertha to tell him the bad news. I knew you were in cahoots with Bertha, because you called me 'my friend' tonight—and the person who slugged me behind Donati's shop said it, too—'my friend.' Bertha addressed me that way when I first talked to him, and I figured you picked it up from him."

She lay silent, her face twisted with pain. She appeared not to have heard me, but I kept on. I had to get it out.

"So I followed you to Bertha's," I went on, "and I busted in on you. Bertha got scared and went nuts. You're deep in the deal anyhow, and so you help him by knocking me silly with a whisky bottle. Maybe the acid part was a little thick for you, but you had to play along. If it hadn't been for Hector Griffith, I probably would have died and your troubles would have been over. Bertha would have all the beauty business in Wheatville, and I would have been just some outsider who broke into his shop and committed suicide by swallowing sulphuric acid. But Bertha was worried, and he hung around outside to make sure that I wouldn't come out of it—and he made you wait with him. When Hector came out of the door, he thought it was me, and he knew that he had to finish the job, so he let loose with a gun." I paused, and then I said, "Bertha killed Donati, didn't he?"

I stopped talking then and stood up wearily. I had had my say and felt weak and dizzy.

"I—I don't know who killed Pete," Joyce Justin moaned. "But the rest is like you said. I—I'm sorry, and I can't help it now. Bertha was drunk, and I couldn't stop him. Please, my leg ... hurts. ..."

I left her and stumbled back down the alley to the court. Hector Griffith was still sitting against the wall. He was smoking a cigarette, and his face was a pale blur in the grayness.

"It's damn quiet," I said. "That shooting should have waked up the whole town."

He chuckled softly. "Not Wheatville. If anybody heard, they probably thought it was a car backfiring."

"I'll have to call the cops, I guess," I said. "Bertha's dead, and the girl's wounded. How do you feel?"

"All right," he said. "The bleeding has stopped. A little sulpha powder should do the trick."

I went back into the beauty shop and called the police. I told them to pick up a dead man and a wounded girl behind Bertha's Beauty Bar, and I hung up before the startled cop could ask any questions. Then Hector Griffith and I walked away from there as fast as we could. It wasn't very fast, because we both were candidates for hospital beds. But we avoided the police, and we made the few blocks to my room at the Wheatville Inn in about ten minutes. The lights of most of the storefronts were turned off, and only a few people were on the streets. As we went up the stairs at the Inn, I looked at my wristwatch.

It was twenty minutes before one o'clock on a Friday morning in July.

CHAPTER EIGHT

When Hector Griffith and I entered my room, we both stopped in surprise. Little Peggy Roark was sitting on my bed. Her hands were folded demurely in her lap and her legs were crossed. The toes of her scuffed saddle oxfords didn't quite reach the floor. She was wearing about a yard of polka-dot material for a dress, and her reddish hair was no longer braided and tied with ribbons. It was parted on the side, and combed smoothly over her shoulders.

I closed the door, said, "Hello, Peggy."

"Hello, Mr. Bennett," she said in a soft, small voice, and she smiled at Hector.

"Hi, Peggy," Hector said, and he headed for the bathroom, carrying his medicine bag. He went inside, closed the door and I heard water running. Carefully I lowered myself into a chair.

Peggy Roark looked down at her hands. "I—I hope you don't mind my walking into your room like this," she said in a low voice. "But the door was unlocked. I've been waiting quite a while. I—I want to talk to you. After you left my house, I got to thinking of the reason for your visit, and I—I wondered—if you thought that I ..."

"Killed Donati?" I finished for her, and I smiled. "I don't think you're quite big enough for a job like that, Peggy."

She shivered. "I'll never forget—how he looked."

"Don't think about it."

She slid off the bed and moved slowly to the door. "Well," she said, "I just wanted to make sure, and I couldn't sleep. Will it—look all right if I start to work for Bertha on Monday? I mean, after what's happened?"

I sighed and said, "Look, honey, you can't start to work for Bertha on Monday—or any other day. Bertha is dead."

"Dead ... Bertha?" Her freckles were big and brown against her suddenly pale face.

I nodded slowly. "You'd better go home to bed. Remember that golf match."

"B-Bertha's dead?" She stammered. "Really?"

I nodded again. "It's nothing for you to worry about. You can find another job."

"B-but who ..."

I stood up and moved over to her. "Never mind," I said, and I patted her cheek. "It'll be in the papers and all over town in the morning. All you've got to do is win that golf game. Your dad would want you to win."

She tilted her face up to me, and her chin trembled. "I—I'll win," she said. She turned abruptly and went out.

Hector Griffith, bare to the waist, came out of the bathroom. Just above his belt, on his right side, was a neat bandage. He sat down carefully in a chair by the bed. "My side's stiffening up," he said. "The bullet missed the muscles but it's sore as hell. How do you feel?"

"Lousy," I said, and ran my tongue over my blistered lips. The swelling had gone out of them, but they still burned, and my tongue felt thick and rough.

Hector gave me his crooked smile. "You could have died, you know."

"So could you," I said grimly, remembering the gunfire in the court and the bullet intended for me.

He nodded slowly.

I sighed and decided that it was time I returned to Sam Allgood's house. I said to Hector, "It's been a long night, and I've got a long day ahead." I peered into a small mirror on the wall. Except for my slightly swollen lips and the neat bandage over my right ear, I didn't look too bad. "Do you suppose I could get along without this bandage on my head?" I asked Hector.

He stood up wearily and came over to me. With deft, gentle fingers he removed the bandage and peered at the cut Joyce Justin had made with the whisky bottle. "It's coagulating nicely," he said. "I would prefer that you keep it covered, because of infection, but you can dispense with the bandage for a while—if you'll let me dress it again tomorrow."

I didn't want Sam Allgood to be asking me questions about a bandage on my head, and I said, "It's a deal, Doc." I smoothed my hair down over the cut in my scalp. I seemed to have accumulated a variety of wounds and ailments, none of them serious, but all together they added up to a definite beaten-up feeling, and the soft bed in Sam Allgood's house was suddenly very attractive.

I put on my hat and placed the gun Hector had given me in my inside coat pocket. "Mind if I keep your gun for a while?" I asked him.

He smiled. "I don't need it."

I went to the door. "I'm supposed to be sleeping at Sam Allgood's house, and I'm going out there now. Stick around as long as you like."

He nodded at my bottle of Bourbon on the table. "Mind if I have a touch of that?"

"Help yourself."

"Will I see you later?" he asked.

"Sure—you'll be at the golf match, won't you?"

He smiled. "I wouldn't miss it."

The telephone rang. I moved across the room and answered it.

A deep voice said, "Bennett?"

"What's left of him."

"This is Swartz."

"Who?"

"Swartz—the chief of police."

"Hello, Chief."

"I just thought I'd tell you we got Pete Donati's killer." He tried to sound casual.

"Nice going," I said. "Who was it?"

"A guy named Bert Homer—called himself Bertha on account of he ran Bertha's Beauty Bar. We got a phone call a while back, and we found him dead behind his shop—two slugs in his face. He had sixteen hundred dollars' worth of cash and checks on him. The checks were made out to Armand's Beauty Salon." He paused.

I swore at myself for not thinking to search Bertha, but I said, "You don't say!"

"That ain't all," the Chief said smugly. "A girl named Joyce Justin was with him. She was shot in the knee. At first she wouldn't talk, but we worked on her a little and she spilled the whole deal—about how she was working with Bertha against Donati—I'll tell you all about it later." He paused.

I smiled to myself. "Don't get cagey now, Chief," I said. "Tell me the rest of it."

"Why, that's about all, I guess," he said innocently.

"Oh, come now, Chief. Didn't you forget to mention that the Justin girl told you that I killed Bertha and winged her, after they laid for me behind the shop? Didn't she tell you that Bertha tried to kill me with sulphuric acid and left me on the floor of his shop—after I'd stumbled onto their racket?"

He laughed. "Well, Bennett, you can't blame me for trying to hog the credit, but now that you mention it, it seems to me that she did say something like that." He chuckled. "I wondered if you were going to mention it."

"Did she also tell you that Bertha slugged me behind Donati's place last night, and warned me to get out of town?" I asked. "And that Bertha tried to gun me out by Peggy Roark's house—because Joyce Justin had tipped him off that I was working for Mrs. Donati?"

"Yep," he said, "she told us that, too. But so far we ain't got a peep out of her about Bertha killing Donati. Maybe Bertha was holding out on her. Anyhow, it's a hell of a mess. You ain't figuring on leaving town right away, are you? We'll need you for the inquest."

"I'll be around. Thanks for calling me."

He laughed. "Thank you." He hung up.

I turned to Hector. "That was Chief Swartz. They found Bertha and the Justin girl. She confessed her part, and they found money and checks from Donati's safe on Bertha."

He had poured himself a drink. He sipped thoughtfully and nodded.

I went to the door again. "Well, I'd better get going. Thanks—for what you did for me. I won't forget it."

"Don't thank me," he said quietly. "I took an oath once, when I passed my state board examinations to practice medicine." He closed his eyes. "The Oath of Hippocrates, taken by all doctors. Let's see if I can remember it." He began to speak, his voice low and clear in the quiet room.

"I swear by Apollo, the physician ... and all the gods and goddesses ... I will keep this oath and stipulation ... I will follow that method of treatment which ... I consider for the benefit of my patients, and abstain from whatever is deleterious and mischievous ... I will give no deadly medicine to anyone if asked, nor suggest any such counsel ... With purity and holiness I will pass my life and practice my art ... Into whatever houses I enter I will go into them for the benefit of the sick ... and will abstain from every voluntary act of mischief ... and, further, from the seduction of females or males, bond or free.

"Whatever, in connection with my professional practice, or not in connection with it, I may see or hear in the lives of men which ought not to be spoken abroad, I will not divulge, as reckoning that all such should be kept secret ..."

Hector paused and opened his eyes. "I still remember," he said, and I thought I saw a hint of tears in his eyes. "I remember the day I took that oath. I was young and filled with ambition and hope and trust in people." He paused, and took a long swallow of his drink. "I thought then," he said bitterly, "that Hippocrates' words were the noblest ever uttered by man." He looked up at me and gave me his twisted smile. "Do you want to hear the rest of it?"

"Sure, Doc," I said gently.

He looked down at the glass clasped tightly in his hand. "I—I never forgot it—after all these years...."

"While I continue to keep this oath unviolated, may it be granted to me to enjoy life and the practice of my art, respected by all men at all times, but should I trespass and violate this oath, may the reverse be my lot."

He looked up at me, and his face was haggard. "Quite touching, isn't it?"

I said, "Can't you practice again—ever?"

He shook his head slowly. "Not in this state—or in this country."

I couldn't think of anything to say.

Hector smiled at me, and said quietly, "You'd better go on out to Allgood's and get some sleep."

"All right," I said. "Take it easy."

"Sure," he said. "Right you are." He got up, went over to the table and poured more Bourbon into his glass. He stood with his back toward me and didn't turn around.

I went out quietly and closed the door.

Down in the lobby the stout lady with the clip-on glasses was still behind the desk.

"Hello," she said to me. "Quite a ruckus in town tonight. A fellow named Bert Horner was shot to death and a girl was wounded." She shook her head. "I don't know what this town's coming to—what with Pete Donati murdered and all. The whole town's buzzing about it. Alvin Sims, he's a cab driver, was just in here, and he'd been at the police station. This Bert Horner, he ran a beauty shop, and—"

"I'll read about it in the paper," I broke in, and went out to the street. I got into my coupé, and drove across town to Sam Allgood's house.

Allgood's new red sedan was parked in the drive, with the door standing open. I got out of my coupé, walked up to the sedan and peered inside. An empty whisky bottle lay on the front seat. I closed the door quietly and went up to the front door of the house. It was standing slightly ajar, and I entered silently and hurried down the hall to my room. I didn't hear a sound in the house as I undressed and stretched out between the sheets.

I fell into deep sleep immediately, and I didn't awaken until I felt the hot morning sun on my face. I climbed out of bed groggily, pulled down the blinds and wrestled with the overpowering temptation to flop on the bed again. I looked at my wristwatch. Twenty minutes after nine. Time to be on the job for Sam Allgood—past time. I stumbled into the bathroom and tried not to look at the bed. A cold shower perked me up a little, and after a glance in the mirror I decided that my shave of the evening before would last a while yet. The bullet groove over my collar bone was sore and my shoulder was stiff, but my acid-burned lips, thanks to Hector's treatment, looked almost normal. With a forefinger I gently probed the cut in my scalp made by the whisky bottle in Joyce Justin's hand. It wasn't bleeding and didn't seem any worse than it was when I had removed the bandage, but I decided that at the first opportunity I'd have Hector give me a general overhauling.

The shirt I had worn was a mess. I put on a fresh one, and when I was combed and dressed I stepped out into the hall. I didn't see anyone, but I smelled fresh coffee, and I followed the aroma through the big house to a sunlit kitchen.

Katherine Allgood was sitting by a screened window in a cheery breakfast nook. There was a coffee cup before her, and she was smoking a cigarette and reading a newspaper. She looked up at me and smiled. She was wearing a sand-colored open-necked blouse, a tan gabardine skirt, white ankle socks and brown moccasins. Her wide brown eyes were clear, but there were dark smudges beneath them, and her thin, handsome face had a faintly drawn look to it. But even with a hangover, she was still one of the most attractive women I'd ever met.

"Good morning," I said, trying to act hearty. "All ready for the big game today?"

She smiled ruefully and shoved a tall glass of orange juice toward me. As I sat down opposite her, she said, "As ready as possible, I guess." She poured coffee for us and flicked the switch on the toaster. "Look, I—" She hesitated, her eyes on the toaster. "I—I'm sorry about last night—and the night before. I'm really not that—cheap." She looked at me, and there was faint color in her cheeks.

I remembered the urgent warmth of her lips on mine, and I took a sip of the orange juice. "Forget it," I mumbled.

She gazed out of the window. "I—I've been rather upset lately, and …"

I changed the subject. "What time is the match today?"

"One o'clock."

Two pieces of toast popped up and I began to butter one of them. She lit a fresh cigarette from the stub of the one she had been smoking. "It's strange that Sam never mentioned you to me before," she said. "But then, he knows a lot of people I never heard of."

"I met Sam in Cleveland," I said. "I'm in town on business, and I saw him at the Beavers'. He was kind enough to ask me to be his guest while I'm in town."

"Business," she said. "That's all Sam thinks about—almost." She laughed shortly.

I could see it in her eyes. She was being eaten alive by jealousy.

She didn't like it, and she didn't know what to do about it. I knew that she had experimented on me the last two nights—coming home from the country club and here in this house the evening before. Sauce for the goose stuff. But I hadn't helped her ego any. She was used to having what she wanted, the way she wanted it and when she wanted it. I didn't doubt that she would win the golf match from little Peggy Roark. She was that kind of woman.

She lowered her gaze to the cigarette between her long slender fingers. "What's going on?" she asked quietly. "Between you and Sam?"

I choked on a bite of toast and took a swallow of coffee. "Why?" I asked.

"He didn't show up for dinner last night—you know that. Then you left. I went to bed, but I didn't sleep. It was after midnight when Sam came home. But this morning he was up early, and he went away—to the office, I suppose. Do you know who he was with last night, where he was?"

I thought about Sam Allgood getting into Marianne Donati's car. I knew where he had been, and whom he had been with. I gave Katherine Allgood what I hoped was a frank grin. "I wouldn't know," I said.

She looked at me thoughtfully. "Sam came home first. Then I heard you come in and go to your room. Were you with Sam?"

I told her the truth this time. "No."

To my surprise, she dropped it. "Oh, to hell with it," she said.

I jumped at the chance to change the subject. "How long have Sam and Jeff Winters been partners?" I asked.

"Ever since they got out of school. They graduated together. They make a good team. Jeff figures the angles, and Sam puts on a good show in court. Between them they make a lot of money." Her lips twisted bitterly. "I suppose I shouldn't ask for anything more."

"What's wrong with money?" I asked her.

"Nothing. It's wonderful—if money is all you need to make you happy."

"It helps," I said.

She shrugged, dropped her cigarette into her coffee cup and spread her fingers in a gesture of finality. I took a last gulp of coffee and stood up.

She smiled brightly up at me. "Are you coming out to the match?"

"I'm going to try and make it."

"I'll win."

I didn't doubt it. "Sure," I said, and I moved to the kitchen doorway. "Will you be our guest long?" she asked in a brittle voice.

I thought of my room at the Wheatville Inn. Whether I finished my job for Sam Allgood today or next week, I knew that I was not going to stay at his house. "I'll probably leave some time today," I said. "I'll pick up my bag later. Thank you for your hospitality."

She shrugged. "Any friend of Sam's ..." She was smiling, but there was a mocking light in her eyes.

I felt like a yokel. She was a beautiful woman, a woman who, on the surface, had everything that any woman would want. And yet, she was desperately unhappy. I wanted to help her, but I knew that I couldn't; not in the way she wanted to be helped. Only Sam Allgood could do that. I lifted a hand. "Goodbye," I said, and turned and left the kitchen.

In the big living room I met Jenny, the colored maid, carrying a vacuum cleaner in from an adjoining room. "'Morning," she said gloomily.

"Good morning, Jenny." I went out the front door and drove down to the business section of Wheatville.

People were gathered in little knots on the sidewalks, and I guessed that they were gossiping about the double killing in the town the day and evening before. I parked close to the office of Allgood and Winters, put a nickel in the meter and entered the big drugstore. I put in a telephone call for Skip Gordon, a sports writer friend on one of the big Cleveland dailies. I was lucky. He was in the office.

"Skip, this is Jim Bennett."

"Hi, Jim. I was just thinking about you. How about having lunch with me today?"

"Can't," I said. "What do you know about that Red Roark deal in the Midwest Open last year?"

"Red Roark is dead," he said.

"I know it. But did he throw that match to the Alabama Kid or didn't he?"

"Well, Jim, the wise guys say he did. But they never proved anything. I was one of the few who stuck up for Red."

"I remember," I said. "Why?"

"Hell, I don't think Red would have pulled a stunt like that. Oh, I know—he was a small-time pro all his life and he probably needed money, but he was a square shooter. I don't think anybody paid him to miss the putt that lost the match for him. I think he missed because he was rattled—maybe sick. And I always had a feeling that somebody got him that way on purpose."

"Tell me more," I said.

"Look, Jim. I was right beside Red when it happened. He played like a champ right up to the seventeenth—it was an eighteen-hole playoff, you know, after Red and the Alabama Kid tied on the first rounds. But just before Red stepped out on the green to putt, a guy steps up beside him and says, 'Red, you're through. Don't forget.' And right after that Red muffed the putt. But not on purpose. He couldn't help it. He lost the match by one stroke—that stroke. He tied the Alabama Kid on the eighteenth, but that one putt licked him. And two hours later he was dead."

"Why didn't you print that?" I asked him.

"Print it? Hell, it was just me against five thousand people, and I didn't know who the guy was who needled him. He disappeared in the crowd. I tried to find him, but I couldn't."

"Would you know him if you saw him again?"

"You're damn right I would."

"Now, don't get excited," I said. "I don't know anything about what happened to Red Roark on the seventeenth, but I've got a story for you. His daughter, Peggy, is playing off a local club championship today. Why don't you climb into your car and come down here? I'm in Wheatville, and—"

"Wheatville?" Skip broke in. "My God, that's sixty miles from here!"

"The agency will pay your expenses," I told him. "Including liquor."

He laughed. "Stop twisting my arm, Jim. I'm on my way. Where'll I see you?"

"At the Wheatville Country Club. The match is at one o'clock."

"Right-o," he said cheerily. "Good excuse to get out of the office. Be seeing you."

I had a pineapple soda at the drugstore counter, and then I drove out the country club road. I turned down a dirt road which ran beside the golf course and parked in a grove of trees below Lem Fassler's farm where it bordered on the sixth fairway. I walked through an acre of second growth pine before I came to the fence separating Fassler's cornfield from the golf course. There I climbed the fence and approached the barn from the rear. When I was fairly close, I reconnoitered from the cover of a bramble thicket. There wasn't a sign of life around the place.

Once more I climbed the fence, crossed number six fairway and walked along the row of poplars until I came to the elevated position of the seventh tee. Here I paused and peered about. Some players were holing out on the eighth green, and a twosome was moving up number five fairway. From where I stood I had a clear view of the sixth tee and the shelter house behind it.

I turned and faced the farm across the fence. The shutters of the little window in the peak of the barn, which I had noticed on my first visit to the course two days before, were still standing open. I stepped down from the tee, skirted the sixth green, climbed the fence again and scooted around back of the barn. There was still nobody about and I ducked into an open doorway. The place smelled the way barns usually smell. A couple of worn-out horses munched in a stall. They gazed at me with dull vacant eyes and kept on munching.

Above the level of the stalls was a hayloft, with an open space in the middle extending to the roof. There was some flooring under the eaves beneath the tiny window in the peak. Birds were shooting in and out of the window, a shaft of sunlight glinting on their wings. A straight ladder was nailed to the flooring under the window and extended down to the stalls. I figured the ladder was used for rigging tackle to pull hay up into the loft.

I took a last quick look around me. Then I climbed the ladder to the little platform beneath the window and peered out. I had a panoramic view of the golf course, and of the entire sixth hole in particular.

A voice from below me said, "What in hell do you think you're doing?"

I turned slowly and looked down. Lem Fassler, the farmer, was standing on the barn floor beneath me. He had a .22 bolt action rifle in his hands.

I climbed down the ladder and stood facing him. He backed up a little and raised the gun. I jerked a thumb toward the window above. "No use going up now," I said. "There's nobody playing the sixth hole right this minute."

He looked puzzled and his mouth hung open. There was about as much expression in his little pale eyes as there would be in a couple of ping-pong balls.

"But don't you worry," I said soothingly. "There's a guy coming up number five."

He shut his mouth then and leaned forward. "Has he got on a red hat?" he asked eagerly.

I shook my head sadly. "No, he hasn't."

"Shucks," he sighed. "That's the one I'm a-laying for."

"Some sport, hey?" I said. "Making them jump."

He doubled over and slapped his hip, his shoulders shaking in silent laughter. I kept a wary eye on the gun in his hand, and I began to wish that I had brought along a straitjacket. Suddenly he straightened up and grinned at me. I saw the gap in his yellow front teeth.

"I sure made that sucker jump. You oughta seen him run."

"Who?" I asked.

"Red Hat. I'll teach him to trespass on my property. But yesterday a fella fooled me. He had on a red hat, but he wasn't Red Hat hisself. I zinged one past him—before I saw it wasn't Red Hat. He run like a scared coon for the shanty." He doubled up again in silent mirth and his hand beat on his pants leg.

I stepped in fast and jerked the rifle from his hand. He straightened up suddenly and his loose mouth flopped shut. His little pale eyes got cloudy, and he took a slow step toward me.

"Gimme the gun," he said, and I got a strong whiff of whisky.

"I'm the guy you shot at yesterday," I told him. "I didn't like it."

He stood still and his mouth opened up again. He shuffled his feet and looked down at the floor. "I thought it was Red Hat," he whined. "He was the worst. I chased him outta my corn a dozen times, and I got sick of it. He was in the field early this week, a-trampling it down, and I told him for the last time. I didn't aim to hit him—I just wanted to scare him a little." He gave me an up-from-under look. "Who be you, mister?"

"The law," I said importantly. "I'll have to take your gun." A crafty look came into his little pale eyes and he got cagey. "Lemme see your badge."

I didn't even have a bottle cap to show him. I moved toward the door, carrying the rifle. "Don't leave the county," I warned him. "The sheriff will want to talk to you."

He jumped to the barn doorway and stood in front of me. I didn't think he could move that fast. He reached behind him, and his big hand closed over the handle of a rusty spade leaning against the stalls. There was a hot glow in his eyes, and a little saliva showed at the corners of his loose lips.

"Gimme that gun," he said in a low voice, and his face took on a sly look. "Anyhow, it ain't loaded, mister."

He shouted at me—something loud and sputtering and without sense, and he swung the spade. I sidestepped, and let him have the rifle butt in his mouth. He slammed up against the stalls and rolled limply to the barn floor. I watched him a couple of seconds, the rifle poised, but he didn't move. I bent over him. His mouth was open and he was breathing heavily. A thick pencil line of blood wormed down over his chin. I figured that a couple more missing teeth wouldn't bother him too much. I left him lying there and walked out into the bright morning sunlight.

When I got back to my coupé, I clicked open the bolt of the rifle and slid it back. Lem Fassler had lied to me. There was a bright brass-bound cartridge in the chamber.

CHAPTER NINE

It was almost eleven o'clock that morning when I entered the office of Allgood and Winters. The thin woman behind the typewriter gave me a cool inquiring glance through her thick lenses. I moved past her to a door labeled *Private*. She half rose from her chair. "Just a minute," she said sharply.

I opened the door, stepped inside and closed it behind me.

Sam Allgood was sitting behind his desk, talking into a dictating machine. When he saw me, he hung up the mouthpiece hastily and swung around in his chair. His face was flushed and puffy, and his eyes looked like two burned holes in a blanket.

"Didn't Miss Hoskins tell you I was busy?" he asked coldly.

"I didn't ask her."

"Well, I am," he snapped. "What do you want?"

I grinned at him. "Let's start all over again ... Good morning."

He sighed and rubbed a hand over his chin, "Good morning," he said wearily. "I guess I'm a little edgy."

"Bad night?"

"I didn't get much sleep."

"Neither did I," I said, watching him.

We eyed each other like a couple of tomcats.

I decided to stop beating around the bush. "You know about the killing of a man named Bert Homer last night?"

He nodded slowly but there was a sudden alert look in his eyes.

"Yes, I know," he said. "I talked with Chief Swartz this morning, and the whole town's busting with it—that, and the killing of Pete Donati."

"Did the chief tell you that I killed Homer?"

"Yes. He gave me the whole story. Nice work."

"Killing is never nice work. I had to kill him—or get killed."

"I'm not criticizing you."

"And you know that I'm also working for Mrs. Donati—or was."

"Of course. I told you that on the telephone last evening. She told me all about it. I—uh—am sorry that I didn't get home for dinner last night, but Mrs. Donati wants to wind up her affairs as soon as possible, and she needed my advice."

"Then you were with Mrs. Donati?"

"Yes," he snapped. "What of it?"

I grinned. "Nothing. Just checking. I saw you get into her car in front of the drugstore."

He smiled bleakly. "You get around." He drummed his fingers on the top of his desk and added with the trace of a sneer, "Your agency should establish a branch office in Wheatville—it appears to be a fertile area for professional snoopers."

"I've finished my snooping for you," I told him. "It was the farmer who was shooting at you."

He frowned. "Are you sure?"

"He admitted it and I've got his gun. I can check the slugs against the rifling to cinch it."

He moved a hand impatiently. "No, no. That won't be necessary. It was his idea of a joke, I suppose. I thought it might be the farmer but I wanted to be sure. Kind of a crackpot, isn't he?"

"He's nuts," I said.

He took a thick wallet from his inside coat pocket. "All right, Bennett," he said briskly. "How much do I owe you?"

"Put your money away. You'll get an itemized bill and a report from Cleveland."

He stood up. "All right." He held out his hand. "Thanks, Bennett."

I ignored his outstretched hand. "What about the farmer?" I asked him. "Do you want to prefer charges?"

"Of course not," he snapped. "What the hell good would that do?"

"He might take another shot at you."

"If he does, I can handle it now. I just wanted to be sure who it was."

"I mussed him up a little," I said. "Next time he might aim

straighter."

"I'll worry about that," he said coldly. "Goodbye, Bennett."

"I'm not leaving right away," I said. "You'll have to pay me for today anyhow, and I think I'll stick around."

"Why?" he snapped.

"Well, for one thing, I want to see that golf match this afternoon."

He turned away and stared out of the window. "That damned match," he groaned. "I'd forgotten about it."

"You're going out and cheer for your wife, aren't you?" I asked.

He nodded without turning around. "I suppose so," he said gloomily.

"There's a couple of other things," I said. "I've got to see Mrs. Donati before I leave, and I'm a little curious about who went through my bag in my car at the club Wednesday evening and stole a gun."

He turned to face me. "Put the price of the gun on your bill," he said impatiently.

"I intend to," I said, "but that isn't what worries me. Who do you suppose swiped it?"

"Some petty thief."

I raised my eyebrows. "At the Wheatville Country Club?"

He flushed. "We can't put up a steel fence and station armed guards, you know."

I moved to the door.

He said coldly, "If you want to hang around town, I can't stop you. But I want it understood that you are no longer in my employ."

I lit a cigarette before I answered. Then I made up my mind to ask him. "Feel like telling me what you really hired me for?"

"I've learned what I wanted to know," he said evenly. "Goodbye."

I went out. Miss Hoskins gave me a mean look. I winked at her and asked, "Is Mr. Winters in this morning?"

"No," she snapped. "Mr. Winters is in court."

"Thank you, Miss," I said, and went out and down the steps to the street.

I walked across the square and saw a pale gray convertible parked a short distance down the street from Armand's Beauty Salon. A curious crowd stood outside, peering into the windows of the shop. I walked down the alley and tried the back door. It was locked. I tried the key Marianne Donati had given me. It worked and I stepped inside. The place was quiet, and I didn't see anyone about. I locked the door behind me, walked through the manicuring and hairdressing rooms to the carpeted corridor leading to Donati's office. The door to the office was standing open and I smelled cigarette smoke. I went silently along the thick carpet and peeked into the office.

Marianne Donati was sitting behind Donati's big desk. A cigarette was burning itself out in an ashtray before her, and her head was resting on her crossed arms, her yellow hair cascading in gleaming folds over the top of the desk. She didn't move, and the cigarette smoke drifted straight up to the ceiling.

I tiptoed back down to the end of the corridor and turned. "Hello," I called. "Anyone here?"

She didn't answer, and I rattled my knuckles on the wall. "Hey," I yelled.

Her soft lovely voice came out to me. "Yes?"

Once more I walked to the doorway of Donati's office. She was sitting erectly in the chair in which Pete Donati had died. Her eyes were hot and dry, and her incredibly scarred face looked naked and ugly in the bright light. And yet, as I stared at her, I had the weird feeling once more that she was beautiful beyond compare.

"Good morning, Mr. Bennett," she said quietly.

"I saw your car outside," I said, "and I came in the back door...."

"Come in." Her voice was almost a whisper. She motioned to a chair.

I stepped inside, took off my hat and sat in a chair facing her. She was wearing a severe black dress with a low V neckline. The skin of her throat was smooth and white and soft, in sharp contrast to the roughness of her scarred face. I felt a deep sadness and a kind of a rage against Pete Donati. And when I thought of Donati, my gaze strayed to the floor, and I saw the wide stain of his blood beside the desk.

I said, "There's a crowd out in front."

She nodded slowly. "I saw them. Vultures."

"Bert Horner killed your husband," I told her, "and took the money and checks from the safe. Joyce Justin was in cahoots with him on the scalp-burning deal—to chase business away from your shop. Horner is dead, and the cops have the Justin girl. I—"

She stopped me by holding up a hand. "Yes, I know," she said quietly. "The police told me early this morning." She looked at me gravely, and for an instant her sad eyes held a glint of warmth. "They told me about what you did. I am very grateful."

I shifted uneasily in the chair. "All part of the job," I said, and the bullet groove above my collar bone gave me a twinge.

She said, "How much do I owe you?"

"We'll send you a bill."

She nodded and crushed out the cigarette. The silence grew in the room, and I cleared my throat. Outside I could hear the traffic in the street, but here in Pete Donati's elegant office it was cool and quiet and remote.

Marianne Donati stood up abruptly and moved to the window. She stood with her back toward me, and I stared at her marvelous figure in a kind of daze. Even the memory of her ugly scarred face faded from my brain.

She said in a low voice, "I'm going to bury Pete on Monday."

I got up and walked slowly over the soft carpet until I stood behind her. The fragrance of her filled my senses, and, like a man in a dream, I place my hands on her shoulders and felt the softness of her skin beneath the thin black dress. Her body trembled a little beneath my hands, and I said huskily, "I'm sorry...."

She turned slowly and I dropped my hands to my side. With the bright sunlight behind her, it seemed to me that the scars of her face were gone, and that her beauty shone through in a shadowed radiance. She moved close to me. The sun glinted on her yellow hair, and her eyes were the color of sea water. I placed an arm around her slim waist and pulled her roughly to me. She turned her face away and pressed her cheek against my shoulder. "Don't look at me," she whispered. "Just hold me."

I held her and I didn't want to let her go.

Presently she pushed me gently away. "Thank you," she murmured. "Thank you."

I reached for her again.

"No," she said gently. "Please …" Her gaze shifted beyond me, and I saw her eyes widen. I turned quickly.

Hector Griffith stood in the doorway, a half-smile on his lean handsome face.

Marianne Donati said sharply, "You might knock, Hector."

"I'm sorry," he said gravely. "I didn't know anyone was here. I had some work to do …"

"Do it," she snapped.

He turned silently and went away. From somewhere in the shop I heard a door close quietly. Marianne Donati turned away from me and took a cigarette from a silver box on the desk. I held a match for her. Her eyes were dark and brooding. She drew deeply on her cigarette and stared out of the window. "Poor Hector," she said. "I shouldn't have been so sharp with him."

"Hector's all right," I said. "He saved my life once last night—and then he stopped a bullet intended for me."

She looked at me quickly, her eyes wide. "The police didn't tell me …"

"Water over the dam," I said.

"Are you—all right?"

"Sure."

She sighed and sank into the chair behind the desk. "I'm very tired," she said.

As I gazed at her I remembered the feel of her body against me and the sweet scent of her hair. And then I thought of Sam Allgood, and I had an unreasoning desire to ask her how much of her relationship with Allgood was purely business, and where they'd spent the time together until after midnight the evening before. But I didn't; I walked to the door.

"Leaving?" she asked.

I nodded.

"Goodbye, Mr. Bennett."

"Goodbye," I said sadly. She was so beautiful, and yet so ugly….

I turned quickly and went out.

I went to the Beavers' Lodge for lunch. It was a mistake. The doorkeeper didn't remember me, and I had to go through the whole silly password routine again. And when I got inside, I discovered that word had got around somehow about my connection with the death of Pete Donati and Bert Homer. A lanky man who needed a shave and who said he was a reporter for the local newspaper tried to get an exclusive interview out of me. I brushed him off with the "no comment" gag and ordered a beef sandwich. But a number of brothers hemmed me in and tried to pump me about Pete Donati's love life.

A fat brother with a long nose leered at me. "Tell us about Mrs. Pete," he said thickly, and I guessed that he'd had too many pre-lunch drinks. "Now, there's a smooth-looking babe—from the neck down." He guffawed loudly.

Another brother said, "I hear you're a big-time private dick. How about speaking at the Civic Advancement Club next Friday noon? Tell us about some of the hot divorce cases you've worked on. You'll get a free lunch, and—"

"No," I said.

Somebody said, "She's got a face that'd make you throw up, but oh, brother, what a shape!"

Two or three of them let out long, low whistles.

The fat brother with the long nose wormed his way behind me and breathed noisily in my ear. "I hear Bert Homer was playing around with Donati's wife. Is that a fact?"

A waiter brought my sandwich, but I didn't eat it. I stood up, pushed through the jabbering brothers and went outside. There I took a deep breath of the fresh air and was surprised to find that I was trembling a little. I walked around the corner to a quiet little bar where I had two dry martinis in peace and quiet. Afterwards, I drove out to Sam Allgood's house. The place looked deserted. Jenny, the maid, answered the bell. She told me that Mr. and Mrs. Allgood were both out. I got my bag, took it down to the Wheatville Inn, had a quick lunch there in the dining room. Then I drove out to the Wheatville Country Club. It was a quarter of one when I parked in the drive beside the clubhouse.

The first person I saw was Peggy Roark. She was getting out of her battered little blue convertible. She waved to me, and I walked over to her. Her small round face looked pale, and there were dark smudges beneath her eyes.

"Golly, I'm scared," she said.

I patted her shoulder. "Just keep your head down and swing easy."

She looked up at me, and there was a hint of sudden tears in her eyes. "Thank you, Mr. Bennett," she said quietly. "That—that's what Red always used to say." She turned and walked briskly away toward the caddy house.

I went up to the clubhouse and found Sam Allgood and Jeff Winters in the locker room. They were sitting at a round table with a couple of other men, and they were working on a bottle of Scotch. Allgood ignored me, but Winters gave me a friendly smile and introduced me to the other men. One of the men handed me a tall glass and I sat down.

Rogan, the white-coated attendant with the thick yellow hair, came in with a bowl of ice. I noticed that his lower lip was swollen and bruised-looking. Jeff Winters kidded him about it. "What happened, Al? Walk into a door?"

Rogan smiled stiffly. "Yes, sir," he said, and he hurried out, not looking at me.

Winters smiled across the table. "You're quite a celebrity," he said, "after last night. Sam never told me that you are a detective."

"It takes all kinds," I said.

One of the men glanced at a wristwatch. "About time for the big event," he said. He looked at Sam Allgood. "How about it, Sam? I've got a hundred bucks that says the little Roark gal will beat your wife."

Allgood grinned at him. "You're talking about the woman I love. Make it five hundred."

The man laughed. "It's a deal." He looked at the rest of us. "You guys heard it."

We all got up and walked out to the first tee. There was quite a crowd on hand for the playoff, and a couple of men were stringing ropes from the tee and out along the fairway. I saw Hector Griffith standing at the edge of the crowd, and he waved to me. Katherine Allgood walked over the grass to the tee, followed by a caddy with a heavy bag of clubs. She appeared to be cheerful and gay, and was waving and speaking to many people. Peggy Roark stood off by herself and took slow practice swings with a driver.

A dusty station wagon wheeled up the drive and stopped. I spotted the Cleveland license and walked over. Skip Gordon got out, and we shook hands. He was a sandy-haired little guy with freckles, a short nose and thick dark-rimmed glasses. He was wearing a gray tweed jacket and pale blue slacks.

"Just in time, Skip," I said. "The battle of the century is about to begin."

"Where's that liquor you promised me?" Like many little men, Skip had a perpetual belligerent look about him.

"Later," I promised. "They're teeing off now. Come on."

The little reporter trotted at my heels. "Damn you, Jim," he panted. "I drive like a bat out of hell to get here, and you ain't even got a drink for me."

"Shush," I said.

The crowd was banked tight around the tee, and Skip and I were forced to go down to the end of the line along the fairway. It was then that I saw Lily Winters. Her tawny hair glinted like ripe wheat in the sun. She waved a bottle of beer at me. "Hi, there, handsome," she called. "Have you seen Jeff?"

I pointed toward the tee. "He's up there—with Sam."

She walked past me with a long-legged stride. "Thanks, pal," she said. "You root for Kate now, hear? Gotta keep this championship in the family, you know." As she walked away, she tilted the bottle of beer to her lips.

Skip Gordon looked at me and said, "Hmmmm."

"Just one of my little Wheatville friends," I said.

"Nice," he said. "Very nice. She married?"

"Sure—and she's too tall for you anyhow."

He looked down toward the tee. "This the usual country club deal? A playoff, you said. I assume it's for the female golf crown—match play, hole for hole?"

"I guess so," I said.

"Look," he said impatiently. "There's medal play and there's match play. In medal play, like in the big national matches, every stroke counts. In match play, the player who has the least number of strokes on the most holes wins, no matter how many he may have on any given hole. Each hole is played separately, see?"

"I see," I said.

The crowd was suddenly quiet, and everyone watched the tee.

Peggy Roark drove first. It was a neat little shot, two hundred yards straight down the middle. Katherine Allgood was right beside her, and they both holed out in par. Then it was neck and neck until the fifth hole. Peggy Roark sank a thirty-foot putt for a birdie four. Katherine Allgood wavered and missed an easy four-footer. Peggy took the hole by two strokes, and was one hole up. The crowd began to murmur.

On the seventh, Peggy holed a short approach shot. Another birdie. Katherine Allgood, playing good steady golf, took her usual par. Peggy was two holes up, and I could see the sparkle of excitement in her eyes. Katherine Allgood's face seemed pale, and she played coldly and silently. The crowd grew restless and beside me a man said, "They're both par golfers, but Mrs. Allgood's got to do better than par. Peggy's two holes are a big lead."

"Yeah," I said.

Skip Gordon said, "That little gal is a champion. She's got this match in the bag."

Peggy Roark was driving. The ball soared straight and true, smack down the middle. Skip muttered, "She swings like Red used to—slow and easy."

Katherine Allgood, visibly tense, sliced her drive into the rough. I saw her bite her lip in anger. She strode out toward the rough, followed by her hurrying caddy. Her recovery from the rough was hurried and ragged—the ball barely made the fairway.

"She's going to pieces," Skip said. "She can't take it." He looked up at me. "This game is all over but the shouting. Let's go and get a drink."

"Stick around," I said. "You'll get a drink—later."

"Nuts," Skip said.

On the thirteenth Peggy was three holes ahead. She was playing smoothly and without apparent effort. By grim determination Katherine Allgood had played Peggy stroke for stroke, but she was losing and she knew it. With only five holes to play, a three-hole lead almost automatically gave the match to Peggy. The thirteenth was a dog-leg, two hundred and ten yards to where the fairway turned. Peggy's drive rolled a little beyond the turn, in perfect position for a shot at the green, a hundred and seventy yards away. Katherine Allgood's ball stopped rolling ten yards past Peggy's and to the left. Peggy unsheathed her brassie, squinted into the sun at the green and took her stance over the ball. Gently she laid the club head behind the ball, and she frowned in concentration.

I was standing behind her and to the left, maybe ten yards away. Skip Gordon stood beside me. Katherine Allgood was directly in front of us, watching Peggy. As Peggy started her backswing, Katherine Allgood turned abruptly and walked past Peggy's line of vision. I saw Peggy's gaze flick for an instant to Katherine Allgood, and her backswing faltered. She tried desperately to recover, and her club whipped up and down far too fast.

Too late I yelled, breaking the course rules, "Wait, Peggy!"

The face of her club cut into the ball, spinning it left across the grass. A miserable shot, a duffer's shot, and a low moan went up from the crowd. Peggy Roark turned, her little face gray beneath the tan, and looked at Katherine Allgood. But the older woman appeared not to see her, and was already standing over her ball, carefully lining up her shot.

Skip Gordon muttered, "That tall babe did it on purpose. She moved, just as Peggy began her backswing—threw Peggy's timing off. That's dirty."

"Yeah," I said. I gazed around at the crowd. No one else had seemed to notice Katherine Allgood's maneuver.

Out on the fairway, Katherine Allgood was smiling. She swung easily, and her ball flew straight and low to the green. She was on in two, with an easy two putts for a par. The best that Peggy Roark could do, after her muffed shot, was to make the green in three—and hope for a short putt to tie Katherine Allgood. But she didn't. She overshot the green, pitched back in four and holed out with a six. Katherine Allgood's par four took the hole. But she was still two holes behind.

They tied the fourteenth, both playing steady, careful golf. On the fifteenth, Peggy's ball took a bad bounce and landed in a marsh. She was forced to take a penalty stroke and lay out. The penalty cost her the hole and her lead was cut to one. Katherine Allgood perked up. Three holes to go, and anything could happen. As they passed me, walking to the sixteenth tee, I said to Peggy in a low voice, "Hold her, honey. You're still on top."

She gave me a faint smile, and Skip Gordon said, "Just swing easy—like Red."

She glanced at Skip in surprise, and he grinned at her. She looked away quickly and moved toward the tee.

"She's cute," Skip said. "As cute a little trick as I've seen in a long time."

Katherine Allgood hit her ball. It was a mediocre shot, a partial hook, but it had a lot of roll, and she was in fair position for a shot at the green. Smiling, she stepped aside for Peggy. As the little girl prepared to drive, Katherine Allgood said distinctly, "I wish I were playing your father, honey. I do believe you want to win."

Peggy Roark stood very still, gripping her club tightly. I saw her small chin quiver, and for an instant she squeezed her eyes shut. Then she took a deep breath, looked once down the rolling fairway—and swung. She was fighting for control, but fighting too hard in the face of Katherine Allgood's taunt, and her stroke showed it. Her ball sliced high and far, and disappeared in a dense thicket to the right of the fairway. Katherine Allgood laughed, and the crowd groaned.

Peggy recovered from the thicket with a masterful iron shot, but it wasn't enough. It was Katherine Allgood's hole, and the match was tied. The excitement in the crowd was almost a live thing. Skip Gordon said bitterly, "We should have left when I wanted to. This is brutal. That little gal hasn't a chance now."

"Wait," I said, but I remembered what Peggy Roark had said to me the afternoon I'd met her. *I guess I can't concentrate when I think of Red. He was such a swell guy....* I knew that Katherine Allgood wouldn't stop. She knew the chink in Peggy's armor and nothing would stop her now. I waited grimly for the end.

It came on the seventeenth and I was standing close when it happened. Katherine Allgood leaned toward Peggy Roark and said pleasantly, "I'm not a bit worried now, dear. The seventeenth is where your father threw away the Midwest Open. Like father, like daughter, you know."

Peggy Roark went pale. Her eyes filled with tears and she turned angrily toward Katherine Allgood. Then she paused, turned slowly away and stood staring down at the grass. The crowd hadn't heard it, but Skip Gordon had, and he swore under his breath. "Foul," he muttered. "Dirty pool. Hitting in the clinches, gouging in a pileup on the two-yard line, spiking a runner sliding into third—all sissy stuff. That tall babe is the master of hitting below the belt."

Smiling confidently, Katherine Allgood stepped up and smacked a sizzling two-hundred-and-twenty-yarder straight down the middle of the fairway. She gazed mockingly at Peggy Roark and stepped away from the tee.

Peggy Roark's drive was pitiful. She topped it, and it bounced down the fairway for maybe fifty yards. Her second shot was better, but her third fell short of the green. Katherine Allgood, on in two, won the hole by two strokes and took the lead.

On the eighteenth Peggy settled down, got control of herself, but it was too late. She parred it with Katherine Allgood. The match was the older woman's by one hole. Once more Katherine Allgood was the woman's golf champion of the Wheatville Country Club. She strode triumphantly away from the green, while her friends ran out to congratulate her. Peggy Roark disappeared in the crowd before I could catch her.

Skip Gordon said, "Who is that black-haired bitch, anyhow?"

"Mrs. Sam Allgood," I said. "And watch your language."

I saw Sam Allgood approach his wife with widespread arms. "My little moneymaker," he called loudly. "Five hundred smackers you won for me. Come to daddy." She stepped into his arms, and he kissed her while the crowd laughed.

I grabbed Skip's arm and pointed at Allgood. "Do you know that man?"

He squinted at Allgood through his thick glasses. "Hell, yes," he said suddenly. "That's the bastard I was telling you about—the one who fouled up Red Roark in the Open."

"The husband of the winnah," I said bitterly.

Skip spat on the grass. "I might have known," he said disgustedly. "A family custom."

CHAPTER TEN

In the late afternoon, at Skip Gordon's request, I drove him out to Peggy Roark's house. She was in the backyard, feeding the chickens. I introduced her to Skip, and she smiled at me. They were about the same size, and I thought that they even looked a little alike.

"You played a great game today, Miss Roark," Skip said, very politely. He was trying to conceal the fact that he'd consumed six Scotch and sodas since he'd left the country club. "You should have won."

"The best golfer won," Peggy said, trying to smile.

"Like hell," Skip said. "Pardon me," he added hastily.

"Mr. Gordon would like to talk with you a little," I said to Peggy.

She looked at me with puzzled eyes. "What about?"

"About Red," I said gently, "and about the Midwest Open." I nodded at Skip. "He is a Cleveland sports writer, and he knows why your father lost to the Alabama Kid. He knows the truth and he wants to print it in his paper. But he needs your help."

"I see," she said quietly. "Come inside."

We followed her into the house.

"Mother isn't here right now," Peggy said. She paused, and added, "I—I'm glad she isn't. Excuse me a minute." She left the room.

"Act sober," I said to Skip.

He laid a finger along his nose and screwed his face into one big wink.

Peggy Roark appeared with an envelope in her hand. She handed the envelope to me. Across its face was written in wavering penciled words: *For Christina and Peggy*.

"Read it," Peggy Roark said in a tight voice. Her little boy's face was pale and her hands were clenched into small fists at her sides.

I took out a single sheet of paper. Black engraving across the top read *Erie Isles Country Club, Cleveland, Ohio*. There was a penciled date, followed by the same wavering scrawl. I read as Skip Gordon looked over my shoulder:

Dearest Wife and Daughter,

I feel pretty bad—you know about those spells I get. If anything happens to me, I want you to know the truth. Already they are saying that I threw the match to the Alabama Kid, that I was paid to do it. I don't have to tell you I didn't. But Sam Allgood bet heavy on the Kid, and he offered me $1,000.00 to let the Kid win. I said, "No." Then Sam said I would lose my job at the club if I didn't do it. I was worried and nervous—you know how I get—but I kept my head down and swung easy, like I always told you, Peggy. On the 17th hole I was tied with the Kid, and Allgood said to me, "Red, you're through, don't forget that," and I told him to go to H. But right then I got that pain in my chest and arms. I began to shake, and I missed the putt. I just wanted you two to know why I missed it—in case I don't come out of this spell. It was Sam Allgood's fault. He won his bets, but I didn't throw the match for him. Peggy, take care of Christina. Chins up.

Red

Skip Gordon began in a low voice, "The dirty—"

Peggy Roark's eyes got big.

"He means Sam Allgood," I explained, and I tapped a finger on Red Roark's note. "How long have you known this?"

"Since Monday," she said. "Mother found it in the ball pouch of his golf bag. We—we hadn't looked at his clubs since he died. He must have written it in the clubhouse in Cleveland right after the match—shortly before he died. It—it was his heart. We didn't want him to enter the Open, but he wouldn't listen, and he said he was going to win it for Mother and me ..." She turned away and stared out of the window.

"By God," Skip Gordon blurted, "I'll plaster it all over the sports page."

She turned to face us and there were tears on her cheeks. "I—I couldn't help it this afternoon. I wanted to win so badly, but when Mrs. Allgood mentioned Red, I couldn't think of anything else...."

"Yeah, I know," Skip said softly. "Can I print it? About your dad, I mean?"

Her chin came up. "Yes. I want you to print it."

Skip rubbed his hands together. "Atta girl. What a story!" He pointed at the paper in my hand. "Can I borrow that?"

"Of course."

I thought of something. "If this story is printed," I said to Peggy, "how will it affect you and your mother? After all, you're living in the same town with Sam Allgood ..."

"I don't care," she said defiantly. "It's the truth. Mr. Allgood can't do anything to me." Her face went white, and there was a flame in her eyes. "Allgood," she whispered, as if to herself. "He ... killed ... Red...." She turned abruptly away.

"Now, now, Peggy," I said lamely. "Don't feel that way about it."

She covered her face with her hands and began to sob brokenly.

I glanced at Skip Gordon. The reporter's lips silently formed an unmistakable six words. I nodded agreement and jerked my head toward the door. He moved over to Peggy Roark and placed a hand on her shoulder. "I'll see you later," he said softly.

She didn't turn around or say anything. Skip looked at me and shrugged. We went out quietly.

As I backed my coupé out of the drive, Skip said, "Let's get a drink."

"Right," I said.

Skip Gordon and I had dinner in the Wheatville Inn, and afterwards he said he had a midnight deadline to make and that the Roark story would break in Monday's paper. "It'll make a terrific story," he said. "Bastards like Sam Allgood deserve to be exposed, and the paper will back me up. The managing editor is a nut on keeping gamblers and racketeers out of sports, and he'll give me a four-column spread if I want it. Red Roark's note is all the proof I need." He grinned at me. "Say, that little Peggy is sure cute, isn't she?"

"And just your size," I said.

"You gonna be in this town long?"

"I'm all finished here," I told him, "but the weekend's coming up, and I'm a tired, battered old man. I may hang around and rest up until tomorrow. Why?"

"If you happen to see Peggy, you might remind her that I said I'd be back."

"I'll tell her. I'll build you up as the best and smartest sports writer in the Midwest."

"Thanks, pal." He grinned at me, climbed into his station wagon, headed around the square and turned into the street leading to the Cleveland highway.

I bought some magazines and sat in the lobby of the Wheatville Inn for a while. The old pappy in the string tie was again on the desk, and he contented himself by looking through the movie magazines, which he carried over from a stand by the cigar counter. Gregory, the high school bellhop, was not around, and in his place was a thin elderly gentleman with a drooping gray mustache. People came and went, and from time to time the old pappy would stir himself to respond to a flashing light on the small switchboard behind the desk.

I was tired and yet I was restless. My chest still ached from the beating I'd taken from Bertha in the alley behind Armand's Beauty Salon, and my head throbbed dully. Except for a dry, puckered feeling, the bullet groove on my neck didn't bother me; my lips, tongue and throat felt almost normal, thanks to Hector Griffith's prompt treatment. Sulphuric acid! I shivered, closed the magazine I'd been reading and stared up at the high ceiling of the lobby. From across the square the clock in the Courthouse tower struck nine times. I thought of my room upstairs, and of the bottle of Bourbon. But a lonely drink didn't appeal to me. I got up, walked across the lobby to the bar and peeked inside. The place was empty, except for a bored bartender and two giggling couples drinking Cokes at a table along the wall. I sighed and strolled back across the lobby.

A telephone booth in a far corner seemed to beckon to me. Almost without thinking, I moved toward it like a moth winging for a candle flame; I found myself inside the booth, thumbing a directory, looking for the D's. I ran a finger down the page and stopped at the name I wanted. *Donati, Peter M.*

I dropped a coin in the slot and gave the number to a cool-voiced operator. As I waited, I was aware that I was trembling a little, and I felt sweat on my forehead.

On the fourth ring she answered. "Yes?" Her voice was soft and lovely.

I gripped the receiver. How to begin? What excuse had I for calling her? Then I blurted, "Can I see you?"

Silence for a second. Then, rather sharply: "Who is it?"

"Bennett."

More silence and I held my breath. She would think I was nuts.

"How nice," she breathed. "Now?"

"Yes. Now."

She laughed deep in her throat. Did they have beauty contests for voices? They held them for shoulders and backs and hands, and even eyes and legs; and, of course, the contests in bathing suits. If they put a brief swim suit on Marianne Donati, and listened to her voice—

and didn't look at her face—she would be crowned Queen of the World, of the Universe.

"Why?" she asked.

"Uh—I thought maybe you'd like to take a ride, maybe, and have a drink, and talk."

She said coolly, "I am afraid you have forgotten that my husband was murdered yesterday afternoon, Mr. Bennett. Thank you for calling, but I don't believe that I care to go out tonight."

I thought bitterly, Damn you, you went out with Sam Allgood and stayed with him until late last night. But that was business, I suppose? Oh, sure! But I said carefully, "All right. I'm sorry. It was just an idea, and I'm leaving town tomorrow."

There was silence on the wire for maybe ten seconds. Then she said hesitantly, "Would—would anyone see us?"

"Just me." Hope flared anew in my breast. "We can stay at your place, if you like."

"No, no. This apartment is driving me crazy. I keep seeing Pete. I see his clothes and his pipes ... I think I'll move into the hotel tomorrow." She paused and then said softly, "I shouldn't, but I'd love to get out of here for a while. I was in bed, but if you want to come over and wait while I dress ..."

"Right away." I hung up quickly, before she changed her mind.

Ten minutes later I parked my coupé a half block beyond the new red brick apartment building where Marianne Donati lived. I spotted her apartment number in the foyer and climbed two flights of stairs. She answered the buzzer immediately, and stood before me in a pale blue silken robe. The light was behind her and her face was in shadow. I was aware of only her shining yellow hair and her marvelous figure.

"Come in," she said in her low, lovely voice. "I'll be ready in a few minutes. There's whisky in the kitchen." She turned and moved away from me.

I watched in dumb admiration as she opened a mirrored door and stepped into a softly lit bedroom. Before she closed the door I had a glimpse of a pair of twin beds covered with silken spreads.

I tossed my hat to a chair and went through the pleasant, tastefully furnished rooms until I reached a big bright kitchen. On a table sat a bottle of bonded Bourbon, a silver soda syphon, a tray of ice cubes and two tall glasses. I took a sip of Bourbon from the bottle. It was as smooth as silk. I made myself a tall drink, half whisky, half soda;

and, in response to the silent invitation of the second glass, I filled it, too, with more emphasis on the soda. I carried the two glasses into the living room and sat down in a deep chair. I placed Marianne Donati's drink on a low table beside the chair, leaned back and gazed about.

There was a wood-burning fireplace, and above it and on each side were shelves of books. From where I sat I couldn't read the titles, but they were mostly new-looking books in bright jackets. I guessed that Pete Donati hadn't been the book reading type, but that his wife read a lot. It didn't surprise me. Because of her disfigurement, she probably spent many lonely hours huddled away from the public's cruel, horrified stare. I felt a sudden deep sadness and a kind of rage against the people who pointed at Marianne Donati and whispered furtively behind the backs of their hands. In their ignorance they could not see that she was beautiful, all of her, from the top of her glossy yellow head to her slim ankles. No surface facial disfigurement could change that; not for me, ever.

I finished my drink; presently I returned to the kitchen and made another, and I added ice to Marianne Donati's glass. I was halfway through the second drink when she emerged from the bedroom, and I stood up.

She looked marvelous. Her slender body was sheathed in soft black, and a sort of small black cap perched on her yellow hair. From the cap a thick black veil hung down, covering her face, and it was tied at her throat with a slender black ribbon. In the soft light the veil hid the horrible scars, and the lovely contours and the delicate bone structure of her face seemed to shine through. Like the sun, I thought, from behind black muddled clouds, and in the same instant I hooted at myself for my flowery comparison.

She stood before me, almost shyly, and when she spoke the black veil moved over her lips. "Shall I wear it?" she asked.

"Take it off," I said. "You don't have to wear it with me."

Hesitantly she plucked at the ribbon at her throat. "Perhaps," she said, "the veil is more conspicuous than ... than ..." There was a note of hope in her voice.

"Of course," I said gently. I smiled, picked up the drink I'd made for her and held it out. "Anyhow, you'll have to take it off to drink this."

She laughed softly, deftly untied the ribbon at her throat and, with a graceful motion of her arms, she flung the veil back over the top of the small cap. She took the glass and said, "Thank you."

The sight of her naked face shocked me; for an instant I was repulsed and a cold horror seemed to creep along my spine. No woman should look like Marianne Donati looked. No living woman should look like that. It showed in my eyes and she saw it; she quickly averted her face and moved away from me, to the center of the room, holding her glass. She stood with her back to me and said bitterly, "Shall we begin our gay evening, Mr. Bennett?" She tilted her glass and swallowed deep and long.

I placed my glass on the mantel and stepped up behind her. I placed my hands on her shoulders, and gently I turned her until she faced me. But still she turned her face away, and I saw her white teeth bite into her lower lip. "You're beautiful," I said. "I know it. I can see it."

"More," she said in a choked voice, still not looking at me. "Tell me more." I saw the tears on her pitted cheeks.

"I don't have to," I said. "You don't need me to tell you."

"I have some photos," she said breathlessly, "taken before ... before ... Would you like to see them?"

"No. I don't need to see them. I don't want to see them."

She gazed up at me and her scarred lips were twisted in a smile. "What shall we do tonight?"

"Ride," I said. "Ride and talk."

"Can we talk about—Pete? Would you mind?"

"No."

Her cool fingers touched my cheek. "You're very nice. Are you married?"

"No."

She sighed. "You should be."

"Why?"

Her shoulders moved beneath the thin black dress, and I dropped my hands to my sides. "All men should be married," she said. "And all women. Ten years ago I married Pete and now he's gone. I—I still can't believe it, really, but I know I've lost something I'll never have again. Poor Pete. He ..." Her voice broke, and she turned away from me.

I stood helplessly.

Abruptly she turned, brushing tears from her eyes. "Pete wouldn't care, would he? I mean, about tonight?"

I shook my head silently, and thought, No, Pete won't care. How can he? Pete's dead, like a dog, and you're here, and I'm here, and tomorrow I'll be gone from this town, and there'll be other women, other towns, other people in trouble—scared, greedy, lost people who will pay money into the coffers of the Agency so that one of us in the vast army of operators will help them. And we are controlled by a sly old man in New York who owns sixty-five per cent of the Agency stock, and who runs its branches from Singapore to Bar Harbor with an iron hand. He's a cunning old man, and he carries in his brain all the evil and all the secret mad thoughts of a million persons who will sooner or later come to him for help, for protection, for advice.

He's a whisky-drinking, cigar-chewing, profane old man, and he knows all the answers. No human failing or weakness or vice is unfamiliar to him, and there is no man or woman without a price tag. Soon I would sit in my office in Cleveland and I would dictate a report to him, describing briefly and coldly the case of Pete Donati, listing expenses, dates and the fee paid, and he will read it and toss it on a pile of other reports from all over the world and think only of the money that had been paid to the Agency. I wondered what he would say or do if he saw the face of Marianne Donati, that horrible scarred mask of a face, with the great beauty underneath, if he could see it. But I knew that he would not see the beauty but only the surface ugliness, and if he were on this job instead of me, he would probably say, "That'll be a hundred and fifty dollars, Madam," and he would go on his eager way in search of other revenue.

And I should be doing likewise, instead of standing here like a high school freshman on his first date. Pete Donati was dead and there was nothing more I could do for him or for his widow, so why in hell was I hanging around?

"Would he?" Marianne Donati said.

"What?"

"Would Pete care that I'm with you tonight?"

I shook my head and took my glass from the mantel. The glass was empty and I said, "Stirrup cup?"

She smiled and handed me her glass. "If you like."

When I returned from the kitchen with fresh drinks, she was standing by the fireplace in a spot where her face was in partial shadow. As I handed her a glass, I said, "Where are your folks? Do they live in Wheatville?"

She shook her head. "I told you—I have no family. Just a brother, but he's somewhere in Australia. He's a ceramist—or was, when he graduated from college. I haven't seen him since before I married

Pete."

"No other relatives?"

"Oh, aunts, cousins and uncles scattered around. Nobody who matters. They haven't bothered me and I haven't bothered them. I've made my own way since I was seventeen. It was just Pete and me." She paused, and then added, "Unless you want to count my first husband."

"Where is he?"

"In Detroit. He's a vice-president of American Motors."

I was a little startled. I said, "What happened between you and the vice-president?"

She lifted her shoulders slightly. "Oh, one of those things. I was working in a beauty shop in Dearborn, and he was an attendant at a big super-service station. We went to beer parlors on Saturday nights and to movies on the nights I didn't have to work. We were mildly happy. And then the daughter of the president of American Motors began to buy gas for her car at the station where he worked. He had wide shoulders, a slender waist and curly black hair. One night he told me he wanted to marry her and I let him go. His name was Gaylord; I called him Gay. They had a big wedding, and a year later he was a vice-president. I used to see his picture in the papers."

"Then what?"

"Oh, I kept on working in beauty shops. One day Pete came in and tried to sell the boss a new line of manicure tools. I was the manicure girl and the boss turned him over to me; before he left he'd made a date with me for dinner. We were married the following spring." She drained her glass. "And now he's dead. Shall we go, Mr. Bennett?"

My glass was still full. I contented myself with two hasty swallows before I picked up my hat and followed her out the door and down to the street.

The night was warm and a million stars were out. Marianne Donati said, "Let's take my car—we can put the top down."

"All right," I said.

Five minutes later I had brought her gray convertible from a garage in the rear of the apartment building, lowered the top and was wheeling it out of town on the lake road. The wind was warm on our faces and the sky seemed limitless. We left the last traffic light, and beyond the road Lake Erie rolled away in the moonlight. I said, "Where to?"

"Just drive."

I drove, and for the first time since I'd arrived in Wheatville I felt contented and relaxed. Ten miles, twenty. We passed through villages and small towns, and the road began to climb and wind to a section of lakefront summer homes known as Erie Cliffs. On several hot weekends, the summer before, I'd been the guest of a client with a summer home on the lake, and I knew this country fairly well. I remembered a small bar on the beach, off the main highway, and I watched for the narrow road leading off to it. On either side of us the wide lawns lay smooth in the moonlight, and off to our left, beyond a dark line of scrub pines on the cliff, the lake rolled and tossed in an offshore breeze. Lights were still on in some of the big summer homes, and once, when I slowed for a curve, I heard music and the sound of laughter. And then the houses thinned out and the woods closed in on either side of the road.

For the first time in a long while, Marianne Donati spoke. "Where are we going?"

"You'll see."

The headlights picked up the sign I was looking for. *Charlie's Cove*, it read, *Liquor, Beer, Fish Dinners*, and an arrow pointed toward the lake. I swung the convertible into a narrow but well-paved road and drove for maybe a mile before I saw the lights of a long low building on the perimeter of a white beach with the pines behind it. Three cars were parked outside, and the music from a jukebox came to us. I braked the convertible to a stop, turned off the motor and lights. "Feel like a drink?" I asked.

She nodded silently in the gloom, and raised her arms to pull the veil down over her face.

Gently I caught her hands and shook my head.

"Please," she said. "There are people in there."

"To hell with the people."

She leaned back in the seat and turned her face toward me. The moonlight softened the scars and made silver glints in her yellow hair. The lovely contours of her forehead and cheekbones were clearly revealed. Her eyes were luminous, with black shadows beneath them, and her red mouth looked dark and soft. Except for an especially deep scar on her chin, her face was like the face of an angel seen through a soft mist.

"Why do you bother?" she whispered. "I mean, about me?"

I couldn't think of an answer and I kept quiet.

"Because you're sorry for me?"

I shook my head quickly.

"Then why? I'm ugly. I've been married twice, and next month I'll be thirty-three years old. People stare at me on the streets, and I frighten children—the small children. The older ones sometimes jeer at me. Pete was all I had, and now he's—"

"Stop it," I said harshly.

She turned away from me, and her body began to tremble with a terrible silent sobbing.

I pulled her against me, and I patted her shoulder awkwardly, as if she were a little girl with a broken red wagon. After a while she was quiet, and she stirred in my arms and raised her face to mine. The moonlight was brighter now, and she was close to me, and her beauty seemed to be fading behind a grotesque mask, but I didn't care.

"Thank you," she whispered. "I won't do that again—I promise."

I brushed a long strand of bright hair back from her forehead, and my fingers felt the roughness of her scarred skin.

"I loved Pete," she said, "and I think he loved me. But after the accident, he—he changed. I didn't blame him, really, but sometimes I was lonely ..." She paused, and gazed out over the lake. When she spoke again, her voice was the barest whisper. "Would you kiss me? Just once? Would you mind?"

I cupped her lovely ugly face in my hands, and her lips parted against mine. She stirred restlessly against me, and my arms went around her. I forgot about her scarred face, and if her lips held a faint roughness, I did not notice or care.

Presently her hands pressed gently against me and she pulled away. I reached for her again. She shook her head. "Not now," she said, and her voice was gentle and soft.

We gazed at each other in the moonlight, and then I smiled.

"All right," I said. I got out of the convertible, moved around to her side and opened the door.

She got out and gazed up at me. Her head came just beneath my chin. "No veil?" she asked.

"No veil."

She laughed almost gaily, and she hugged my arm as we walked over the sand and into the place called Charlie's Cove. Except for a new bartender, it looked the same as it had the summer before. Dim lights, a long bar, tables, booths around the walls, a small dance floor. A few people were sitting quietly at the tables and in the booths. Through an alcove the myriad lights of a jukebox glowed softly on the dance floor. Two couples danced slowly and intimately. There was the pleasant smell of whisky and lemons and beer, and when a white-uniformed waitress came out of the swinging doors leading to the kitchen, there was the added smell of frying fish.

Marianne Donati and I sat down in a corner booth. The waitress came over. "Evening, folks. What'll it be?"

Marianne Donati quickly averted her face.

I said to the waitress, "Two Bourbons with soda."

The waitress nodded and left. I touched Marianne Donati's hand. "Don't do that."

She turned her face toward me. "I'm sorry. When people are near me, I—I want to hide."

"Do you want to hide from me?"

"No," she said soberly.

"Good," I said.

She looked down at her hands folded on the table. "If I could just forget Pete—how he looked ..."

"You've got to forget him," I said, and I thought of Pete Donati, the wavy-haired Armand. Once more I saw him as he sat drenched in his blood behind his desk. His death had been the end of the world for his wife, and he had left her alone with her ugliness. I felt a surge of rage against Pete Donati, and then I remembered that he was beyond rage, beyond the bittersweet reproach of his wife. Nothing could touch Pete Donati now.

The waitress brought our drinks, said, "Anything to eat, folks?"

I shook my head, and the waitress went away. It was then that I saw the tears in Marianne Donati's eyes, and I thought dismally, What the hell are you doing here, Bennett? Why are you with a new widow who is eating out her heart for the love of a cheating husband who couldn't be bothered with her after her looks were gone? Where does it add up for you, you dumb yokel? Out squiring around a woman with a marvelous shape—and a face that scares kids. That's what she said. You should be getting some sleep so that you can drive back to Cleveland tomorrow and make out reports for the boss in New York. Two jobs—Allgood and Donati. But here you are, close to midnight, miles from the home office, dilly-dallying around in a beach bar with a woman bleeding inside for a murdered husband. What's the score, anyhow, Bennett? What's in it for you?

Marianne Donati brushed a hand over her eyes. "Let's talk about you," she said brightly. "About your work. I know you're a—a detective, a private investigator. Is it like in the movies and in books?"

"No," I said, "but it's a living."

"Tell me about it."

I told her as best I could. It helped pass the time while we finished our drinks. I told her that I worked for a big international agency, that I was the chief district agent for the Cleveland territory and that I was merely a cog in a vast business machine engaged in private investigation. I told her about the tyrannical old man in New York who was my boss, and how my job was mostly leg work—asking questions, snooping, checking court records, the morgues, police blotters, running down insurance beneficiaries and missing heirs. Dull work, most of the time, with maybe a little excitement occasionally, but not much. Mostly just deadly routine for different people with different private worries and secrets.

"Like the FBI?" she asked.

"Yes—except that we work for private individuals and organizations."

"That is very interesting," she said. "I guess I never thought about it before."

I motioned to the waitress to bring us two more drinks. The jukebox began a slow love song, all muted brass and muffled drums. It was a song that had been new in my second year of college, fifteen years before, and which was now, like so many other old songs, enjoying a popular revival. There were no good new songs anymore, I thought—but the old ones stood up against the years, and the kids who danced to them thought they were new, never dreaming that their parents had probably romanced to the strains of the same music. I remembered this song in particular, because the year it came out I'd been in love with a redhead from Toledo. But she had quit college to marry a wealthy wholesale grocer from Columbus, and I had been brokenhearted for all of several months. Although I had never forgotten the song ("Our song, Jim," she used to murmur in the moonlight), I hadn't thought of the redhead in a long time. I thought of her now, remembering a tiny mole behind her left ear. I sighed. What had happened to the years?

Marianne Donati said suddenly, "Would you like to dance?"

"Sure."

I led her past the dim lights to the tiny dance floor. We were alone on the floor and I danced slowly, holding her close. The nostalgic song was like a drug, and my mind wavered back to the time in my life when everything had been simple, before I'd decided to study law—and then chucked it after two years to work for a wicked old man in New York. After a few years he had grudgingly let me buy some stock in the agency, and now I was privileged to vote in the annual election of officers. But the old man still considered me just one of his gutter-rolling, thumb-in-the-eye private dicks. Some day, I told myself grimly, as I'd told myself many times before, I'd get out of this dirty racket and get a decent job. But I knew I never would. It was like driving a truck—in the end it jars your kidneys loose, but you stay with it. Or like the newspaper business, or flying a plane. It gets in your system, and you can't get it out. I held Marianne Donati tighter.

She lifted her face, and her lips moved against my ear. "You dance beautifully," she whispered.

"I haven't danced in a long time."

"Neither have I. I used to dance a lot with Pete, before …" She stopped abruptly, and I felt her fingers dig into my shoulder.

The music stopped, and we stood silently in a corner, close together, waiting to see what the jukebox would offer next. It started again, and a lonesome cowboy began to twang a guitar and sing a nasal song about his purty gal on the Rio Grande. Marianne Donati led me quickly back to our booth.

Our fresh drinks were waiting, and as I lifted my glass I saw that her eyes were shining.

"That was fun," she breathed.

"Want to dance some more?"

She shook her head. "Not tonight. Let's go now."

"And leave our drinks?"

"Of course not. I don't want to leave that quickly." She smiled at me.

We drank silently, gazing at each other, and presently she said soberly, "I'm glad you called me tonight."

"So am I."

"Are you really leaving tomorrow?"

"Probably."

"What will they do with Joyce Justin?"

"For helping Bertha—Bert Homer?"

"Yes."

"Accomplice to murder? I don't know. She's a pretty girl—she might get off with maybe twenty or thirty years."

She said, in a suddenly hard voice, "It's not enough."

I shrugged. "Maybe not. But I don't think she had anything to do with it—the murder part. At least, she couldn't help it." But even as I spoke, I remembered Joyce Justin swinging the whisky bottle at me, while Bert Homer's crazed brain hatched the scheme of pouring sulphuric acid down my throat.

Marianne Donati drained her glass, and the ice clinked in the bottom as she placed it on the table. "Shall we go?"

"If you like." I stood up.

I wheeled the convertible down the winding road away from Erie Cliffs. The soft night wind fanned our faces, and the moon made ghostly gardens of the fields around us. On our right the lake glittered and rolled, and far off I saw the tiny lights of a freighter bound for Duluth. After a while the road leveled out, and the traffic grew thicker, and I saw the beacon light of the Wheatville airport sweeping the sky. I glanced at Marianne Donati. She sat quietly, her head against the back of the seat, the wind tossing her yellow hair.

I touched her arm. "Almost home."

She turned her head. "Already?"

"I'm afraid so."

She sat up straight and took a cigarette from her purse. I held the dash lighter for her, and the wind whipped sparks behind us. She settled back in the seat once more, and her voice came to me faintly over the wind. "Park behind the apartment house."

We came to the outskirts of Wheatville, and I drove fast through the deserted streets. The clock on the dash told me that it was a quarter of one in the morning as I turned into the alley behind the apartment building where Marianne Donati lived. I eased the convertible into the garage and turned off the lights and motor.

Her high heels clicked on the cement as I followed her to a rear entrance. We went up a dimly lit stairway. At a small landing at the top she took out a key and unlocked a door. We stepped into her kitchen. A small light over a gleaming stove cast a soft yellow glow over a refrigerator, the bright linoleum and an enameled table. She entered the dark dining room, and I followed her, guided by the glow from the kitchen. Ahead of me I saw her slender shadowy figure enter the big living room, and I hurried after her. I stumbled over a chair, and I almost fell headlong. I cursed under my breath.

Marianne Donati laughed softly from the darkness.

"You must have cat's eyes," I grumbled, rubbing my shin.

She laughed again, but I couldn't see her, and I fumbled for a wall switch. My fingers found one and I flicked it on. An overhead light flooded the room with dazzling brightness. She stood in the living room, beyond an archway, but in the path of light, and she turned her face away.

"Don't," she said sharply.

I turned off the light and stood still.

I couldn't see her, but I heard her moving softly toward me. And then I felt her hand on my arm. "This way," she whispered, her lips close to my ear.

She led me across the length of the living room. It was lighter here, and through the wide window I could see the street below and an occasional car moving past. We moved past the window, and as my eyes became more accustomed to the gloom, I saw that we were entering a small alcove beyond the living room. She stopped before a closed door, a door with a mirror covering its full length, and she turned to face me.

"It's been perfect," she whispered. "I needed a night like this. Even with Pete gone, even with my ugliness, it's been perfect. Thank you very much."

The ringing of a telephone startled me, and Marianne Donati's lovely voice answering it, said, "Yes?"

I waited woodenly. I knew who was calling.

I heard her say, "No," in a sharp brittle voice. "I'm sorry, but it's late ... I've been out, and I'm very tired ... Yes, out ... Never mind ... No ... No!" There was a sharp click as she hung up.

I stood waiting. I could see her shadowy form standing across the room from me. The light from the street below shone faintly on her yellow hair. I moved over to her, placed my hands on her shoulders and said, "To hell with Sam Allgood."

I felt her stiffen, and there was a deep silence in the room. Then she said, "You know a lot, don't you?"

"I know he was with you last night, when he was supposed to be having dinner with me—and his wife. I saw him get into your car late in the afternoon."

She twisted her shoulders away from my hands and stepped back a little.

"Mr. Allgood is my attorney," she said coolly.

"Is that why he calls you at one o'clock in the morning?"

"Why else would Mr. Allgood call me?"

"Call him Sam," I said wearily. "It makes no difference to me." A faint unreasoning anger was stirring in my brain.

She didn't speak for maybe two seconds, and then she said distinctly, "Good night, Mr. Bennett."

"What happened to our perfect evening?"

"It's gone. I'm sorry."

I was sorry, too, as sorry as all hell. But since the damage had been done, I decided to go whole hog. "How long has Sam Allgood been your attorney?"

"For a long time—long before my husband was killed, if that's what you mean."

I said harshly, "Before his throat was cut, maybe, but after he got drunk and spilled you through a windshield. After his love grew cold because of your ugliness. Is that when Sam Allgood entered your life—as your attorney, of course?"

She spoke in a deadly quiet voice. "Mr. Allgood was our attorney long before the accident. And he was more than just a lawyer—he was our friend, Pete's and mine."

"Hah!" I said. I felt mean and nasty. This was a miserable, bickering ending to a pleasant interlude, but I couldn't help it now, and I realized that Sam Allgood had been in the back of my brain all evening. "So he telephones you at one o'clock in the morning? On a legal matter, no doubt?"

She turned away from me, and I heard her dry, broken sobbing. "Go away.... Please ..."

I felt like the grandfather of all the heels in the world, but a cold little ice pick kept jabbing my brain, and I couldn't forget the sight of the awkward angle of Pete Donati's head above his severed throat. Maybe he deserved to die. I didn't know or particularly care, but I had killed a man named Bert Homer whose pockets had been stuffed with money and checks from Donati's safe. Robbery, Chief Swartz had said. It was a good motive but commonplace. Still, I hadn't thought of any better motive—until now, I thought bitterly, until this moment. Jealousy was a swell motive for killing someone, and so was love. And revenge. And a combination of all three made a wonderful motive for murder. One of the best. More people killed for love, in one form or another, than for any other reason. For love, or the absence of love; for jealous love, for revengeful love; for freedom to love another. The combinations were infinite.

Marianne Donati sobbed quietly, her slender figure silhouetted against the window, and I remembered with a sharp regret the pleasure of our evening together. What was the matter with me? The reason for Pete Donati's death had been established to the satisfaction of the law, and it was no longer any concern of mine. And if Sam Allgood found pleasure in Marianne Donati's company, and she in his, what was that to me? I was just a crude private dick and soon I would be leaving this town, and Marianne Donati would be just an exciting and pleasant memory. I would remember only her beauty, the soft loveliness of her voice, and the scarred ugliness of her face would be like a mask to me, a mask donned for those too gross and too insensible to see beyond it.

I said humbly, "I'm very sorry."

Slowly her sobs ceased and she turned to face me. The dim light from the window was behind her, and her face was in deep shadow, with the pale hair framing it. I stepped close to her, and my hands caressed her arms. I felt her tremble a little, and I waited silently.

"I—I'm sorry, too," she said.

"Don't be. It was that damned phone ..."

She shook her head. "Not just the phone. Sam Allgood is in love with me. He told me so last night. He said he has been in love with me for a long time."

A cold bleakness seemed to settle over my soul. I said, "Do you love him?"

"I don't know. He is the first man in a long time who has treated me like—like I want to be treated. Oh, I know—Sam is married, and all that. But if you were as lonely as I have been ..."

"I don't blame you," I said, and my hands tightened on her arms. "I don't care."

"But I care," she said softly. "I want to be alone now and think of my husband, of Pete. It was very wrong of me to go with you tonight."

"You went with Sam Allgood."

"That was wrong, too. Good night."

"Look—" I began helplessly.

Her arm moved quickly to a wall switch, and an overhead light flooded the room with brilliance. It shone down with a merciless cruel glare upon the nightmare of her scarred, pitted face, and I had a quick feeling of sick revulsion. She tilted her face to the light, so that I could see it better, and she closed her eyes. "Good night," she said in a dead voice.

"Good night," I said miserably, and I moved to the door, opened it and half stumbled down the stairs.

Down on the sidewalk, in the soft early morning air, I looked up and saw that her apartment was already dark. For one frantic moment I fought the desire to run back up the stairs. And then her hideous, scarred face floated across my mind's eye, and I sighed and walked slowly to where I'd left my coupé.

As I drove away, I thought suddenly of Katherine Allgood, and it occurred to me that Sam Allgood and his damn telephone calls had crossed me up twice in two days.

When I reached my room at the Wheatville Inn I knew that I was dead tired. My whole body felt sore and battered, and my head felt numb and dull. The evening's whisky had died within me and I moved about like a man in a daze. I hung a *Do Not Disturb* sign on the outside knob of my door and crawled into bed. But sleep didn't come. I was too keyed up.

The people and the events of the last three days formed a ghostly parade behind my closed eyes, and I couldn't shut them out. People and places appeared in precise order, beginning with the town of Wheatville itself. Then came Miss Hoskins, the prim secretary for the firm of Allgood and Winters, and others followed in turn. It was like watching a movie in a dream. Sam Allgood, handsome and jittery, told me about bullets on a golf course. The scene shifted, and I was at the Wheatville Country Club, talking to Rogan, the yellow-haired attendant. I met Jeff Winters, the lean, grave, friendly partner of Sam Allgood, and I talked with Katherine Allgood, the dark beauty who was Sam's wife, a woman who was all but consumed with love and a fierce jealousy. There was little Peggy Roark, walking by my side on the fairways, loyally defending the memory of her dead father, Red Roark, a small-time golfer who almost made the big time. I saw Lily Winters, the wife of Jeff, slim and tawny, friendly as a kitten, and I heard Jeff Winters say, We call her Annie Oakley Winters. She's deadly with a gun, any kind of a gun....

Once more in my half-dream I stood on the sky-blue rug of Armand's Beauty Salon and talked to Joyce Justin, a cool, lovely girl, playing both Pete Donati and Bert Homer for what she could get out of them. She was behind the bars now; poor Joyce. I thought of Pete Donati, faithless after his wife had lost her beauty, but dead now and beyond all reproach. And then I thought of Marianne Donati, and my brain seemed to falter, slowing the parade, and for a long time she lingered in my mind's eye. What was she doing now? Asleep? Awake? Alone? Her lovely, ugly face faded at last, and the end of the parade came into view. I saw Hector Griffith's quiet crooked smile, and his tall distinguished figure, a man marked for tragedy, living out his days with only the bitter memory of his surgeon's training, his skill and his knowledge. I felt a deep sadness for Hector. I owed my life to him, and I told myself that I must see him before I left this town called Wheatville. The figure of Skip Gordon wound up the parade. He didn't linger long. He was just a little freckle-faced sportswriter on a Cleveland paper, and I smiled as I remembered the soft look in his eyes as he watched Peggy Roark, and I thought of his question after Katherine Allgood had defeated Peggy Roark: Who is that black-haired bitch?

The parade was ended and I stirred restlessly, not wanting it to begin again. But it did, with the face of Marianne Donati. I got out of bed and poured a glass half full of Bourbon. I stood by the window in the dark room and drank it slowly, and stared out at the quiet town. After a long time I returned to my bed.

No parade this time, and sleep came quickly. I was glad.

I awoke at noon, looked at my wristwatch and rolled over again. The soft bed felt wonderful, and I toyed with the pleasant idea of sleeping until Sunday morning before I started back to Cleveland.

At two o'clock in the afternoon a gentle rap on my door aroused me from a blissful world of half-sleep. I crawled out groggily, crossed to the door and opened it.

Hector Griffith smiled at me. "How's my patient?" he said.

"He'll live, I guess. Come in." I went back to the bed, sat down and yawned.

Hector said, "With the shop closed, I didn't know what to do with myself, and I wanted to look you over. You took quite a beating, you know."

I yawned some more. "Yeah, I know."

He came over and stood beside me. "Let's check," he said.

I took off my pajama jacket, and Hector's deft fingers probed and felt my chest. He peered at the healing bullet wound on my neck and felt the tender spot on my head. Then he peered intently into my eyes and straightened up.

"Any reaction from the sulphuric acid?" he asked.

"My mouth and throat feel a little dry, but that's all."

He nodded. "Good. I got to you in time. You'll be all right."

I grinned up at him. "Thanks, Doc."

He smiled, and once more I saw the gleam of pride in his eyes. "Go on back to bed," he said, and he started for the door.

"Don't go, Hector," I said. "I'm going to get dressed. Stick around."

He turned and smiled. "Sure you don't mind?"

I motioned to the Bourbon bottle. "Have a drink."

He shook his head. "No, thanks." He sat down and filled his pipe.

I called the desk and asked them to bring up coffee, toast and orange juice. Then I went into the bathroom and shaved and showered. While I was dressing, Gregory, the bellhop, brought in a tray. While I ate, Hector drank a cup of coffee. I said, "I didn't see you after the big golf match."

"I left before the kill," he said. "I saw what Katherine Allgood was doing to Peggy, and I didn't want to watch."

"Katherine Allgood won," I told him.

He nodded. "So I hear. Mrs. Allgood is a very determined woman. I feel sorry for Peggy."

"Yeah," I sighed. "Poor little Peggy. She wanted so badly to win."

As I finished eating, my telephone rang. It was Jeff Winters. "Sam told me you had left town," he said in his quiet friendly voice, "but I thought I recognized your car parked in front of the Inn. Are you going to be around a while?"

"I don't know. I just got up."

He laughed and then asked, "How about some golf this afternoon?"

"Thanks, but I think I'll rest up some more. I'll probably drive back into Cleveland tonight."

"Oh, no, you can't do that," he said. "There's a big dance at the club. I'd like to have you come ... with dinner at my house first."

"That's very kind of you, but if you don't mind, I'll take a rain check."

"I'm sorry," he said, and he really sounded sorry. "But I won't coax you. If you get to town again, be sure and call me. And if you change your mind about the dance, just come on out."

"Thanks, I'll do that." I hung up and said to Hector, "Jeff Winters wants me to go to a dance at the country club tonight."

"Why don't you? I'll probably go out for a while."

"I'll see," I said. "I'm kind of at loose ends."

He stood up and held out his hand. "Well, if I don't see you again, good luck."

"The same to you, Hector. And I won't forget what you did for me."

He smiled his grave smile. "Forget it. I was glad to help." He went out and closed the door quietly.

I lit a cigarette and moved to the window. Presently I saw Hector moving along the tree-lined sidewalk toward the square, his tall figure erect in the afternoon sunlight. I watched him until he was out of sight, and then I crushed out my cigarette, crossed the room and sat down by the telephone. I sat there a long time, thinking of many things. Once I reached for the telephone, and changed my mind. It would look silly if I called her now, after what had happened the night before. Silly as hell. What was the matter with me? Why wasn't I burning the highway for home? My business was finished in Wheatville, all wound up.

I suddenly remembered Chief of Police Swartz's request that I stay in town. Something about the death of Bert Homer—an inquest, that was it. I called Swartz. "Chief, this is Bennett. How long do you want me to hang around this burg?"

He laughed. "You still here?"

"You said you wanted—"

"Yeah, I know, but everything's squared away. If I'd wanted you, I'd have had you brought in before this. The county prosecutor says it's open and shut. He may want you later. We'll let you know."

I was disappointed. "All right, you know where to find me." He chuckled. "You're damn right." He hung up.

I sat and stared at the ceiling a while. Something didn't fit. What was it, what was it …

I sat up straight. I had it.

Who had stolen my gun? And why?

Some petty thief, Sam Allgood had said. But if it had been a petty thief, why hadn't he taken my bag—instead of pawing through it? And why just my gun and nothing else? I sat and thought about it a while. It wasn't important, and yet it bothered me. Surely, it wasn't important enough for me to stay in Wheatville any longer. But I had nothing to do until Monday, and my room at the Wheatville Inn was comfortable.

The afternoon wore on, and presently my room was in shadow. I moved to the window. The sun was low and yellow, and the lawn of the Inn was in deep green shade. On the street beyond, the afterwork traffic was spewing out of the square. I glanced at my watch.

Twenty minutes before six o'clock. I put on a coat and necktie, picked up my hat and went down to the lobby.

The dining room was already half-filled, and I decided that people ate early in Wheatville. I entered the bar. It was doing a booming pre-dinner business. I ordered a dry martini, and as I drank I toyed with the idea of having dinner at the restaurant where the snub-nosed brunette worked. I toyed with the idea, but I didn't do anything about it. After my second drink, I left the bar and ate in solitude at a corner table of the Wheatville Inn's dining room.

After dinner I lingered at my table, killing time. I drank a second cup of coffee and watched the people. After a while I went up to my room, and on Wheatville Inn writing paper I outlined a preliminary report of my doings in Wheatville, listing names and addresses, to help me when I dictated a complete report to the boss in New York. Then, for a while, I stretched out on the bed and stared at the ceiling. At ten o'clock I got up and went out.

I drove to the Wheatville Country Club. I knew that I'd intended to go there all along. I should have accepted Jeff Winters' invitation in the first place.

The place was lit up like a Hollywood premiere, and I had to wheel my coupé all the way down the drive before I found a place to park. I walked back in the darkness to the clubhouse. The porch was swarming with people. I squeezed my way inside and set my course for an improvised bar in the ballroom. Nobody stopped me to ask for an engraved invitation, and I grinned to myself as I contrasted my old blue suit with the draped white dinner jackets and the filmy summer evening gowns.

I had struggled halfway across the floor when a woman's voice shrieked in my ear. "Mr. Bennett!"

I turned. Lily Winters was close beside me. She was wearing a black dress with a couple of threads for shoulder straps and a wide V almost to her waist. Her tawny hair was cut in a straight bob across her forehead, and it hung in long folds over her shoulders. She was dancing with Sam Allgood, and he wasn't careful where he put his hands. Allgood ignored me and tried to lead her away. But she wouldn't be led. She wiggled from Allgood's arms and grasped my arm with both hands.

"You look awfully sober," she shouted at me above the blare of the music. "How about a drink?"

"Sure," I shouted back at her.

She threw back her head and laughed and pulled me toward the bar. Allgood trailed along behind with murder in his eyes.

"I thought you had left, Bennett," he muttered in my ear.

"Not me," I said. "I like this town."

We reached the bar and Lily elbowed a space clear for us. Three bartenders were working like madmen. I finally got a Bourbon and soda. At least it was something liquid and faintly amber-colored in a small glass with an ice cube. I cuddled it in both hands and tried to gulp it down before it was splattered on the ceiling.

"To hell with this," Lily Winters shouted in my ear. "Come on."

She grasped my arm and pulled me away from the makeshift bar barricaded by a swarming horde of thirsty people, and led me between the dancers back across the big room. Allgood stumbled after us sullenly. We emerged into a cleared space in a foyer beyond the dance floor, and entered the locker room.

Lily Winters went straight to a locker with a brass-bound card bearing her typewritten name. From a tiny sequin bag she took a small ring of keys and unlocked the door. "I'm supposed to keep golf clubs in here," she said over her naked shoulder, "but I use it mostly for guns—and whisky." She stooped down and took out a bottle half full of Scotch.

I peered past her into the locker. I saw a leather golf bag filled with assorted gleaming clubs. Leaning beside it was a fancy .22 bolt action rifle with a tooled stock and fitted with a telescope sight. On the floor of the locker were three boxes of .22 long rifle cartridges, and beside them lay a long-barreled .22 target pistol with an inlaid ivory oversize stock.

Sam Allgood, standing behind me, muttered, "Ugly things, guns."

Lily Winters laughed and held the bottle over her head. She swayed her slender hips in the tight-fitting black gown and hummed a few bars of a rumba. Allgood leaned against the locker and watched her. He was almost drooling.

"Rogan!" Lily shouted. "Hey, Rogan, my boy."

The locker room attendant appeared from somewhere. His lip was still swollen.

"Set-ups, handsome," Lily said to him. "Ice, soda, glasses."

Rogan nodded silently and retreated. He was back almost instantly with a loaded tray, and he was carrying an extra quart bottle of soda in his hand. As he leaned forward to place the tray on the table, the heavy bottle fell from his hand. It landed squarely on my right foot, across the toes. It hurt.

"Oh, I'm sorry, sir," he said, and he stooped to pick up the bottle.

I looked down at the top of his sleek blond head, and wanted to kick him in the teeth. I said, "How did you hurt your lip, Rogan?"

He straightened slowly and placed the bottle on the table. His face was red, but carefully composed, and he didn't say anything.

Sam Allgood laughed. "Did her husband come home too early, Rogan?"

Rogan avoided my gaze and managed a tight grin. "Yes, sir," he said. "That must have been it." He went out quickly.

"My foot hurts," I said.

Lily Winters handed me a glass. It was about two thirds Scotch and one third soda. "That'll fix you up," she said. "Drink 'er down."

The locker room door swung open, and Katherine Allgood and Jeff Winters came in together. Katherine Allgood glanced sharply at Sam and Lily Winters. "What a cozy little party," she said.

"And with my liquor, too," Jeff Winters said.

"You mean you paid for it, darling," Lily Winters said. "Anyhow, it was in my locker."

Jeff Winters took the bottle from her. "Well," he sighed, "it's Saturday night, and I've gotta get drunk—God, how I dread it!"

Sam Allgood took Lily Winters' arm and pulled her to the door. "Come on, Lil," he said. "The party's lost its class." The two of them went out into the din of the dance floor. Lily was swaying her hips and snapping her fingers.

Jeff Winters grinned after her. "She's riding high tonight," he said to me, "but come the morn and she'll wish she was dead. And she's supposed to compete in a rifle match in Toledo tomorrow morning."

"Never worry about Lily," Katherine Allgood said. "She'll always come out on top."

There was a thin edge of bitterness to her voice, and I glanced at her.

She said to me, "I thought you'd left our fair city, Mr. Bennett."

"I couldn't miss this party," I told her.

"Did you see the match yesterday?" she asked.

"Yes, I saw it."

"I won, you know."

"Congratulations," I said.

She looked at me coolly. "You're not very convincing."

"I'm sorry." From the corner of my eye I saw that Jeff Winters was watching us silently.

Katherine Allgood turned abruptly away and poured whisky into a glass. With her face averted, she said in an unsteady voice, "All right, Mr. Bennett-from-Cleveland—it was a dirty thing to do. But I won."

"That's all that counts," I said.

Jeff Winters leaned his long frame against a locker and took a slow drink from his glass. He winked at me, and said to his partner's wife, "You played beautifully yesterday afternoon, Kate."

She moved up close beside him and took his arm. "Thanks, Jeff. You're a sweetheart. Shall we go find Lily and Sam?"

He put his arm around her and pulled her close. "To hell with 'em," he said. "Let 'em go—they're old enough." He raised his eyes to me and smiled. "Glad you made it after all, Bennett. How about some golf in the morning?"

The invitation, like the one earlier in the afternoon, surprised me. But I had nothing better to do—except maybe sleep—before I headed back for Cleveland. I made up my mind and said, "Thanks. I'd enjoy it. Can you dig up some shoes and clubs?"

"Sure. About seven-thirty?"

I sighed. "That's kind of early, isn't it?"

"That's the best time on Sundays—before the course gets cluttered. I'll pick you up. At the Wheatville Inn?"

"Yes," I said, avoiding Katherine Allgood's quick puzzled glance.

Jeff Winters smiled. "It's a date."

Katherine Allgood pulled him to the door, and they went out, leaving me to drink alone. I was taking a last swallow when Rogan poked his head around the corner of a locker.

"Boo!" I said.

He jerked his head back.

"Hey," I said. "Come here." I jumped around the locker and grabbed him by the back of his white jacket. He struggled briefly, but I held him with a firm grasp. He stood still. He turned slowly to face me, and there was cold hate in his eyes.

"Sonny," I said, "why didn't you just take my bag, and be done with it?"

"What do you mean, sir?"

I sighed and gathered the front of his jacket in my fist. He stood very still and kept his gaze on the points of my collar. "Tell me about it," I said gently. "Why did you search my bag and steal my gun?"

He didn't say anything. Only the corners of his mouth twitched.

I slapped him across the cheek.

He began to tremble a little, but he didn't raise his sullen gaze above my chin. I slapped him again. He turned his head sideways, kept it that way. I waited.

"May I go, sir?" he said in a choked voice.

My toes still ached where he had dropped the bottle on them—intentionally, I knew. I pushed him away from me. He turned silently and disappeared behind a row of steel lockers. I had a bad taste in my mouth. That hardboiled stuff never did get me any place.

CHAPTER ELEVEN

As I shouldered my way through the crowd toward the porch, I caught sight of Hector Griffith standing in a corner. He had a tall glass in his hand, and he was watching the dancers with a half smile on his intelligent bony face. In his well-tailored white dinner jacket, his soft white shirt and black bow tie he looked more than ever like a best-selling author in a whisky advertisement.

I wormed my way between the dancers and stood beside him. There was too much noise to speak without shouting, and so I just grinned at him. He lifted his glass in a friendly salute and turned his gaze once more on the crowd. I spotted Lily Winters standing in the middle of the floor. I was surprised to see that she was alone, with the dancers swirling around her. Her eyes were hot and angry-looking, and there was a bitter twist to her red lips. I followed her gaze and saw the reason for her anger. Sam Allgood was dancing with a tall black-haired girl in a tight flame-colored dress with a low strapless top. Allgood held her tightly, and he guided her clumsily through the dancers, his eyes glazed with liquor. The girl was laughing gaily, and Allgood lowered his head and kissed her naked shoulder. The girl stopped laughing and Allgood held her closer, and they disappeared in the crowd at the far end of the room.

I shifted my gaze to Lily Winters. She was standing on tiptoe, trying to see where Allgood and the girl in the red dress had gone. A fat man with a gray mustache pranced up, grabbed Lily's arm and tried to dance with her. She brushed him away viciously, and started a swift long-legged stride around the edge of the floor. I saw her shining blond head bobbing in the crowd, and then I lost sight of her.

The fat man who had wanted to dance with her stared open-mouthed for an instant, and then he turned in the direction of the bar.

I glanced at Hector standing beside me. I saw by the amused expression on his lean face that he had also observed the little drama. He winked at me and shook his head sadly. I jerked my head toward the porch, and Hector followed me outside to the lawn above the drive. I sat down on a bench and he sat beside me. The ice tinkled gently in his glass.

He leaned back and stared up at the stars in a blue-black sky. He murmured, "The stag at eve had drunk his fill ..."

"Yeah," I said. "We're just a couple of stags—but we haven't drunk our fill. At least, not me. But Sam Allgood seems to have had plenty.... I didn't know you went in for this sort of thing." I nodded at the clubhouse.

He chuckled quietly. "I don't—but as long as I'm paying dues I figure I'm entitled to a little entertainment. I play golf occasionally, and it sometimes amuses me to come out and watch the dances." He paused, took a swallow of his drink and said musingly, "I was once interested in anthropology, and I spent a year in the Congo, before I took up medicine. These dances remind me of some of the savage tribes' love rites. They're quite similar, you know." He turned to me suddenly. "Would you like a drink? I've got a bottle in my locker."

"All right," I said. "And then I'm going to leave this mad, gay whirl and go to bed. I've got a date to play golf with Jeff Winters early in the morning." I paused and then asked, "What do you make of Jeff's wife?"

"Lily?" he said. "She's all right—friendly, and not too intelligent. But she'd better stick to Jeff. Sam Allgood will lead her a merry chase. I hate to see it ... Jeff's such a hell of a swell guy. Everybody in town likes him."

"Doesn't he know what's going on?" I asked. "You live in this town. What's the official opinion?"

He laughed shortly. "Don't ever bank on a small town's official opinion. Sometimes the gossip is true—and often it isn't. Either way, it's vicious. But I told you before—it's pretty common knowledge about the affair between Lily Winters and Sam Allgood. If Jeff Winters knows it, he apparently has decided to ignore it—at least in public."

"What about Sam?"

He gave me his half smile. "You're persistent, aren't you? It seems to me that I told you all this the day before yesterday, but I'll tell you again. Sam's a chaser, pure and simple. He'll never change. He likes 'em all."

"Even Mrs. Donati?" I said, and almost instantly I was sorry.

Hector frowned. Then he said carefully, "I wouldn't know about that."

I was faintly ashamed of my remark, and I hastened to say smoothly, "While we're gossiping so cozily, what about Sam's wife, Katherine?"

He shrugged. "She and Lily Winters appear to be friendly enough. All that seems to interest Mrs. Allgood is golf—and parties."

I sighed. "And so Lily is married to Jeff, but she's got a yen for Sam. Sam is married to Katherine, but likes Lily—and all the girls. In algebra, Katherine and Jeff would be unknown quantities—Mr. and Mrs. X. But I don't know why I'm bothering about it. I'm going to play some golf with Jeff Winters in the morning and then head for home."

"Work all finished here?"

I nodded. "Yep. Sam Allgood fired me and Pete Donati is dead. I've run out of clients. By the way, it was the farmer who was taking pot shots at Sam—just to scare him so that he'd stay out of the cornfield."

Hector laughed. "People—they're wonderful." He stood up. "Come on. Let's get that drink."

From the road below the clubhouse lawn, beyond a clump of pine trees, I heard a sharp report. And then another. I gazed down toward the road. Above the trees a string of lights stretched out to the main highway, and as I stared, the report came again and one of the lights popped out.

"Come on," I said to Hector, and ran across the grass toward the road.

As I rounded the clump of pines I saw a slender bright-haired figure in a black evening gown, aiming a rifle at the lights. The rifle cracked; I saw the slim pencil of flame and another light bulb shattered. The girl laughed shrilly and the rifle spoke again. The bulbs were going out at evenly spaced intervals all along the wire to the highway. I ran forward and yelled, "Hey!"

Lily Winters turned toward me, and stood swaying, the rifle held easily in the crook of her arm. I approached her warily until I stood facing her. I was aware of Hector Griffith standing quietly behind me. Lily Winters giggled and a strand of her bright hair fell over one side of her face.

I smiled at her. "Nice shooting," I said.

"Let me try." I reached for the gun.

She jerked back, a sudden hot light in her eyes. "Oh, no. This is my gun. Little target practice. I'm practicing to shoot a skunk."

I heard a sharp voice behind me say, "Lily!"

I turned to see Jeff Winters. His face was pale, and he was staring at his wife with worried eyes. "Come on, Lily," he said quietly. "I'll take you home."

She shook her head violently. "Don't wanna go home. Wanna practice shooting. Big shoot in Toledo tomorrow. Remember?"

"Sleep will do you more good than practice," Winters said patiently, like a father reasoning with a small child. He glanced at me with a mixed expression of apology and embarrassment.

"Sure," I chimed in, and once more I reached for the gun. She stepped back quickly and the light glinted on the rifle barrel.

There was a stumbling step on the gravel, and Sam Allgood came down the road. His black hair was ruffled, and his black bow-tie was hanging loosely over his white shirtfront. When he saw the gun in Lily's hand, he stood still and stared stupidly. Slowly his gaze swung away from her, and he looked at Hector, Jeff Winters and me. "What the hell?" he muttered thickly, and he lurched for the girl.

She raised the rifle to her shoulder with professional grace and pointed the muzzle directly at Allgood. "Stand still, my little playmate," she said. "Stand still while I make a bull's-eye of your cheating heart."

Allgood stood still. His eyes bugged out, and I could almost see his knees shaking. "Lily," he whispered hoarsely. "Lily ..."

"Where's Red Dress," she demanded, "the sexy number you chased—and left me standing with my thumb in my mouth in the middle of the dance floor? Get her out here, and I'll have two bull's-eyes."

Jeff Winters said sharply, "Lily! Put that gun down."

"Stand clear, darling," she said. "Stand clear, everybody. This concerns Sammy Boy and me."

Allgood's body seemed to have turned to jelly. "Lily," he croaked. "Don't ..."

She steadied the gun.

Then I saw Hector. I had forgotten about him, and now I saw that he had quietly moved around behind Lily Winters. Suddenly he jumped forward, grabbed the rifle and twisted it from her hands. He stepped away quickly, a bright alert look in his eyes.

Lily Winters flung out her arms and laughed shrilly. "Act's over, folks," she cried. She did a dance step and snapped her fingers. "Let's all have a drink." She started across the grass.

Jeff Winters ran after her and caught her arm. She leaned against him, and I saw them disappear beyond the pine trees.

Sam Allgood laughed shakily and passed a hand over his forehead. "That Lily," he said. "She's quite a gal."

"Yeah," I said. "Quite a gal."

Hector looked at the rifle in his hands. "What'll I do with this?"

Allgood said quickly, "I'll take care of that." He took the gun from Hector and walked toward the clubhouse. Hector and I followed him into the locker room. Allgood fumbled a key from his pocket, unlocked the locker with his name on it and put the gun inside. I saw his golf clubs and the red cap I had worn the previous afternoon. He locked the metal door, pocketed the key and started for the door. "Come on," he said. "Let's all have a drink."

"No, thanks," Hector said quietly.

Allgood turned and glared at me. He had sobered a little, and his face was covered with sweat. "How about you?" he said to me. "I don't know why the hell you're still snooping around, but I'll buy you a drink anyhow."

I grinned at him. "Go ahead and enjoy yourself. It's safe now."

He didn't like it. His lips tightened and his eyes narrowed. He took a sudden step toward me.

A voice said, "Sam, where have you been?"

Katherine Allgood stood in the doorway of the locker room. She looked cool and sober and her eyes met mine casually. I smiled at her and she glanced away quickly.

Allgood attempted a hearty laugh. "Hi-ya, honey." He moved over and put an arm around her. I saw her lips twist in distaste, and she shrugged away from him. Suddenly she turned and went out.

Allgood lurched after her. "Aw, honey—"

The door closed behind them and I looked at Hector. He raised his eyebrows, and smiled faintly.

"Trouble in camp," I said.

He nodded gravely.

"Well," I said, "I've had enough of this rat race. Me for bed."

Hector walked with me down the dark drive to my car. As I opened the coupé door, he held out a hand and said seriously, "I probably won't see you again. It's been nice knowing you."

I shook his hand. "Good luck, Hector. When you come to Cleveland, look me up."

"Sometime, maybe." He paused and gave me a crooked smile. "Tomorrow, and tomorrow, and tomorrow ..."

I remembered my high school Shakespeare, and I added, "Creeps in this petty pace from day to day...."

He laughed softly. "Life is a petty pace, isn't it?"

In my mind the parade began again, and I thought of Jeff Winters, that quiet, friendly man, and of his cheating wife, Lily; and of Katherine Allgood, who wanted to be first in everything, no matter what the cost; and of Sam Allgood, handsome and arrogant, with a roving eye. I thought once more of Joyce Justin, playing two men for what she could get out of them; and of Bert Homer, greedy and revengeful, dead in an alley with my bullets in his face; and of little Peggy Roark, loving the memory of a dead father who had died following the goading of Sam Allgood. I thought of Marianne Donati, marvelously lovely, yet ugly, with the figure of a goddess; and the parade slowed down again. And then I saw Pete Donati as he sat behind his desk, with his blood drenching everything ...

I said to Hector, "Life wasn't petty for Bertha and Pete Donati."

"No," he said slowly. "There is nothing petty about death. But, still, for a time, Pete had Marianne ..." He gazed away into the night.

I knew what he meant, and once more her ugliness was just a bad dream; not real; a surface thing not to be noticed in connection with her personality, her figure or the beauty veiled behind her eyes....

I said briskly, "Well, so long." I got into my coupé and drove into town to the Wheatville Inn.

Before I went to sleep that night, a soft summer rain began to fall.

CHAPTER TWELVE

At seven-thirty-two in the morning Jeff Winters' black sedan stopped in front of the Wheatville Inn. I had finished breakfast and was reading the Sunday comics. As I got in beside him, I said, "I didn't think you'd make it—after that party last night."

He smiled. "I didn't stay so late. I like to drink but not all night. And I wanted to talk to you. I didn't have a chance last night."

"All right," I said. "Go ahead."

He swung the sedan left at the Courthouse. He was freshly shaven, and his blond mustache glinted red in the morning sunlight. He was wearing a gray flannel suit, a crisp white shirt and blue polka-dot tie.

He said, "What kind of trouble is Sam in?"

"Why do you think he's in trouble?" I asked him.

He showed his white even teeth in a grin. "Hell," he said, "everybody in town knows you're a private dick—and you came here in the first place as a guest of Sam's."

"I should have worn my false whiskers and putty nose," I said.

Winters laughed. Then he said seriously, "No kidding. Sam's my partner, and he's been acting jumpy lately. If he's in trouble, maybe I can help."

I thought about Sam and Lily Winters, but that was none of my affair and I said, "It's kind of silly, but I'll tell you what Sam hired me for." I told him about the farmer shooting at Sam on number six tee at the golf course.

When I had finished, Winters nodded slowly. "I can see how a thing like that would worry anyone. But it seems to me that Sam could have figured it out for himself and acted accordingly, without going to the trouble of hiring you."

"That's what I thought," I said. "Anyhow, I cornered the farmer and he admitted shooting at Allgood—to scare him. When I told Allgood, he seemed satisfied and fired me."

"Fassler's kind of a nut," Winters said. "Is Sam going to do anything about him?"

I shook my head. "He said not—he just wanted to know who it was—and, naturally, he doesn't want any publicity." I paused, and then I added, "I warned Sam that the next time the farmer might aim better."

Winters sighed heavily. "Well, I can't do anything about it. I'm not supposed to know about it so I can't mess in." He braked the sedan and turned into the grounds of the Wheatville Country Club.

We parked in the drive. The whole place was silent and deserted in the early morning sunlight. Winters took a key from his pocket, went up on the porch and unlocked the clubhouse door. "Want to come in?" he asked me over his shoulder.

I shook my head, and while I waited in the car I smoked a cigarette. The sun shone on the distant woods and glistened on the wet grass of the fairways. I thought about a lot of things, and I felt a little sorry for Jeff Winters—he seemed like too nice a guy to have a fast-stepping babe like Lily for a wife and a cheating partner like Sam Allgood.

I felt sorry for little Peggy Roark, and I hoped Skip Gordon would do a good job on the story clearing her father of taking money to throw the Midwest Open to the Alabama Kid. I didn't feel sorry for Katherine Allgood. She was the kind of a woman who would never be happy unless she was holding four aces with the lid off the limit. I thought of all the people who had crossed my path in the few days I'd been in Wheatville, and once more the sad, scarred, tragic face of Marianne Donati crossed my brain. Suddenly I wished that I had refused Winters' invitation, and that I was out of the town of Wheatville and headed for Cleveland and home. When I thought about it, I didn't see any good reason why I was still hanging around.

Winters came out of the clubhouse carrying two golf bags and a pair of spiked shoes. He had changed his clothes and was again wearing the white terry cloth pullover. He handed me the shoes and I tried them on. They were a little tight for my size eleven feet, but they would do.

"They belong to Lily's brother," Winters explained. "He's about your size. Do you mind playing without a caddy? It's a little early for them."

I said I didn't mind. I left my hat and coat and tie in the car, and shouldered the bag of clubs Winters had brought me. We went out to the first tee. As I drove my first ball, the sun lifted clear of the woods and I decided that maybe I was going to enjoy myself after all.

We were the only persons on the course. The ground was a little soggy from the rain of the night before, and blades of freshly cut grass clung to our shoes. The soft turf cut down on the roll of our drives, but it helped our approaches to stop dead on the greens. By the time we had finished the fourth hole Jeff Winters and I were talking and joking together like a couple of old pals, and we decided that we ought to bet a quarter a hole, with a dollar on each nine. He had a quiet, friendly, easy manner about him, and he played about the same brand of Sunday golf that I did.

We holed out on the fifth green and climbed a little hill to the sixth tee. We were walking side by side, and we both saw it at the same time.

A man was lying face down on the green grass of the tee. The sun glinted on the shiny steel spikes in the soles of his golf shoes. He was wearing tan gabardine slacks and a dark green sport shirt. On the back of his head was a bright red baseball player's cap. One arm was doubled beneath him. The other was stretched out at his side.

Jeff Winters and I exchanged glances.

"Allgood?" I asked.

He nodded and said in a low voice, "I'd know that red cap anywhere."

"Drunk?" I asked, but suddenly I knew that I was just making conversation.

"He was hitting it pretty heavy last night," Winters said. "He must have had a crazy idea to play golf—got this far and passed out." He stepped forward.

I followed him.

"Sam!" Winters called.

I put a hand on Winters' arm and pulled him back. "Drunks don't flop like that," I told him. "He's dead."

Winters stared at me with shocked, puzzled eyes. Then he shook my hand away, moved swiftly to the form of Sam Allgood and knelt down. Gently he turned the body over. I stepped up and knelt beside Winters.

Sam Allgood hadn't been dead very long—maybe an hour or two. I laid the back of my hand against his cheek. The flesh was still faintly warm, but chilling fast. There were two bullet holes in him—one under his left eye and one over the left breast pocket of his shirt. The holes were small and there wasn't much blood. A number five iron lay beneath the body, and a little to the right a small yellow wooden tee protruded from the ground with a golf ball lying beside it. On the edge of the grassy elevation where Sam Allgood lay was a white-painted wooden arrow upon which was printed in black letters: *No. 6, 170 yds., Par 3.*

"Well," I said, "Sam's one under."

Winters glanced at me. "What?"

"Only two shots in him," I said. "It's a par three hole."

Winters stood up. "That's not funny, Bennett," he said in a ragged voice.

"Sorry," I said.

He lit a cigarette with an unsteady hand. "All right," he said harshly. "You're the big-town dick—what do we do now?"

I gazed across the fence at the buildings of the Fassler farm, and I saw a telephone wire leading in from the highway to the house. "You stay here," I said to Winters. "I'm going to see a man."

His eyes followed my gaze and he nodded grimly. I walked away from him.

It was eight-thirty of a bright Sunday morning. As I climbed the fence, I heard cows mooing in the barn and a collie barked at me from his place in the sun on the back porch. I walked around the house and pounded on the front door. I pounded long and hard, and I was still pounding when the door was jerked open.

A woman in a long flannel nightgown peered out at me. She was maybe thirty, but she looked forty, and her long tangled hair was beginning to gray. She had probably been a rather pretty girl once, but the wind and the sun and the lack of dental care had changed all of that.

"Well," she said sullenly, "carry him in."

"I haven't got him," I said. "I'm looking for him."

She squinted up at me. "And who are you?"

"Never mind," I said. "I'm afraid your husband is in trouble. Isn't he at home?"

"No," she said, and she started to close the door.

I stuck a foot inside, in the approved door-to-door salesman technique. "Where is he?"

She shook her head. "He went to town right after supper last night, and I ain't seen him since."

"All right," I said. "May I use your phone?"

"We ain't—" she began, and then she saw me glance at the wires slanting over the porch. She stepped aside and pushed a lock of hair from her eyes. "It's on the radio," she said wearily.

I stepped inside.

"Is it about that shooting of his?" she asked me. "I told him that he'd get in trouble, but—" She turned away from me and covered her face with her hands. The heavy nightgown very effectively concealed the lines of her body, but the shape of her head was good, and I wondered what circumstances had prompted her to marry a lout like Lem Fassler.

I looked around the bare room. There was a big coal stove in the middle of the floor, and along one wall was a large old-fashioned radio with a telephone on top of it. I called the Wheatville Police Department. A sleepy voice answered, and I told the voice who I was, where I was and what had happened.

"Pick up a farmer named Lem Fassler," I said. "Lives out here on the south side of the golf club. His wife says he went to town last night and hasn't come home yet. Check your booze joints."

"Listen," the cop complained. "That's outta the city limits. You better call the sheriff. He—"

"You call him!" I snapped, and hung up before he could argue with me.

I heard a shrill sound behind me. The woman in the nightgown was sitting by the coal stove with her face in her hands. She was sobbing as a child does—spasmodically, holding her breath. The heels of her bare feet were resting on the lower rung of the chair. Her toenails had chipped red lacquer on them.

"Goodbye, Mrs. Fassler," I said gently. She didn't look up or make any answer, and I left. As I closed the door, I could still hear the whimpering sound of her sobbing.

I found Jeff Winters leaning against the sunny side of the shelter house. A few flies were buzzing around Sam Allgood's head, and I shooed them away with my hand as I passed. Winters looked a question at me.

"Looks like the farmer's on a drunk," I told him. "I put the cops on his tail. They ought to be out here pretty quick."

He nodded silently. I lit a cigarette and moved over to Allgood's body. The bill of his red cap protruded upward from his thick black hair. His eyes were half open, and the pupil of his left eye was turned in slightly toward his nose. The flies had settled again and I flicked them away.

Behind me Winters said softly, "He was just getting ready to drive when the farmer shot him."

I nodded. "It looks like it."

After that, Winters and I just stood around, smoking and not talking much. Winters' face held a gray tinge, and he kept looking across the fairway toward the road. Presently we heard the sound of a car coming up from town. It was coming fast, and in a second I saw it. Its brakes squealed as it came to a stop in front of Lem Fassler's house. Three men got out and hurried toward us.

"Here comes the law," I said to Jeff Winters. "Get your answers ready."

It was ten o'clock before Jeff Winters and I were through with the local law. The sheriff was a little dried-up man in a cowboy hat and a silver star on his vest. He bustled about, shouting orders to his deputies, asking questions and chewing tobacco; he seemed to enjoy himself immensely. An ambulance from Wheatville came out and hauled the body of Sam Allgood to an undertaking parlor, and the sheriff warned the ambulance driver not to do any embalming until the coroner, Doc Hendricks, had examined it.

At last Jeff Winters and I were heading toward town in his car. He hadn't changed his clothes, and was still wearing his spiked shoes. I changed my shoes as we rode along.

"I've got to tell Katherine," Winters said.

"How about getting Lily—Mrs. Winters—to tell her?"

He gave me a quick glance. "I can't. She went to a shoot in Toledo."

"That's right," I said. "I remember now. So she made it, huh?"

He nodded grimly. "It'd take more than a hangover to keep Lily from a rifle match."

"Doesn't Sam's wife have any relatives in Wheatville?"

He shook his head. "None that I know of. She came from up around Detroit."

"I guess you're elected," I said.

He nodded gloomily.

When we got into town, I told him to drop me at the Wheatville Inn. He swung his head toward me. "Hell, aren't you coming with me?"

I shook my head. "Sorry. I've got a chore to do."

His gray eyes regarded me steadily. "About ... Sam?"

"Maybe," I said. "When do you expect your wife home?"

He averted his gaze and shrugged his lean shoulders. "Lord knows when she'll get back." He paused and then said in a tight voice, "She—she left before sunup."

"Sure," I said carelessly. "That was before Sam was killed."

He nodded. "Long before." He turned his eyes upon me and said in a level voice, "Let me know when they pick up the farmer."

"All right," I said. "I hope you don't have too much trouble with Sam's wife."

He sighed deeply. "I wish to God Lily was home." He gunned the motor of his car. "Well, see you later." He drove away.

I walked around the block, unlocked my coupé and drove out to Peggy Roark's house on the edge of town. A thin-faced woman with tired eyes answered my knock. She was small and slender, and her black hair held streaks of gray. I asked her if Peggy was at home, and she told me that Peggy had gone to Sunday school, was staying for church and would be home shortly after twelve o'clock.

I asked her what church and she said, "St. Paul's, on Monument Street."

I thanked her and started to leave.

She stopped me. "Aren't you Mr. Bennett?"

I nodded.

"Peggy has told me about you," she said. "And about Mr. Gordon, the newspaper man. I want to thank you. It means a lot to us—to have my husband's name cleared."

"Thank Mr. Gordon," I told her. "It should be in the paper tomorrow." I hesitated and then I said, "Did Peggy—uh—leave early this morning?"

She gave me a wan smile. "I really don't know, Mr. Bennett. I haven't been feeling very well and she was gone when I got up. But she always leaves early on Sunday mornings—she teaches a nursery class."

"Good for her," I said, and I tipped my hat. "Goodbye, Mrs. Roark."

As I got into my car and drove downtown, I felt once more like the grandfather of all the heels in the world. But that didn't stop me from driving down Monument Street past St. Paul's church. A faded blue convertible was parked out in front. I glanced at the dash clock. Half past ten o'clock in the morning. I had an hour and a half to wait—unless I wanted to crash a church service. I decided to get a cup of coffee.

I frittered away maybe half an hour at a lunch counter, drinking coffee and reading the Sunday papers. Then I began to get jittery. I walked along the quiet street to the Wheatville Inn and sat in a leather chair in the lobby, facing the window. Hector Griffith came around the corner and started across the street.

I jumped up and stepped outside. "Hey, Hector!" I called.

He turned, saw me and waited. I walked over to him. He was wearing a light tweed coat, an open-necked white shirt and gray flannel slacks. The morning sun glinted on his close-clipped hair. He smiled at me gravely, waiting for me to speak.

"Where are you going?" I asked him.

He shrugged. "Just killing time. Going to get a paper, and then back to my room ... I thought you'd be in Cleveland by this time."

"Come in and talk to me," I said. "I've got the jumps."

"All right," he said quietly, and he followed me into the inn. As we crossed the lobby, the old pappy who was again on the desk, called to me. "Telephone, Mr. Bennett."

I walked over to the desk and picked up the phone. "Yes?"

It was Jeff Winters. He sounded tired. "Can you come over, Bennett?

I've got Katherine here at my place—she's in pretty bad shape. Took it hard about Sam. I called her folks in Detroit, and I've just now talked her into going upstairs and lying down. Lily isn't back from Toledo, and I can't get hold of her up there. And Chief Swartz called. He wants to talk to me, and you, too, about Sam. He's helping the sheriff."

"Have they picked up the farmer yet?" I asked.

"Yes," Winters said. "Swartz said they found him in his car on the river road—sleeping off a drunk. He was in no shape to talk, and they've got him in the county jail."

I glanced at my wristwatch. It still lacked forty-five minutes of twelve o'clock noon. "All right," I said. "I'll be out." I hung up.

I walked over to where Hector Griffith stood by the window. "I've got to go out to Jeff Winters' house," I told him. He turned to stare at me gravely.

"Look," I said, "I may as well tell you. It'll be all over town anyhow. Sam Allgood was shot dead on the golf course early this morning. Jeff Winters and I found him. Jeff's wife is out of town, and Jeff's got Sam's wife at his house. She's taking it pretty hard."

His eyes widened a little. "Sam Allgood? Shot?"

I nodded.

He sighed. "Which husband was it?" he asked wearily.

"It was a half-wit farmer named Lem Fassler," I said. "The cops have got him now. He was the one who had been shooting at Sam on the golf course. I told you about it."

He nodded slowly and filled his pipe. As he struck a match, he said, "That makes two murders in Wheatville within twelve hours."

"Two murders—and a killing," I said gloomily, remembering the dead body of Bert Horner in the alley. I turned to the door and went out to the sidewalk. Hector followed me.

"Why don't you come along?" I asked him. "You're a doctor. Maybe you can give Mrs. Allgood something to quiet her down."

"Was a doctor," he said. "No, thanks." He puffed on his pipe, and looked away.

"You're good enough for me," I said. "Come on. We'll pick up your pill bag."

He removed the pipe from between his teeth, and I saw a glint of eagerness in his eyes. "All right," he said quietly. "If Mrs. Allgood won't object."

We went to my car, and I drove to a small brick apartment house and waited while Hector went in to get his bag. When he carried it out, he looked very serious and professional. I grinned at him. "Hi, Doc," I said.

He smiled quietly, but I saw the pride in his eyes.

Hector gave me directions and I drove to Jeff Winters' house. It was bigger and fancier than Sam Allgood's, and boasted a tennis court on the side lawn. Winters met us at the door. He was still wearing his golfing clothes, but had changed his spiked shoes for soft leather house slippers. He had a half-finished highball in his hand. The morning sun lighted up the deep red of the carpets and the walnut paneling of the big living room.

I said, "You know Hector Griffith?"

Winters nodded. "Of course. How are you, Hector?"

"Fine, Jeff," Hector said quietly.

"I thought maybe Hector could give Mrs. Allgood something to quiet her," I said. "He used to be a doctor, you know."

Jeff Winters looked doubtful. "I didn't know," he said. "But I think she's quieted down now. Maybe later ..."

"Of course," Hector said stiffly. He turned to go.

I grabbed his arm. "Stick around. I'm going back downtown pretty soon."

"Sure," Jeff Winters said. "I'll make a drink. The Chief should be here before long." He moved across the room to a lacquered liquor cabinet. "What'll you have?"

"Anything," I said, and I meant it.

Winters glanced inquiringly at Hector.

"Same here," Hector said. He placed his bag carefully on the floor and sat down in a deep chair.

As Winters busied himself at the cabinet, I looked at my watch. Church would be out in twenty-five minutes. I knew what I had to do, and I moved restlessly about the room. I said to Winters, "You couldn't get in touch with your wife, huh?"

He hesitated a second before he answered. Then, without turning, he said, "Yes, I did. Right after I called you. She's on her way home."

"Did she win the match?" I asked him.

He shook his head. "No. She withdrew when I called her. But she was leading in points on rounds fired."

"Too bad," I said. "Sam should have gotten murdered at a more convenient time."

Winters turned slowly, and his blue eyes were as hard as marble.

"This is no joking matter, Bennett," he said coldly.

"Murder is never a joke," I said.

He turned back to the cabinet, and there was the clink of ice in glasses.

From above a stairway at the end of the room I heard a low sobbing wail.

Winters turned, handed a glass to me and one to Hector.

Winters said, "Sam's folks are all dead—except a married sister in Zanesville. I've wired her." He sighed and took a long swallow of his drink.

The gun Hector had given me was nestled in my inside coat pocket. I pressed my arm against it to make sure it was still there, and I sipped at the drink Winters had given me. Scotch. Smooth and mellow and smoky. Good Scotch, a gesture of friendliness from a good man. A good man with a cheating wife named Lily. A man with a partner named Sam Allgood who threw the rules overboard when they interfered with his desires. I stood in the middle of the room with a drink in my hand, and I sighed a deep sigh.

I said to Jeff Winters, "Could I see your wife's rifle? The one she kept in the locker?"

He jerked his head toward me. "Why?"

Watching him, I said carefully, "I wanted to see if it has been fired recently, and if there are any fingerprints on it. And then I think the police would like to compare the bullets in Sam Allgood with the rifle."

His face went gray, and for an instant I saw the naked fear in his eyes. He took a deep, shuddering breath, and I could almost see him pulling his nerves into line. "Lily didn't kill Sam," he said in a level voice, "if that's what you mean."

"I'm sorry," I said, and I really was. "I'm not a cop, but I've got a cop's mind. A dirty, suspicious mind, maybe, but I can't help it. Your wife threatened Sam last night, and if Hector here hadn't taken the gun away from her, she might have killed Sam then and there. She passed it off as a joke afterwards, but I'm not so sure it was a joke. I hope you'll forgive me, but it was obvious to me that she was wildly jealous of Sam, and I think she killed him. And I don't think she's in Toledo at all. I think you're covering up for her." I took a step toward a telephone on a small table in the corner. "Anyhow, I'm justified in calling the police and asking them to arrest your wife—on suspicion, of course, until her gun is checked—for the murder of Sam Allgood."

"Damn you!" Winters blurted. "To hell with you and your cop's dirty mind. Lily didn't kill Sam. I killed the double-crossing son-of-a-bitch."

CHAPTER THIRTEEN

For maybe three seconds there was quiet in the room. I felt old and tired and discouraged. This was something I hadn't expected, and I was sorry for Jeff Winters. It was a hell of a rotten deal for him. And yet, I knew, somehow, that he would not duck it, and once more I thought grimly of the hairline between Right and Wrong. I glanced at Hector Griffith. He sat silently, his shocked gaze flicking from Winters to me.

I said to Winters, "I'm sorry. Really, I'm sorry."

He turned abruptly away to the liquor cabinet.

"Tell us about it," I said gently.

Jeff Winters turned slowly to face me. He had a blue steel Smith and Wesson .38 revolver in his hand. I recognized my own gun—the one which had been taken from my bag, I thought dismally. He had it in the liquor cabinet all the time, and I shot a quick glance at Hector. But he was too far away to be of any help.

Winters held the gun very steadily, and he said in a flat strained voice, "Don't move, Bennett. Or you, Hector. I'm a lawyer, and I know what I'm up against. In this state it's the chair, and they can only burn me once."

"Put that gun away," I told him, and I took a slow step toward him. "You're among friends. Maybe we can figure something out." If I can stall him, I thought, and get that gun.

"Stick to snooping, Bennett," he said harshly, "and stand still. I know what they'll do to me. I killed Sam because he needed killing. I've hated him for a long time. It wasn't only because of Lily—she was only one of his women. If he had been serious and Lily wanted him, I wouldn't have stood in their way. But Sam wasn't a one-woman man and Lily was just one of his affairs. Oh, I knew all about it, and I couldn't let Lily throw herself away on him. He had other women ..." He paused and I saw sweat on his forehead.

"Marianne Donati?" I said softly. "For one?"

He nodded grimly. "For one." The hand which held the gun was now trembling a little.

From the corner of my eye I saw Hector carefully place his glass on the floor and rise slowly from his chair. He stood very still, a bright, alert look in his eyes.

I took one more slow step toward Jeff Winters.

He backed away and raised the gun. "Stand still, damn you," he said raggedly. "And remember this—I don't blame Lily. She isn't very bright, and sometimes I've felt more like a father than a husband, but I happen to love her. Last night she ran away from me, and later I saw her sneaking away with Sam. I followed them here—to my house. They came in, and they were in here a long time with the lights out. I waited. I was ninety years old before the door opened and Sam came out. I was hiding behind the porch, and I saw that he was still drunk. He got into his car and drove away. I followed him. He went out to the club and entered the locker room. He came out dressed in his golfing clothes, and was carrying a single golf club. He walked to the first tee and hit a ball. He's done it before—gets a crazy idea to play golf when he's drunk."

"Was it daylight?" I asked him.

He nodded. "Yes. But before sunup." He paused and passed his free hand over his eyes.

"Go on," I said.

He looked at me with calm cold eyes. "All right. I want you to know. I got Lily's gun from my locker and I followed him. When he reached the sixth tee, I had my chance. The sun was just coming up, and I had a clear view of him as I stood behind the poplars on the fairway. I shot him—twice—and I saw him fall. I walked over to him and saw that he was dead. I was glad.... Can you understand how I felt, Bennett?"

"Maybe," I said. "Did you hire Rogan to search my car?" He nodded slowly. "Yes, I did. I was curious about your business with Sam. That was before the whole town knew you were a private detective. But Miss Hoskins tells me everything, and she told me about you coming into the office and asking for Sam. You showed her your membership card in the Beavers' Lodge, and she noticed your name and address. When she told me, I made a telephone call to friends in Cleveland, and they told me that you worked for a detective agency. Sam is—was—my partner, and so I paid Rogan to search your car. I thought maybe I could learn something from your belongings—a letter, maybe. But all Rogan brought me was your gun. This gun." He moved the barrel in a half circle.

"You should have asked me before this morning," I said, "when I told you about Sam Allgood hiring me. He suspected that the farmer named Fassler was shooting at him, but he had a guilty conscience and he wasn't sure. Sam was afraid it might even be you—or some other husband. Maybe Pete Donati. Guys who are chasing other men's wives don't sleep easy. He was worried, and he hired me—if only to find out for certain that it was the farmer." I paused and added curiously, "Why didn't you try to blame it on the farmer? He's a perfect frame. I told you this morning on the way to the course that he'd admitted taking shots at Sam."

Winters sighed. "I didn't think fast enough, I guess. Besides I had already killed him. I couldn't think of anything else. After I killed him I put Lily's rifle back into my locker, went home, shaved, changed clothes and picked you up." He gave me a twisted smile. "Now that I think of it, Sam was killed on the spot where you told me the farmer had shot at him. Maybe the farmer did kill him, after all."

I shook my head. "You're too late. You should have thought of that before you confessed to killing Sam."

"Look, Bennett," he said, and there was a note of desperation in his voice. "I'm serious. I can pin it on the farmer—if you'll help."

"No," I said. "I'm sorry. Anyhow, Hector is in on it, too."

"Five thousand," Winters said. "For you and Hector. For each of you."

"Don't make it hard for us."

Winters sighed heavily. "No harm in trying." He motioned to the liquor cabinet. "Have a drink, both of you. I'm walking out of here, and I'm going to get into my car and drive away."

"No," I said.

"Yes." His voice was soft, and I saw his teeth gleam beneath his neat yellow mustache. "If you try to stop me, I'll kill you."

I moved away from him to the telephone on the table. Beside the table there was a spindle-legged chair with a bright needle-point seat. I placed one hand cautiously on the telephone and the other on the back of the chair. Winters watched me silently. Hector Griffith stood like a stone statue.

Winters steadied the gun. "Damn you, Bennett," he said from between his teeth.

I flung the chair at him. It struck his knees, and in the same instant the gun exploded and the bullet buzzed past my ear. I ducked low and jumped for him. But Hector was ahead of me. He moved with surprising speed, and I saw him lean forward and jerk the gun from Winters' hand. Winters was tangled in the chair and he fell awkwardly to the floor. Hector stepped clear and leveled the gun at Winters. There was excitement in his eyes but his hand was steady.

I hadn't risked reaching for it before, but now I took from my inside coat pocket the .32 Hector had loaned me. I held it loosely in my hand and stared down at Jeff Winters. He rolled over on the rug, pushed himself to a sitting position and stared at me with hot, bitter eyes.

I shot a glance at Hector. He shook his head sadly, but he kept the gun leveled. I dropped the gun I held back into my pocket. I heard a slight sound and glanced behind me.

Katherine Allgood stood on the stairway. Her face was the color of dirty snow, and her brown eyes looked almost black. She stared wildly, her fingers gripping the railing.

Outside the house a car door slammed and through the wide windows I saw Lily Winters hurrying up the walk. The sun struck pale glints in her long tawny hair. Beyond her a black police cruiser turned into the drive. The cruiser stopped, and Chief of Police Swartz and a uniformed policeman got out. Swartz glanced at the house, hitched at his belt and started for the porch. The policeman stayed by the cruiser.

For a few seconds the house was very still. The scene in Jeff Winters' big living room reminded me of the first-act curtain of a fifth-rate play—a man on the floor, one standing with a gun in his hand, a wild-eyed girl on the stairway and me by the telephone.

I heard the faraway bonging of the big clock in the tower of the Wheatville Courthouse. It struck twelve times. Church was out now, I thought, and little Peggy Roark was probably climbing happily into her battered blue roadster.

I looked at Jeff Winters. "The law is outside," I said.

"Do your duty," he said harshly, "by all means."

Katherine Allgood leaned forward on the stair railing and began to sob brokenly.

The door opened and Lily Winters stepped inside. She was wearing gray flannel slacks and a tight pale blue sweater. Her silky hair clung softly around her shoulders, and, except for dark hollows beneath her eyes, she looked marvelous. Her startled gaze took in Hector and me, and then she saw her husband. She ran to him and knelt down. "Darling! What's wrong?"

Winters tried to smile at her. "Shush, baby," he said.

Chief of Police Swartz loomed in the doorway. "Bennett," he said heavily, "we found out that Sam Allgood was killed by a blow on his head. Doc Hendricks says the slugs didn't kill him. He was already dead. You—" He stopped, and I saw him stare at Hector holding the gun and at Jeff Winters and his wife on the floor.

Winters looked up at Swartz. "Lock me up, Irvin," he said evenly. "I killed Sam."

Lily Winters cried, "Oh, no, Jeff! No!"

Swartz looked bewildered.

"Take over, Chief," I told him. "I'm tired."

CHAPTER FOURTEEN

An hour and a half later Hector Griffith and I sat in the office of Chief of Police Swartz. Hector sat in a chair along the wall with his pipe in his mouth, and I had my feet on the chief's desk.

Swartz gave me a crooked grin. "Let me know when you're coming to town again, Bennett," he said. "I'll call out the National Guard. You hit town and all hell breaks loose." He held up a pudgy hand and began to count on his fingers: "Pete Donati, Bert Homer, Sam Allgood—all dead. Joyce Justin in the hospital with a murder accomplice charge hanging over her. Jeff Winters in the jug for the murder of Sam Allgood. The only good thing about the whole mess is that we won't have any expense in sending Donati's killer to the chair. Bert Horner is dead—thanks to you. But I'll want you back here for Winters' trial."

"Hector heard his confession," I told him. "He'll be all the witness you need."

Swartz shook his head. "Winters might fight it. He's got his side, you know. Anyhow, we'll need both of you before this deal is off the books."

I sighed and took my feet off the desk. I said to Hector, "I'm going out and say goodbye to Peggy Roark. Want to come along?"

He stood up and went to the door. "Sure," he said.

To Swartz I said, "So long, Chief," and Hector and I went out.

As we drove across town, I said to Hector, "If Mrs. Donati sells the shop, what will you do?"

"I've been thinking about that," he said quietly. "Maybe I can get a job in a hospital or in a laboratory." He paused, and when he spoke again there was a bitter edge to his voice. "After all, I am a doctor—maybe they'll let me do something where I can be of some use to my profession."

"Even if they won't let you deliver babies?" I said, trying to be cheerful.

He nodded gloomily. "I should have made the break before. But I felt obligated to Marianne—Mrs. Donati. She was so damned nice to me."

"Look," I said. "I know the Chief of Staff of a big hospital in Cleveland. Maybe he could use you—research, or something. Want me to speak to him?"

"Would you?" There was a sudden hopeful gleam in his eyes.

"Sure," I said, and I stopped my coupé in front of Peggy Roark's house.

There was a car parked in the drive and I recognized Skip Gordon's dusty station wagon. And then I saw Skip. He was sitting on the front steps close beside Peggy Roark. They looked like a couple of high school freshmen on their first date. When Skip saw me, he looked embarrassed and stood up. Peggy Roark just smiled happily.

I said to Skip, "What're you doing back in town?"

He grinned at me. "I needed a follow-up story on Red Roark, and I—I thought that Peggy—well ..." He waved his arm helplessly.

Peggy Roark said, "We're going on a picnic this afternoon."

Skip Gordon shot her a reproachful glance. Then he said to me, "I can take notes while Peggy fights off the ants and flies, and stuff ..."

I introduced Hector to Skip Gordon. They shook hands, and Peggy Roark stood up and linked her arm with the young reporter's. Looking at the two of them, I decided it was the prettiest sight I'd seen in Wheatville. I said to them, "I'm heading home. Hector came along with me while I said goodbye." I winked at Hector and added, "I'd ask you both to come down to my room for a farewell drink, but I wouldn't dream of interfering with your picnic."

"Thanks, Jim," Skip said seriously, "but I gotta help Peggy make the lemonade."

Peggy looked happily up at him and I said, "Sure. So long." Hector and I returned to my car, and I drove down to the Wheatville Inn.

As I parked in the drive, Hector sighed. "Ah, young love," he said.

"Peggy's a nice kid," I said. "And so is Skip." I looked sideways at

Hector, and added, "Do you suppose I ought to see Mrs. Donati before I leave?"

"Do you want to?" he asked gravely.

I didn't know whether I wanted to or not. My business with Marianne Donati was finished. The parade began again, and I remembered the warm softness of her body, the clean smell of her hair and I heard her husky voice. And then the characters in the parade changed abruptly. I was seeing old Doc Hendricks in Pete Donati's office, and was hearing his gruff voice on the telephone: *An ear-to-ear incision ... severed external jugular vein on both sides, the internal jugular vein, and the carotid artery ...*

I thought with compassion of Jeff Winters and of Katherine Allgood, freshly widowed, and of Peggy Roark and Skip Gordon, and I wished, for Hector's sake, that I really did know the Chief of Staff of a Cleveland hospital. The parade became mixed up, jumbled and faded away. I was glad that I was leaving Wheatville and the people who lived there.

"No, I don't want to see her," I said to Hector. "To hell with it. Come on up with me and have a drink while I pack."

"All right," he said quietly. "Thank you." We got out and he followed me up to my room.

I poured a drink of Bourbon for Hector and one for myself, and then I piled clothes into my bag. As I packed, Hector stood by the window, his glass in his hand, and silently watched the lazy Sunday afternoon traffic in the street below. I peeked into the bathroom to make sure that I had my toothbrush and razor, and then I said to Hector, "Well, I guess I'm ready for the road."

He turned slowly and gave me his grave smile. "Take it easy," he said.

The telephone began to ring.

I looked a question at Hector and he shrugged his lean shoulders. I crossed the room, picked up the receiver, said, "Yes?"

"Mr. Bennett?"

I knew that soft, lovely voice. "Yes," I said. "How are you?"

She hesitated a second and then she laughed a little uncertainly. "You—you knew my voice?"

"Of course."

"How nice."

I waited and she said, "I was afraid you'd be gone."

"I'm just leaving."

"Now?"

"Yes," I said.

"Would—would you have time to stop for a few minutes?"

"Why?"

"You make it very difficult for me. I—I just wanted to tell you that I'm sorry about last night. You were so nice to me, and I—I spoiled it …"

"That's all right." I felt sweat on my temples, and I was aware of Hector's half-mocking gaze upon me.

"But it isn't all right," she said softly. "I'd like to—to make amends. I—I'm so lonely. Couldn't we have a quiet drink together and talk?"

Grimly I wondered if she knew that Sam Allgood was dead. I decided that she didn't, and I also decided that I wasn't going to tell her. Not now, anyhow. I said, "Isn't your husband's funeral tomorrow?"

She was silent for a second and then said, "Yes. Why do you ask that?" There was a faint hard edge to her voice. When I didn't answer, she said in a softer tone, "You said when I was with you, that Pete wouldn't care—that he would want me to be happy. Have you forgotten?"

"No. Would it make you happy if I came over?"

Silence. Then, softly, "I think it would make me very happy."

"All right." I hung up quickly. But I knew I would not go to her apartment. Not anymore. I would never see her again if I knew what was good for me. I looked at Hector. He was gazing discreetly out of the window again. I saw that his glass was empty and I drained mine.

I sighed deeply, and I said, "Well, here I go."

He turned, placed his glass on the table, reached into his inside coat pocket, took out my .38 and handed it to me. "You might need this," he said.

I had forgotten that he had taken my gun from Jeff Winters, and that he still had it. A lot had happened since I'd stood in Jeff Winters' living room and listened to the church bells.

I took the gun. "Thanks." And then I remembered that I was still carrying the .32 he had given me in Bert Homer's shop. I took it from my pocket and handed it to him.

He dropped it carelessly into the pocket of his tweed coat. "A fair exchange," he said, smiling.

I didn't answer him. I was thinking of Marianne Donati, and, thinking of her, I remembered Pete Donati's dead face, drained pale of blood, and once more the voice of the coroner, Doc Hendricks, droned through my brain. What had he said?

... My God man, you saw him, didn't you? ... External jugular vein ... internal jugular, vein ... carotid artery ... Medical mumbo-jumbo. Once more I saw the hot desperate light in Jeff Winters' eyes, and his ragged words came back to me: *I killed Sam... Got Lily's gun from her locker ... I shot him—twice...*

And Chief of Police Swartz's words suddenly made sense. *Sam Allgood was killed by a blow on the head ... The slugs didn't kill him ...*

Once more I saw the body of Sam Allgood lying on the damp grass with the sun glinting on the shiny clean spikes of his golf shoes. No mud, no damp blades of grass sticking to those shoes, and I suddenly knew what I had to do. But I had to be sure. Very, very sure.

I placed my empty glass on the table, and I said to Hector, "All through this you haven't said much. You're a queer person, Hector. Three people have died, and I would have made it four—if you hadn't saved my life. You heard Jeff Winters tell how he killed Sam Allgood. What do you make of it?"

"Sam Allgood was only human," he said gravely, "with a human weakness. And he died with a bullet in his heart."

"He was dead before that," I said. "A blow on his head killed him in the first place—according to Swartz. Winters didn't say anything about hitting him."

He shrugged. "What difference does it make? Whether Jeff Winters struck him first, or not, Sam's dead—because he cheated on his wife and on his partner. It's tragic, really, it is. Sam may have had his faults, but, after all, it isn't what you do, but what you get caught at. Sam was just unlucky. He got caught, and—"

"Like me," I broke in harshly. "Like when you walked in on me and caught me with my arms around Marianne Donati."

"I wasn't going to mention that," he said quietly.

"I'm mentioning it," I snapped. "She was beautiful once—still is, if you can see it. But she needs someone to tell her, to make her feel that she is still beautiful, desirable. Sam Allgood made her feel that way, and maybe I did in a small way, and I don't know who else. Maybe you."

He nodded slowly. "Yes. Maybe me. Anyhow, I felt her beauty."

"All right," I said. "But her husband didn't. He forgot and he neglected her, and he found other pastures greener. So she hated

Pete Donati and she had a strong reason to kill him. Maybe she didn't really hate him—maybe it was just jealousy. But still she killed him."

"No," Hector said. "No, no. You're wrong. Bert Homer killed Pete Donati. The money and the checks were found on Homer, and—"

"Stop it, Hector," I broke in. "I know how you feel, but don't try to protect her. You're in love with her, aren't you?"

He stared at me steadily, and then he said in a level voice, "Of course. I've been in love with her for a long time—since the night that she talked to me in the bar, I guess. What's that got to do with it?"

"Nothing," I said wearily. "Not a thing. But you must know that people kill other people for many reasons. The three most common reasons are money, love, revenge. Mrs. Donati had all three motives. And Joyce Justin told me that she, Mrs. Donati, was the last person to see him alive. I thought she was lying when she told me, but now I know she was telling the truth. And Donati carried fifty thousand dollars' worth of life insurance, and Mrs. Donati is the beneficiary. Jeff Winters killed Sam Allgood because of jealousy and love for his wife, but jealousy is the brother of hate, and they both are the brothers of revenge. I'm going over to see Mrs. Donati now—and I imagine that Chief Swartz would be interested in hearing what she has to say. Would you care to come along?"

The room was quiet and the traffic in the street below sounded far away. I started for the door and repeated my invitation. "Coming along?"

Hector shook his head slowly. "No, no...." He turned away. "Poor Marianne ..."

"So you would?" I said.

He turned and gazed at me with puzzled eyes. "Would what?" he asked quietly.

"Let Marianne Donati take the rap for you."

His lips tightened. "What are you talking about?" he asked coldly.

"For a while I figured you were a square shooter who had gotten a bad break," I said, "but I was wrong. I just gave you a chance to confess to the killing of Pete Donati and Sam Allgood, but you didn't take it. I don't blame you for that. But when the chips were down, you were willing to let Marianne Donati take the blame—in spite of your professed love for her. You killed Donati and Allgood, and you almost got away with it."

He said harshly, "Jeff Winters has confessed to the murder of Allgood."

"Sure," I said. "Sure—to shield his wife, Lily. He's nuts about her, and he was sure she had killed Sam Allgood. He knew about their affair and he knew they had quarreled. And when I accused her, he was convinced that she had killed Sam, and he tried to protect her. Some men are like that, you know. But I realized that he was lying when I remembered that he said he took his wife's gun from his locker. That's where it was usually kept, but last night Sam Allgood put the gun in his own locker—remember? And after Chief Swartz said that Sam had died from a blow on the head, I knew that Sam Allgood hadn't walked to the spot where we found him. The spikes of his golf shoes were clean and shiny. If he had walked, there would have been some mud, or at least some wet grass, clinging to his shoes. It rained last night, you know—that's another reason I knew Jeff Winters was lying. And you slipped up just now when you said that Sam Allgood had a bullet in his heart. How did you know he was shot there? Nobody told you, and you weren't supposed to have seen him. But you knew how he died—because you killed him. Jeff Winters invented the whole confession—to keep his wife's name out of it. But you killed them both ... Feel like telling me about it?"

"You're telling it," he said stonily. "Go on."

"All right, Hector," I said. "I may be wrong in a few details, but I know you killed Pete Donati, because it was a professional job. Only a person with training in surgery could do it so completely. Both external jugular veins, the internal vein and the carotid artery. An amateur in a hurry would have botched it up—maybe hit one or two veins, but not the whole works.

"You're in love with Marianne Donati, and, as bookkeeper for the shop, you knew about the fifty-thousand-dollar insurance policy Pete Donati carried. Mrs. Donati was beautiful once, and she needed to be loved. You could supply the love, even if she was ugly, and share in the fifty grand besides. So you killed Donati and took the money from his safe to make it look like robbery. And then Bert Homer played right into your hands. Two nights ago, after I shot Homer, you planted the money and checks on him—while I was talking to Joyce Justin out in the alley. It was perfect, you thought—Donati's murder pinned on a dead man. But I should have tumbled right away when Doc Hendricks told me about the thorough job performed on Donati—I just remembered a little while ago what he had told me."

I turned quickly to the door, locked it and pocketed the key. I moved to the telephone. "I'm sorry as all hell, Hector, but I'm calling the cops."

He turned slowly to face me. "Is this a trick, Bennett? Or do you really think I killed those two men?"

"No trick," I said, "and you sure as hell killed them." I reached for the telephone.

He leaped for me, and there was a shining instrument in his hand. He came in fast, half stooping, and I started to grab for my gun, but I changed my mind. He was coming too fast. I lifted my foot and he ran straight into it. My heel caught him on the chin and he sprawled sideways to the floor. I jumped for him, grabbed his wrist and twisted a bright razor-edged surgeon's scalpel from his hand. He rolled over and crawled away from me. I let him go. He bumped blindly into a chair, and he pulled himself slowly to his feet. He turned to face me. His mouth was bloody where I had kicked him, and there was despair and hate and pain in his eyes.

"Damn you," he muttered. "Damn you to hell ... You knew ... all the time ..."

I had my .38 out now, and I held it in my hand, watching him. "You're wrong," I said wearily. "I was dumb as hell. It's like I told you—I didn't tumble until a little while ago." I paused, and then I said curiously, "You've got a gun in your pocket. Why didn't you use it just now?"

He gave me a sly smile. "The scalpel is silent—and more certain. But I thank you for reminding me of the gun. I may use it yet."

"All right," I said. "Go for it."

He shook his head. "You'd like that, wouldn't you, Bennett?"

"No," I said, "I wouldn't. I'd hate to kill you, Hector."

"I saved your life," he said raggedly. "Remember, Bennett?"

"I remember," I said sadly, "and I thank you."

"Listen, Bennett. Don't be an idealistic fool." His voice was hurried, desperate. "Pete Donati had no right to be Marianne's husband, and Sam Allgood was a cheap woman-chaser. The police think Horner killed Donati and that Winters killed Allgood. We can leave it like that. I'll make it worth your while."

"With Donati's money?" I sneered.

"Money is money," he said. "Donati deserved to die and so did Allgood. The world will never miss them. Maybe Marianne doesn't love me now, but she will, later on, when I have her all to myself—without Donati, and without men like Sam Allgood pursuing her. Donati and his sordid affairs—with a wife like Marianne!"

He paused, and his eyes held a hot, bright light. "Listen, Bennett, I'll tell you how it was and then you decide. I've wanted to kill Donati for a long time. That afternoon, after you had been there in the morning, I went to his office to have him sign some payroll vouchers. He was in an ugly mood, and he snarled at me as if I were a dog. I saw that the safe was open, and it came upon me suddenly—the resolve to do it then. In that moment I knew I was going to kill him." He paused, and added harshly, "Can you understand that, Bennett?"

"Maybe;" I said grimly, "but you picked a bad time. You knew that Donati had hired me; that I was snooping around."

"Of course I knew," he said impatiently, "but I didn't care. In that moment, I didn't care about anything—except that Donati should die. Nothing would have stopped me. I carry a small scalpel in a case in my pocket, like some men carry a pocket knife. I sprang for him, and I hit him on the head with the bronze ashtray, and I did it—with the scalpel. As you say, I performed a complete incision.

"With the insurance money I knew Marianne would get, and the money from the sale of the shop, I could take her away, to Mexico, or South America, and I could practice medicine and surgery again. I could make her the most beautiful woman in the world, like she once was. I could do it, I swear I could, with plastics, with what I have learned. I have kept abreast of the advances in surgery. And she would learn to love me. I'd make her love me."

He paused once more, and then went on fiercely, "Don't you see, Bennett? Let them blame it on Bert Horner—he was a gross, ignorant person. Let them convict Joyce Justin as an accomplice—a cheap, double-crossing woman, playing both Donati and Horner for what she could get out of them. What is it to you, Bennett? What do you care? Think what it will mean to Marianne and me—and to the people I will heal and make well again.... This has been my dream, my life, and you—"

"What about Winters?" I broke in. "Let him take the rap for a killing he didn't do?"

"To hell with Jeff Winters!" he almost shouted. "If he wants to go to the chair for a cheating wife, let him!" He paused, and then said in a quieter voice, "I killed Sam Allgood and I'm glad I killed him. I watched him at the club last night, after you left. He sneaked away from his wife and drove into town. I knew where he was going, because he was with Marianne Thursday night—he got into her car in front of the drugstore. I wanted to kill him then, but I decided to wait for a better opportunity. It came—after you told me about the farmer, Fassler, shooting at Allgood. Last night I followed him to Marianne's house and I waited outside. They were there a long time. I was suspicious and saw red." He paused and he began to tremble. There was sweat on his face. "I saw red Friday morning, too, when I caught you embracing Marianne at the shop. I should have killed you then."

"Why didn't you?"

"I've killed enough," he said in a tired voice. "And you weren't really a threat—not like Sam Allgood. You were leaving town but Sam lived here, and I could not allow anything to come between Marianne and me. All I want is Marianne, to go away with her, to make her beautiful again, to practice my profession. I killed Donati to make my dream come true, and I killed Allgood. You can't stop me now, Bennett. Nobody can stop me."

"So you followed Allgood last night to Marianne Donati's house, and you killed him there and took him out to the golf course?" I asked him.

"Yes," he said bleakly. "He was dead, and I took him out there."

I said, "And you wanted to make it appear that the farmer had shot Allgood?"

"That's right," he said in a tired voice. "I didn't plan it too well, and I made mistakes, but it might have worked out if it hadn't been for you." He made a hopeless gesture. "It doesn't matter now. Early this morning, just before dawn, as I crouched in the darkness by Marianne's apartment, I realized that I held a heavy wrench in my hand—a wrench I'd taken from my car. When Allgood came down at last, I wanted to hit him, to tear him. I leaped on him, and we struggled, and I struck him in the face with my fist. He went down, and in my rage I smashed the wrench against his head. He died very quickly. I was glad. I wanted him to die. Then I carried him to my car and took him to the country club. I got his keys from his pocket, entered the club and opened his locker. I changed his clothes and took Lily Winters' rifle from Sam's locker. I knew it was there, because last night I'd seen Allgood put it there after I'd taken it away from Lily. Then I slung Allgood over my shoulder and carried him out to the sixth tee, propped him against the shelter house and went down the fairway in the direction of Fassler's farm and waited for daylight. As soon as I could see clearly enough, I shot Allgood twice. Then I laid him on the tee and planted the props—ball, wooden tee, club. I replaced the rifle in the locker, took the keys back and put them in Allgood's pocket. Then I went home. The sun was just coming up. I slept very well."

He cocked an eyebrow at me, and gave me his crooked smile. "Does that satisfy that policeman's mind of yours?" He began to move slowly toward me, still smiling.

I leveled the gun at him. "Stand still, Hector. Don't make me shoot."

He kept coming. "Shoot," he whispered. "Damn you, shoot."

I was tired and frazzled and beat up, and sick of the whole business. I lowered the muzzle of the gun and pulled the trigger. Hector's body jerked as the bullet smashed into his leg just above the knee. But he kept coming.

"Higher, Bennett," he rasped. "Higher. Here." He tapped his chest. And still he moved toward me, dragging his wounded leg, his lean handsome face a twisted mask of pain.

"No," I said, and I backed up a little. "Dammit, stop."

He lunged for me awkwardly, his hands reaching for me like claws.

I stepped forward quickly, and swung the gun against the side of his head. He stumbled to his knees and raised a haggard, bloody face to me. "Shoot," he panted. "Quickly."

I felt a little sick. "No, Hector," I said.

"What is it to you?" he cried. "Kill me now—or let me go on with my dream ..."

I backed away from him and picked up the telephone. "Police Department," I said, and my voice sounded harsh and queer in my ears.

Hector Griffith sank to the floor, and his broken sobbing filled the room.

THE END

SLEEP, MY LOVE

Robert Martin

For JILL

CHAPTER ONE

I suppose that every bachelor has his favorite among his friends' wives. Kay Canfield was mine. For one thing, she was the prettiest woman I knew—tall and slender, but not too slender—with copper-colored hair and deep-blue eyes fringed with dark lashes. But it was more than looks; I had respected and liked her grave, quiet character since the days when she and Don Canfield and I had gone to high school together.

It wasn't quite dark on a Saturday night in September when I parked my car in the drive of the house Don Canfield had built in a grassy rolling section on the southern fringes of Cleveland. Lights shone in the big living room and as I crossed the grass to the terrace I could see Kay and Don standing by the fireplace. I moved to the screened door opening on a small reception hall and was about to press the bell button when I heard their voices—not the voices of a happy husband and wife talking together before their guests arrived, but the voices of a couple in bitter argument.

I turned away and moved silently and quickly back across the lawn toward my car, wondering what could possibly have come between those two good friends of mine. My work for the agency had kept me on the run in and out of town and I hadn't seen or heard from either of them for a couple of months, until Kay's invitation to this Saturday night party.

I suppose all married people have arguments, but hearing Don and Kay quarreling shocked me more than a little. I knew that Don had a violent temper when goaded too far, but he was usually quiet and easygoing. He and Kay had been my idea of the perfect happy couple. Don was a successful salesman for the Connors Electric Company, and Kay, after her marriage, had continued to design dresses for the city's largest and fanciest department store. They had a small daughter named Annie, also a combination housekeeper and nurse named Mrs. Mahoney, a Buick sedan, and a Ford convertible. I sometimes envied them a little.

When I reached my car I opened the door, slammed it loudly, and walked back to the house, whistling. They couldn't help hearing my approach, but as I passed the window I saw they hadn't moved from their positions by the fireplace.

"Hey!" I called through the screen door.

"Come in, Jim," Kay answered, but there was no warmth in her tone and that told me that the matter was serious.

I stepped into the hall, tossed my hat onto a table, and entered the living room. It was attractively furnished and decorated with Kay's unfailing taste and feeling for color. Autumn flowers brightened the mantel and the portable bar had been wheeled to a position in a far corner. Ash trays and cigarettes were placed at strategic spots on low tables near chairs and divans; the whole house had a neat, expectant, waiting-for-the-party look.

"Hi, folks," I said cheerfully.

They both looked at me without speaking. Kay was wearing a black linen dress which made a sharp and pleasing contrast to her milky skin. She smiled at me fleetingly and returned her gaze to Don. He was a former All-Ohio halfback, and he looked it; wide, heavy shoulders, long legs, and a round compact head. His eyes were blue like Kay's and his yellow hair was clipped short, the way he'd worn it all the years I'd known him. His jaw was set and there was an angry glint in his eyes.

"Jim," Don said, "you're just in time to join the big fight. Go ahead—pick your side."

"If I did," I said, "one of you would be outnumbered."

"Hell," Don said, "with three women in the house, I'm outnumbered anyhow." He tried to smile, but he didn't quite make it.

Kay said, with an attempt at lightness, "Nothing like dragging your friends into a family argument. Jim, you may as well know that the Canfields are feudin'."

Don moved over to the bar. "Drink?" he said to me over his shoulder.

"All right," I said, watching Kay.

Her lips smiled again, but there was no smile in her eyes; they were cloudy and troubled. Don moved away from the bar, handed me a glass, and said to Kay, "Would you like a highball, darling?" He put a little too much emphasis on the last word.

She shook her head, turned away, and began to rearrange the flowers on the mantel. Don cocked an eyebrow at me and said distinctly, "Sociable, isn't she?"

I said, "How're things out in the territory?"

"All right," he answered carelessly. "Been a little slow the last few weeks, but it'll pick up." He paused, gazed into his glass and added, "I'm going to get out of the selling end, Jim."

Kay turned away from the mantel. "Maybe," she said quietly.

I asked Don, "Is that what you want?"

"It's what we both want," Kay said, "but we aren't going to get it."

Ignoring her, Don said to me, "It's been hanging fire for a long time, Jim. Dale Everett, the general manager, is retiring the first of the month. It's the job I've been working for. I'm qualified and I've earned it, and Jesse Connors knows it. It will mean that I can stop sleeping in hotel rooms and stay at home with my family—at least, most of the time. Then Kay won't have any excuse for continuing this silly business of dress designing, and—"

"Stop it, Don," Kay said sharply. "My work isn't silly, and you know you won't get that job."

"I'm in line for it," he said stubbornly. "I worked in every department in the plant before I went on the road. I know production, cost, engineering, and personnel. I even worked in advertising, accounting, and research, and I know sales."

"Yes," Kay said, "but Roger Quinn will be the new general manager of the Connors Electric Company. Why shouldn't he? He's Jesse Connors's son-in-law, isn't he?"

"Of course he is," Don said hotly. "But Roger Quinn doesn't know a drill press from a boiler stack—and he can't get along with the workers. I've got nothing against Roger, but he can't handle that job—and Jesse knows it."

I thought about Roger Quinn. He would be at the party tonight. He and his wife, Helen, were regular members of the group which included Kay and Don Canfield and myself. Both Don and Roger had started work for the Connors Electric Company at the same time. Two years later Roger had married Helen Connors, the only child of Jesse L. Connors, owner and founder of the company. Roger's present title was a vague one—vice-president of something or other, maybe public relations. He was a handsome, gregarious man, attractive to women. It didn't matter to any of us that he'd married Helen Connors; it's just as easy to fall in love with a rich girl as a poor one, and he and Helen seemed to be reasonably happy—in spite of the rumors of Roger's extramarital adventures with women, ranging from a college professor's wife to a waitress from the Railroad Café. They had two children, a boy and a girl, and they lived a few blocks from Kay and Don in a big house that Jesse Connors had built for them.

"Don," Kay said, "let's face it."

He gazed at her bleakly, the flicker of anger still in his eyes. Then he rattled the ice in his glass, swung away abruptly, and strode to the bar.

"I'm sorry, Jim," Kay said. Her face was whiter than I'd ever seen it, and her blue eyes seemed almost black.

"All in the family," I said carelessly; and in a weak attempt to ease the tension I added, "How does Annie like nursery school?"

Her eyes were on Don and she ignored my question. "I can't stand it anymore," she said in a strained, tight voice. "I *won't* stand it."

The room was suddenly quiet. Don turned slowly away from the bar, a fresh drink in his hand. He looked at me and then at Kay. Their eyes met across the room and he moved over to her and touched her arm. "Let's stop this, honey," he said quietly. "We'll work it out."

She moved her arm slightly and he dropped his hand. The muscles along his jaw tightened, but still he tried to smile. "We're arguing over nothing," he said. Both he and Kay seemed to have forgotten that I was in the room.

Kay hugged her bare arms as if she were cold. "There's more," she said in a dead voice. "Don, I think you know there is more."

He stared at her blankly.

Kay looked directly at him. "Please don't pretend," she said coldly. "I would gladly give up my work for you. You know that. But I wish you had told me."

"Told you what, Kay?" Don's voice was deadly calm, but I saw a tiny flame of violence in his eyes, and I remembered, suddenly, a college football game when he'd tackled a player, a quarterback, with such viciousness that he'd broken the man's leg. Don's team had been losing, and on the play before the quarterback had gouged Don's eye under cover of a pileup.

"About the woman," Kay said wearily. "The one you see in Toledo every week. I wish you had told me about her."

Don went pale and he said in a ragged voice, "Kay, do you think—"

The doorbell rang.

Kay turned away and moved across the room to admit the first guests of the evening.

Not counting myself, there were fifteen people at the Canfields' on that Saturday night, seven couples and one girl, all of them associated in one way or another with the Connors Electric Company. In the flurry of arrivals and the ensuing small talk I lost track of Don, but

Kay was always near me, smiling, gay, and gracious. Around ten o'clock, after everyone had arrived, I carried my glass out to the terrace and took a deep breath of the cool night air.

A soft voice said, "Hi, Jim," and I turned to see Kay standing alone in the shadows at the far end of the terrace. I moved over to her. She raised her glass and said, "My first drink tonight. Happy days, Jim."

"Happy days."

We drank. Behind Kay I could see the party swirling slowly in the big living room and I could hear the laughter and the talk drifting out through the screened door.

"What about this woman in Toledo?" I asked.

"It's true," she said in a brittle voice. "He's been with her often—for a long time. I just found out yesterday, but I didn't mention it to him until tonight. He takes her to dinner, to nightclubs, dancing—" Her voice broke.

"Not Don," I said.

"Yes," she said. "Don, my husband. I have a photo of them, taken at a table in a nightclub—you know the kind of picture. The friend who sent it to me bought it from the girl who took it, and she wrote me a letter—" She turned and pressed her face against my shoulder. "Why, Jim?" she asked brokenly. "What have I done? He resents my work, but I've never neglected him because of it. He's gone all week—why shouldn't I keep on with it?"

I put an arm around her and I felt her trembling a little. "We're old friends," I said, "Don and I, and that includes you. What can I do to help?"

"Nothing. Nothing can help now."

"Let me check on it," I said. "That's what a detective is for—that's my business. Who is the woman?"

"I don't know—I don't want to know."

"Maybe Don can explain it. Maybe—"

"Stop it, Jim," she said sharply. "Stop trying to defend Don. My mind is made up. We—we haven't been happy for a long time, and this finishes it."

"Let me talk to him."

"No, no. He'll deny it, and I couldn't stand that—not on top of everything else, and it doesn't matter now."

Someone inside the house, a female, called, "Kay! Where are you, Kay?"

She moved to the door and I followed her inside the house.

Don was behind the bar and he reached for my empty glass. "Drink up, pal," he said, grinning at me, as if he hadn't a care in the world. He laughed and responded easily to the remarks and the banter of the people around him. Kay moved across the room, bright-eyed and smiling, and joined gaily in the conversation of a group of women seated before the television set. The program on the screen was a dull one, involving an energetic master of ceremonies and an interminable succession of incredibly mediocre vaudeville acts.

Don handed me a full glass. "There you are, Jim."

I started to speak to him, but he turned to a guest holding an empty glass. He was still smiling, but there was a hot, bright light in his eyes. I drifted through the room, speaking to people on the way. As I passed the group around the television, Kay did not look at me and I had a dismal feeling of bewilderment and sadness.

A girl was standing in a corner, talking to two women, and smiled at me. She was Rebecca Foster, Jesse Connors's secretary, and the only unmarried female at the party. Rebecca was almost six feet tall and built in proportion, everything to scale. Her skin held a ruddy outdoor look and her hair was brown with lighter sun streaks in it and it was pulled severely back from rather prominent cheekbones. She excelled in outdoor sports, I had heard, in everything from golf and tennis to swimming and softball. I had seen her at a number of semi-official gatherings and parties given by Don Canfield, Roger Quinn, and other Connors Electric associates, and as far as I knew she had no men friends—at least, she never brought any to the parties. She had always called me Mr. Bennett and I had observed that she never drank anything but Coke or ginger ale. Jesse Connors was of the democratic one-big-happy-family school of industrial relations and I suppose that Rebecca felt obliged to attend the parties to which she was invited, but I sometimes suspected that they bored her.

I nodded to her, smiled, and moved into the room beyond, a combination dining room and library. Here Roger Quinn was entertaining a small group of men with a story about a traveling salesman and a female midget. Roger was a big man, beginning to get fat, with a fleshy, handsome face and deeply cleft chin below full lips. Black brows met in an almost straight line over his gray eyes. As always, he was immaculately dressed, and he held a glass in one hand, a cigarette in the other. It was an English cigarette, gilt-tipped, with the brand name of Lord Nelson, the kind he always smoked. Maybe he even preferred them to the common American brands, for all I knew.

I decided I'd heard the midget story and I moved to a corner where two men were seated in deep chairs. One of the men was a young attorney named Owen Harris who, in addition to conducting a private law practice, was legal counsel for Connors Electric. The other man was Ralph Bixby, purchasing agent for the company.

"How about some golf in the morning, Jim?" Harris asked.

"All right," I said absently. But I wasn't thinking of golf. I was thinking about Kay and Don Canfield.

The three of us talked a little, and then excited exclamations from the group around Roger Quinn caused us to turn our heads. Men were shaking Roger's hand. Bixby, Harris, and I went over to the group. One of the men was reading a paper and Bixby peered over his shoulder. Then Bixby stepped forward and grasped Roger's hand.

"Congratulations, Roger," Bixby said sincerely. "I'm proud of you."

Somebody handed me the paper. It bore a mimeographed message on a Connors Electric Company letterhead. Owen Harris and I read it together.

To All Departments, Branches, and Distributors:
I am pleased to announce that Mr. Roger V. Quinn has been appointed to the position of General Manager of this company and on October 1st will assume the duties of Mr. Dale Everett, who is retiring after many years of loyal service.

J. L. Connors
President

Owen Harris said in a low voice, "That should have been Don's job—but I guess blood is thicker than ability."

I looked up at Roger Quinn. He was smiling modestly and saying, "Thanks, fellows. It's a real break for me. But please don't spread it around yet. J. L. doesn't want it released until Monday."

I became aware of someone standing at my side. I turned and saw Don Canfield. He was peering at the paper in my hand. Silently I handed it to him, and he read it with a stony expression. The room went quiet. When Don looked up, his face was gray. He held out a hand to Roger. "Congratulations," he said quietly.

Roger seemed a little embarrassed as he took Don's hand. "Thanks, Don," he said hesitantly. "I—I guess I won't have to worry as long as the company has salesmen like you."

Don turned and left the room.

Somebody said, "Well, that calls for a drink."

I entered the big living room. Don wasn't there. The television set had mercifully been turned off, and Kay was talking to a group of women at a bridge table. She gave me an inquiring look as I went past. I grinned at her and moved to the door. Rebecca Foster was standing alone by the mantel, leafing the pages of a *Life* magazine. As I went out, Ralph Bixby came into the room and I heard him say excitedly, "Did you hear the news about Roger, girls?"

I found Don standing in the shadows at the far end of the terrace.

"Big night for me, huh, Jim?" he said.

"I'm sorry about the job," I said.

"To hell with it. It doesn't matter now."

"What about this woman business, Don?"

"Do you believe it?"

"I don't know. I'm asking you."

"Did Kay tell you to ask me?"

"No. She asked me not to." I hesitated, and then I said, "We've been friends for a long time, Don. If what Kay said is true, you can tell me. We're grown men. Those things happen."

"It doesn't matter whether it's true or not," he said bitterly. "What matters to me is that Kay believes it, that she doesn't trust me."

"It's true, then?"

"About my seeing a woman in Toledo? Of course it's true. I see her almost every week. She's Isabel Rawlings, a plenty shrewd career woman and a purchasing agent for Lawson-Ware and Company. Isabel likes to do business over cocktails and steaks, and that's all it is—business. Hell, half the time her husband comes along. Isabel likes to be entertained and I entertain her, and that's why all of the washing machines sold under the Lawson-Ware label are made by Connors Electric. It's one of the biggest accounts the company has, and it's my job to see that we keep it."

Lawson-Ware, as everyone knew, was the largest mail-order house in the world. I said, "Then, for God's sake, tell Kay that."

"Why?" he snapped. "She's already condemned me, without giving me a chance to explain. She listens to what some snooping busybody tells her, and she believes that I'm cheating on her. Listen, Jim, if I wanted to cheat, I've had plenty of chances, believe me. But I haven't." He lit a cigarette with hands that trembled. "Maybe I should have," he added bitterly.

"I'll tell her, then," I said.

He grasped my arm. I felt the sudden fierce strength in his fingers and I saw the flame in his eyes. "No," he said from between his teeth. "Damn you, Jim, stay out of it."

"I want to help, Don."

He released my arm. "Forget it," he said wearily. "The damage is done. If she believes that of me—" He turned away and stared out over the lawn.

I stepped down off the terrace. "Good night, Don."

"So long, Jim. I'll be seeing you."

"Sure."

I walked across the lawn, got into my car, and drove away. But I didn't go straight home. I stopped at the office and looked in a Toledo classified directory. *Rawlings, Isabel R.*, was indeed a purchasing agent for Lawson-Ware and Company.

I reached for the telephone, intending to call Kay, but I paused, thinking wryly that perhaps I'd already overstepped my doubtful privilege to meddle in my friends' affairs. Then I decided to call Kay anyhow.

She answered, and I was glad it wasn't Don. "Kay, I'm sorry to have left without saying good night or thanks for the party."

"I don't blame you, Jim. I'm afraid it's a boring party."

"Listen, Kay, I talked to Don, and—"

"But I told you not to," she said quickly.

"I know," I said, and I told her about Isabel Rawlings. When I had finished, Kay said coolly, "That's his story."

"I'm sure it's true, Kay."

"Why didn't he tell me then?"

"It meant nothing to him. It was just business, and—"

"Never mind, Jim. Please just never mind."

For the first time in all the years I'd known Kay I felt a stirring of anger against her, and against Don, too. On the surface it looked like a pure case of stubbornness, and then I thought, with a small shock, that maybe I didn't know the whole story, either Kay's or Don's, and I knew that I'd meddled far too much. But I hated it, all of it. It happened every day, but it shouldn't have happened to Kay and Don.

"Good night, Kay."

"Good night," she said shortly. The click of her phone was loud in my ear.

Monday morning Kay telephoned me at my office.

"Jim, it's over," she said. She sounded as if she had been crying. "He left Saturday night, right after the party. We—we had a terrible row—it was awful. I have never seen Don so—so violent. At one time I was afraid he would—" She paused, her voice breaking.

I gripped the phone tighter. "Would what, Kay?"

"N-Never mind. It's over now—I thought you'd want to know."

"I'm sorry." It was all I could think of to say.

"Please don't be." She had gained control of her voice and it sounded brittle and cold, not like Kay's voice at all. "We settled everything yesterday. The divorce is all arranged and Owen Harris will handle it." She paused, and then said, "There's something else, Jim. The store wants me to go to Paris—they just told me this morning. I'm leaving next week. Mrs. Mahoney will stay with Annie and everything will be fine."

"Congratulations. Will I see you before you leave?"

"I'm afraid not, Jim. I'll be busy—"

"Well, good luck, and all that."

"Goodbye, Jim."

She hung up and suddenly the world seemed a bleak and lonely place.

During the following weeks I saw Don a few times. He was living alone in an apartment on the west side and I knew that he was drinking too much, something that Don had never done before, and he had taken to hanging around some rather frowzy nightclubs on the north side. One night, when I was tailing a suspected embezzler for an uptown loan company, I saw Don and Roger Quinn at a table in a St. Clair Street bar. There were two girls with them and all four were a little drunk. They didn't see me. I thought Roger and Don were a strange alliance, particularly from Don's viewpoint. Knowing Roger's proclivities, I wondered if he had found Don a convenient alibi for his escapades, but I felt nothing but sadness for Don's part in it.

Kay returned from Paris, and once, during the first week in December, I had lunch with her. She talked of her work with a kind of shining-eyed excitement. She was being sent back to Paris, she said, and there was a chance that she would get the job of head designer for the store. The Kay Canfield label in a dress was beginning to be talked about and was already being noticed by the top people in the world of fabrics, dress models, and high fashion. She didn't ask about Don, and I didn't mention him.

The holidays came and went. In March, at a Saturday night poker party at Roger Quinn's house, I heard about Don's marriage. Roger told it with a just-between-us-men manner. "I introduced Don to this little babe," he said confidingly. "I knew she was on the make, but I didn't think she'd hook Don. But she gets him liquored up and then talks him into driving down to Kentucky for a quick marriage. She's a little French gal, a dancer, and, boy, what a shape! Her name is Louette, and—"

On a Friday night a week later, in a restaurant where I sometimes had dinner, I encountered Don and his bride. They were sitting at the bar, drinking Martinis and they were both quite drunk.

Roger Quinn had been right. The girl was small and slim and perfectly proportioned, with a dancer's curved calves and slim ankles. I could see that much as she perched on the high bar stool. Don turned his head and saw me. "My God," he said. "Jim! Good old Jim."

He got down from the stool and shook my hand. He had taken on weight and the flesh beneath his eyes was puffy. "Meet Louette, Jim," he said, and he added with what I thought was a trace of mockery, "My wife."

She turned away from looking at herself in the mirror behind the bar, and I saw that she was pretty in a dark, smoldering way. She had sleek black hair pulled back over small flat ears and gathered in a tight bun at the of back of her head. Her eyes were big and brown, almost he too big for her small pointed face, and her plump red mouth held a velvety, petulant look. She was wearing a tight black dress with a plunging neckline and gathered at the waist by a wide patent leather belt with a huge silver buckle. Louette, I thought, was a sharp contrast to Kay's fair, blue-eyed Nordic beauty.

I smiled at her. "Glad to know you, Louette."

"Call me Lou," she said. "Please call me Lou. I hate the name Louette." Her voice held the whisper of an accent and it was surprisingly husky. She gazed at me thoughtfully, coolly, appraisingly, and a little smile played around her mouth. "What is the name, please?"

"Jim," I said. "Jim Bennett."

She placed a cigarette between her lips, struck a match, and attempted to connect the flame with the cigarette.

But the match wavered in a slow circle.

Don laughed, steadied her hand, and said to me, "Have a drink,

Jim."

I sat on a stool and ordered a Martini. Don kept up a steady chatter and we talked across Louette, who sat sullenly smoking. Once our gaze met in the mirror and she stared at me steadily, almost insolently, until I looked away.

"How's the old crowd, Jim?" Don asked. "How's the old Saturday night crowd?"

"Just the same," I said.

"I see Roger Quinn now and then," he said. "For a while I saw quite a lot of old Roger, the son of a bitch."

"Now, now," I said.

"Old Roger got the job I should have had, but we're still buddies. He introduced me to Lou, you know."

"We miss you, Don," I said, changing the subject.

"Hell with the old crowd. Hell with all of 'em. Not you, though." He finished his cocktail in one long swallow.

Louette said abruptly, "I want to go home, Don."

He sighed and got off the stool. "All right. Anything you say. Come and see us, Jim."

"Sure."

They went out. Louette didn't say goodbye or look at me.

A week later Don called and invited me to dinner at his apartment. It was a dismal evening, and I felt sorry for Don. He was trapped and miserable and his jovial attempts to make everything seem all right were pitiful. He drank too much, while Louette sat sullenly, talking very little.

Once, when she was out of the room, Don said, "I get to see Annie on Sundays."

"Good," I said.

"Have you seen Kay?" He didn't look at me.

"Not lately. She's away a lot."

"I know," he said. "It's what she wanted." He looked at me then, and I saw the pain in his eyes. "Her damned work—that started it all."

I didn't say anything.

"What am I going to do, Jim?" His voice was pleading. I didn't have an answer for him and I was glad that Louette came back at that moment.

Around eleven o'clock, when I decided that I'd stayed long enough to leave politely, Don said suddenly, "Roger Quinn has been coming to see us— Did I tell you that I met Louette through Roger?"

"Yes. Roger told me and you told me."

"My buddy," Don said bitterly.

Louette broke a long silence by saying, "I think Mr. Quinn is nice."

Don looked at her, and the contempt and distaste were naked in his eyes. "Nice like a snake," he said softly. "He may be my boss, but I don't want him coming here."

Louette shrugged her slim shoulders, her red mouth sullen.

I stood up.

"Aw, don't go, Jim," Don protested. "Have another drink."

"No, thanks. Got a heavy day tomorrow." I looked at Louette. "Thanks for the dinner."

She smiled faintly.

In the hall, after I'd closed the door, I heard their sudden voices, shrill and angry. I moved away quickly, not wanting to hear their bickering, not wanting to think of the contrast between the old happy evenings with Kay and Don before their quarrel and the evening I'd just spent. And then, from out of nowhere, I remembered what Kay had told me of that last quarrel when Don's violence had frightened her. He hadn't struck Kay then or harmed her, I was certain, because he loved her. But I knew his temper and I grimly hoped that Louette, who had tricked him into marriage, would be smart enough not to push him too far.

CHAPTER TWO

In May, I went to Chicago to do a delicate and special tax investigation job for the Treasury Department, and after that I spent a week in Cincinnati, returning on a Friday night and spending all day Saturday at the office, cleaning up an accumulation of reports and desk work, a dreary job. At noon on Sunday I made myself some breakfast, read the papers, napped a little. At four o'clock I became bored and got the agency Ford from the garage behind my apartment building. It was a warm and golden day, with the leaves almost a full green and the sky a clear blue.

I drove along the lake boulevard for a while, and at 105th Street swung south across town and into the rolling hills and valleys on the southern edge of the city. I passed the house where Roger and

Helen Quinn lived, the house that Jesse Connors had built for them, and then I came to the house which Don Canfield had built and where Kay lived with little Annie and Mrs. Mahoney. It looked quiet and deserted in the afternoon sun and the shadows were dark and cool across the terrace. A child's red wagon stood on the walk, and I had a sudden impulse to stop, but I drove on. I hadn't seen Kay in a long time, but even if she were at home I decided that I wasn't in the mood to answer her inevitable questions about Don and his new wife—Louette, of the smoldering eyes and the sullen red mouth.

At five o'clock I found myself on the lake highway west of town and approaching the Lake Shore Amusement Park, a place where I'd spent many happy hours during my high school days. I turned into the drive leading to the park, feeling a sense of nostalgia, a happy-sad remembrance of days gone by. I parked the Ford outside the gate and strolled along the winding cement walks, watching the kids and the people and enjoying for the first time in years the sight and the sound and the smell of the place. It was early in the season, but many of the concession stands were open and most of the amusement rides were operating. I came to the merry-go-round and sat down on a nearby bench. As always, the kids on the painted wooden animals were having a wonderful time.

A little blond girl with blue eyes and flying pigtails was riding a green horse with golden eyes. A fat yellow pig was chasing her and before her a red rooster undulated sedately. A chubby boy was riding the rooster and waving a plastic pistol.

"Bang!" yelled the chubby boy above the strident music. "Bang! Bang!" He was aiming at a skinny kid astride a zebra.

With a small start of surprise, I recognized the little girl with the pigtails. It was Annie Canfield. I looked about and saw Don sitting on a bench a few yards away. He was gazing thoughtfully at a paper cup in his hand. Beside him on the bench was a small wicker basket with a white napkin folded over it. He was wearing a gray tweed jacket and gray flannel slacks, and I noticed for the first time that his short yellow hair was the exact color of the little girl's, and that his eyes held the same clear blue. I got up and walked over to him.

He turned his head and his eyes lit up. "Jim!"

We shook hands and I nodded at Annie. "She's grown. What is she now—four?"

He nodded. "Last month." He looked tired and the dying sun made deep shadows beneath his eyes. As I sat down on the bench beside him, he said, "This is a queer place for you to be on a Sunday afternoon. Where've you been? I called your office a couple of times, but the girl said you were out of town."

"I just got back from Cincinnati. Before that it was Chicago." I nodded at the kids on the wooden animals. "I haven't been this close to a merry-go-round in years."

"They call them carousels in France," Don said.

I remembered then that his wife was French, and I said, "How's Louette?"

"She's left me," he said bluntly. "First Kay, now Lou. I'm sure hell with the women."

I gazed out over the park. People were all around us, enjoying the last of the golden May day, laughing and talking and having fun. In a nearby field a noisy softball game was in progress, and beyond a line of trees I saw the curving skeleton frame of a roller-coaster and heard the freight train roar of the cars and the delighted screams of the passengers. There was the smell of hot popcorn and frying hamburgers. A few feet away a white-whiskered old man was inserting a penny in a scale contraption bearing the inscription, *Your Weight—Your Fortune—The Time—One Cent*. A boy and girl strolled past, holding hands and licking at ice-cream cones.

"I'm sorry, Don," I said, but I had no sense of sorrow, and I had the feeling that Don hadn't, either.

"Don't be, Jim," he said. "I asked for it. It was a crazy mistake in the first place, you know that. I suppose Roger told you that—"

"Yes, he told me," I broke in. "She kind of tricked you into a wedding, didn't she?"

"Don't blame Lou," he said. "It was as much my fault as hers. And she's all right—nice in a lot of ways. At first I tried to make a go of it, but we just didn't get along. I talked divorce a couple of times, but she just laughed and said she wouldn't give me one." He gazed down at the cup in his hand and added bitterly, "But I can damn well divorce her now."

"What happened?"

He shrugged. "The usual thing. I caught her with a man."

"When?"

"A little before noon yesterday. A deal in Toledo held me up and I telephoned Lou Friday night that I wouldn't be home until late Saturday. But I finished up sooner than I'd expected and came home. She was with a man named Paul Reynard, a skinny little Frenchman with greased hair—one of her nightclub pals. They were both pretty drunk on my bourbon, and the Frenchman got nasty. I went wild. I slapped him around a little and booted him the hell out. Then I had a fracas with Lou and she left. I let her go." He took a drink from the paper cup.

I wasn't really surprised, and I didn't say anything. What had he expected? From the first Louette had looked to me like trouble. But I remembered Don's temper in moments of extreme emotion, and I felt a faint uneasiness. I tried to remember how long after his divorce from Kay he'd married Louette. Four months? Six, maybe? Too soon, anyhow. Rebound was the word. Rebound and heartache and loneliness, and much whisky and laughter and a soft little body—a pair of wise, smoldering eyes and a velvet, sullen mouth.

The merry-go-round stopped. Annie slid off the green horse and came running up to us. "More tickets, Daddy," she cried, holding out her hand confidently. "I gave the man my red fortune tickets, but he said he needed yellow tickets for the merry-go-round." She looked at me with wide friendly eyes. "Hello, man."

"Hi, Annie," I said.

She gazed at her father in surprise. "He knows my name, Daddy. Why?"

Don said gently, "He's a relic of happier days, Annie. You've just forgotten him." He reached into his shirt pocket and handed her two small pieces of cardboard. "Here are tickets for two more rides. Then we'll have our picnic and I must take you home."

Her blue eyes clouded. "Why, Daddy? Is Sunday over? Is next Sunday a long time away?"

"Not long, honey. You'd better grab that green horse before some other kid gets him."

She ran back to the merry-go-round, her pigtails flying, and climbed back on the green horse. A young fellow in a white T-shirt took her ticket, grinned at her, tore the ticket in two, and then walked around the perimeter of the platform, collecting tickets from other juvenile passengers. Then he jumped to the space in the center and pulled a lever beside a gasoline engine. The merry-go-round began to revolve, and he dropped the torn yellow tickets into a big metal can beside the engine.

Don said, "Lou has her faults, but I didn't think she'd cheat on me. That damned Reynard has probably been hanging around for a long time." He reached into the basket and brought out a quart Thermos bottle and unscrewed the cap. "How about a drink, Jim?"

I grinned at him. "Lemonade?"

"Dry Martini." He filled a paper cup and handed it to me.

I took a sip. It was a Martini, all right, very cold and very dry. We drank silently, and then I said, "What are you going to do?"

"Divorce her," he said shortly. "Get rid of her—if I can." He stared at his cup with brooding eyes. Then he turned to me with a crooked smile. "To hell with it, Jim. I shouldn't be boring you with my domestic problems." He lifted the Thermos. "Drink up."

We talked about his work as a salesman for Connors Electric and he asked about Owen Harris and Ralph Bixby and other members of the Saturday night crowd. I told him about my jobs in Chicago and Cincinnati, and both of us very carefully avoided mention of Kay or of the general manager's job which Jesse Connors had given to Roger Quinn. Presently the shadows grew long on the grass and the air turned cool. Annie's two merry-go-round rides stretched into five, and Don stood up and called to her. As he lifted the basket from the bench he said, "Why don't you stay and eat with us, Jim? We have plenty."

The Martinis had made me mellow and agreeable and I wasn't particularly anxious to return to my lonely apartment. "Thanks," I said. "I'd like to."

The three of us walked across the park to a comparatively secluded table in a grove of trees. On the way I bought Annie a bottle of orange soda. Don told me that a delicatessen had packed the lunch for him and, as he had said, there was plenty. When we had finished eating I walked with them to Don's car.

Annie climbed into the front seat and said to me, "Goodbye, Uncle Jim."

Don winked at me. "You got promoted fast."

I said, "Thanks for the drinks and the lunch."

"Glad to have you—Uncle Jim." He smiled at me. "Look, you're not going anywhere; how about coming along with me while I take Annie home, and then coming up to my place? I've got some bourbon—anyhow, I *had* some bourbon. Want to take a chance?" Behind his smile I saw the pleading look in his eyes.

"All right," I said. "I'll follow in my car."

"Good."

Forty-five minutes later I stopped behind Don's car in the drive of the house where he'd once lived with Kay. An elderly pleasant-faced woman rose from a chair on the terrace and stood smiling. Don carried Annie over to her, said, "Home again, Mrs. Mahoney," and kissed the little girl before he put her down.

Annie stood gazing up at him, trying hard not to cry. He spoke briefly to the woman, patted Annie's cheek, turned abruptly, and came back to his car. I backed out and followed him to his apartment. Evening traffic was heavy and it took us maybe a half hour. We parked side by side in a court at the rear, and as we walked back to the front entrance, Don said, "Go on—say it. You always liked Kay and you think I was nuts for letting her divorce me, don't you?"

"Yes," I said.

"So do I," Don said, "and to hell with you. Let's get that bourbon."

I followed him up the stairs to the second floor and down the hall to his apartment. The carpeted hall was muffled with a dusky Sunday evening quiet. From somewhere a radio or TV was playing softly and there was the smell of frying steak. Above us a woman laughed gaily, a door slammed, and then there was quiet again, with only the faraway traffic sounds coming up to us. I stood beside Don as he unlocked a door upon which was a small brassbound card printed with the words, *3C—Mr. and Mrs. Donald R. Canfield.*

He swung the door open and we stepped inside.

Bright light hit my eyes. Every bulb in the place was blazing. Louette Canfield was on a cream-colored divan; not sitting on it or lying down—she looked as if she'd been thrown on it. One delicately curved nylon-clad leg was flung over the edge. The other leg was twisted beneath her. One arm hung down, the limp fingers touching the carpet. The other arm was bent awkwardly behind her. Her head was flung back over the low armrest, her long black hair hanging motionless almost to the floor. The wide V of the neckline of her black dress slanted down from her white shoulders away from the taut line of her throat and the sharp contour of the tilted jaw.

In the point of the V of the dress, and a little to the left, toward the heart which beat no more, protruded the handle of a knife. It was a black handle, smooth and polished, with bright brass screws flush with the wood. Just the handle protruded, none of the blade. The blade was buried in the chest cavity, in flesh and tissue and tendons. There wasn't a lot of blood, just the little that had escaped and seeped up and out of the body and around the hilt of the knife, and had dripped thinly and gently to the divan and the rug below.

CHAPTER THREE

The divan reached across the far wall, with shaded lamps on small tables at either end casting a bright rosy glow over the still body. Don was slightly ahead of me and to my left. I stepped forward and grasped his arm. He shook off my hand and took a slow step toward the divan. I swung him around until he faced me.

"Jim—" he said.

"Shut up!" I said sharply and loudly. I went to the divan.

The blood wasn't fresh—she'd been dead for some hours. I didn't touch her, but I leaned over and peered into her back-flung face. The eyes had been pretty once, big and brown and liquid; they were still pretty, except for the vacant, faintly amused expression in them.

I turned to face Don. He was gazing at the divan, his face expressionless. I watched him a moment, and then I left him standing there and made a quick tour of the apartment—bedroom, kitchen, and bath. There were unwashed dishes in the sink and the whole place was not very neat or clean. Louette had apparently not cared for housework. The place was cozy and compact, ideal for two people without children, plenty big enough for a salesman and a wife who was alone, or presumably alone, for five days of each week. Plenty big enough for a couple without love and who only wanted a place to eat and sleep, a place to come to when the parties were over and the bars were closed.

I went back to the living room.

Don was standing where I'd left him. He had lit a cigarette and as he inhaled he watched me silently. Behind me the telephone jangled. Don's eyes widened and I almost jumped. I turned, saw the phone on a table in a corner. I moved over to it, picked it up. "Yes?" I said.

A woman said, "Mr. Canfield, this is Mrs. Mahoney. I'm sorry to bother you, but Annie left her Teddy bear in your car." She laughed. "I guess you know what a tragedy that is—she won't go to sleep without it. Would it be too much trouble for you to send it over—in a taxi, perhaps?"

"I'll see that she gets it," I said.

"Thank you, Mr. Canfield." She hung up.

I cradled the phone, but kept my hand on it, and I said to Don, "Annie forgot her Teddy bear." The words sounded fantastic in that quiet room with Don and the dead body of his wife.

He stared at me stupidly. "What?"

"Don't worry about it," I said. My gaze caught a tiny bright gleam of something in an ashtray on the telephone table. I picked up the stub of a cigarette with a gilt tip. I held it up to the light and read the brand name: *Lord Nelson*. An English cigarette. Something stirred in my memory, and I dropped the stub back into the ash tray onto a pile of other stubs, most of them stained with lipstick.

I said to Don, "Is there anything you want to tell me before I call the police?"

"Police?"

"Murder," I said, gently.

He shook his head slowly. "I—I guess not."

I said, "She probably died sometime this afternoon—I would guess around three o'clock. The police lab boys will hit it pretty close. Were you with Annie all afternoon?"

He nodded. There was a little color in his face now, but his hand shook as he took the cigarette from his mouth. "Yes. I picked her up right after lunch, around one o'clock, and was with her from then on." In spite of the hand trembling his voice was steady.

"At the park?"

He nodded again, drawing on his cigarette.

"Can you prove it?"

"Only by Annie—and you. Listen, Jim—"

"I'm no alibi," I said. "It was after five o'clock when I saw you by the merry-go-round."

He averted his eyes. "I—I see," he said in a low voice. "The police will want to know—"

"Yes. They'll ask a lot of questions." I paused, and then I suggested, "Would you like to rehearse a few of them with me first?"

"No. My God, Jim, I didn't—"

"Is there anything you haven't told me?"

"No, no." His gaze roved to the divan and skittered away. "What are you getting at, Jim?"

"Nothing. It would make things simpler if I could say that I met you at the park at, say, three o'clock this afternoon, but I can't."

"I don't suppose you can," he said hopelessly. "But I was there. I—I don't know anything about—" He gestured toward the divan without looking at it. "To walk in on— Who—"

I lifted the phone and called Detective Sergeant Dennis Rockingham of the homicide division.

CHAPTER FOUR

Flash bulbs popped, busy men swarmed over the apartment, the fingerprint boys went to work, the medical examiner peered and probed and tentatively fixed the time of Louette Canfield's death at approximately three o'clock in the afternoon, subject to laboratory confirmation. Mentally, I patted myself on the back for guessing it so closely. The knife turned out to be one from the kitchen of the apartment, and Don Canfield identified it.

Sergeant Rockingham, in his quiet way, asked a couple of dozen questions. He was a tall, lean, freckle-faced man with a carefully trimmed red mustache. Over the years we had become fairly good friends, but I knew him well enough not to try any tricks on him. I answered his questions truthfully, and I assumed that Don did, too. At least, his story checked in every detail with the one he'd told me; he had come home unexpectedly a little before noon the day before, found a man named Paul Reynard with his wife. They both had been drinking. He had struck Reynard several times and forced him to leave. Then, naturally, he had quarreled with his wife. He had not struck her nor touched her at all. His wife left, and she hadn't returned while he was in the apartment. Yes, she had her own key. Today, Sunday, he had gone to his ex-wife's house at one o'clock in the afternoon to pick up his daughter Annie, and had taken her to the Lake Shore Amusement Park. He had remained there until a little after seven o'clock. He had met me shortly after five o'clock. We had taken his daughter home, come to his apartment together, and had found his wife dead on the divan.

Rockingham listened gravely and politely, and presently, after his men had carried Louette out, he asked Don not to leave town for a few days. Then he left. I was a little surprised; he had taken the whole thing too casually. He had learned, of course, that Don and I were friends. I thought, on the whole, that Don had behaved very well. During Rockingham's questioning his voice had been steady and strong, his answers quick and positive. Now, when we were alone, he said, "How about a drink, Jim?"

"Not now. I have an errand to do. I'm going to return Annie's Teddy bear."

He sighed and pulled a hand down over his face. "Come back, Jim," he said. "Stay with me tonight."

"All right."

I hated to leave him there alone, but a Teddy bear is an important animal to a four-year-old, and I wanted to deliver it in person. I got it from Don's car and as I drove out to the street I saw one of Rockingham's men reading a newspaper under a streetlight on the opposite corner. His name was Riggio. I waved to him as I drove by, but he pretended not to see me. I knew then for certain, in spite of Rockingham's polite and casual manner, that he was taking no chances with Don Canfield.

Twenty minutes later I parked once more in the drive of the house where Kay Canfield lived. Carrying Annie's Teddy bear, a bedraggled object with one glass eye and a torn ear, I went up to the terrace in the early-evening darkness and pressed the bell button. The elderly woman appeared behind the screen. When she saw what I had under my arm, she smiled and opened the screen door. "Mr. Canfield asked me to drop it off," I said. "I hope it's not too far past Annie's bedtime."

A tall, slender figure appeared in the hall and a familiar voice exclaimed, "Jim Bennett! Where did you come from?"

Mrs. Mahoney moved aside, and I stepped into the hall. Kay grasped my hand in both of hers. "It's nice to see you, Jim. How have you been?" She hadn't changed much since I'd last seen her. A little of the warmth had left her blue eyes, maybe, and there were tiny, almost invisible, lines at the corners of her full red mouth, but she was still the prettiest woman I knew.

"Hello," I said.

She linked her arm in mine and led me into the familiar living room. "I've missed you, Jim, and I've been saving a bottle of Scotch just for you. How about a tall one with ice and plain water?"

"Kay," I said. "Listen—"

She turned slowly to gaze at me with puzzled eyes.

In that instant Annie came into the room. She was wearing blue pajamas covered with prints of pink rabbits. "Did you bring my Teddy bear, Uncle Jim?" she asked, rubbing her eyes sleepily.

Kay glanced at me with an amused smile. "'Uncle?' When did this happen?"

"I met Don in the park this afternoon," I said, "and I've been with him ever since. Kay, I have something to tell you—"

Annie jumped about and said excitedly, "We had lots of fun, Mommie. Daddy took me to the zoo in the park, and we saw the real live bears and the funny little monkeys, and Daddy let me stay in his car all by myself, and I played his car radio and went to sleep and Daddy waked me up. Wasn't that funny, Mommie?"

A cold feeling crawled slowly up my spine. "Annie," I said, "when did you stay in your daddy's car all by yourself?"

She looked up at me with big eyes. "Why, when Daddy went to his house. He said I was a big girl and could wait in his car and play the radio. I wasn't scared. And then Daddy came out, and I was asleep, and he waked me up and we went to the park and I rided the green horsie five-teen times." She turned to her mother and clapped her small hands. "And, Mommie, Uncle Jim got me some orange pop, and we had cookies and 'tato chips. Is next Sunday a long time away?"

"No, dear," Kay said. "Not very long."

Mrs. Mahoney handed the Teddy bear to Annie. "You can tell your Mommie about the picnic tomorrow." She led Annie out of the room.

Kay said quietly, "Sit down, Jim. What's wrong?"

I sat down and lit a cigarette. "It doesn't really concern you, but I wanted to tell you before you saw it in the morning papers. Don's wife is dead. She was murdered."

Her face paled and she stared at me silently for maybe ten seconds. Then she took a cigarette from a silver box on a low table and rolled it gently between her long slender fingers. "Yes?" she said. "Tell me about it."

I told her. When I had finished, she flicked flame from a silver lighter with a steady hand. "How's Don?" she asked coolly. "How's he taking it?"

"It was a shock to him at first. Me, too. But he was better when I left him."

"Jim," she said evenly, "Don should never have married her. She tricked him, trapped him. I blame myself for that."

I agreed with her. But the divorce hadn't been all her stubbornness; it had been Don's, too. They both were to blame, I thought, and now there was hell to pay.

She gazed thoughtfully at the end of her cigarette. "Do they have any idea who—"

"The police are looking for this Paul Reynard." I picked up my hat and moved toward the hall. "I'll take a rain check on the drink, Kay. Don's waiting for me. I'm staying with him tonight."

She followed me into the dark hall. "Come back, Jim. I'll want to know about everything." She hesitated, and then said, "Call me tomorrow—at the store."

"Still designing dresses?" I asked. "Those nine ninety-eight jobs which sell for a hundred dollars just because they have the Kay Canfield label in them?" I smiled at her.

"I'm the head designer now," she said quietly. "The store is going to spend a lot of money this year, advertising Kay Canfield originals."

"The top," I said. "Congratulations. Where do you go from there?"

She averted her eyes. "I—I don't know. It's what I've wanted since I was in the fourth grade, what I've lived for. I couldn't make Don understand. But now—"

"You've got the rainbow," I said, "and now you're wondering if the price tag was too high?"

"Maybe," she said. "But it wasn't only my work. You know that."

"I know."

"Good night, Jim. Call me."

"Sure," I said again and went out.

CHAPTER FIVE

I met Sergeant Rockingham on the front walk. He was carrying a fuzzy stuffed rabbit under one arm and a doll with yellow hair under the other. Behind him at the curb I saw the red glow of the port light of a police cruiser. Rockingham stopped and eyed me narrowly.

I jerked a thumb at the house. "Your witness, Rock—but it's past her bedtime."

He shifted the rabbit to the arm which held the doll and scratched a corner of his red mustache with a little finger.

I nodded at the toys. "Bribing a witness, huh?"

"What're you doing here?"

"Delivering a Teddy bear—but I didn't buy it for the kid. And I told the first Mrs. Canfield that the second Mrs. Canfield is dead."

"Was she happy about it?"

"She didn't say."

He gazed thoughtfully at the house. "That little girl of Canfield's is his only alibi," he said softly. "A four-year-old's testimony may not be legal, but she might give me something to work on. Kids are smarter than you think. Now, take that oldest boy of mine. The other day—" He checked himself and gave me a beady look. "Jim, tell me the truth. Do you believe his kid was with him all afternoon—every minute?"

"Ask her," I said.

"Did you?" he snapped.

"No," I said truthfully. "I didn't."

He scratched his mustache some more. "What kind of woman is her mother? Will she object to my talking to the kid?"

"Want me to pave the way a little?"

"You a friend of hers?"

"Of the family, let us say—when she was married to Canfield."

For an instant he was tempted to take me in with him. Then he remembered that he was the majesty of the law. "I'll handle it," he said shortly, and he started to move past me.

I said, "You can take Riggio off that corner. Canfield won't run away tonight. I'm staying with him."

He gave me a wolfish leer. "Riggio stays." He stalked up the walk to the house.

I moved out to the curb. There were two cops in the front seat of the cruiser. As I passed, I said, "Evening, boys."

They replied softly, in unison, "Hi, Jim."

It was ten o'clock when I arrived back in Don Canfield's apartment. He was seated in a deep chair in a corner with a glass in his hand. Beside him on the floor was a bowl of ice cubes, a pitcher of water, and a bourbon bottle. He had turned the cream-colored divan around to the wall and thrown a sheet over it.

"This place is giving me the crawling horrors," he said. "Did you give Annie her Teddy bear?"

"Yes."

"Was Kay there?"

"Yes," I said again, and I decided to get it over with. "Don, Annie said you came back here sometime this afternoon and left her in your car. She said she went to sleep, that you returned, woke her up, and then went to the park."

He gazed at me steadily. "That's right, Jim," he said quietly. "After I'd picked up Annie, I discovered that I hadn't brought any money with me. I came back here to get some, and I told Annie to wait in the car. I didn't want to bring her up here, not if Lou had maybe come back." He ran his fingers through his short yellow hair. "She was here, all right, packing a bag, and she wouldn't talk to me. Then

I had a phone call from Ray Cooper—he's in charge of personnel at the plant—and he asked me to come to a party that Jesse Connors and Roger Quinn are throwing for the salesmen next Saturday night. I said I would come. Then I went to the bedroom and asked Lou what she was going to do. She flared up and said, among other things, that she was sick of me, that she had gotten me to marry her because she was tired of working for a living and that she was going back to Paris and drink champagne. She was still a little drunk. I saw that there was no use in trying to talk to her, and I left." He gave, me a crooked smile. "A lovely, charming girl, don't you think?"

"What time was that?"

"Around one-thirty." He took a long swallow from his glass and added bitterly, "No later—if that's what you're thinking."

"Why didn't you tell me this before?"

He sighed. "I don't know, Jim. Seeing her—like that—I guess I was kind of dazed. And then, later, when I saw the look in that cop's eyes, I knew that he was trying to connect me with—with what happened. So I took a chance on Annie not remembering, if she were questioned, and—oh, hell, Jim, have a drink." He nodded at the bottle.

"In a minute," I said. "How do you feel about Louette?"

"I don't know," he said slowly. "I can't tell yet. We weren't happy, you know that. How the hell could we be? I'm sorry that she is—is dead, of course, but—"

"Rockingham has men watching you," I broke in.

"To hell with him," he said hotly, and I saw the hot flame in his eyes.

"Look, Don. This is murder. Cops like Rockingham don't fool around. He's smart, and believe me, you're number one on his list. You had a strong motive and the only alibi you have is Annie. Rockingham is at Kay's house right now, probably listening to Annie tell how you came back here and left her down in the car—"

"But Louette was killed at three o'clock," he said stubbornly.

I shook my head slowly. "Don't count on the time angle. The best they can do is approximate it. And you haven't established that you were not here at around three o'clock. If you could do that, it would help very much."

"Oh, Lord," he groaned, "what a mess." He looked up at me. "What about that damned Reynard? He could have been here—after I left."

"They have probably picked up Reynard by now," I told him. "I know how Rockingham works, and he won't overlook anything. To him it's simple murder, with the most obvious motive. Husband catches man with wife. Husband beats man up, kicks him out, kills wife. It happens all the time—murder pattern number D-1416—Y, or something like that. He's got you covered now, and he'll move in fast when he thinks he has enough against you. Now, think hard—wasn't there anything that happened this afternoon, say between two and four o'clock, that you could prove? Did you see anybody who would remember? The park is over an hour's drive from here, and if you could just establish the fact that you were there— Think hard, Don."

He shook his head slowly. "You were the only person who saw me there, and that was too late in the afternoon to help. Annie is the only person in the world who knows that I was at the park at three o'clock." There was sweat on his forehead.

From out of nowhere I remembered something and I moved to the telephone table. The ashtray was still there, but the cigarette stubs were gone. Nothing remained but a smudge of fingerprinting powder. The laboratory boys had been thorough. I turned to Don and said, "Before the police came I saw a gilt-tipped cigarette butt in this ashtray, an English cigarette called Lord Nelson. Roger Quinn is the only person I know who smokes them. Has he been here lately?"

"He stopped in last weekend."

"Would cigarette butts remain in an ashtray for a week?"

"Yes," he said wryly, "in this house. Lou never emptied an ashtray until it was overflowing."

I was about to ask him another question, but the buzzing of the doorbell stopped me. Don looked at me with startled eyes. I moved to the door, opened it.

Sergeant Rockingham pushed past me, strode over to on. "Come on, son," he said.

"Rock," I said, "you can't hold him long. Annie is a little young to be sworn in as a witness, and besides, she's related to the defendant."

Rockingham's teeth showed beneath his red mustache. "That little gal told me plenty. We'll work it out."

Don stood up and said to him, "Can I talk to Jim for a minute?"

"Sure, but make it quick."

I followed Don into the bedroom. He was a little pale and he took a deep breath. "Do you think I killed her?"

I looked him in the eyes. "I hope not, Don."

"I didn't. She roped me into a marriage, but I tried to a make the best of it. At the last I think I hated her—but I didn't kill her."

"All right. That's good enough for me."

"You—you won't tell them about Lou being here, when I came back this afternoon?"

"Not unless I have to." I touched his arm. "Take it easy. I'll do all I can for you."

"Thanks," he said in a low voice and moved to the door. "Let's go."

In the living room, I said, "Rock, I think you're pushing things too fast. Why don't you pick up this Reynard?"

"We have, Jim," he said pleasantly. "The boys brought him in a half hour ago. He was quite intoxicated, but I am sure that we will be able to have some words with him before morning."

"I'm sure you will," I agreed. "Could I come down and join in your—uh—conversation with him?"

"I'm awfully sorry, Jim, but visiting hours aren't until tomorrow afternoon. Rules, you know."

"To hell with you," I said.

He grinned at me and turned to Don. "Ready?" Neither of them looked back as they went out.

I sat down in a big chair and thought things over. The sheeted divan looked like some huge, pale animal. From somewhere a clock chimed the half-hour. Ten-thirty. I got up, crossed the room, and raised a Venetian blind. I stood for a while in the cool night breeze, looking down at the traffic in the street below. Then I went to the telephone stand and thumbed the book until I found the name I wanted. *Cooper, Raymond D*. He lived on the south side. I dialed his number and a man answered.

"Mr. Cooper?" I asked.

"Yes."

"I'm calling for Don Canfield. He asked me to tell you that he is sorry, but he can't make the party Saturday night after all."

"Oh, that's too bad. But—"

"You called him today, I believe?"

"Yes, but—"

"What time?"

"Around one-thirty this afternoon, but—"

"Goodbye," I said. He got in one more "but" before I hung up.

I went back to the chair and sat down. It didn't mean much, except that Don had been telling the truth about the call. I picked up the bourbon bottle and had two short nips before the phone began to ring. I let it ring. I didn't want to talk to Raymond D. Cooper again. I'd had all I wanted from Cooper, the eager and alert personnel manager of the Connors Electric Company, who was curiously trying to call Don to do a little checking on a rather unusual telephone conversation. I knew Cooper vaguely, a pale young man with a chattering wife who had attended one or two parties at Roger Quinn's house, along with Ralph Bixby, and Owen Harris, Rebecca Foster, Don and Kay Canfield, and other Connors employees. As I recalled, Cooper had talked incessantly and boringly, especially in Jesse Connors's presence, of employee morale, job training, and aptitude tests.

There was a soft knock on the door, and when I opened it Kay Canfield was standing there. She moved past me, her gaze searching the room. When she saw the sheeted divan she stood still and her face paled. "Is that where—where—"

"Yes," I said, closing the door. "That's where we found her. By the way, Don isn't here."

She turned toward me quickly. She was wearing a thin print dress with a wide flaring skirt and a low, square neckline. A Kay Canfield original, I thought, and I gave her credit. She had an eye for line and simplicity, and the pale-green background of the dress was just right for her copperish hair and milky complexion. Beneath one arm she held a dark-green linen purse with yellow flowers embroidered on it. Her deep-blue eyes looked a question at me.

"The police took him downtown," I said. "They wanted to talk to him."

"Jim, we can't let them do that," she said quickly.

"They have," I said.

"But Don didn't—didn't kill her. Don't they know that? A policeman came to see me tonight, right after you left, a Sergeant Rockingham. He wanted to talk to Annie. What's going on, Jim? Is it because she was with Don all afternoon, and they think she can tell them something that will connect Don with—"

"I'm afraid that's it. Annie is his only alibi—so far."

"I wanted to see Don," she said. "I felt that I should talk to him, help him if I could. I—I feel sort of responsible. I know that Don has changed since our divorce; people have told me. And that woman who married him—" Her red mouth twisted slightly in an expression of distaste. "Listen, Jim, this is your kind of work. Find the person who killed her and clear Don. And I want to pay you. Forget our friendship. This is a business proposition."

I wanted to remind her that I had once offered to investigate Don's association with a woman in Toledo, but I didn't. I said, "I'll do what I, can, of course, but—"

"But what?"

"What if I learn that Don killed her? He had plenty of motive, and he has a wild temper sometimes."

"No," she whispered. "No, no."

"Why not?" My voice was harsher than I'd intended.

She turned abruptly away from me. "Just forget it," she said in a brittle voice. "If you think that Don is capable of murder, if that's what you think—" She moved to the door.

I stepped forward and touched her arm. She turned slowly and brushed a hand over her eyes. There were tears in them. I said, "I'll help, but you don't have to pay me."

"And you won't do anything to—to hurt Don?"

"Not if I can help it."

"You've always liked me, haven't you, Jim? I mean, aside from the fact that I was Don's wife?"

"Yes, Kay."

"And Don is your friend?"

"Since we played football together in high school."

"Help him, Jim."

The doorbell let loose with two sharp buzzing sounds.

CHAPTER SIX

Kay's eyes grew big. I moved away from her and opened the door.

A small woman with a vivid red mouth stared at me with eyes the color of amber ice. Her hair was like bleached straw and it hung over her shoulders in gleaming folds. She was wearing a white silk dress and white ankle-strap shoes with incredibly high heels, no stockings, and through the straps of the shoes I saw red lacquer on her toenails. Over one shoulder was slung a white leather purse.

"Mr. Canfield?" she said. The words held a faint accent, and her voice was low-pitched and musical. It reminded me of Louette's voice.

I shook my head. "He isn't here."

Her odd yellowish eyes gazed past me and fixed upon Kay for an instant. Then she looked at me again. "And who are you?"

"My name's Bennett."

She eyed me coolly and silently and moved slowly and gracefully into the room. I caught an illusive scent of lilac.

Kay said, "I'll see you later, Jim." She turned to the door.

"Kay," I said, "wait."

But she was gone. The door closed gently and firmly. I turned to the blonde with the yellow eyes.

Her red mouth curved into a smile. She had small white teeth, a little crooked. "I am sorry if I interrupt something," she said. "Did I?"

"What do you want?"

"I want Mr. Canfield. Where is he?"

"In jail."

Her eyes widened. Then she smiled. "I like that. Perhaps now they will release my Paul."

"Paul?"

She nodded vigorously, and her pale-yellow hair danced on her shoulders. "But, of course. Paul Reynard. He is my husband."

I said, "You should train your Paul to stay away from other men's wives."

She lifted her slim shoulders. "You know how husbands are—but always he comes back to Francine. It only becomes complicated when he gets into trouble—like now." Her red lips twisted. "Perhaps this will teach him to be true to Francine. Do you perhaps have a drink?"

"No," I said.

She glanced around the room, spotted the bottle on the floor by the chair where I'd left it, and went toward it, her small hips swaying. She picked up the bottle, briefly examined the label, and then tilted it to her lips. It was a long swallow. Bonded bourbon whisky, one hundred proof, and she never fluttered an eyelash. "Thank you so much," she said, and moved around the room, carrying the bottle. "So this is the rendezvous," she said musingly, and she paused at the sheeted divan. "And this is where the foolish and greedy Louette met her death?"

"Yes," I said.

She laughed, a low, pleasant sound, deep in her throat. "And to think that the stupid police suspect my Paul. He does not have the courage. He cannot take a mouse from a trap, even. I must always do it. We had many mice in our rooms in Paris, and in the winter we had rats. Big brown ones. One night we caught a rat in a trap, by a leg. He screamed like a baby and tried to bite me. Paul ran into a closet and hid. But I, Francine, killed the rat with a hammer. Then I threw him by his tail into the fireplace, and he burned with much sizzling. You see, if you burn one, the smell keeps the other rats away for a long time." She smiled at me brightly. "Did you know that, mister?"

"No," I said.

She took another long swallow of the bourbon and held up the bottle to the light. "One nice thing about America," she said, "is the whisky. In France we drink mostly wine, but now I like the whisky better." She smiled at me. "Do not look so—so sad. I told you I was sorry to interrupt. She is very beautiful. Your sweetheart—or merely your wife?"

"Neither. Why do you want to see Mr. Canfield?"

She sauntered over to me, still carrying the bottle, and stood close. The top of her blond head was about three inches below my chin. She said, "I want to see him because I know that he killed Louette. My Paul did not kill her. I wanted to ask Mr. Canfield to go to the police and confess his guilt so that they will release my Paul."

"Why do you say that Canfield killed her?"

She took another step toward me, which put us very close together indeed. I couldn't move away from her, because my back was against the wall. Her eyes narrowed and her full red mouth took on an ugly hardness. "I do not know who you are. Possibly you are of the police, but I do not care. I am telling you that I know Mr. Canfield killed Louette because I saw him leaving this apartment at three o'clock this afternoon—and that is the time the police say she died."

"And where was your Paul this afternoon?"

"With me!" she snapped. "With Francine—except for the short time I lock him in our room. He went away yesterday, and he did not come home until noon today. He was hurt. I question him carefully, and maybe I slap him a little. He can never lie to Francine, not even when he has been very bad. He tell me all—about his visit to Louette and how Mr. Canfield beat him. I slap him some more, and then I forgive him. He is like a little boy. So I lock him in our room and I come here to tell Louette that I do not want her to see my Paul any more. That was at three o'clock, and that is when I see Mr. Canfield coming out the door."

She pointed dramatically at the door. "That door. He did not look at me and he went down the stairs quickly. I ring the bell. I do not get an answer, and so I go back to Paul, quickly. We make love and we drink much and we are happy again. But this evening the police come and take my Paul from my arms. They ask many questions, then they drag him away. I cry and scream. Then I come here." She smiled up at me. "I have told the police that I saw Mr. Canfield leaving here this afternoon. Perhaps that is why they have taken him into custody."

"Perhaps," I said.

She held up the bottle. "Would you like a little drink with me?"

I reached for the bottle, but she drew it back, laughing. The white leather purse slipped from her shoulder and fell to the floor. I let her keep the bottle and picked up the purse. She made a grab for it, and her fingernails scratched my wrist. I held her off and opened the purse. She lifted the bottle by the neck and swung it at me. I ducked. Whisky spouted over both of us and splattered against the wall. I got hold of her wrist and twisted. She moaned a little and dropped the bottle. Her lips pulled away from her small white teeth and she sprang for me, silently and swiftly, her fingers clawing for my face.

I slapped her, feeling the sharp edges of her teeth against my fingers. She stumbled away from me, her long pale hair falling over her face. I kept one eye on her and pawed through the contents of her purse. The first thing my fingers encountered was a tiny nickel-plated automatic with a mother-of-pearl grip, a German make, small caliber, less than a .22. I dropped it into my coat pocket, rummaged some more. I found a lipstick, cigarettes, matches, handkerchief, hairpins, a five-dollar bill, and some silver and pennies. And then I uncovered a thin little book with a cover of imitation red leather. I removed the book and tossed the purse to a chair.

Francine turned to stare at me with glittering yellow eyes. Her fingers were spread against the wall behind her, the red nail polish glinting in the light. She reminded me of a tawny cat ready to pounce. There was a smudge of blood at the corner of her mouth, and the low neck of the white dress had slipped down over one white shoulder. She saw the little red book in my hand and she began to spit words at me. I don't know much French, but I recognized a couple of very uncomplimentary phrases.

I opened the little red book.

She sprang for me screaming, *"Non, non!"*

I hated it, but I had to slap her again. She stumbled to a chair, sobbing, and covered her face with her hands. I opened the book. It was a savings-account passbook on a Paris bank. In flowing script in black ink on the fly leaf was the inscription, *Paul M. Reynard et Louette A. Reynard*, followed by a brief paragraph in the same handwriting. I thumbed the pages. They were filled with dates, starting in 1946, and the entries of deposits. The last entry was a year old and carried a total amount forwarded of over twenty million francs. I didn't know exactly what a franc was worth at current exchange, but I guessed that twenty million of them was a substantial amount.

I said to the blonde, "So Louette was married to Paul Reynard—the man you say is your husband?"

She lifted her face from her hands. There was cold hate in her eyes. "What is a husband?" she said scornfully. "A husband is nothing, a thing. Paul loves me, Francine. We came from France together—after Louette ran away with a man she thought was an American millionaire. He was not a millionaire, and he soon tired of her. She was forced to find work here as a dancer. She wrote to Paul in Paris and asked him to take her back. He did not want her back, but he wanted the money which was his. He had made it honestly on the black-market, after the liberation, while he was living with Louette, and he very foolishly let her persuade him to place it in a joint account. But he was wise enough to have her sign a document at the bank, saying that no money could be taken unless *both* signed a withdrawal statement. Do you understand?"

I looked at the first page of the little book again and in the statement beneath the names I saw the word *mort*, and I said, "But if one of them dies, then the other can draw the full amount? Is that in the agreement, too?"

"Yes," she said. She stood up and took a step toward me, her small hands clenched. "But my Paul did not kill her. All he wanted was to get her to sign the proper paper, so he could get his rightful money. That is why we came to America. Then we were going back to France together, Paul and Francine."

"And now that Louette is dead," I said, "all Reynard has to do is get a death certificate, go back to Paris, and collect his money."

"I will not listen to you! My Paul did not kill Louette. Mr. Canfield killed her out of jealousy. It was merely a business affair with Paul, but Mr. Canfield thought Paul was her lover. Is not that funny?"

"Very," I said. I picked up her purse and dropped the bankbook into it. Then I took the little automatic from my pocket and pulled out the clip. It was empty, and the firing chamber was empty. I tapped the gun with a finger. "Where did you get this?"

"An American lieutenant gave it to me, in Berlin, last year. I—I was working there. The lieutenant was very handsome—and very jealous."

I replaced the gun in the purse, closed the clasp, and handed it to her.

Her eyes widened in surprise.

"I'm sorry I had to hit you," I said. "Where do you live?"

"With my Paul, of course." She moved up close to me. The blood at the corner of her mouth was drying, but there still were red marks from my fingers on her cheek. "It is all right that you struck me," she said. "Perhaps I angered you unduly." She patted my cheek. "You Americans—so cold, so hard, so—so violent. Do you not ever have pleasure, enjoy life? Why do you care about Louette? Were you her lover?"

"I'm nobody's lover."

She pressed against me. "That is a shame," she murmured.

She pressed more closely against me. Too late I felt her hand slip beneath my coat. I grabbed for her, but the danced away with a delighted little laugh. She had my wallet in her hand. Pocket-picking, it seemed, was one of her accomplishments. I let her go. I was weary of wrestling with her.

"Now," she said triumphantly, as she opened the wallet, "we shall learn the identity of this big strong man who is nobody's lover." She read my name aloud from one of the cards in the wallet, probably my driver's license, and then she saw the small silver shield issued me by the state highway patrol. "So," she exclaimed, "you are of the police."

I held out my hand. As she returned the wallet there was a thoughtful look in her yellowish eyes. "You have been posted here to guard this place?"

"No. I'm leaving now." I opened the door.

"One minute." She ran into the bathroom and closed the door.

As I waited my gaze fell upon a photograph on a table. It was of a young man in a U.S. Army uniform, with sergeant's chevrons on the sleeve. The blonde came out of the bathroom. She had wiped the blood from her mouth and applied fresh lipstick. I nodded at the photo. Recognize him?"

She hesitated only an instant. "But, of course," she paid. "It is Mr. Canfield—the man I see leaving here this afternoon."

I pushed her gently into the hall and closed the door, making sure that it was locked. As we walked down the hall to the stairs I saw the doors of three apartments open a crack and I felt the eyes of the neighbors upon us.

Down on the sidewalk she turned to me and held out her hand. "We part friends, Mr. Bennett?"

I took her hand. It was small and cold. "Sure, Francine," I said, and I glanced across the street. Detective Riggio hadn't moved. He still had the newspaper, but now it was tucked under his arm and he was gazing up the street like a man waiting for a bus. His hat was pulled down over his eyes and his round fat figure was turned away from me.

"Truly," Francine said, "Mr. Canfield should not have killed his wife."

"You mean Paul Reynard's wife."

She lifted her shoulders. "Wife, husband—what are they? It is the person one loves who matters. I love Paul and he loves me. A wife?" She snapped her fingers. "Pooh!"

"That's a cozy attitude," I said.

She laughed softly. "Cozy. An American word. I like it. My Paul and I are very cozy."

"You can't be cozy when he's in jail."

She snapped her fingers again. "He will be out by morning. And then we will return to France and live a cottage in Normandy."

"On black-market money?"

"Money is money, Mr. Bennett."

"Well," I said, "so long."

She lifted her hand in a brief salute, turned, and walked briskly away, her high heels making pleasant clicking sounds, her small body erect. Her head was held high and her long pale hair lifted gently in the night breeze.

I looked across at Riggio. He had shifted his position so that he could watch Francine and me, too. I crossed the street toward him. He began to shuffle away.

"Hey, Riggio," I called.

He slowed his steps and half turned. I moved up to him.

"Who you tailing? Me or the blonde?"

He grinned. "I ain't worried about you, Jim." He gazed up the street. Francine was passing under the streetlight and her pale hair looked like silver.

"You'd better get going," I said. "She's Rockingham's star witness—she and a little four-year-old gal."

"Yeah, we know. Jake Brady is on the next corner."

"Rock's not taking any chances, huh?"

"Does he ever?" Riggio's dark fat face leered at me as he moved away.

I had learned what I wanted to know. I went back to where the Ford was parked and got in behind the wheel. I thought of the photo in Don's apartment. It was of Don's younger brother, Steve. He had been a sergeant, a mechanic, based in England during the war known as World War II, and he now operated a gas station in Akron.

There was no resemblance between Don Canfield and his brother Steve.

CHAPTER SEVEN

As I drove north to the lake road and headed east toward home, I thought of Don and Kay, Roger and Helen Quinn, of Louette and Francine and her Paul, and it occurred to me that perhaps it was just as well that I was still a bachelor. It was lonely, maybe, but it had its compensations. Sometimes I had thought of getting married and having kids and living in a house in the suburbs and going to work from nine until five. But I'd worked for the agency too long, and I often wondered if even my soul was not owned by a wicked and greedy old man in New York. He frowned upon his men or his women getting married; it divided their interests, he insisted, and rightly, I suppose. All of us were supposed to live and eat and drink for the agency twenty-four hours a day.

But he paid well, and as head of the Cleveland branch I had a comfortable office, a brown-haired secretary named Sandy Hollis, two late model Fords at my disposal, and one full-time assistant named Alec Hammond. Also, I had several specialists on call when I needed them in the never-ending business of investigation for the corporations and the private citizens who could afford to pay the agency's fees for help when the problems of life, or the bitter battle known as business, became too complex or too secret or too embarrassing to entrust to the sturdy minions of the law.

It was a nice life for me, boring sometimes and lonesome, it is true; exciting, sometimes, and occasionally dangerous. I liked it. But when

I thought of a woman like Kay Canfield, I would wonder and grow restless, and think that I was missing something special and rewarding, something I would never have as long as I stayed on the agency payroll. And yet, Don Canfield had had something special, and he had let it get away from him.

Traffic was thick, as it usually is on a Sunday night, especially in the spring, and it was eleven-thirty when I entered my apartment. I took off my coat, loosened my tie, sat down beside the telephone, and called Sergeant Rockingham. He was at the station.

"Rock," I said, "how are you making out with Canfield and Reynard?"

"I let 'em both loose a half hour ago."

"Giving them a little rope?"

"What's on your mind, Jim?"

"Listen—did you know that Paul Reynard is the legal husband of Louette Canfield and that Don Canfield has been living in sin with her all these months?"

"No," Rockingham said stonily.

"And did you know that Reynard has a pile of frozen dough in a bank in Paris he couldn't get his hands on as long as Louette was alive, and that Reynard is currently shacked up with a blonde named Francine, who carries a passbook for the money and also a small-caliber rod? And I suppose this very same blonde has told you that she saw Canfield leaving his apartment at a very suspicious hour this afternoon, and—"

"Never mind, Jim," he broke in wearily. "I know that Canfield is a pal of yours, and his ex-wife is, too, but for my money he's guilty as hell. The only alibi he has is that kid of his, and that backfired on him. She told me about how he went back to his place this afternoon and left her in the car."

"But that was at one-thirty," I said. "A long time before the killing. A man named Raymond Cooper telephoned him then. I checked on it."

"So did I," he said smugly. "He gave me that story, too. But it doesn't prove that he didn't hang around until three o'clock. And you're correct about the blonde. She's willing to swear under oath that she saw Canfield leaving the apartment at three o'clock."

"She's trying to protect her sweetheart, Paul Reynard," I said desperately. "Can't you see? Both of them had reason to kill Louette, and—"

"Just go to bed, Jim," he snarled. "Just go the hell to bed. The police department will handle it."

"I just wanted you to—"

The phone clicked in my ear. When Rockingham was tired and irritated and baffled there was no use in trying to talk to him. I would tell him later, maybe, about Don's brother Steve, and go into more detail about the black-market francs, if he would give me a chance. He was always complaining about cooperation, but sometimes when I tried to cooperate he seemed to resent it. Like tonight. He had his own ideas and he didn't want anything to change them. Or maybe he had something else on his mind. After all, cops are human, too, and they have the same personal problems that other people have. They have certain quirks, too; if they didn't, they wouldn't be cops, because the pay certainly did not compensate them for being cops, and I thought wryly that if the pay were better I would probably be on the force myself.

I undressed, brushed my teeth, listened to a news broadcast, and went to bed. I had turned over twice and was dozing off when the phone rang. For a while I let it ring, but it didn't stop. At last I crawled out of bed and groped my way in the darkness to the living room.

"Yes?" I said, making no attempt to conceal the irritation in my voice.

"Jim?" a man's voice said.

"Yes."

"This is Roger."

"Who?" I snapped.

"Roger Quinn, Jim." The words slurred a little and I guessed that he was drunk.

"Hello, Roger." It had been maybe three weeks since I'd seen him.

"Can I see you, Jim? Now, I mean?"

"What about?"

"I'll tell you when I see you. It—it's very important."

When people call to say that they want to see me about something important, it invariably means that it is important to them and not to me. So I said, "Roger, I've had a hard day. Can't you see me in the morning?"

"No, no. I've got to see you tonight." I had the impression that he was trying to keep his voice under control, and that he was not drunk, after all—at least, not as drunk as I'd first thought.

"Where are you?"

"In a drugstore at Ninety-third Street."

"All right. Come on out."

"Thanks, Jim," he said hurriedly and hung up.

I put on slippers and a robe and made a pot of coffee. It was almost midnight and I was on my third cup when I heard his soft knock on my door. I let him in, and he stepped quickly past me and stood quietly while I closed the door. I said, "Hi, Roger," and when I looked at his eyes I knew that he was so scared that he could taste it. But he was fighting the fear, trying to keep his nerves in line.

"Jim," he said unsteadily, "I'm sorry as hell to bother you so late—"

"That's all right, Roger. Sit down."

He glanced quickly around. "Are you alone?"

"Sure. I try to get the weekend blondes out of my place by Sunday night."

"I—I didn't mean that—"

"I'm alone. You'd better sit down."

He shook his head impatiently and a strand of thick black hair fell down over his white forehead. There was a bruised spot the size of a half dollar below his left eye.

He was wearing a gray cashmere suit, a soft white shirt, and a blue-and-red-speckled bow tie. The collar of the shirt was open and the loose ends of the tie hung down across his chest. There was mud on his brown shoes and the knees of his trousers were soggy and damp with a dark-brownish stain. He lit a cigarette and his hands shook so much that the flame flickered.

I said, "Would you like a drink?"

"No. No, thanks." He took a deep, shuddering breath and drew deeply on his cigarette.

I nodded at his knees. "Did you have an accident?"

He looked down and stared dumbly, as if he were seeing the stains for the first time. He reached a hand toward his right knee, and then he drew it back quickly, his fingers spread. He looked at me, and there was a hint of wildness in his eyes. "Jim," he said desperately, "I—" His mouth worked soundlessly.

"Go on, Roger," I said gently. "Tell me."

"I'm in a jam," he blurted. "A bad one."

"I guessed that," I said, thinking that Roger Quinn, in spite of our long association, meant nothing to me, really. I had been a guest in his house, as he had been in mine, and I owed him nothing. We happened to be thrown together in the same strata of society, and he'd married a girl I'd known in high school. To me he was just a person, no better and no worse than many others I knew who were living out their lives in whatever niche they had carved for themselves. It did not matter to me that Roger, by dint of energetic bootlicking and buttering-up of Jesse Connors, had found himself in a particularly lush niche, but perhaps I subconsciously resented the fact that he held a job that Don Canfield should have had, and that he did not appreciate his niche, or the girl who had made it possible.

"Jim, could I—I have that drink, after all?"

I went to the kitchen, got a half-full bottle of bourbon from the cupboard, filled a glass with water, and carried the bottle and the glass in to him. I was fairly familiar with Roger Quinn's drinking habits. He drank from the bottle, and then from the glass, and offered the bottle to me.

I shook my head. "I don't need any courage."

"But I do?" There was a little color in his face now.

"You're scared stiff, Roger. Is it a woman?"

"You know me pretty well, don't you?"

"Pretty well, Roger. We all know one another."

"Sure." He avoided my gaze and looked at the bottle in his hand.

"Does she want money—or what?"

He took a long swallow before he answered. "She doesn't want anything. It—it isn't that." He looked at the bottle, but he didn't drink right away.

"Then what?" I snapped. "Speak up. We're two grown men." I pointed at the stains over his knees. "What's that? It looks like blood."

"Yes," he said in a queer voice. "It's her blood—she's dead." He wanted another drink, but I was watching him, and he said the word again with a rising defiant inflection. "Dead."

The room seemed to settle into a shocked silence. Then I said, "Who?" thinking of Louette Canfield or Louette Reynard, or whatever her name was.

He took a drink then, quickly, a small drink, and he said, "Just a— a girl. I don't know her name. She—" He waved the bottle in a helpless gesture, and his eyes looked everywhere but at me. He hated the thing that had driven him to me, but it was something he couldn't cope with, something beyond him, entirely out of the sphere of his experience. But he had his pride and I sensed that he hated me because he was reduced to asking me for help.

Suddenly I felt sorry for him and I said quietly, "All right, Roger.

People die. Where is she?"

The tone of my voice seemed to give him courage. "In a hotel room," he said, "over in East Grange. I wanted help, advice—not the police—and I thought of you—"

"How did she die?"

"Her—her throat— It—"

I turned away from him, remembering the knife in the white flesh of Louette, and thinking that trouble always comes in bunches. Behind me Roger said shrilly, "What are you going to do?"

At the bedroom door I turned. "I'm going to get dressed. Then we'll go to East Grange. You can tell about it on the way."

"I—I can't go back there," he said in a ragged voice. "I can't look at her again. You handle it, Jim. I'll pay you whatever you want—"

I peered at him closely. He really meant it; he was serious. I said, "I haven't said I'd handle anything, no matter what you pay me. But I'll take a look. I don't want to do that. But you have a nice wife and two nice kids, and we've known each other for a long time. But you've got to go with me."

"All right, Jim," he said humbly. "It—it wasn't my fault. I just took her to the hotel and—"

"On second thought," I said, "I think you need a lawyer. I know a couple of good ones. How about Owen Harris?"

"No, no." There was sweat on his face. "I want you. You know about these things, know how to cover it up. If it takes money—"

I went into the bedroom and slammed the door. When I came out, he was standing before the mantel mirror combing his thick black hair.

We left Roger Quinn's gray Cadillac on the street in front of my apartment and drove out of town in the agency Ford. Traffic was light and the night breeze cool on my face. At an intersection of Route 20, close to Elyria, I turned south and we were soon in softly rolling country and headed for East Grange, Ohio, some thirty miles southwest of Cleveland's Public Square. The moon came up and its white light was bright on the fields around us.

All the way across the city and into the country Roger Quinn sat quietly. He didn't speak until I said, "Give me the story—all of it."

"It began a couple of months ago." His voice was quiet and controlled. "I was on my way home from Pittsburgh and I pulled into a hamburger drive-in south of East Grange. This girl, a carhop, came out in white shorts and a calico shirt—you know how they dress—and she was cute, really nice, stacked, you know, and she had yellow hair, and—"

"Never mind," I broke in. "You made a play for her. Then what?"

He said angrily, "Maybe we'd just better skip the whole thing."

"Fine," I snapped. "Good." I braked the Ford and began to look for a place to turn around.

I felt his hand on my arm. "Damn it, Jim, don't get sore. I know I'm asking a hell of a lot of you, but I—I didn't know what else to do. It's like having a nightmare—worse than that—" He took a deep, shuddering breath.

I fed gas to the Ford. To hell with Roger Quinn and all the faithless Roger Quinns, from Long Island to Los Angeles. But my night's sleep was gone, and I was involved in Roger's trouble now, whether I liked it or not.

"It's my fault, I suppose," he said helplessly. "I've never pretended to be an angel. You know how it is."

I didn't know how it was. I wasn't married, and I took my fun where I found it. If ever I married I would know that the fun was over, and I would be glad that it was over; if I hadn't been glad to leave the fun behind I would not have married. That's the way it was with me. Of course, I wasn't married, with no prospects of being married, and I could have been wrong.

So I said, "Sure, Roger, I know how it is."

"It was just one of those things," he said. "I made a date with the little blonde for when she got through working. I had a bottle, and we ended up in this dinky hotel in East Grange. I was with her once after that. Then last Friday I went to Detroit on business, expecting to be gone over the weekend, until Monday or Tuesday." He paused and I heard him sigh. "Well, it turned out that I did not need to stay, and—"

"But instead of driving home to your wife tonight," I broke in, "you stopped at the hamburger drive-in. You figured you might as well, since Helen wasn't looking for you home for a day or two. Is that it?"

"Yes," he said in a tight voice. "I picked her up, and I we went to the same hotel. Around ten o'clock she said she was hungry, and I went out to buy some sandwiches. When I came back, she was on the floor—dead—" Something like a groan escaped him.

I didn't look at him. I didn't want to look at him. He was going through a little private hell. Presently he said, "She was all bloody.

There was blood on the floor. I kneeled beside her, in the blood—Then I ran out."

I said, "Did you lock the door?"

"I—I don't think so. It was a hell of a shock, and just left—"

"Did anyone see you go in—or leave?"

"Just an old man on the desk when we registered. He was asleep when I left."

"What do you know about the girl?"

"Not much." His voice was calm and flat now. "He name was Melissa. She never told me her last name, and I didn't ask her. I called her Lissy. She—she was rather nice. She did tell me that she was married to a truck driver from Columbus. She said he drank heavily and frequently abused her, and she left him. We—we didn't talk much." He flung his cigarette out of the window. "Jim, you hear about these things, you read about them, but—"

"Yeah," I said. "It's like a bad accident on the highway—it can never happen to you."

I thought about Don Canfield. It had happened to him, too, the last part of it, the coming into a room and finding death, and the two happenings had occurred only a few short hours apart, on a Sunday evening in May. They said that Louette had died at three o'clock and if what Roger had told me was true, the blonde had been killed around ten o'clock. I felt a sense of uneasiness, and then I came to the turn I had been watching for. I swung the Ford from the state highway to the county road leading back to East Grange.

In a couple of minutes I came to a white sign at the edge of the road.

EAST GRANGE
TRAFFIC LAWS ENFORCED
SPEED LIMIT 35

I slowed the Ford as we entered the long main street. It was a small place in the middle of the corn belt, not quite a town, but still bigger than a village, with streets crossing the main one, a movie theater, more than a few bars and beer taverns, quite a few stores, some of them with modernized entrances and plate glass windows, and a sprawling residential section composed mostly of two-story frame houses built by retired farmers. On the fringes of the town there were small farms and truck patches and beyond them the cornfields stretched like a prairie. The clock on the dash of the Ford told me that it was a quarter after one o'clock in the morning.

"Where's the hotel?" I asked Roger.

"Keep going. It's at the end of the main street. The Avalon."

Presently I saw it, a red brick building flush with the sidewalk, with a neon sign reading, *Hotel Avalon—Rooms by Day or Week*. I parked a half block away and Roger and I walked back to it. The town was quiet and deserted, with most of the business establishments dark, even the bars and beer joints. I wear rubber heels, but Roger's hard ones made a disturbing clatter on the cement. He didn't speak as we walked side by side. I glanced at him. He was staring at the neon sign and his face was pale. At the door of the hotel I stopped.

"Roger," I said, "you realize that I can't keep you out of this, whatever it is—not for long. I'll have to report it to the law."

He began to tremble. "Jim, you can't do that," he said in a pleading voice. "It would ruin me—with Helen and with J.L. That's why I came to you. If I hadn't thought you'd help me, I would just have gone home and kept quiet—"

"Maybe you should have, Roger," I said gently. "But *somebody* knew you were in the room with that girl. You did the right thing in reporting it, but I wish you'd go to the police. You've got me into it, and I can't back out. The fact that I'm here now involves me. I'm a little like the law myself. I can't promise you a thing. I have an obligation to the law—call it duty if you want to. I want you to understand that."

He stared down at the sidewalk, his face contorted and his mouth quivering. For a second he looked like a small boy about to cry. Then he lifted his head and his mouth tightened. "All right, Jim," he said quietly. "Let's go up."

He followed me into the Avalon Hotel. There was a small lobby, with a wide stairway leading up to the floor above. The steps were covered with worn red carpet. A row of straight wooden chairs sat before a wide window facing the street, with heavy brass cuspidors beside them. Behind a small high desk in a corner an old man with thick yellowish hair was snoring loudly on a chair tilted against the wall. He was wearing a soiled-looking white shirt, pink elastic sleeve holders, and a cheap red-green-yellow-splashed necktie. The shirt pocket bulged with an assortment of fountain pens and automatic pencils. His sallow, narrow head was sagged sideways, his mouth open, disclosing shrunken and toothless gums. A little saliva dripped over his chin. On the left side of his head, in the spot where his left ear should have been, was a shapeless lump of red puckered flesh.

I glanced at Roger Quinn and laid a finger to my lips. He nodded stiffly, and moved very carefully past me to the stairway. I followed him up to the second floor and down a narrow hallway. I smelled dust and peeling paint and old cooking odors and the stale reek of dead and soggy cigar butts. We passed five closed doors. Roger stopped before the sixth and I saw the painted number *206*. He turned to look at me, his hand on the knob. When I saw the expression on his face I felt sorry for him.

I nudged him gently aside and turned the knob. Slowly I pushed the door inward. The room was dark, but I could see a faint glow from a window. My fingers felt along the wall for a light switch. I didn't locate it right away and I became aware of a hot, close smell, as if the window had been closed against the May night. There were other smells, too; a faint perfume, and a blend of whisky fumes and stale cigarette smoke, and a sweetish, clinging smell that was not unfamiliar to me—the smell of blood. My fingers found the switch, pressed it. The weak, sickly glow from three naked and dusty light bulbs hanging from a dirty brass chandelier cast a yellow glow over the room. A high old-fashioned brass bed stood against a far wall. Something was on the bed, covered with a sheet.

Behind me Roger Quinn's breathing sounded strangled and his fingers plucked at my sleeve.

"My God," he said hoarsely. "She's been moved!"

CHAPTER EIGHT

I shook off Roger's hand and moved to the bed. She lay serenely with the sheet pulled up to her chin. All I could see of her was her head, her bare arms, and her hands folded demurely on top of the sheet. A small bunch of wilted violets was clasped in her fingers. Pale hair was fanned out over the pillow. Her eyes were clear blue. Death had made one pupil slightly off center, but she appeared to be staring fixedly at a spot on the opposite wall. A heavy coating of lipstick on her half open lips looked almost black against the white edges of her teeth. The upper half of the sheet, the pillow, and the ends of her hair were soaked in blood. Once she had been rather pretty, but she wasn't pretty now.

From the way the sheet had settled over her small body I knew that she was naked beneath it. With a thumb and forefinger I gently lifted the sheet from her throat. The gaping wound and the blood told me all that I needed to know, or wanted to know, about the way she had died. One artery, maybe several, had been severed with a knife or some other sharp instrument.

Her clothes were on a chair beside the bed; a cheap little black dress with a white starched collar, a small brassiere, a pair of pink rayon panties, all folded neatly. Beneath the chair was a pair of small-sized, black, high-heeled shoes with slim ankle straps, side by side, with a rolled-up nylon stocking in each one.

Roger Quinn whispered beside my ear, "She was on the floor when I left." He pointed a trembling finger at a wide damp stain on the carpet close to the wall. There was a dark dribbling trail from the stain to the bed.

I said, "You're sure she was dead when you left her?"

He nodded dumbly, his eyes avoiding the bed. There was sweat on his forehead and his cheeks looked pinched and gray. "I—I'm sick," he blurted, and he crossed swiftly to a door beyond the bed, jerked it open. I saw the edge of a high old-fashioned bathtub. He closed the door.

I lit a cigarette and waited, feeling a little sick myself. On top of a dresser I spotted a black leather purse, and I picked it up. It was a cheap little purse, worn and cracked, with a tarnished metal clasp. Inside were the usual female items—lipstick, nail file, hairpins, cigarettes, matches, and chewing gum, plus a dollar bill, sixty-seven cents in change, and a little heart-shaped locket on a thin gold chain.

I lifted the locket up and held it to the light. The name *Melissa* was engraved on one side, with *Tony* on the other. I opened it with a thumbnail and saw a tiny photo, the head of a man, cut from a snapshot taken in the sun, a dark, black-haired man with a broad, swarthy face and thick black brows. I closed the locket, dropped it back into the purse, and rooted some more. But all I found were more hairpins and some tobacco crumbs. No identification, not even a Social Security card.

Roger Quinn came out of the bathroom, dabbing at his mouth with a handkerchief. His face was very pale. He didn't look at me, but moved straight to a small table by the wall and picked up a whisky bottle. Also on the table were an empty ginger ale bottle, two glasses, and a bowl which I guessed had contained ice cubes. Roger lifted the bottle to his lips and swallowed twice. Then he lowered it and began to cough. I thought he was going to be sick again but he wasn't. He stopped coughing and held the bottle out to me in mute invitation.

I shook my head, moved to the bed, and placed the back of my hand against the dead girl's cheek. The flesh was cool but not cold, and I guessed that she had been dead about as long as Roger had said. I looked around the room. Half out of sight beneath a chair near the door was a brown paper bag. I walked over to it, picked it up. Inside there were four sandwiches wrapped in wax paper—two hamburgers and two ham, with mustard and catsup. I rewrapped them, put them back in the bag, and told myself to take them with me. A short-order cook might remember a handsome black-haired man buying two ham sandwiches and two hamburgers at ten o'clock on a certain Sunday night. Not that I intended to cover up for Roger Quinn; it was just something that I decided to do until I knew for sure what I was going to do about Roger and his dead playmate.

I said to him, "Anything of yours lying around?"

He lowered the bottle from his lips, peered carefully around the room, avoiding the bed; he pulled a wallet from his pocket, flipped through it, and put it back. He shook his head at me.

"There'll be fingerprints all over," I told him, "but we can't worry about that now. All we can do now is get the hell out of here. Did the old guy on the desk ever ask questions or get nosy?"

"No. I paid for the room in advance the three times that we came here. I always registered as Mr. and Mrs. A. J. Holman, from Detroit. He never asked any questions."

I said, "And while you were out buying sandwiches somebody came up here and killed her. And then, after you left, somebody came in and laid her out like that with the violets in her hand. And *that* somebody knew that she was here with you. That's bad, Roger."

He drank more whisky.

"You're in a tight spot," I said.

He lowered the bottle and waved it. The whisky was hitting his empty stomach and he was getting a little drunk. "You can fix it, Jim. You know how to handle these things. I'll pay you—a couple of thousand, five thousand—"

"Shut up," I snarled, feeling a sudden revulsion for Roger Quinn. "I know you're heeled—after all, your daddy-in-law made you general manager—but money won't help you now. As far as I'm concerned, you can face the music. You can come home with me, or you can stay here with your girlfriend until the cops come."

He eyed me angrily. The whisky was making him brave again. "Since when did you get so damned virtuous? I just got a bad break, that's all—it could happen to anybody. I came to you because I thought you were my friend and I trusted you. You're supposed to be a big-time operator, a guy who knows the score. My God, I didn't kidnap her and drag her up here! She came because she wanted to. She was glad to come. She—"

"Please shut the hell up," I said wearily. I moved to the door.

Panic showed in his eyes then and he moved forward and plucked at my sleeve. "Don't you see, Jim? I'm just a guy, an ordinary guy who likes a little fun. My fun doesn't hurt Helen—as long as she doesn't know about it. She's all right, but—well, if you were married you'd know what I mean. A man has to cut loose once in a while. Some men drink, some gamble, some—well, where's the harm? This girl liked me and I liked her, and I made it worth her while. She had nothing to lose—"

"Nothing but her life," I said, and I grasped the doorknob. "Come on, Casanova." It wasn't a nice thing to say, but that's the way I felt.

Somebody pounded on the door.

I looked at Roger. He stood frozen, and then his gaze darted around the room, looking for a way out. But there wasn't any way out, except the window, and it was two stories above the street. Savagely I motioned him to go to the door and I flattened myself against the wall. He looked a silent question at me, and again I pointed at the door. He moved to it then, and opened it about an inch.

I heard a thin, high voice. "I was making my rounds, and I saw your light. Is anything wrong, Mr. Holman?"

"My wife has a little headache," Roger said, "that's all." I gave him credit. His voice was steady.

"Didn't sound like your voice in there just now, Mr. Holman."

Roger laughed, a kind of croaking sound. "Get that good ear of yours tested, Pop. Good night." He made a move to close the door, but the scuffed toe of a brown shoe protruded into the room.

"As long as you're up, Mr. Holman," the voice in the hall said, "I may as well fix that leaky faucet in the bathroom."

"Tomorrow," Roger said. He was going to pieces fast and his voice was faint now.

The thin voice complained, "I go off duty at seven and if I don't fix it now, I'll have to do it tomorrow night."

I could see the sweat running down behind Roger's ears. He held the door with one hand and reached into a pocket with the other. His hand came out with a five-dollar bill and he shoved it out the door. "Tomorrow," he said.

The shoe withdrew slowly. "Well, all right. I hope your missus feels better."

Roger closed the door and leaned against it, his head down.

I said, "He was just shaking you down a little because he knows you're not A. J. Holman, from Detroit. If he knew what was on the bed, he wouldn't settle for any five bucks."

He raised his head and looked at me blankly. "What?"

"Never mind," I said, moving away. I found a *Do Not Disturb* sign in the top dresser drawer, and I said to Roger, "Where's the door key?"

He fumbled in his pockets, peered at the top of the dresser. "I—I don't know," he mumbled.

I moved to the door, opened it cautiously, and peered out. The old man from the desk was not in sight, but from behind a door at the end of the hall I heard the sound of running water. I picked up the bag of sandwiches and the *Do Not Disturb* sign and nodded to Roger. He moved past me into the hall. I hung the sign on the outside knob, turned off the lights, and closed the door. Roger stumbled a little as we went down the stairs and I held his arm. The lobby was deserted. We crossed it quickly, went out to the sidewalk, and down the street to where the Ford was parked. The moon was high and bright over the town of East Grange.

We didn't talk as we drove through the cool night to the highway leading back to Cleveland. At a bridge over a small creek I stopped the car and threw the bag of sandwiches into the water. Roger sat quietly and did not seem to notice what I was doing. As I drove on, I glanced in the rearview mirror. There was a pair of headlights a long way back on the deserted road. They were still behind us when we merged with the city traffic, and then they were lost in the myriad lights. It was three o'clock in the morning when I stopped behind Roger Quinn's gray Cadillac parked across the street from my apartment building.

I sat with my hands on the wheel, feeling the tiredness creep over me. "Go home," I said to Roger. "Go home and get some sleep."

He didn't answer and I looked at him. He was slumped beside me, stupid with whisky and fatigue and the events of the night.

"Go home," I said again.

"Jim," he said in a dead voice, "I hate it—about her. She was all right—she didn't deserve—"

It was the first time he'd expressed regret for what had happened to Melissa, and for the third time that night I felt sorry for him. Roger Quinn was just a guy, as he had said, and there were millions like him, no better and no worse, and I thought sadly that often it did not matter what a man did, but what he got caught at. That mattered very much.

"What are you going to do, Jim?" he asked.

"I don't know."

"I want to do what's right," he said, "but if Helen finds out, and J. L.—"

"Go home, Roger; go home to your wife. You just came in from Detroit. Don't say anything to anybody. I'll see you in the morning."

"You'll help me, Jim?" His voice was wistful, pleading.

"If I can, Roger. But don't count on it."

"I'll pay you—"

"Shut up," I said.

"Jim, you don't think that I—"

"Killed her? Hell, no."

He sat silent for maybe a minute, staring out at the dark street. Then he took a deep breath and said in forlorn voice, "Jim, if this gets out, it'll mean the end of everything for me. There must be something that you—" His voice trailed off.

"Let me think about it," I said. Since the moment that I had stood in the hotel room at East Grange and looked at what was on the bed, a tiny insistent something had been prodding at my brain, and I had thought of another woman lying on a cream-colored divan thirty miles away. Two women, both dead within a few hours of each other, both murdered with a knife. And here was Roger Quinn, husband, father, lady's man, sitting beside me scared blue, reaping the harvest of his folly, as well he should.

"Roger," I said, "have you been seeing Louette Canfield—Don's wife?"

He swung his head quickly toward me. "Why do you ask that?"

"Have you?"

"I know Louette," he said carefully. "In fact, I introduced her to Don, and I've been to see them a few times since they've been married."

"Stop hedging," I said sharply. "Have you been seeing her—when Don is out of town?"

"Of course not." There was an edge to his voice.

"You're lying," I said. "Tonight I saw one of your cigarette stubs in their apartment. You're the only person I know who smokes Lord Nelsons."

"I see," he said. His repentant mood was gone, and his voice was mocking, faintly sneering. "The famous detective finds a clue."

Anger flared within me. "All right," I said, "you damned woman chaser. You got yourself in a nasty mess and you come crying to me for help, but I can't help you, not the way you want to be helped. I can't keep it quiet, keep you out of it, and that is what you want. I'm way out on a big fat limb right now because of you, and yet you lie to me. You've been seeing Don's wife, haven't you?"

"Of course," he said coldly. "Don't be naïve, Jim. What did you think? Louette and I were pals before she met Don. Just because she was smart enough to get Don drunk and trick him into marrying her—well, that didn't change things between us. Don's away a lot, and she asked me to come and see her. Why should I pass it up?"

"She didn't ask to be murdered," I said.

"W-What?"

I told him quickly about Louette, and I said, "In the last few hours I've looked at two dead women, both of them killed with a knife, and both of them friends—shall we say?—of yours. Maybe you didn't have anything to do with the killings, but the cops will sure as hell think you did, and you're in for a bad time, any way you look at it."

He didn't speak and his body seemed to have shrunken in the seat. All of his arrogance was gone again and he was back where he had been a few minutes before, a scared and beaten and hopeless man. And once more, in a softer tone, I told him to go home. "Get what sleep you can and be at your desk at the usual time. I won't promise you a thing, Roger, but I'll do what I can."

He fumbled for the door latch, opened the door, and got slowly out to the sidewalk. He stood there, a dark and lonely figure, peering in at me. "Thank you, Jim." he said clearly and distinctly. "Thank you very much for nothing."

I watched him walk slowly to the Cadillac, get in, and drive away.

I decided to leave the Ford on the street for the few hours until I'd be needing it again. I locked it and went up to my apartment. My door was standing slightly ajar and there was a light inside. I stopped and thought it over. Then I walked in.

Helen Quinn sat stiffly on the divan, facing the door. She didn't have a drink in her hand, or a cigarette or a purse or anything. She was just sitting there with her hands folded and she had the appearance of a person who has waited a long time and is prepared to wait longer. She was a plain, quiet woman with soft brown hair, grave brown eyes, and a fragile delicate figure with small breasts, like a young girl's. I'd known her for a long time, as I had Kay and Don, long before she'd married Roger. Now she looked more fragile than ever, sitting on my big divan with the light shining on her smoothly combed hair and her small oval face. She wore no rouge, but her small mouth was painted a vivid red. Her eyes looked sad and haunted and there were dark shadows beneath them.

Helen Connors Quinn, wife of Roger, mother of his children, heiress to Jesse Connors's washing machine fortune.

She was wearing a plain black skirt, a white nylon blouse buttoned to her thin throat, with her pale narrow shoulders and the white straps of her slip showing through. On her feet were high-heeled black shoes, and I thought of another pair of black shoes in a hotel room thirty miles away.

"Hello, Jim," she said quietly. Her voice was soft and low, like music, and I remembered that it had always been one of the most attractive things about her.

I decided to give it the light touch. "Helen," I said, as I closed the door, "I almost forgot our early breakfast date this morning."

She didn't smile. "Where is Roger?" she asked.

"Roger?" I tried to think fast.

"Yes, my husband," she said patiently, like a woman speaking to a child. "I've been looking for him, and I saw his car down in front so I came up. Your door was not locked, and I came in. I've been waiting a long time. Where is he, Jim?"

Pure male instinct put words in my mouth and I tried to cover up for Roger, at least for the moment. "He's gone home, Helen. I just left him." I paused, trying to remember whether or not I'd locked my door, but knowing that it didn't make any difference. "We had a little game tonight. You know—poker?"

"I see," she said. She stood up and regarded me gravely.

I saw the beginnings of lines in her face and the tiny wrinkles in her throat, and I thought sadly that in another ten years Helen

Quinn would be an old woman. There was no reason for it; she was younger than Kay and Don, younger than any of us, and with a trace of bitterness I wondered if Roger had done this to her.

"I'm sorry that you were worried," I said.

A faint flush touched her cheeks. "Jim," she said gravely, "you're looking at a jealous and worried wife."

"I know. Why else would you be out looking for him at three o'clock in the morning?"

"And you'd protect him, wouldn't you?" she asked "Lie for him. You men must stick together, mustn't you?"

I didn't answer her. What answer could I give her? All through the years Helen Quinn had been to me just a quiet, soft-speaking girl, the wife, the mother, always in the background at parties, saying the right things, wearing the right clothes, giving the prescribed number of parties a year, talking with other mothers about mumps and whooping cough and measles and immunity shots; about clothes and bridge and the new teacher in the second grade; always pleasant and serene, sometimes a little shy.

I suddenly remembered that I liked Helen Quinn, that I had liked her for a long time.

She said, "Where has Roger been, really?"

"Helen, I told you."

She shook her head slowly. "Jim, something is very wrong. Roger was supposed to be in Detroit on business until Monday or Tuesday. Yesterday afternoon I had a call from friends in New York, an invitation to go to Bermuda. I wanted to tell Roger about it, thinking that he would be pleased, and so that he could rearrange his schedule. They told me at his hotel that he'd checked out shortly before noon. I thought that he had finished his business sooner than he expected and was on his way home. I waited dinner for him, but he didn't come. I ate alone after the children were in bed and I waited some more."

She paused and looked down at her tightly clasped hands. "We've been married for twelve years, Jim. I love Roger, but there have been—things. When he didn't come home last night I felt that the time had come for me to learn what he was doing to me. I didn't want to, but I had to. I've tried to fight against becoming the suspicious wife—I'm not the type. But it got to be too much for me—especially after I received this in the mail on Saturday afternoon." She handed me an envelope. "You are the only person I know who would understand, maybe explain it to me. Do you mind, Jim?"

"Of course not, Helen."

It was a cheap envelope, the kind that can be purchased in any dime-store, and was addressed in heavy black pencil to Mrs. Roger Quinn at her address in Cleveland. It was postmarked at East Grange, Ohio, at 9:30 p.m. the previous Friday. I took out the single ruled sheet and read the wavering penciled handwriting.

Dear Mrs. Quinn, Your husband is carrying on with Other Women and my heart bleeds for you. If you wish more detailed information meet me at the Hotel Avalon in East Grange at 11 P.M. Sunday night and I will tell All. I will wear a bunch of violets in my coat so you will know me. A Friend. P.S. Please bring One Hundred Dollars. This has been going on for some time.

I read the thing twice before I handed it back to her. "Did you go?" I asked her.

She folded the paper, put it back in the envelope before she answered. "Of course not."

I said, "It's obviously from some screwball. Forget it."

She picked up a light tweed coat from a chair and moved to the door. "I'm sorry to have bothered you, Jim."

"No bother, Helen."

She opened the door. The haunted look was in her eyes. "Jim," she said, "of course you are aware that I know you lied to me about Roger?"

"Helen," I said, "listen—"

The door closed quietly in my face.

CHAPTER NINE

I let her go. There was nothing I could do for her now. I had known her and Roger, and Kay and Don, since a time in my life when everything was simple, when everyone was reasonably happy. The memory of those days was hazy and pleasant. It is only after you are older and deep in the jungle warfare called living and after you become involved with the things that people do that the early memories come back, and then it is too late and it is no good. I felt sorry for Helen Quinn, but she had too much trust and too much faith. She was bound to be hurt sooner or later.

I went straight to the telephone and called Roger's house. I didn't get an answer, although I knew that an extension had been placed in his bedroom after he'd been appointed general manager of Jesse Connors's factory. After ten rings I gave up and called the Connors Electric Company.

A man answered. "Connors Electric. Main gate."

"Is Mr. Quinn there?"

"No, sir, not at this time of night. Call at nine in the morning."

"Can you ring his office for me?"

"No. The switchboard don't open until eight."

"Could you go to his office and see if he is there?"

"Ain't allowed to leave the gate, mister, except at clock-punching times. Anyhow, if he was here his car would be in his parking space. It ain't there."

"All right. Thanks."

I didn't know where else to call and I wondered where he had gone. Anyhow, I told myself wryly, I had tried to do my duty as a fellow male.

It was after four o'clock in the morning, but the sky was still black. I pulled the blinds against the coming light, undressed, and got into bed. I didn't sleep much, but I dozed a little, and in my half-sleep I thought of all that had happened since five o'clock of the afternoon before, and of the trouble that had exploded into divorce between Don and Kay Canfield, the previous September. I thought of little Annie Canfield, riding a green horse with golden eyes, and of the ugly suspicion hanging over Don, with only the word of a four-year-old girl between him and a murder charge. I thought of Louette, sprawled on a cream-colored divan, and of Kay, tall and cool and lovely, wanting to help Don now—after she had left him because of jealousy and pride and stubbornness, and because she wanted to follow the rainbow trail of ambition.

I thought of the blond Francine, who had killed a rat with a hammer in Paris, while her lover, Paul Reynard, cowered in a closet; and Helen Quinn's pale, thin face with its haunted eyes floated across my brain. And then once more I was seeing the girl in the Hotel Avalon, lying dead and alone, with a bunch of violets in her hand. I saw Roger Quinn's scared, dissolute, handsome face; and my thoughts returned to the girl in the Avalon and I stirred uneasily and opened my eyes wide. Something would have to be done about her and soon.

Then I remembered the note Helen Quinn had received and all sleep was gone. I got up, heated the coffee I'd made the night before, and sat huddled in the kitchen, drinking it while the dawn crept in the window. Presently the sun came up and after a while it was seven o'clock on a bright morning in May.

I had shaved and showered when Helen Quinn telephoned. Her voice was strained. "Jim, he hasn't come home, and I just now discovered that his car is in the garage—I—I don't know how long it's been there. Had he—been drinking a lot?"

"No," I said.

"I'm worried, Jim. Won't you tell me what really happened last night?"

"I told you." My voice sounded as hollow and as false as a back-alley pawnbroker's.

"You don't have to protect him, Jim. I—I know what Roger is. I just want to find him, to know that he's all right."

I said carefully, "He said he was going home when I left him. Would you like me to look around a little?" As I spoke something in my brain seemed to turn over sluggishly and I felt a kind of chill along my arms and shoulders. Two people were dead, thirty miles apart, killed within the same seven-hour period, and Roger Quinn was a slender link connecting them, maybe more than a slender link. I wondered where Roger had gone and an ugly thought came to me—blackmail. Louette, from what I knew of her, would be capable of blackmail, and maybe the dead blonde, too. Maybe—

"Would you, Jim?" Helen Quinn said.

"Sure. Don't worry."

She said something I didn't understand, and I said, "What?" but she had hung up.

I finished dressing, put on my hat and coat, and went down to the Ford. It was a cool morning, but bright and sunny, with a lot of blue sky and a few white clouds showing over the tops of the buildings. I drove north toward the lake and then east to a long stretch of factories in a concentrated industrial area. The plant of the Connors Electric Company was not one of the largest, but it was modern and efficient-looking, all glass and steel and brick, and I guessed that it covered about six acres. It was built a good hundred yards from the highway and was surrounded by a wide expanse of weedy ground—plenty of room to expand. The plant itself was entirely surrounded by a high steel fence with three strands of barbed wire leaning inward at the top. Inside the fence on the east side of the plant was a wide parking area filled with cars. Before the entrance, just inside the main gate, flowers and shrubbery bloomed on an expanse of well-kept lawn.

I stopped the Ford in a space outside the fence marked *Visitors* and moved along a sidewalk to the gate. A uniformed guard came out of a small white-painted building and stood waiting for me. He was a thin little man with a long nose and a round chin the size of a golf ball. A small plaque on the shelf of an open window of the gatehouse said, *Alvin E. Semms on Duty*.

"Good morning," I said.

"Morning." He hitched at his belt. A shield pinned to his gray shirt was inscribed, *Connors Electric Company—Special Police*. He peered at me with small black eyes behind steel-rimmed glasses. "Kinda early for visitors," he said.

"Mr. Quinn around?"

"Nope. Come back around nine, ten o'clock. He *might* be here then."

I teetered on my heels and jangled some silver in my pocket. The flowers on the lawn were blowing in the cool morning breeze; the sun was bright on the glass and steel of the plant, and from inside I heard a continuous roaring sound.

I said, "How many shifts you working?"

"Just two now. They cut out the graveyard shift in 1946. You the fella that phoned a while back?"

I nodded.

"Thought you might be, seeing as you're here so early."

"Maybe he's in his office," I suggested.

He shook his head. "Naw. I looked. He ain't around." He gave me a sly look. "After you called I got worried and took a peek. Us guards like to know when any of the big brass is here."

"Could I go to his office and wait for him?"

"Afraid not. Anyhow, not until the office opens at eight-thirty."

I leaned against the gatehouse and looked up at the bright-blue sky. I saw the high boiler stack rising from behind the factory and my gaze idly followed the roof of the big sprawling building. Far to my left I saw the aluminum-painted ball on the tip of a high flagpole and my eyes followed the pole down to the jutting edge of the roof. Just above the roof something swayed gently back and forth in the breeze. Abruptly I stood up straight and brushed a hand across my eyes. It was still there, very clear and dark against the morning sky, the head and shoulders of a man with the head tilted forward at an impossible angle; the rest of the body was obscured by the roof.

I glanced at the guard, this Alvin E. Semms who was on duty, and he, too, was staring at the flagpole, his eyes big behind his glasses.

"*Yipe!*" he gulped.

He began to run and I followed him, running, too, although I knew there was no need to hurry. We pounded around the corner of the building. I looked upward then and I saw what was hanging almost halfway up the flag pole and I slowed to a walk. When I reached the pole the guard was breathing hard and frantically unwinding the rope from a metal hook riveted into the bright steel.

I placed a hand on his shoulder and pulled him away.

He stared at me blankly, his mouth open. Then he gazed upward, his Adam's apple moving convulsively. "Lordy, Lordy," he breathed. "It's Mr. Quinn."

I followed his gaze. Alvin E. Semms was correct. Roger Quinn was indeed hanging about thirty feet above our heads. His hands and feet were tied with a rope, with the hands behind his back. He was still wearing the gray cashmere suit, and the loose ends of his blue-and-red-speckled bow tie lifted gently in the breeze. The knees of his trousers, where he'd knelt in the blood of the blonde named Melissa, looked stiff and brown. His toes pointed downward and his head tilted forward, the thick black hair hanging over his dark congested face. Through the tangled hair I saw the eyes, bulging and white, and the tongue protruding from between the white teeth. There was a big clumsy knot of rope at the base of his skull.

"He—he musta been a-hanging there all the time," the guard stuttered. "I never saw him, nobody saw him up there." He turned, doubled over, and began to run.

He was almost to the gatehouse before I caught him. I grabbed his arm and swung him around. "How long you been on duty?" I snapped at him.

He shook his arm violently and his feet skidded in the gravel. "Lemme go! I gotta call the cops or somebody—"

Up at the main entrance a green Buick Roadmaster came to a stop beside the gatehouse. The guard saw it and he groaned. "Oh, my God—it's the big boss."

A tall gray man got out of the Buick. Gray hair showed over his ears beneath a gray hat. He wore a severe gray suit and he had a narrow gray face. He stood erectly by the car and gazed coldly at the guard and me.

I released my hold on the guard's arm and he ran forward. "Mr. Connors," he bawled, "an awful thing! It's Mr. Quinn, sir— That's him a-hanging up there!" He turned and waved his arm wildly at the flagpole. "We just found him, honest to God—"

Jesse Connors, owner and president of the Connors Electric Company, the father of Helen, the father-in-law of Roger Quinn, gazed at Alvin E. Semms with eyes the color of raw oysters. Then he shifted his gaze to the flag pole. Except for a spasmodic tightening of his jaw muscles, his expression didn't change.

The guard closed his mouth, stopped pointing, and shuffled his feet. "I didn't see nothing, Mr. Connors," he whined, "and I didn't hear nothing. I made my rounds on time and nobody came in the gate. I didn't even know Mr. Quinn was here. Honest, sir—"

"Shut up!" Jesse Connors snapped. "Get him down, you fool."

"I started to, Mr. Connors," the guard blurted, "but this fella—" He pointed an accusing finger at me.

Jesse Connors seemed to become aware of me for the first time. His narrow head began to vibrate from side to side in tiny jerking movements. "Hello, Bennett," he said in his crisp cold voice. "What—"

"He's dead," I said. "There's no rush now. It's a job for the police."

He looked once at the flagpole and then his gaze turned to me. "What are you doing here?"

Under the circumstances it seemed a rather silly question. Before I could answer he swayed and one thin mottled hand groped for the Buick. Then he fell slowly forward. I jumped and caught him in my arms before he hit the gravel. For a man of his height he was surprisingly light and I guessed that he didn't weigh much over a hundred and twenty pounds. His hat fell off, and the guard, who had been standing bug-eyed, picked it up and then scurried around and helped me carry Jesse Connors down the sidewalk to the office building. With our burden we entered a deserted reception room with blown-up photographs of Connors washing machines on the walls. The guard kicked open a door and we entered a long corridor. No one was in sight.

"This way," the guard grunted. "There's a couch in his office. Oh, Lordy, Lordy—"

We passed a row of doors and stopped before a frosted-glass one labeled *J. L. Connors, President*. The guard opened it with a key from a ring. We carried Jesse Connors inside and laid him on a leather couch against a wall.

I said to the guard, "Call a doctor—and the police." He nodded vigorously and ducked out. I guessed he was glad to get out.

I bent over the thin, gray old man and loosened his stiff white shirt collar. Suddenly he opened his eyes and stared up at me. He began to breathe hard and there was sweat on his face. He gasped, "Right—coat—pocket—"

I felt in the pocket, found a small glass vial filled with little round black pills the size of buckshot, unscrewed the cap, and shook two of the pills into my palm. Connors opened his mouth wide, like some gaunt fledging bird waiting for the worm, and I saw the fake pink of his upper plate. I dropped the black pellets on his tongue, and he swallowed convulsively. Then he closed his eyes and stretched out with a deep, rasping sigh. I placed my fingers on his scrawny throat and felt for an artery. His pulse was very weak, but as I waited I could feel it growing subtly stronger beneath my fingers. When his breathing became regular I stood up and looked around.

The office was big, but sparsely furnished. A plain oaken desk sat before a wide window overlooking the front lawn. The floor was polished hardwood, with no carpet. There was a row of straight wooden chairs along one wall and a big green metal filing cabinet in a corner. Except for a telephone, the top of the desk was bare.

Behind me a weak voice said, "Thank you, Bennett."

I turned. Jesse Connors's eyes were open and his hands were folded over his flat stomach. His face looked grayer than ever but his eyes were very clear and bright. During all the years that I'd known him he had always called me Bennett.

"Feeling better?" I asked.

He nodded slightly. "It's my heart. Get these spells every so often. Guess the sight of Roger—out there—"

He paused and in the silence I could hear the rumble of machinery from the plant.

Jesse Connors said, "How— Why—"

The door opened and the guard, Alvin E. Semms, poked his head in. "Pardon me, but the police just got here and Doc Eaton is on his way."

"All right." I motioned for Semms to leave and his head disappeared. Connors said, "Bennett, maybe you'd better get on out there."

"Will you be all right?"

"Of course." He closed his eyes.

I went out, quietly closed the office door, and moved down the corridor. The office help was beginning to arrive and the place was filled with a high excited chattering. A small group of men and women were crowded around a window, peering out. Others were running up and down the corridor and in and out of the reception room. A tall, sturdy girl was walking rapidly toward me. Her head was down and she seemed oblivious of the excitement around her. She brushed against me and I said, "Sorry."

She stopped and gazed at me blankly.

"Hello, Rebecca," I said.

She recognized me then. "Oh," she said, "Mr. Bennett." She brushed a thick strand of her tawny hair away from her tanned face. "Did—did you see what's out there?"

I nodded, thinking it a shame that Jesse Connors's secretary did not have a husband, or at least a lover. In spite of her husky stature she seemed very feminine to me—but I always did like big girls.

"They've got him on a canvas stretcher," she said. "I—saw him before they covered him up. His eyes were open and his tongue was sticking out—" She closed her eyes and shivered a little.

"Death is always ugly," I said.

She opened her eyes. They were blue-gray and very clear.

"Mr. Connors saw him," I told her, "before they took him down. He had an attack. He's on the couch in the office."

She looked distressed. "Oh, *dear*." She turned and moved swiftly down the corridor toward Jesse Connors's office. She had firm square shoulders and long strong legs and her waist was slim, in pleasing proportion to the width of the hips and shoulders. She entered the office and closed the door. For the first time I noticed the lettering on the glass door of the office across the corridor. It was bright and new-looking and it said *Roger V. Quinn—General Manager—Private*.

As I turned and moved away I wondered what the V in Roger's middle name stood for. And then I remembered that it was for Victor.

The day's production of washing machines at the Connors Electric Company was shot to hell. Every man and woman in the place was either standing outside the plant or leaning out the window. There was a police squad car parked by the flagpole and two cops were trying to keep the mob away. A death wagon was just pulling out of the gate, and a lieutenant of detectives named George Bronski was standing quietly on the fringe of the crowd. The little guard, Alvin E. Semms, was standing beside Bronski, and when I approached Semms pointed at me and I heard him say, "That's him. He's the fella who saw him first."

Bronski regarded me gravely. He was a stocky man in his fifties with a flat smooth face and thick black brows. He was dressed very neatly in a dark-blue suit, a maroon knit tie, and a gray hat with the brim turned up all around. He looked more like a banker than a veteran homicide cop.

"Hello, Jim," he said.

"Hi, George."

He nodded at the flagpole. "This is a new one—I thought I'd seen all the ways a man could die. Hanging, sure—from a cellar beam, an attic rafter, a hook on a wall, from a tree, from a cell window, a bridge, and even a bedpost. And now a damned flagpole." He sighed. "Did you know him?"

"Yeah, I knew him; Roger Quinn—married Jesse Connors's daughter."

"Oh?" He raised his thick black eyebrows. "And how did you happen to be out here?"

I was expecting that and I gave him the same story I'd given Helen Quinn. It would do for the present and I wanted a little time to think about things. I knew that he would check with Helen and I wanted our stories to jibe, at least temporarily. East Grange was out of the Cleveland police territory and there were things I wanted to do before I revealed the facts of Roger Quinn's love life. I hated it, holding out on George Bronski, but I was thinking of Helen Quinn and of Don Canfield and I wanted to go back to the Hotel Avalon before the East Grange law moved in, if they hadn't already. And there was Kay to think of, and little Annie, and the murder of Louette—

"Is that all?" George Bronski said gravely.

"Yep."

"Are you—uh—retained by Quinn's family?"

"Not officially. I told Mrs. Quinn that I'd try and locate her husband." I jerked a thumb at the flagpole. "Well, I located him."

"You sure did," Bronski agreed. "We'll do an autopsy, but the way it looks now he was knocked cold, trussed up, and then strung to the flagpole."

"Death at half-mast," I said.

Bronski smiled. "Very clever. You should write murder mysteries."

"How's Rockingham making out on that Canfield business?"

"I don't know. I haven't talked to him. He's home sleeping now. Anything else you want to tell me about this deal?"

"I guess not."

"You know, Jim, one thing I always liked about you—you cooperate with the police, don't you?"

"That's me," I said stoutly.

He patted my arm. "Keep it that way. I'll see you later."

As he moved away I knew that I hadn't seen the last of Lieutenant George Bronski.

A police lab truck pulled up and busy little men swarmed out and warily approached the flagpole with their kits of equipment. Two men in executive-looking dark suits came out of the plant, and with the aid of a squad of foremen they herded the gawking employees back into the building. Work must go on. Connors washing machines must continue to spew from the assembly lines, no matter if the boss's son-in-law was lying cold and stiff in the morgue, probably at this moment under the curious probing scalpel of the medical examiner.

I drove away, not wanting to do what I had to do.

CHAPTER TEN

I found Helen Quinn in the backyard of her big house. There was a lot of lawn and a big double garage, with a black-top drive winding up to a portico supported by white pillars. I parked near the garage and saw that Helen's blue Mercury and Roger's gray Cadillac were inside. I opened the door of the Cadillac. A half-full smashed package of Lord Nelson cigarettes lay on the front seat. The glove compartment yielded nothing but a pair of sunglasses, an Ohio-Michigan road map, and a pint bottle three-fourths full of bourbon whisky. I left the garage, circled a rose trellis, and saw Helen Quinn digging in a half-hearted manner in a tulip bed. She saw me coming and stood up.

She was wearing brown gabardine slacks, brown moccasins, and a soft tan sweater. The sweater was a mistake, because she didn't have the figure for it, but still she was attractive in a frail, delicate way, and I thought that she resembled the photos of those lean angular women in the slick fashion magazines. Her small face was pale and her eyes seemed sunken in the dark hollows of their sockets. I guessed that she hadn't slept since I'd seen her at four o'clock in the morning. She tossed a trowel into the tulip bed and began to pull off a pair of thin leather gloves, and all the while her eyes asked a silent question.

"Yes," I said, "I found him."

Her hands emerged from the gloves, white end thin and smooth; and she took a cigarette from a package in her slacks and placed it between her lips. As I struck a match for her I saw the glint of the morning sun on her hair. It was smoothly combed, parted on the side as always, and hanging in a loose curl just short of her frail shoulders. There was a faint clean odor of soap about her.

She drew on her cigarette and said lightly, "Does he feel badly? After slaving over a hot poker table all night?"

I placed my hands on her shoulders. Her skin felt cold beneath the fine wool of the sweater and I realized how thin she was, how vulnerable. She didn't move, but her gaze was on me and I could see the little cloudy flecks in her brown eyes. Some lipstick on her small, rather thin-lipped mouth would have helped; she looked too much like a little girl, a half-starved little girl.

I said, "This is bad news, Helen."

I felt her body stiffen but her voice was quiet, as always. "Tell me, Jim."

"He's dead."

She squeezed her eyes shut and she swayed a little, but she made no sound and she held on to her cigarette. I put an arm around her and led her into the house. She moved silently beside me as we went through a big bright kitchen and into a long living room. I pushed her gently to a deep divan and sat down beside her; I told her quickly about Roger, how and where I'd found him. She sat very still, her eyes closed, her head against the back of the divan. The cigarette burned close to her fingers and I took it and crushed it out in a glass ashtray on a low leather-embossed table. Still she didn't move and I began to feel uneasy. I was steeled for a different reaction and I wasn't getting it.

From somewhere in the house door chimes tinkled softly. I got up and moved across thick carpeting to the bare polished floor of the hallway. Lieutenant George Bronski peered through the screen at me.

"You get around fast, don't you, Jim?"

"She's a friend of mine. Somebody had to tell her."

"How's she taking it?"

I shrugged and opened the door. He entered and stood aside politely, waiting for me to lead the way. He was a cop, but he was human, and I saw that he didn't like his job any more than I had. We entered the living room. Helen Quinn hadn't moved. She opened her eyes and looked at us.

"Helen," I said, "this is Lieutenant Bronski. He wants to talk to you a little. Feel up to it?"

"I—I guess so." She nodded gravely at Bronski. "Please sit down, Lieutenant."

Bronski gave me a sidelong look and I knew what he meant. He didn't want any old family friends hanging around when he talked to her.

I said to Helen Quinn, "I'll see you later."

"All right, Jim. And—thanks."

A police car with a uniformed cop at the wheel was parked beside my Ford. I didn't know the man, but he said, "Hello, Jim."

"Hi," I said. I got into the Ford and drove slowly away.

It was after nine o'clock when I entered my office downtown. Sandy Hollis was pounding away on her typewriter and Alec Hammond was tilted back in a chair, reading the morning paper. He was a tall lean man with a freckled face, red hair, and pale-greenish eyes. He looked more like a Wyoming cow puncher than what he was—my star assistant. He lifted two fingers at me, "Morning, Jim."

"Hello, Alec."

Sandy Hollis handed me a slip of paper and said, "Hi, boss. Call that number." She was long-legged, brown-haired, gray-eyed, and she'd been with me since the day the old man had assigned me to run the Cleveland branch.

I looked at the paper. Kay Canfield's number was written on it.

I turned to Alec. "Ready to go?"

The legs of his chair hit the floor. "Yep."

I gave him a quick description of Don Canfield and told him the address. "Stay with him. He may not leave his apartment, but if he does I want to know where he goes, who he talks to. The cops probably have him staked out, too. Don't let them shove you around."

"Right, Jim." Alec went out.

I called Kay's number from my desk in the inner office. Mrs. Mahoney answered. "Mr. Bennett?" She sounded breathless.

"Yes."

"Mrs. Canfield asked me to call you. A terrible thing has happened.

She's been hurt."

"When? How badly?"

"Not too bad, praise the Lord. It was Providence that saved her. It happened early this morning, just before daylight. It's just her arm, but it could have been awful. Doctor Stein says it may leave a scar. They took her to the hospital, but they brought her home a while ago. She would like you to come out, if you could."

"I'm leaving now."

"Oh, thank you, Mr. Bennett. I'll tell her."

As I hung up I heard Sandy's phone ring and when I came out of my office she said, "It's a Miss Foster."

I took the phone from her. "Hello, Rebecca."

"Mr. Bennett," she said crisply, "Mr. Connors would like to see you. Can you come to his office right away?"

"Not right away, but maybe within the next hour or so. Will that be all right?"

"Just a moment." I heard a low mumbled conversation. Then she said, "Yes, but Mr. Connors asks that you come as soon as possible."

"I'll be there as soon as I can."

"Thank you."

I told Sandy Hollis where I'd be until noon; at Kay Canfield's first, and then at the Connors Electric Company. On my way to Kay's house I caught myself crowding the traffic lights and doing sixty in the thirty-five-mile zones. As I stopped in Kay's drive I saw Annie walking awkwardly in a scuffed pair of her mother's high-heeled shoes and pushing three dolls and the Teddy bear across the lawn in a toy baby carriage.

"Hi, Uncle Jim," she greeted me.

"Hi, Annie."

"When are we going to the merry-go-round again?"

"Soon, maybe."

"My mommie is hurted," she said soberly. "She's in bed."

"That's too bad, Annie."

"Where's Daddy? Will he come to see me pretty soon?"

I thought of Don and realized that I should have called him, but things had been happening too fast. "Sure," I said. "Soon."

Mrs. Mahoney came to the door. "This way, Mr. Bennett," she said in the hushed voice customary in a sickroom or a funeral parlor.

I followed her into the cool house and up the carpeted stairway into a sunny hall. She moved to a half-open door, peered into a room, and said softly, "Here's Mr. Bennett." Then she turned and nodded to me.

I moved into the bedroom, my hat in my hand. Behind me I heard Mrs. Mahoney going quietly down the stairs.

It was the first time I'd been in the bedroom that Kay had shared with Don. Venetian blinds were closed against the morning sun and it held a dusky twilight look. It was an attractive room, warm and intimate, with soft. tinted walls, a deep-rose rug, and two lounging chairs. Against one wall stood a high masculine chest of drawers of dark gleaming mahogany. Beside it was a very feminine dressing table with winged mirrors and a dazzling array of brushes, combs, jars, and bottles on its glass top. There were low twin beds, side by side, with a small table between them bearing a bronze lamp with a parchment shade. One of the beds was covered with a silken spread. Kay Canfield was on the other.

Her right arm was bandaged and held at an upright angle against her chest by a slender sling looped around her neck. Her bronze hair looked a deep red against the white pillow and it brought out the milky white of her skin. Above the top of the sheet and a light-green blanket pulled up beneath her bare arms I saw the top of a thin white nightgown. Even with no make-up and her arm in a sling she looked marvelous.

She smiled at me. "Hello, Jim."

I moved over to the bed and stood beside it. "Kay, what happened?"

She motioned me to a chair. I pulled it up beside the bed and sat down.

"I don't know, exactly," she said. "This morning, before daylight, I awoke suddenly. Annie was crying in her room and I started to get out of bed to go to her. Then I saw a black form rushing toward me and I screamed and slung up my arm. I felt pain in my arm and screamed again. Then I heard somebody running down the stairs and the front door slammed. Mrs. Mahoney came running in and saw the blood on my arm. She screamed, too. I told her to go quickly and see if Annie was all right and I looked at my arm. It—it made me a little sick and I guess I kind of fainted." She smiled up at me. "Don't look so—grim."

"Then what?" I asked.

"The next thing I knew, Mrs. Mahoney was bandaging my arm with a pillow case. She said Annie was all right and that she had called Doctor Stein. He came very promptly, looked at my arm, and hauled me off to the hospital in his car. He said it took ten stitches—I guess it's a rather bad cut. He brought me home a little while ago." She turned her head on the pillow. "There are cigarettes on the table, Jim. Would you light one for me?"

I lit a cigarette, placed it between her lips, and then lit one for myself.

"Did you get a look at the person in your room?"

"No—just a dark figure."

"Man?"

"I don't know."

"Anything stolen?"

"I don't think so."

"Do you lock your doors at night?"

She smiled ruefully. "Sometimes—when we think about it. But it's such a quiet neighborhood—"

I said, "It seems that Annie's crying awakened you just in time."

"Mrs. Mahoney thinks that Annie saved my life. But I hardly—"

"Have you told the police?"

"Doctor Stein called them before we left the hospital. An officer from the local station came over. He said it was attempted burglary, that my awakening surprised the intruder, that he became frightened and struck at me with a knife before he ran out. The policeman looked for fingerprints and all that." She smiled at me and reached with her good arm and touched my hand. "I'll be all right—I just wanted to talk to you, to tell you about it."

It seemed to me that there was a sudden chill in the room. I thought of Louette stabbed to death, of Melissa with her throat cut, of Roger Quinn hanging by his neck from a flagpole, and I said to Kay, "Have you seen Roger lately?"

A startled light flickered across her blue eyes. "Why do you ask that, Jim?" she asked in a quiet voice.

"Have you?"

"Yes. After my divorce from Don he started to come here. I couldn't stop him. Most of the time he was drunk. But Mrs. Mahoney and I managed to handle him. Then he became—persistent. The last time he was here I told him that if he didn't stop bothering me I'd call the police. I didn't want him here and I hated it because of Helen—she's such a swell girl. He hasn't been back."

"When was the last time?"

"Last week one night. Wednesday, I think."

"He won't bother you anymore," I said. "Roger is dead."

Her eyes grew big. "Roger—dead?"

I told her about it quickly, just the last part about how I'd found him on the flagpole. When I finished, I added, "It'll be in the afternoon papers."

"I—I can't believe it," she said, turning her face away. "It's—horrible. Poor Helen. Whatever Roger was, she loved him."

"I know." I stood up and gazed down at her. "Lock your doors from now on."

She turned her head and gazed at me gravely. "If you say so, Jim."

"Do you have a gun in the house?"

She looked puzzled. "Gun?"

"Do you have one?"

"I think there is one that Don had in the service—almost all of his things are still here." She pointed at the tall chest of drawers. "Look in the bottom drawer."

In the drawer beneath a pile of socks and shirts with frayed collars I found an Army .45 automatic wrapped in flannel. A film of oil glistened on the blue-steel barrel. I searched some more and found a box of cartridges. I filled the clip and carried the gun and the clip over to Kay's bed. She listened intently while I instructed her in its use. When I had finished she repeated what I had told her and awkwardly held the gun in her left hand and went through the motions of unclicking the safety and firing. It was a big gun for a woman, but I was satisfied that she was able to use it if she had to, even with one hand. Then I inserted the clip, set the safety, and slid it beneath her pillow.

"It's loaded now," I warned her. "If you have any more trouble, use it."

She smiled up at me. "It seems so—so melodramatic."

"Do as I say, whether it's melodramatic or not." I moved to the door. It was all I could do for her, short of camping on the terrace or having Alec Hammond sleep in the spare bedroom. But I didn't want to scare her with the thoughts I had and the things I knew, and I smiled at her. "I'll see you."

"Jim," she said soberly, "that's awful—about Roger."

"Yeah. A hell of a way to die."

"Have you seen Don?"

"Not since last night. Rockingham released him."

"Does that mean—" she asked quickly.

"I'm afraid it doesn't mean anything. They just don't have quite enough to hold him, or else they let him go for a reason. They're probably watching him."

She closed her eyes. "Who killed Roger—and Louette?"

"How would I know?"

"Are you still on my side, Jim? And Don's?"

"You know I am."

She opened her eyes. "Come and see me. Soon."

"All right, Kay."

She stirred restlessly. "I'm tired already of staying in bed. I think I'll get up for lunch. Mrs. Mahoney will help me."

"You'd better take it easy. Goodbye, Kay."

"Goodbye. Thanks for coming out."

Mrs. Mahoney was waiting for me in the downstairs hall. Her plump face was one big expression of anxiety. "It's an awful cut, Mr. Bennett," she said in a hoarse whisper. "Clear to the bone. And the blood! I like to fainted. But little Annie saved her. If she hadn't cried, Mrs. Canfield would never have waked up, and that man would have killed her, I know it."

I knew it, too, or thought I knew it, and I said, "Did you get a look at him?"

"Lands sake, no! I heard her screaming and I came running. Then I heard the front door slam and I didn't see anything."

"Keep the doors locked," I told her.

"I will! My brother is coming to stay with us tonight. He's a boiler fireman and he's on the day shift this week."

"Good." I went out.

Annie was still parading around in her mother's shoes. She waved at me as I got into the Ford. "Goodbye, Uncle Jim."

"Goodbye, Annie."

As I drove away I thought of Kay, pale and beautiful in the white nightgown, and of how she had asked Mrs. Mahoney to call me. As I said, she was my favorite among my friends' wives. And then I remembered that she was no longer anybody's wife. But I had never felt anything but friendship for Kay and I drove steadily on. There is a time and place for everything, and it was time for my appointment with Jesse L. Connors.

CHAPTER ELEVEN

Another guard was on duty at the main gate of the Connors Electric Company, a fat one, this time, with a red face and a white mustache. The plaque on the window ledge now read, *John M. Rice on Duty.*

I said, "Bennett's the name. Mr. Connors is expecting me."

John M. Rice waved me on in. "Go ahead. They called from the switchboard."

In the reception room a pocket-sized redhead behind a small desk greeted me with a brisk "Good morning." She had freckles and a humorous quirk to her red mouth.

I told her good morning, who I was, and whom I wanted to see. She nodded, picked up a phone, pressed a button, and gazed at me brightly.

"I'll just go on in," I told her. "I know where his office is."

She shook her head emphatically. "No, sir. You stay here until I contact the proper party." She smiled. "Standard procedure, you know."

I waited.

She turned her attention to the phone. "Miss Foster? Mr. Bennett is here to see Mr. Connors."

There was a muffled crackling from the phone and the redhead said, "Yes, Miss Foster." She cradled the phone and said to me, "It'll be about five minutes."

There was nobody in the reception room but the redhead and me. I leaned on her desk and asked innocently, "Miss Foster is Mr. Connors's secretary?"

"Now she is—exclusively. She used to do work for both Mr. Connors and Mr. Quinn, but since Mr. Quinn—you know about *him*, don't you?"

"Why, no. What about Mr. Quinn?"

She shivered with pleasure. "They found him hanging from the flagpole this morning—right out in front of everybody. Dead, you know. I saw him. It was awful, and the police were here and all. Mr. Quinn was general manager. He's Mr. Connors's son-in-law—was, I mean. It was a terrible thing. Didn't you *know?*"

"Suicide?"

"Oh, no, no. Murder. He was all tied up, hands and feet. And his eyes stuck out, and his tongue—it was simply *ghastly*." Her eyes danced.

"That's too bad," I said. "I'll bet you people were all pretty shocked about it."

"Oh, yes," she said quickly. "We certainly were. Poor Mr. Quinn."

"And Miss Foster was secretary for both Mr. Connors and Mr. Quinn, and now she's secretary to Mr. Connors alone?"

"Yes. Becky is very efficient."

"Becky?"

"Sure. Becky the Brute." She clapped a hand to her mouth. "Oh, I shouldn't have said that. Excuse me."

I waved a hand. "Forget it. You're among friends. What's your name?"

"Marcella, but my girlfriends call me Sally. My boyfriends, too."

"That's a nice name. Why do you call Miss Foster 'Becky the Brute'?"

"Well," she said seriously, "for one thing, she wears size eighteen dresses. Not that she's abnormal or anything, but she's *big*. All over, if you know what I mean."

"I know what you mean," I said.

"And besides," the redhead went on, "she's the athletic type. She don't drink or smoke and she don't care anything about men, can you *imagine?* But she just loves sports; bowling and golf and tennis and swimming and all that stuff."

"Is she really good?" I asked. "I mean, a champion swimmer or something?"

"Oh, yes! She's got just trunks of trophies. She prizes them greatly, but if you ask me, there are other things in life more important than trophies on a mantel."

"Like what?" I asked, following the script.

"Hah!"

The phone on her desk tinkled gently. She held a finger to her lips, winked at me, and lifted the phone. "Reception," she said in a carefully modulated voice, "Yes, Miss Foster, right away." She replaced the phone and said to me, "Go on in. Third door on your left."

"Thanks, honey." I moved out into the corridor and down to the door with Jesse Connors's name on it. I knocked softly and Rebecca Foster opened it immediately.

"Hi, Becky," I said. "I mean Rebecca."

She frowned slightly and stepped aside. Her tawny streaked hair caught a thin shaft of sunlight from the window beyond Jesse

Connors's desk. He was sitting at the desk, looking grim and grayer than ever.

"Sit down, Bennett," he said in a firm voice and motioned to a chair by his desk.

I sat down, holding my hat on my knees. Rebecca Foster took a chair at Connors's left, crossed her long sturdy legs, and flipped open a stenographer's notebook. She poised a pencil and didn't look at me. I thought of the redheaded receptionist's description of her and it seemed to me that it was unkind. Rebecca Foster was big, but she didn't look brutish. Far from it. I thought of a better word. Amazon was the word for Rebecca, a very feminine Amazon. Her broad shoulders looked strong and firm beneath her bright attractive dress and her skin held a clear golden glow. There was no polish on her closely clipped nails and her hands were brown and strong with no rings on the fingers. She wore no jewelry at all, I noticed, but her dress fitted her snugly and her stockings were of the sheerest nylon.

I said to Jesse Connors, "I hope you are feeling better, sir."

During the war called World War II, I had been obliged, by military regulations, to address my so-called superiors as "sir," and when I returned to civilian life I sometimes found the term helpful in certain situations and with certain men. It showed that I was sincere, polite, and respectful of my elders.

"Yes, thank you." He indicated Rebecca Foster with a slight movement of his narrow head. "This is my secretary, Miss Foster."

"I have the pleasure of knowing Miss Foster," I said.

She looked up and smiled at me. Her lips were full and nicely shaped and her teeth were big and white.

"I see," Connors said. "Also, I believe you were a friend of my son-in-law." He paused and his head began to jerk from side to side in almost imperceptible movements. "I mean, my late son-in-law."

"Yes, sir," I said, gazing at him respectfully.

He clasped his thin hands before him and his cold grey eyes bored into mine. "Roger is dead. That policeman—Bronski, is that his name?—tells me that it was murder. The police in this city are efficient and I hope they will find and bring to justice the person responsible. Last September I appointed Roger to an important position with this company. I'll confess that I did it over my better judgment. There was another man who was much better fitted—"

"Don Canfield?" I broke in.

"Yes. How did you know?"

"Don's my best friend. He counted on that job."

The old man sighed and his eyes shifted away from mine. "I know, I know. But sometimes in my position I must do things that—well—I must do things. I thought if Roger were given some responsibilities it would be good for him, steady him, and my daughter wanted him to have the job—hell, Bennett, you understand those things."

"Yes, sir."

"Don Canfield will be the new general manager now," Connors said bleakly. "I'll issue a memo right after Roger's funeral."

I thought of the trouble Don was in, but I didn't say anything. If Jesse Connors didn't know it, he would find out soon enough. "He's a good man," I said.

"I know it," Connors snapped. "I'm thinking of Roger now. My daughter loved him, he was the father of her children, of my grandchildren. I want his murderer caught—I owe that much to Helen. I know that you represent a reputable organization engaged in the business of investigation. You, personally, in the times that we have been in contact, have impressed me as a man of integrity, of character, a man to be trusted. My daughter has always spoken of you in the very highest terms. I believe you went to school together?"

"That is correct," I said, thinking of Helen Quinn with a faint sadness. "I finished my last two years of high school here."

His head had stopped its vibrating and his steady eyes never wavered. "Bennett, I want you to seek out and find, by whatever means and methods you possess, the person who killed my daughter's husband. I want him brought to justice for her sake. Will you undertake such a commission?"

"Yes, sir," I said. This was more like it, the right kind of a job, the kind of a job I liked. No haggling about the price, no strings to it—so far—a straightforward assignment from a man who knew what he wanted. His son-in-law had been murdered. He wanted the murderer caught. This wasn't a dubious deal in which I might or might not accept money from Kay Canfield, or an out-and-out favor for Don. Not that I wouldn't do my best for both of them, because they were my friends, but Jesse Connors's proposition was a strictly business deal with cash on the line. I'd do a job for him and he would pay me. That was the way I liked it, and the way the old man in New York insisted that it should be.

"Does your firm require an advance payment?" Connors asked.

"No. You will receive a statement from our office, itemizing the expense involved and the cost of services. If you wish to know the basic rates—"

"No, no." He waved a hand impatiently. "Frankly, Bennett, I like your manner and the way your firm operates. I did not realize that the profession of private investigation had been advanced to such a businesslike basis. It gives me confidence."

"Thank you," I said, smiling. "Did you expect me to have a pint of rye in my coat pocket, a blonde at my heels, and a .45 automatic in a shoulder holster?"

His thin gray face cracked in what might have been a smile. "Something like that, Bennett, I must confess."

I said, "You are aware that the police will probably find Roger's killer before I do?"

"If they do—fine. The sooner the better. But I don't want to take any chances. When will you start?"

"I'm working for you now," I said.

CHAPTER TWELVE

"Good," Connors said with grim satisfaction. "Ask me anything you need to."

I glanced at Rebecca Foster. All during our conversation she had been writing in her book, never glancing up. Now she looked up inquiringly.

Connors said, "It has been my practice for many years to keep a transcript of all conversations pertaining to business transactions or contracts in which I engage. I hope you do not object?"

"Not at all," I assured him, thinking of certain questions I wanted to ask Jesse Connors and wondering how far he wanted to go on the transcript of our particular contract. Now was the time for the discussion of certain delicate and personal matters and once more I glanced at Rebecca Foster, raising my eyebrows for Connors's benefit. Rebecca Foster was a nice girl, perhaps slightly frustrated and inhibited due to her sturdy stature, but no doubt entirely trustworthy in her secretarial capacity. Still, I hesitated to ask in her presence the questions I wanted to ask Jesse Connors.

He caught my glance and he said to Rebecca Foster, "Uh— that's all for now, Miss Foster."

She folded her notebook and stood up. Even with the low-heeled shoes she wore to lessen her height she was almost as tall as I. Without looking at me she went out, walking with a free and graceful movement, and quietly closed the door.

Jesse Connors said plaintively, "I wish I had a cigarette."

I offered him one from my crumpled pack, but he shook his head sadly. "No, I don't dare. However, I am permitted a little whisky." He opened a lower drawer of his desk and placed a bottle of bonded bourbon before him. "In the hall," he said, "there is a water cooler with a paper cup dispenser."

I jumped up like any junior executive, went out to the corridor, and got two paper cups. Connors poured mine full, his half full. I sipped at the aged whisky, savoring the smooth hot taste. He tossed his off and shuddered a little. Then he looked at the bottle longingly, but he didn't pour again, and he crumpled his cup with a swift final gesture and tossed it into a wastebasket.

"Help yourself," he said to me grudgingly.

"No, thanks," I murmured. "It's a little early in the day for me."

"It's never too early for good whisky," he snapped. "Drink up, Bennett."

"Thank you," I said, filling my cup again.

He watched me with sad eyes and he sighed and said, "Begin the questions. Let's get 'em over with."

I took a swallow of the whisky and said carefully, "How deeply do you want me to go into the murder of Roger?"

"What kind of a question is that?"

"Shall I be frank?"

"By all means." He lifted the bottle and took a tiny sip. "Don't tell my doctor," he said.

"I won't," I said gently. "It's *your* heart."

"To hell with my heart. I'm old enough to die. It's my daughter I'm concerned about. She really liked the son of a bitch."

That was my cue. All of my delicate instincts vanished and I told him quickly and positively about the dead blonde in the room at the Hotel Avalon. I didn't say anything about Louette or Don Canfield or about his daughter, Helen Quinn, and her early-morning visit with me. This was not the time for that, not yet. He listened gravely, his brows knotted over his deep-set gray eyes.

When I had finished he lifted the bottle and took another small drink. Then he said, "That's a shocking story, Bennett, but I believe you. Do the police know about it?"

"Not unless the cops at East Grange have found her. And if they have, they won't connect it with Roger." I thought of the note Helen Quinn had received and I added, "At least, not right away."

"Do you have any idea who killed this—this woman?"

"No."

"All right," he said briskly. "My only interest is to keep my daughter from being hurt further, and from being exposed to unpleasant publicity."

"I understand your feelings," I said. "If it comes out it will be unpleasant for Helen, of course. For me, too, I don't mind saying that for Helen's sake I have exposed myself to considerable criticism, both from the law and my superiors, but I am hoping that it will work out."

"I appreciate that, Bennett." He glanced at the bottle, but he didn't reach for it. Suddenly I felt sorry for him. He was Jesse L. Connors, a self-made man, a man who had clawed and double-crossed and worked his way up in the ruthless world of industry, and all he had to show for his life span was a multimillion-dollar business, a wife, a house, a widowed daughter, two grandchildren, a car, and a bad heart. I hoped that he'd had time for a little fun along the way.

He said slowly, "I know what Roger was. I knew about his women. He had a weak character. Helen is our only child and her mother and I thought he would make a good husband for her, but we were wrong. He embarrassed me before my associates and he antagonized my employees. But because of Helen I still stood for it. Oh, I raised hell with him, but he just laughed at me because he was sure of Helen's love and protection. When I made him general manager he promised to reform. But he failed me again. I had no love for Roger, I confess, but I want to protect Helen. Thank God, she didn't know what he was."

I thought of Helen Quinn, searching for her husband at four o'clock in the morning, but I didn't say anything

Connors said bluntly, "Tell me the truth. Do you think Roger had anything to do with that woman's death?"

"I don't know, but I don't think so."

He pushed himself back in his chair. Once more his head was vibrating from side to side, but his eyes were cold and steady. "You've got a job, Bennett. Let the chips fall. I place only one restriction upon you."

"What is that?"

"I want to be informed of any developments before you go to the police with them. I am thinking of my daughter, naturally."

"All right," I said and I stood up. My paper cup was empty and I tossed it into the wastebasket.

"Good luck," he said bleakly.

I moved to the door. "I'll keep in touch with you. Do I have your permission to question persons here at the plant?"

"Certainly. Go where you please, talk to anybody. I'll instruct the personnel office to give you full cooperation. If anybody balks, just call me."

"Thanks." I went out.

In the reception room two men with briefcases on their laps were waiting for Connors Electric executives to finish a conference, a cup of coffee, a comic book, or whatever an executive does to keep callers waiting. Marcella, the redheaded receptionist, called Sally by her friends, was talking on her telephone. She gave me a bright smile as I passed by.

John M. Rice, the red-faced guard, let me use the phone in the gatehouse. I called Sandy Hollis and told her that I would not be back at the office until sometime in the afternoon. She said that Don Canfield had called for me, also Sergeant Rockingham, who wanted me to call him back. I didn't want to talk to Rockingham, not for a while yet, and I said, "If he calls again, tell him you can't get in touch with me. I'll call Canfield later. Alec report in yet?"

"Not yet."

"All right, hold the fort." I didn't tell her where I was going because I didn't want anyone to know, not even Sandy.

As I crossed the drive to the Ford I noticed that the two police cars were pulled up along the far wall of the factory, and I wondered if Lieutenant Bronski was inside, questioning the employees. And I noticed something else. Someone had strung up a flag on the pole. It was snapping briskly in the breeze against the bright-blue sky. At half-mast.

It took me forty minutes to drive to East Grange. A kid with a crew cut and wearing a T-shirt with *East Grange Hi* lettered across the chest was behind the desk of the Hotel Avalon. He stopped reading a love confession magazine to sell me some cigarettes. Then I went up the stairway to the second floor and down the hall to room 206. The hall still smelled of soggy cigar butts and the *Do Not Disturb* sign was on the knob. I opened the door and poked my head inside. Everything appeared to be the same. One look at the bed was enough. The blonde named Melissa was still staring vacantly at the far wall. I closed the door and went back down the stairs. The kid on the desk didn't look up from his magazine. When I was outside the fresh air felt good and I took a deep breath of it.

A man came across the street, headed for the Avalon. It was the old man who had been on the desk the night before. He was still wearing his red-green-yellow necktie and the pink sleeve holders, and the pencils and pens sagged from his shirt pocket. On his head was a faded stiff straw hat, and a seersucker coat was slung over one arm. The puckered lump of flesh that had once been his left ear looked raw and ugly in the sunlight.

I touched his arm. "Good morning."

He whirled as if I had struck him. It was then that I saw the wilted bunch of violets in the lapel of the coat slung over his arm.

I flicked a finger against the violets. "Did she meet you last night?" I asked.

He twisted like a snake and made a dive for the hotel doorway. I grabbed his skinny arm and held on. He struggled briefly and then turned slowly to face me. "I don't get you a-tall," he said.

"I think you do."

His eyes shifted. "Who are you?" he asked sullenly.

"State police." I gave him a quick look at my special highway patrol shield.

He backed away, but I held on.

"I—I—I—" he stuttered.

"Don't get excited," I said soothingly. "I just want to ask you a few questions."

A sign up the street proclaimed that the Grange Bar dispensed beer, wine, and liquor. I guided the old man toward it. He moved jerkily, his gaze on the sidewalk. "Buck up," I said. "I'm going to buy you a drink."

The Grange Bar was long and narrow with tables in front and booths in back. Three men in overalls sat on stools at the bar. The tables and booths were deserted. I steered the old man to a rear booth. When we were seated the bartender came back. Ignoring me, he said, "The usual, Cornelius?"

The old man nodded.

I said, "Bourbon and water."

The bartender moved away. The hair on the back of his neck was shaved in a perfect half circle.

I said, "Cornelius what?"

"Hogmyer." He was sullen, his gaze on the table top.

"So she came to meet you, and for a hundred dollars you tipped her off that her husband was bringing women to the Avalon?"

He kept his eyes on the table and he didn't answer me. "What did she do then—after you told her?"

His thin lips worked in and out over his toothless gums. Then he said in a low voice, "She drove away."

"What kind of a car?"

"Blue Mercury."

The bartender came back with a tray and placed whisky and beer in front of Cornelius Hogmyer, whisky and a glass of water before me. I gave the bartender some money, but he didn't go away. He stood watching the old man, who poured the whisky into a glass, filled up the glass with beer, and drank it in three swallows his Adam's apple bobbing convulsively.

"The same, Cornelius?" the bartender asked.

Hogmyer nodded. The bartender looked at me.

"All right." I poured my whisky into the water.

When the bartender was gone Cornelius Hogmyer looked at me slyly. His eyes were bright and his lips had stopped working. "You ain't no cop," he said.

"Why not?"

"If you was, you'd run me in—not buy me a drink"

"I like to be sociable," I said.

The bartender returned with more whisky. Hogmyer made another beer-and-whisky highball and drank it. The bartender waited as before, but I waved him away.

I drank a little bourbon and said, "Tell me about it."

"I don't have to talk to you."

I shrugged. "All right. Then you can talk to the police." I made a move to get out of the booth.

He plucked at my sleeve. "Maybe one of them women is your wife, or your gal friend. Is that it?"

"No." I stood up.

"Oh, sit down," he said impatiently. "Maybe if I had another drink—"

I motioned to the bartender and sat down. More whisky and beer arrived and Cornelius Hogmyer's eyes became very bright indeed.

I said, "So he brought other women to the hotel, too—not just the one he had with him last night?"

He waved a hand expansively. "Hell, yes. He had a string of 'em, that boy, all kinds. The first time he came he had a skinny black-haired one, and then a little chunky one, and a big mixed-blond one—even a gray-haired one with a young shape." He laughed in a high falsetto. "And the son of a gun always winked at me and signed the register 'Mr. and Mrs. A. J. Holman,' from Detroit." He smacked the table. "Yes, sir," he said gleefully, "always Mr. and Mrs. A. J. Holman, from Detroit. He had more wives than a sow has pigs. It got to be a joke between him and me."

"What was your take?"

"Ten dollars each time. I always work the night shift."

"Why did you finally double-cross him?"

His lean face took on a sad expression and he eyed my extra shot glass of whisky with his bright little eyes. I shoved the glass across to him. He drank it straight this time, following it with a long swallow of beer. Then he ran the back of a hand over his mouth.

"I kinda hated to do it," he said. "I really did. But last week I saw his picture in a Cleveland paper with his real name and address, and—well, they're closing the hotel the first of the month. A new feller bought it and I'll be out of a job, and—" He lifted his narrow shoulders.

"So you decided to make a killing while you could?"

"I ain't as young as I used to be," he said gloomily. "I got myself to think of." He sighed. "It don't make no difference now, even if you are a cop, which you ain't."

"No," I said, thinking that I would need Cornelius Hogmyer eventually, and thinking, also, of the dead girl at the Hotel Avalon. "I appreciate what you have told me. Will you have another drink?"

"Sure. Why the hell not?"

Once more I motioned to the bartender. Then I nodded at the violets in the lapel of the coat lying on the seat beside Hogmyer. "Where did you get the posies?"

"They grow in back of the hotel—a big mess of 'em, this time of year. They smell nice. Roses are red, violets are—"

More drinks arrived. I finished my first one while Hogmyer mixed and drank another beer-and-whisky highball. He fixed me with a beady eye. "I went up the hill with Teddy," he said.

"What hill?"

"San Juan, in '98. Got my ear shot off. Teddy Roosevelt hisself wrapped his sword sash around my head." He turned his head so that I could see the lump of flesh where the ear had been. "A dirty Spic did it with a Springfield rifle. I thought I was kilt."

"You were in the Spanish-American War?"

He pounded the table. "Yes, by God! The Rough Riders. I got malaria, too."

I stood up. "Don't leave town, Cornelius. I may want to see you again."

"To hell with you," he sneered. "You can't do nothing to me. That woman, Mrs. Quinn, and me had a straight business deal. She paid me money and I told her what she wanted to know. Nothing wrong in that and I don't care who knows it now. I told her the truth. Go over to the hotel and see if I didn't. They're in Two-O-Six. If they've checked out, just look at the register." He cackled loudly. "Old A. J., the lady's man. You just mosey over there. It don't make no difference to me. He won't be coming anymore, not with the hotel closed. Gonna make a damned tearoom outta it, I hear. Better get over there. They got a 'Do Not Disturb' sign on the door." He giggled and some saliva ran down over his chin.

I could have told him that old A. J. wouldn't be bringing any more women to the Avalon, but I didn't. He was still giggling when I left him.

CHAPTER THIRTEEN

I didn't go to the Hotel Avalon. There was no need for me to go there anymore. Five miles out of East Grange I stopped at a gas station with a *Public Telephone* sign out in front and called the East Grange police department.

To the voice that answered I said, "There's a dead woman in Room Two-O-Six at the Hotel Avalon. It's a warm day and you better get her out."

After that I headed south on the main road leading to East Grange, on the route to Pittsburgh, and in a few minutes I saw what I thought I was looking for, a low glass-and-cement-block building surrounded by a wide expanse of black-top parking area. A big sign told me that it was *The Ranch House, Hamburgers of Distinction, Car Service.*

I hadn't turned off the Ford's motor before a tall girl in a long-sleeved open-necked calico shirt, scanty fringed white shorts, short white cowboy boots, and an imitation ten-gallon hat came out of the building and jounced toward me. She had reddish hair worn long over her shoulders, and a face that would have been pretty if she'd toned down her make-up a little. She stopped at the car window, smiled at me brightly. "What'll it be, partner?"

"One hamburger and a cup of coffee—black."

"Yes, sir." She hooked her thumbs in the waistband of the shorts and jounced back to the building. I had a ringside view of her long legs and compact hips.

There were four other cars parked by The Ranch House, with parents and kids in three of them. The fourth car was occupied by an elderly couple drinking malted milks. The clock on the dash told me that it was ten minutes after twelve o'clock noon. The tall girl came back with a tray bearing my sandwich and coffee and hooked it over the car door. I handed her a dollar and told her to keep it.

"Thanks, partner. Will there be anything else?"

I thought that over for a couple of seconds and decided to skip it. "Where's Melissa today?" I asked.

"Oh—you like blondes?"

"Sometimes. But I'm not choosey."

She tilted the big hat to the back of her head, took a sack of Bull Durham and cigarette papers from a shirt pocket, grooved the paper with her fingers, sprinkled tobacco evenly in the groove, and rolled a cigarette. She slid a pink tongue along it, deftly twisted one end, and put it between her lips. Then she lit a match with a thumbnail and held it to the end of the cigarette.

"That's a cute trick," I said admiringly.

She grinned like a kid with all A's on her report card. "A trucker from Texas taught me. The boss says it gives the place atmosphere. You know? Ranchy and cowboyish?"

"And cheaper than tailor-mades," I said.

"You a friend of Melissa's?" she asked.

"Sort of."

"I got bad news for you. She don't work here no more."

"Since when?"

"Since this morning. She's missed too many mornings lately. The boss said once more and she was finished. She's finished."

"So she didn't show up this morning?"

"Not even with bags under her eyes and butterflies in her tummy.

She just didn't show." She smiled at me and her teeth looked very white against her too-red lips. "But I get off work at three o'clock."

"Maybe I'll be back at three."

"What do you mean—'maybe?' Make up your mind."

"Okay. Three o'clock. Where does Melissa live?"

"If I tell you," she pouted, "maybe you won't be back."

"Sure I will." I laid a five-dollar bill on the tray.

She clapped a hand to her breast and her mouth was a red O. "For me?"

"Sure. We'll spend it for beer when I see you at three. Where does Melissa live?"

She slipped the bill into the shirt pocket which held the Bull Durham. "Well, she's got a room somewhere in East Grange, but I don't know where. The name and address she gave the boss was Melissa Kovak, 1428 Puxatawny Drive in Columbus. I help with the books sometimes, and I remember it because it's such a funny name. Puxatawny. Melissa is kind of a queer kid. She don't talk much, but she sure has the boyfriends." She sighed. "One of 'em drives a Caddy. He picked her up yesterday afternoon."

"You don't know her address in East Grange?"

"Nope. Sorry."

"Well, thanks, anyway. I wanted to see her on a little business matter. What's your name?"

"Why?" she asked coyly.

"We've got a date at three. Remember?"

"What kind of business did you have with Melissa?" she asked suspiciously.

"Life insurance," I said, thinking grimly of a trite underwriter's advertising slogan: *You Can't Buy Insurance When You Need It.*

"My name's Ethel," she said, casting an apprehensive glance over her shoulder. "Oh, oh," she muttered.

I followed her gaze. A big dark man in a white apron was glaring at her through the front window of the lunchroom.

"See you at three, partner," the girl murmured. She moved away to a station wagon that had just pulled in.

I ate my hamburger, drank my coffee, and then tooted the horn politely. Another girl, a rangy brunette this time, came out and got my tray. She gave me a nice smile. "Everything all right, partner?"

"Just lovely," I said, and as I drove away I decided that all of the girls at The Ranch House were real friendly.

At the next crossroads I used a phone in a highway garage to call the postmaster in East Grange. He had never heard of Melissa Kovak, had never had any mail for her, and naturally did not know her address.

Columbus was a good sixty miles south. I got into the Ford and swung in that direction.

It was a small soot-gray frame house on a long narrow street lined with soot-gray frame houses. There was a factory district at one end of the street and the Olentangy River at the other. In the distance against the sky I could see the buildings of downtown Columbus and the tower of the Deshler-Wallick Hotel. I stopped the Ford at the curb and went up a cracked and broken sidewalk. There was no grass in the tiny front yard—just bare yellow clay. I climbed three rotting steps and rattled my knuckles against the frame of a rusty screen door. There wasn't any mailbox, but a card was sticking out from beneath the screen. I leaned down and peered at it. It was a bill from the gas company addressed to Anthony S. Kovak. I pounded on the door with a fist. Nothing happened. I opened the screen and tried the brass knob of a blistered door. The door swung open, squeaking a little.

I poked my head inside and yelled, "Hey!"

I waited maybe a minute before I stepped inside and closed the door. I was in a small front room filled with cheap worn furniture. In the middle of the floor was a neat little pile of articles; a folded black lace nightgown with holes in it, a small pair of scuffed and dirty saddle Oxfords, three sheer stockings with wide runs in them, a small bundle of letters tied with a brown shoelace, a dusty paper gardenia with a red ribbon on it, a photo of a girl. I looked at the photo closely. It was in a cardboard frame printed with the words, *Souvenir of Cedar Point, Ohio*. The girl's face smiled up at me. It was the face of the blonde on the bed in Room 206 of the Hotel Avalon.

I straightened and gazed around the room. Against a wall was a small leatherette suitcase with the price tag dangling from the handle. I lifted the suitcase. It was heavy. I took four steps and peeked into an adjoining room. The floor of this room was piled with junk of all kinds—old clothes, buckets, mops, worn-out shoes, stacks of newspapers and magazines. Beyond was another doorway and through it I saw the edge of a stove and the drain pipe of a sink. I picked my way through the litter and entered the kitchen.

I had time to see a table piled with dirty dishes before a bright light exploded behind my eyes. Then the worn and greasy linoleum heaved up and smacked me in the face.

I don't know how long I was out before I rolled over and opened my eyes. I saw cobwebs in a corner of the kitchen ceiling and stared at them blankly for a while before I pushed myself to a sitting position. The back of my head felt spongy and wet. I got to my feet, staggered to the sink, turned on the cold water, and held my head beneath it. Water ran pink into the sink. After a while I turned off the water and dried myself as best I could with a handkerchief. Then I lurched through the room piled with junk and stood swaying in the doorway of the front room.

The new suitcase was gone and so was the pile of articles which had been in the middle of the floor. I gazed out of a dusty window and saw that the Ford was still at the curb. Then I went back to the kitchen and ran more cold water over my face and head. As I combed my hair before a wavering mirror over the sink I saw that my white shirt was soaked with water and blood and that my gray flannel suit looked like dirty blotting paper. I picked up my hat from the floor and put it on, tilting it well forward from the tender lump behind my right ear.

Out on the front porch I saw that the bill from the gas company was still lying beneath the screen door. I figured it would be lying there for a long time. Let them turn off the gas—what the hell did Anthony S. Kovak care? I moved carefully down the steps and out to the Ford. As I drove slowly away, the street seemed to be bobbing up and down before my eyes.

I stopped at Worthington and had a slow drink of bourbon and water. It didn't help my head any. I bought some aspirin, took a couple of tablets, and had another bourbon. I felt worse. By the time I reached the fringes of Cleveland, my head was one big ache and I had trouble focusing my eyes on the road. In Rocky River I stopped at the office of a doctor I knew and pressed the bell beside his back door. His nurse let me in, and the doctor left a fat woman and a crying baby in an adjoining room to look at my head and shine a bright light into my eyes.

"Nasty bump, Jim," he said. "Maybe a slight concussion. I think maybe I'd better take a picture."

"Not now, Doc."

He looked dubious. "I'd better." He dabbed at my head with alcohol.

"Just give me something for the pain."

"Okay," he sighed, "but if it hurts you by tonight, call me. What did he hit you with?"

"I don't know. I didn't see him."

The nurse went to a cabinet and came back with a small envelope, two capsules, and a glass of water. I took the capsules and pocketed the envelope. At the door the doctor said, "Take it easy, Jim. You hear?"

"Sure."

It was almost four o'clock in the afternoon when I reached my apartment. The pain in my head had let up a little. I took a shower, changed clothes, and drank some hot black coffee. Then I drove to Helen Quinn's house.

It was a warm afternoon, but it was cool on the wide green lawn. Roger's gray Cadillac was still in the garage beside Helen's blue Mercury. I went around to the front door and pressed the bell. Helen's mother came to the door. She was stout, red-faced, and gray-haired. Helen, it seemed, had inherited her thinness from her father.

"Why, hello, James," Mrs. Connors said. "How have you been?"

"Fine, Mrs. Connors," I said, thinking it odd that, in all the years I'd known the Connors family, she had always called me James while her husband called me Bennett. With my hat in my hand I stepped into the cool dusky hall. "Could I see Helen for a few minutes?"

"Of course. Jesse told me what you are trying to do for us." She leaned forward and spoke in a lowered voice. "Just between us, James, it's a blessing, in a way. I'm sorry for the children, but Jesse and I will make it up to them, and to Helen, too. Jesse thought she didn't know about Roger but she did, and now Roger has reaped the harvest of his sins. It's God's will, I say. For years I've watched Roger ruin that poor girl's life." She shook her head. "A shame, a shame."

I mumbled something sympathetic and moved to the archway leading into the living room. "She's in there, James," Mrs. Connors whispered. "I've sent the children over to my sister's. Try and cheer her up." She patted my arm, smiled knowingly, and went heavily up the stairs.

Helen Quinn was sitting in a corner of the big divan. Her legs were doubled beneath her and her eyes were closed. She was wearing a simple black dress with long sleeves and a high neck. It made her look thinner than ever, and brought out the waxy pallor of her skin.

But her brown hair was carefully combed and her small mouth was red with lipstick. On the low table before her a half-inch of cigarette smoldered on the edge of a glass ash tray. Across the room a small ivory radio emitted muted dance music. I leaned down and stubbed out the cigarette.

She opened her eyes. "Hello, Jim."

"Hi."

"I heard you and Mother whispering in the hall. I'm all right, really."

"Good." I tossed my hat to a chair.

"There's whisky in the cabinet."

"I don't like to drink alone."

"Of course you don't." She closed her eyes again.

I crossed to a liquor cabinet and opened it. There was everything inside, from Scotch to sherry. In Roger Quinn's house there had always been a good supply of alcoholic beverages. I selected an open bottle of Vat 69, took two glasses from a rack inside the door, and carried them back to the divan. I poured two inches of Scotch into the glasses and held one out to Helen. Her eyes were still closed.

"Helen," I said.

She opened her eyes, gave me a faint smile, and to the glass. "Mother never liked Roger," she said, "but Daddy did—at first."

"How about you?"

"I loved him." She took a sip of the Scotch. "I still love him." Her eyes avoided mine.

In my mind I had a long-ago picture of drab little Helen Connors dressed in a too-expensive formal gown, all green taffeta and ruffles, from which her thin little body emerged like a pale flower, and I saw again her thin shoulders and her narrow chest above the gown, white and delicate, with a big cameo on a gold chain falling to just above her small breasts encased in the stiff bodice. She was standing alone along the wall of the high school gymnasium while the senior prom swirled past her, standing forlorn and alone, trying to pretend with a pitiful fixed look of expectancy that she was just waiting for her partner. But I knew that she had no partner, that Jesse Connors had brought her in a big Packard with side curtains up against the rainy night, and that he would come and bring her home. And once again in my memory I was dancing with Kay Canfield—her name had been Kay Starr then—and Don was in the locker room having a drink from a pint bottle of bootleg whisky which we had purchased jointly for the occasion.

"Kay," I said, "go powder your nose. I'm going to dance with Helen Connors."

"That's sweet of you, Jim. I tried and *tried* to get her a date but—"

We danced to the wall and Kay joined a group of laughing couples, confident and secure in the knowledge of her beauty and popularity, and a boy had grabbed her and swung her to the dance floor. I had zigzagged through the dancers to where Helen Connors stood and when I spoke to her she turned big startled eyes upon me.

"Dance, Helen?" I had tried to make it casual.

But she had known why I'd asked her. It shone in her eyes and I'd had a quick odd feeling of sadness, of embarrassment.

"Thank you, Jim, but I—I have this dance—"

"Aw, come on." I had pulled her to the floor. I remembered after all the years the light and slender feel of her body within the circle of my arm and I'd been afraid to hold her too tightly. We hadn't danced very well together and I'd been glad when the music stopped.

Thinking of that spring night, and seeing Helen as she was now, made me realize how quickly the years went by. They hadn't changed her very much; she was still forlorn and alone, with only the bitter memory of a faithless husband. She drank now, and smoked, and made correct conversation; and she had acquired a certain polish. She had a big house and two children, and her picture appeared frequently in the Sunday society sections, but to me she would always be little Helen Connors, standing alone at a party, trying pitifully to look as if she expected someone breathless and exciting to happen along the next moment.

Her breathless moment was past now, I thought sadly, and she was alone again—standing alone at the ball. She took a cigarette from a box on the table and as I struck a match for her she said in a plaintive voice, "Who killed him, Jim—like that—such a horrible way?"

I drained my glass and poured more Scotch. I don't think she expected me to answer.

"Let's go somewhere, Jim. Let's get in a car and drive and drive. I—I can't stand sitting around here anymore. And soon relatives and friends will come to see me and I will have to face them. I will be the bereaved widow—"

I gazed at her silently.

"I am bereaved, Jim," she said quietly. "Really and truly."

I looked into the amber depths of the Scotch and I thought that now was the time to bring it out into the open. I said, "Helen, you must have known about him. Why did you stay with him so long?"

She lifted her thin shoulders. "There was nothing else to do. He was my husband, my children's father. What would I have done without him? He was my husband, the only husband I'll ever have—" Her voice broke and she drank some of the whisky.

"You're still young, Helen," I said, thinking that it was a hell of a thing to say to a new widow, but I meant it, and I really hoped that she would get married again to some nice plain guy who would love her and protect her from the world.

The soft dance music had stopped and I became aware of a voice coming from the radio. *"The body was found at noon today by East Grange police after an anonymous telephone call, and has been identified as Melissa Kovak, a waitress at The Ranch House, a roadside restaurant near East Grange. Police are searching for Anthony S. Kovak, the murdered woman's estranged husband, and a mysterious man who registered with Mrs. Kovak at the hotel at seven o'clock last evening as A. J. Holman, of Detroit. Cornelius Hogmyer, night clerk at the hotel, testified that this man was in the room early this morning. Police say—"*

Helen Quinn stood up, crossed the room quickly, and turned off the radio.

I swirled the Scotch around in my glass and gazed at the tips of my shoes. I decided they needed polishing. Helen came back to the divan and sat down. I looked at her. She lifted her glass to her lips. Her hand was trembling.

I said, "Today I talked with a one-eared man with violets in his coat lapel."

She leaned forward and carefully crushed out her cigarette. "All right, Jim," she said in an odd tight voice. "I lied to you. Of course I went to East Grange after I received that note. Any wife would."

A small cold feeling started at the base of my skull.

She leaned back and closed her eyes. "I saw her, Jim—that woman." She took a deep, shuddering breath. "I'll see her until I die."

I took a big swallow of the Scotch. "Helen," I said, "your father has hired me to find the person who killed Roger."

"I know. Mother told me."

"Tell me about it, Helen. All of it."

CHAPTER FOURTEEN

She said in a dead voice, "I went to East Grange last night and met that old man. He told me about the women Roger had brought to the hotel, and about the one he had there then, the blonde. I paid him and drove around a long time, thinking. At last I went back and parked behind the hotel. I found a back door and I went up to the room. I—I wanted to face Roger and get it over with. The door wasn't locked and I went in. I saw her—on the floor—"

"Go on," I said.

She opened her eyes, but she didn't look at me. "Roger wasn't there. I left and drove around some more, trying to decide what to do. I wanted to find Roger. I came back home. He wasn't there. I drove past your place and I saw Roger's car parked in front and I went up to your apartment." She looked directly at me. "I lied to you, Jim," she said quietly, "but you lied to me, too."

"Yes, Helen. I saw her, that woman. Roger took me there." I told her briefly about it. There was no longer any point in attempting to shield her.

She said, "Do you think that Roger—"

"Killed her?" I shook my head. "No."

"Then who— And who would do—do that to Roger?"

I finished my Scotch and stood up. My head ached and I felt old and tired and sick at heart. "I'm trying to find out, Helen. I'm worried about you. If anyone saw you go into that room—"

"Nobody saw me," she said quickly.

"You never know," I said. I looked at my glass and decided against pouring more Scotch. "Did Lieutenant Bronski bother you much?"

"He was very polite and considerate. He just asked a few questions— about when I saw Roger last, if he had any known enemies, things like that. I—I didn't tell him about East Grange. Was that wrong of me, Jim?"

"Bronski would think so," I said grimly, thinking that I hadn't told him about East Grange, either. "But don't worry about it now. We've got a little time, but not much, and maybe something will break before you have to tell him." I picked up my hat and moved to the archway leading to the hall.

"Must you go, Jim? Can't we take a ride or something?"

"Not now, Helen. I'm sorry."

"Is there anything wrong? Are you angry with me?"

"No, Helen. Did you tell Bronski that Roger was with me last night, playing poker?"

"Yes. I—I didn't know what else to—"

"It's all right." I sighed. "At least our stories jibe. But if Bronski gets too inquisitive, I may have to rig a poker game."

"Can—can you do that?"

"Yes," I said bleakly, "but I won't unless I have to."

"Will I see you soon?"

"Yes. Try and take things easy, Helen."

She gave me a wan smile. "I'll try."

In the hall by the front door I paused a minute and from the living room I heard her quiet sobbing.

It was almost five o'clock when I entered my office. Sandy Hollis was waiting with some letters and reports for me to sign. I signed them and telephoned Sergeant Rockingham. He was at the station.

"Rock, I just got back to the office. What's on your mind?"

"What's the idea of tipping off Canfield that we're watching him?" He sounded unfriendly.

"Why do you say that?"

"After I let him loose last night I got to thinking, and this morning I put a man on him, thinking maybe Canfield would lead us to the other woman—but he won't leave his apartment."

"Other woman?"

"Sure—the one he killed his wife for. There has to be a woman in it some place. I think you're covering up for him, because you're a pal of his, and I think you told him that we got him staked out and to lay low."

"Hell, I've got a man on him, too. Does that look like I told him to stay home?"

"Who?" he snapped.

"Alec Hammond. Didn't your man spot him?"

"No." On top of being mad, he was now irritated.

"Rock, I'm working for Jesse Connors on his son-in-law's killing. I thought you'd like to know."

"Who?"

"That Quinn killing this morning."

"Oh. Bronski's on that. So you're working for old man Connors, huh? You ought to be able to string that out for a long time—at fifty bucks a day."

"Rock, what's the matter with you?"

I heard him sigh. "Don't mind me, Jim. I've had a bad day. I've got this killing on my hands, and my wife went to the hospital for a gall bladder operation. I had to send to Toledo for my mother-in-law to come and stay with the kids. They're going to operate in the morning."

"That's too bad, but I'm sure she'll get along okay. Give her my regards."

"Thanks, Jim."

"Is Bronski there?"

"Yeah. He just came in."

"Let me talk to him."

"Sure."

In a couple of seconds Bronski's quiet voice said, "Hello, Jim."

"George, I wanted to tell you that Jesse Connors hired me today to work on Quinn's killing."

"He's got a good man."

"How did you make out today?"

"Well, we made a start, but it looks tough. I spent the whole damned day at the plant. The medical report shows that he was knocked cold first and then strung up, like I said. He died on the flagpole."

"Any ideas?"

"There are only about a thousand suspects, Jim," he said dryly. "Every employee of the Connors Electric Company is all. From what I can find out, every man and woman in the place hated him. Being the big boss's son-in-law, he threw his weight around considerable—from the top on down, especially after he got the job of general manager. I've talked to a hell of a lot of those people out there, and my men have talked to a lot more, and not one of 'em had a good word for Quinn. Ain't that hell? And they weren't bashful about saying so, either. Jim, somewhere in that plant is a man with a perverted sense of justice and a real or imagined grievance against Quinn. That's the man I've got to find—some screwball with the kind of quirk that would make him want to string Quinn up where everybody could see him."

"How do you figure to approach it?" If I could keep Bronski's mind on Connors Electric employees maybe he wouldn't get too inquisitive about a mythical poker game.

Bronski said, "The personnel office out there has a complete file on all employees, past and present—their conduct, background, hobbies, family status, and all that, plus photographs and fingerprints. I'll start with the prints, weed out those with records, and take it from there."

"Sounds good, George." He was a bulldog, I knew that, and I began to wonder if I was on the right track or on any track at all. "If I can help, just let me know."

"All right, Jim. Thanks."

As I hung up I wondered how long it would be before Lieutenant Bronski and Sergeant Rockingham would get together and begin to connect a few details, like Roger Quinn's visits to Louette Canfield and to Kay, and to a hotel in East Grange. Details like a dead blonde named Melissa Kovak, and an attempt upon Kay Canfield's life and no poker game, and maybe Helen Quinn's visit to East Grange with a hundred dollars for a one-eared old man named Cornelius Hogmyer. Not long, I decided, and I began to sweat. It wouldn't be too damn long before two smart cops would be digging up things and starting to add them up. Time was running out. If I was going to help Don Canfield or anyone else, if they could be helped, it would have to be quickly.

Behind me Sandy Hollis said, "How did you get the goose egg behind your ear?"

"A wound received in the course of duty," I said, picking up the phone again. I called the Connors Electric Company and asked for Miss Foster.

Her voice was crisp and businesslike, as befitted the secretary to the president. "Mr. Connors's office. Miss Foster speaking."

"Rebecca, this is Jim Bennett."

"Hello."

"Look, Rebecca, as you know, Mr. Connors employed me this morning for a special job and maybe you can help me, if you will. How about having dinner with me?" She hesitated, and then she said, "I have a dinner engagement with a business girl's group at the YWCA. I'm awfully sorry."

"Then meet me for a drink first. Do you have a car?"

"I have a car, but it's at home. I ride to work with some other girls from the office. And I don't drink. Remember?"

"Well, I'll pick you up and buy you a Coke before I take you home, if you're going home."

She laughed. "All right."

"I'll be there as soon as I can."

As I replaced the phone, Sandy Hollis said, "Is *that* in the course of duty?"

"Miss Hollis, the ways of investigation are devious and winding."

"I'll bet," she said. "Oh, sure."

I helped her lock up and we went down to the street together. She said she wanted to do some shopping before the stores closed, and I left her and got the Ford. It was slow driving across town in the late-afternoon traffic, and it was after five-thirty before I stopped at the gate of the Connors Electric Company.

Rebecca Foster was waiting for me by the gatehouse and I thought that for a big girl she wore her clothes well. The sun glinted on her sun-streaked hair as she ducked her head to get in beside me, and I remembered again the redheaded receptionist's description of her as Becky the Brute. I still thought it unkind and I would never have called her that. She was big, all right, but all of her was in the right places. She had everything a girl should have, only more of it.

"Just take me home, please," she said. "We can talk there. I'm to meet the girls at seven o'clock. We're organizing a softball team and they want me to be captain."

"Good for you." I was aware of the clean soapy smell of her. No perfume—just the wholesome odor of an outdoor girl who probably took two cold showers a day. "What's your batting average?"

"I thought you wanted to talk about Roger—Mr. Quinn?"

"I do, I do. We'll get to him. Where do you live?"

She told me. It was on the east side, close to Euclid, and as I headed the Ford in that direction, I said, "I hope your boyfriend won't care that I'm taking you home." I was pretty certain that she had no men friends, and I was curious.

She laughed. "I don't have time for boyfriends. I had one once—he used to work in the laboratory at the plant, but I'm afraid he wasn't my type. He just wanted to talk about poetry and his stamp collection. He didn't care anything about sports, not even baseball. He thinks the Indians live in tepees and go on the warpath. He didn't even know that they won the World Series in 1948." She laughed again. "Really, I'm too busy to have dates. I'm practicing now for the northern Ohio women's golf tournament next month, and then comes a swimming meet. In between I want to get in some tennis, and, of course, the softball schedule will keep me busy two nights a week."

"My, my," I said, "that all sounds very interesting and wholesome and worthwhile, but there are other things in life, Rebecca, believe me."

"What things?" she asked mockingly.

"Oh," I said, "things like dancing and picnics, moonlight nights and champagne cocktails, push-button kitchens and automatic washing machines, a husband and two or three kids, a television set and payments on a little bungalow—things like that, to name a few."

"Not for me," she said firmly. "That's for the masses, for the poor little girls who need someone to protect them, to pay their bills and assure them a soft life without working."

"Oh, come, now," I said, "every girl wants to get married."

"What for?" she asked almost fiercely. "So that they can meekly submit to the biological pattern of reproduction, with a man their lord and master? The girls who get married would be helpless without a husband, and they console themselves for their slavery by thinking that they are providing a home for a man, cooking his meals, darning his socks—but without a man they are lost. That's not for me, ever. Turn right at the next corner."

I turned and she pointed out a big red brick apartment building. I pulled over to the curb and stopped. We went up a wide walk to the entrance and into a small foyer. She took some mail from a box on the wall and I followed her up a short flight of steps to a cool carpeted hell. She took a key from her purse and opened a door. The apartment was small, but sunny and pleasant, with softly tinted walls. And then I saw the dog.

He was a big gray-and-black German shepherd and he was coming for me like a bat out of hell. He raced across the room silently, his yellow eyes glued to a spot just below my chin.

I swung around and ran for the door.

Behind me Rebecca Foster said sharply, "Eric!"

I heard a scratching sound as the dog skidded to a stop. I turned slowly, still poised to run. I like dogs, but I guess I'm not a true dog man. When they lunge for me with a fixed look in their eyes I don't know enough about them to say, "Heel, Rover," or whatever the hell you say to dogs to make them behave. This dog was now crouched down three feet away from me and his eyes were still focused with a steady intensity on my throat. His jaws were closed, but a low rumbling came out of his chest and the hair over his powerful shoulders was standing up straight.

Rebecca Foster laughed. "You're strange to him," she said.

I wiped my forehead with a damp palm. "Maybe you'd better introduce us."

She laughed again and pointed a finger at the dog "Eric, lie down."

Eric backed away, still crouching. When his hindquarters hit the wall, he sank down, his big head on his front paws. He continued to growl deep in his throat and his yellow wolf's eyes never wavered.

"His full name is Eric Bismarck Von Tonder the Third," Rebecca said. "He's just a puppy."

"He's playful," I said. "I can see that."

"But he's well-behaved, really, and very well trained. But I'm afraid I'll have to get rid of him. I take him for walks at night, but he gets restless in the apartment all day. When he was small, it was fine, but big dogs should have space to run. Would you like a nice German shepherd, Mr. Bennett?"

"No, no," I said. "But thanks."

She smiled. "How about a drink?"

"I'm in dire need of one."

"I'm sorry I can't offer you a cocktail, but there's some whisky."

"Fine—with water."

She left the room. I heard a refrigerator door open and close and the clink of ice in a glass. Eric and I silently eyed each other. I lit a cigarette and tried to ignore him, but he continued to make low ominous sounds. I was glad when Rebecca returned.

She was carrying a bottle and a glass containing water and two ice cubes. The bottle was about a quarter full—rye, if the label meant anything.

"Pour your own," she said. "I'm afraid I'm not very familiar with drink mixing. I happened to have the whisky because some friends left it here ages ago."

I drank some of the water, filled the glass with the rye, and stirred it with my finger. She went to the kitchen again and returned with a tall glass filled with a thick orange fluid. She sat down on a divan and I sat there, too, with a good three feet between us. I gazed around the room. It was attractively furnished and surprisingly feminine for a girl like Rebecca Foster. Bookshelves filled one wall and a quick glance from where I sat told me that most of the titles dealt with sports and the outdoors. Two which caught my eye were *Professional Tennis* and *The Handling of Small Sail Craft*. I didn't see any fiction, no books about anything so silly as love. On a mantel above a gas-burning fireplace shone a glittering array of silver trophies.

I nodded at the trophies. "All yours?"

"Yes," she said carelessly, sipping from her glass.

I said curiously, "What're you drinking?"

"Carrot juice—lots of vitamins."

I suppressed a shudder and poured more whisky into my glass. Across the room Eric made hoarse throaty sounds.

I decided it was time to get down to business. "Rebecca," I said briskly, "I don't want to make you late for your softball meeting with the girls. Can you tell me anything which might help me to catch the person who killed Roger Quinn? Anything at all? You worked with both him and Mr. Connors for some time, I believe. Did Roger have any particular enemies—that you know of?"

"No," she said, shaking her head slowly. "I'm afraid I can't be of much help. Of course, he wasn't very popular with the employees, and he and Mr. Connors did not always agree on policy regarding discipline for misconduct. You know—discharge, or other punishment. But anyone in Mr. Quinn's position, especially after he was promoted to general manager, is bound to make enemies, but as for anyone disliking him enough to—"

"How was he to work for? As far as you personally were concerned?"

She lifted her sturdy shoulders. "All right, I guess. He was impatient sometimes, and demanding, but I got along with him."

"How long have you worked for Connors Electric?"

"A little over five years—ever since I finished business, school. It was my first job. After the first year I was assigned to Mr. Connors, and I did secretarial work for both him and Mr. Quinn. Mr. Connors was away a lot, leaving the plant in charge of Mr. Quinn."

I thought a couple of seconds before I asked the next question. Then I decided that there was no reason why I shouldn't ask it; Rebecca was attractive and feminine, in spite of her size, and what I had in mind was not at all impossible, knowing Roger. Mere proximity to any female had been like a green light to Roger Quinn. I said, "Did he ever make any passes at you?"

She looked startled. "Pardon?"

"Did he try to make love to you?"

Her tanned cheeks took on a deep ruddy glow. "No," she said. "He was never like that—not at all. Why do all ask?"

"Just wondered," I said, giving Roger mental credit for not mixing business with his love life. "To your knowledge had he received any threatening phone calls lately or letters? Anything like that?"

"Oh, yes—quite a few during the past year, all of them obviously from employees or ex-employees—no doubt from persons he had discharged or punished for breaking a plant rule."

"I thought that things like that were delegated to foremen or supervisors."

She smiled faintly. "Not at the Connors Electric Company. Mr. Connors is very—well—democratic, and he believes in the personal touch. He feels it's good for labor-management relations."

"To have the top brass fire a man?"

She smiled again. "Yes, even that."

"You mentioned rules. What rules?"

"Oh, there are rules and punishments for drunkenness on the job, stealing, habitual tardiness or absence, insubordination, loafing, concealing spoiled work, smoking in restricted areas—we have a lot of rules. Perhaps the workers felt that Mr. Quinn was unreasonable and maybe too severe at times, but he had heavy responsibilities."

"Do you have the threatening notes Roger received?"

"Not at present. Mr. Connors told me that the personnel department turned them over to the police."

"Oh," I said, thinking that Lieutenant Bronski was at holding out on me; he hadn't mentioned any threatening notes when I'd talked to him. Then I remembered that I was sure as hell holding out on him, and on Sergeant Rockingham, too, and I smiled wryly to myself. "Then the police apparently think that the killer is somewhere in the Connors organization. Do you agree?"

"It's possible," she said. "When you have a thousand people concentrated in one place there are bound to be some—well, crackpots."

"Yeah," I said, and I sighed. I wasn't getting any place. I finished the whisky and stood up. "I won't detain you anymore. Thanks very much, Rebecca."

"Have I helped any?"

"You never know."

"I wish you luck, Mr. Bennett. Do you have anything to go on? I mean—what do you call them—clues?"

I laughed. "Plenty of clues, but they don't mean anything. I just snoop and ask questions and dig around and maybe I come up with something and maybe I don't. But I keep trying. It's pretty dull work."

She raised her eyebrows. They were smooth and blond and heavy and a little plucking would have improved them. "Really?"

"Yes, but it's a living."

She stood up. Her carrot juice was all gone and she placed the empty glass on a table. There was something that I'd been wanting to find out about her for a long time. I stepped close to her. She didn't back away.

"You're quite a girl, Rebecca," I said.

She smiled.

I placed my hands on her firm shoulders and pulled her gently toward me. She fixed her gaze on my necktie and I felt her big body tremble a little. I dropped an arm to her waist and held her closely. She stood still, with only the faint trembling. She was tall and substantial, just about the biggest girl I'd ever been this close to, but all of her was nice and when I kissed her, her lips were warm and clinging. Some man, I decided, was missing an opportunity for quantity and quality in one generous package, and I kissed her again.

She pushed away from me then and she said breathlessly, "Please—" Her cheeks were flushed and her eyes were veiled and cloudy.

"Skip the softball meeting with the girls," I said.

"You said it was dull work," she said mockingly.

"Not this work." I reached for her again.

She shook her head and lightly held my arms. "Can I see you again?"

"To talk about Mr. Quinn?"

"To talk about you. About us. I'd like to bring you up to date about a lot of things."

"What things, Mr. Bennett?"

"Call me Jim."

"What things, Jim?"

"I'll tell you—and show you."

"And you think I would like them?"

"Sure—if you were exposed to them. How about dinner tomorrow night?"

"I'm busy."

"Doing what? Practicing for a channel swim?"

She smiled. "Gym class at the Y."

"My God! Skip the gym class."

"All right— You know, you're the first man who has kissed me in a very long time."

"A hell of a note."

She gazed at me thoughtfully. "I haven't kissed many men. I'm too big for most of them." She laughed shortly. "They would have to stand on a box or something."

"Not me," I said.

"I know. Are you really serious about my having dinner with you?"

"Of course."

"Thank you," she said soberly. "It's nice of you to ask me."

"Tomorrow night, about six? Here?"

"All right."

"Fine," I said. "May I kiss you again?"

"Let's leave it like this—for now."

"All right. For now." I moved to the door and opened it.

"Goodbye, Jim."

"Goodbye."

Eric growled a goodbye to me, too.

CHAPTER FIFTEEN

It was five minutes after six in the evening. I was sleepy and tired and my head still hurt, and I suddenly realized that I hadn't eaten anything since the hamburger at the drive-in south of East Grange before my ill-fated trip to Puxatawny Street in Columbus. I thought longingly of my soft bed and of a sirloin I'd been hoarding in my refrigerator, but I still had things to do and now wasn't the time to let the trail grow cold—if I had a trail.

Since early morning I'd talked to a number of people, had been knocked cold, consumed a little whisky, smoked a pack of cigarettes, been half propositioned by a sexy cowgirl, kissed a husky athletic girl who hadn't been kissed much before, learned a few things which didn't fit with anything else. I had gone through the motions of a man trying to flush a killer, but I was still way out in the wild blue yonder all alone and with a bump on my head.

The worst of the traffic was over and I made it to Don Canfield's apartment in twenty-five minutes. I parked around the corner, walked back, and spotted Alec Hammond down the street a little way, standing with a group of people at a bus stop. Riggio, Rockingham's man, was loitering in the door of a candy store across the street. He saw me and I waved to him, but he looked the other way.

I walked up to Alec and stood beside him. He knew I was there, but he didn't look at me as he said softly, "He hasn't showed all day. Babe went in a half hour ago. She's in his apartment, still there. Tall babe, hair like a new penny, nice legs, arm in a sling, smooth dresser."

"All right, Alec, relax. Riggio saw me, and he sure as hell is seeing you now."

He grinned at me, his greenish eyes glinting in the yellow sunlight of evening. "He didn't spot me until I followed the babe in," he said. "I had me a nest across the street upstairs. Apartment of a gal friend of mine. She let me sit by the window all day. Worked out real nice." His grin grew wider. "I'll be glad to take this beat tomorrow."

"I'll bet," I said. "You can knock off now. Call Red Drake to take over until morning. If he's tied up, get Homer Shippen. I'll stick around until one of them gets here."

"Right, boss." As he moved away I thought that he even walked a little like a cowpuncher, slightly bowlegged, his arms swinging free, as if he were ready to draw a six-gun as he trod the dusty streets of Abilene.

I walked back to the apartment house. I didn't look across at Riggio, but I knew that he'd observed my conversation with Alec. I went up to Don Canfield's apartment and pressed the buzzer. Nothing happened. I waited a little and pressed it again. Don opened the door. He was wearing a yellow pullover sweater, cord slacks, and crepe-soled shoes. He needed a shave and his eyes looked tired.

"Oh, hello, Jim. I was just getting a little shut-eye." He yawned and pulled a hand over the stubble on his cheeks.

I stepped inside and closed the door. He took a crumpled pack of cigarettes from his slacks pocket, extracted a cigarette, and lit it. "Sit down, Jim. What's on your mind?"

"You. Getting tired of being cooped up?"

"God," he said.

I looked around. The divan where Louette had died was still covered with the sheet and turned to the wall. A window was open and a breeze gently blew the curtains, but the room seemed hot and smelled of stale cigarette smoke. A stack of newspapers were on the floor. I could see part of a black headline: *Police Hunt Flagpole Slay*— That would be the story on Roger Quinn.

I sat in a deep chair and stretched out my legs. It felt very good to sit down.

Don said, "What's going on in the outside world?"

"Rockingham still thinks you killed Louette."

"But *why?*" There was a desperate edge to his voice.

"He says you're in love with another woman and wanted to get rid of your wife."

"Jim, you know damn well—"

I held up a hand. "Sure, I know, but Rockingham doesn't. He's not a friend of yours. He's just a cop. He also thinks that I'm covering up for you, holding out on him."

He gazed at me quietly for a brief moment. Then he said quietly, "Are you, Jim?"

"How could I?" I asked, watching him. "What is there for me to cover up?"

His gaze shifted away from mine—"Nothing, Jim. I've told you everything."

"Everything?"

"Yes."

I said gently, "Where is she?"

He swung quickly toward me. "What?"

"Where's Kay, Don?"

He flushed. "Jim, I—"

A voice from the bedroom doorway said, "Here I am, Jim."

She stood there, tall and cool in a belted rust-colored dress and a tiny straw hat on her bronze hair. In spite of the bandage on her arm and the slender sling looped around her neck she looked like a model in a gold-plated dress shop, and she was so beautiful that for a second I caught my breath. She was every man's dream of the perfect woman; very feminine and yet not clinging or soft, not small and dainty, but full-breasted, slim-waisted, long-legged, with clear, steady eyes bright blue against her white skin.

"Hello, Kay," I said and stood up.

Don said to me, "How did you know she was here?"

"One of my men told me. He's been watching your place all day."

"Why?" he asked quietly.

"Because I wanted to know where you went, who you talked to, what you did."

"I see," he said bitterly.

"You don't see, damn it," I said sharply. "The police are watching you and I don't want them to know anything I don't. I'm trying to keep them from getting the jump on me and on you."

"I see," he said again. "Just like in the movies."

"Listen—" I began.

"Jim," Kay broke in, "I'm afraid we owe you an explanation—and an apology."

I looked at her, "I think so, too. This is the worst possible time for you to be here. Rockingham knows it by now, and it won't take long for him to add things up—the way he wants to add them up. He thinks there is a woman in the woodpile, and to him you'll be that woman. If you and Don wanted to talk over old times you could certainly have picked a more suitable place—and time." I felt mean and bewildered and somehow betrayed.

"Don't talk like that," Kay said. "We weren't trying to deceive you or anyone else." She glanced at Don and he shrugged and nodded grimly. "Jim, Don and I are going to get married again."

I thought about that in the silence for maybe thirty seconds. And then I said, "You might wait until Louette is buried."

Don got half out of his chair. "Jim, damn you—"

I looked at him, feeling meaner and nastier by the second. I didn't say anything, but just looked him in the eyes, and I think at that moment I almost hated him. He'd had Kay once and he'd let her go, and now he was going to get her again.

He leaned back in his chair, "Oh, hell," he groaned, "what a mess."

Kay said firmly, "Now, listen, Jim. I won't have you thinking what you're thinking. A long time ago Don and I decided that we'd made a mistake. We both were to blame, but I was the most to blame. It was silly of me to be jealous of him, to suspect him. I know that now. We wanted to get married, start over again; but he was married to Louette, and she wouldn't divorce him. A week ago she finally agreed, but she wanted a lot of money, more than we have. Twenty thousand dollars. I offered to sell the house, but Don wouldn't let me. He said he'd talk to Louette some more, find a way. And then Louette was killed and—"

"My God," I almost shouted, "if Rockingham knew that he'd have you both in jail, and I wouldn't blame him."

"Wait," Kay said quietly, "listen to the rest of it. It's not only Louette—Roger Quinn was killed, too. And when Don came to see me the other night he found Roger there. They quarreled, naturally, and Don struck him. We couldn't tell you *that*, not after what happened later. We couldn't tell you anything, don't you see? We wanted to keep our marriage plans secret until after Don's divorce. You can understand that, can't you?"

"I understand a number of things," I said, remembering the bruise on Roger Quinn's cheek. I could have told them that Don and Louette had not been legally married, that Louette had already been married to Paul Reynard, that they could have gotten married any time. But I didn't tell them and I thought to hell with them. I was dead tired and discouraged, and as lonely as I ever felt in my life.

"Don," I said wearily, "of course you know that Roger Quinn has been murdered?"

"Yes," he said in a tight voice, "Kay called me this morning after you told her, and it's in all the papers tonight." He lit a fresh cigarette from the stub of the one he was smoking. "Do you want a drink?"

"No," I said.

He sighed. "Well, I do." He looked at Kay and she shook her head. He got up and went out to the kitchen.

Kay said, "Jim, I'm very sorry. We should have at least told you."

"You sure as hell should. Rockingham will know you've been here, and that'll bring you into it. It'll be cut and dried with him—ex-wife visits former husband in murder apartment. Planned to remarry, but husband's second wife refuses divorce. Second wife murdered to clear way for reunion. And he'll connect other things, maybe. Roger Quinn makes passes at ex-wife. Ex-husband catches him. Fight. Then Quinn murdered and—"

"Stop," she said sharply. "Stop it, Jim. I—I didn't realize—"

The apartment buzzer let loose.

Kay stared at me wide-eyed. Don came into the room with a glass in his hand. He stood still, his gaze shifting from the door to me. I moved to the door and opened it.

Rockingham stepped quickly inside. From the way he held his right arm away from his side I knew that he was prepared to go for a gun in a shoulder clip. He was carefully dressed in a tan tweed suit with a dark-brown hat. A green-figured silk necktie was neatly knotted in the slot of a crisp white shirt collar. But his lean face looked haggard and his eyes were tired. I wondered fleetingly how his wife was getting along. He stood alone in the room, but with the door open behind him, and I knew that he had helpers outside.

"Hello, Rock," I said.

He caressed his red mustache with the little finger of his left hand, his gaze shifting from Don to Kay to me, "Quite a cozy little gathering," he said. "The ex-husband, the ex-wife, and the trusted old family friend."

"So Riggio called you," I said.

"You're damn right. That's what he's down there for." He nodded at Don. "You're under arrest for the murder of your wife."

"Rock," I said, "you can't do that. You're just grabbing in the dark. You think you've got it all figured out, and that's the way it's going to be, the way you're going to make it. But you're wrong."

"Jim," he said, "I told you there was another woman some place. I thought he would go to her, sooner or later, but she made it easy by coming to him, his ex-wife. That's enough motive for me. He'll open up."

"You don't have any real evidence against him."

He gave me a wolfish leer. "The hell I haven't." He called over his shoulder. "All right, send her in."

The blonde named Francine stepped into the apartment. She was wearing the same white dress she'd worn the evening before, and she was still carrying the white purse. The dress looked faintly soiled but her straw-colored hair was neatly combed and it fell in smooth waves over her shoulders. She glanced quickly at the three of us, and then stood quietly with her odd yellowish eyes downcast. I wondered if she'd killed any rats with a hammer lately.

Rockingham's voice was oily. "Now, miss, please point out the person you saw leaving here at three o'clock yesterday afternoon."

Francine raised her eyes and without hesitation she pointed at Don Canfield. "That is the man," she said dramatically.

A gleam of triumph showed in Rockingham's eyes. "Thank you," he said with satisfaction. "You may go now."

Francine, her eyes again demurely downcast, turned and went out.

"Rock," I said, "she's lying. I tried to tell you last night, but you wouldn't listen. I showed her a photograph of Don's brother, Steve, and she said it was Don. They don't look anything alike."

He gave me a pitying smile. "Never mind, Jim. Just don't worry about it." He stepped to the door, spoke briefly, and two plainclothesmen came inside. I didn't know either of them. Rockingham jerked his head silently at Don and the two men moved over to where he stood stiffly. He hadn't had a chance to drink his highball. He placed his glass carefully on a table and glanced at Kay. A look, a something, passed between them and Kay turned away. I think she realized that any demonstration of affection at this time would be out of place, to say the least.

As Don moved away between the two plainclothesmen, I said, "I'll see you."

He didn't answer me until he was in the hall. Then I heard him say, "Don't bother, Jim."

Rockingham, after a speculative look at Kay, turned to the door. At the last minute I said, "Rock, you're making a mistake," but the words were just a baby's cry in the wilderness.

"Maybe I am, Jim," he said cheerfully. "Maybe I am." He went out and closed the door very quietly behind him.

CHAPTER SIXTEEN

I telephoned Alec Hammond and asked him if he'd called Red Drake, the other operative we used. He said he had just finished talking to him. I told Alec that the job was canceled, and I told him why. Alec promised to call Red right away. Then I closed the windows in Don's apartment, turned off the lights, and Kay and I stepped out into the hall. I locked the door and handed her the key. She accepted it without comment.

I drove her home in the dusk of the early evening. She didn't talk and neither did I. When we stopped in the drive at her house I saw that the lights were on in the living room. Through the screen door we heard Annie's gay laughter and Mrs. Mahoney's quiet voice.

Kay said, "I've got to help him, Jim."

"Somebody has to."

"What will they do to him? Can they really—"

"I don't know. So far, it's circumstantial, but Rockingham will build it up. That witness he has is lying, but I can't prove it. It all points to Don, and God knows what Rockingham will uncover next."

"You mean—about Don coming to see me and his fight with Roger?"

"Yes. A Lieutenant Bronski is investigating Roger's death, but he and Rockingham are bound to compare notes—and they both know that Jesse Connors has hired me to find Roger's murderer."

"He has?" she asked quickly.

"Yes."

"Jim, is there anything you haven't told me? Something I should know?"

"You didn't tell me things I should have known." It was childish, but I couldn't help saying it.

She touched my hand. "I'm sorry, Jim, really and truly."

"It's all right." Her fingers were cool and soft on my hand.

I thought about Don. He was in trouble, bad trouble, and Kay might soon be in trouble, too. It was a bad time for all of us. I thought of the attack on Kay the night before and of her wounded arm, and it occurred to me that of all the jobs I'd had this was the first time that close friends had been involved. I wished that I was out of it, way the hell and gone out of it, and working for strangers, people who didn't know me and who didn't matter to me, just people who paid me to do what I could for them. If I couldn't do what they wanted and they got hurt, it would mean nothing to me, except for the professional pride in my work.

I was like a surgeon, I thought, performing a serious operation on a friend, knowing that if my friend died I would feel more than just regret at my lack of skill, or maybe knowing that no skill could have saved him but feeling the regret and the helplessness and the sadness just the same.

Kay fumbled at the car door with her good left hand and I leaned across her and opened it, aware of her closeness and the clean scent of her. She slid out quickly and together we walked across the grass to the house. The dusk was gone and it was now black dark, the hour before the first moonlight. On the terrace before the door she turned to face me, the light from the window falling on her bright hair and the slim curves of her shoulders.

"Would you like to come in, Jim?" she asked. "Annie would love to see you, and I know you haven't had your dinner."

"No, thanks."

"Some other time—soon?"

"Sure."

"Help Don, Jim."

"I'll do my best."

"They can't hold him very long, can they? Can they?"

"I don't know. If there was just something, *anything*, that would even tentatively place him at the park at the time Louette was killed—"

"I know," she said. "It's Annie. Poor little innocent Annie. *She* knows where Don spent the afternoon. Last night she told that police detective about Don going back to the apartment. I didn't realize the implication of it until too late—before I could stop her—"

"We can't help it now," I said. "They can't use that in itself against him, but it's another link in the chain of circumstances."

"Keep in touch with me, Jim."

"I will."

"Good night." She went inside and the screen door closed.

I had meant to remind her to be sure and lock her doors, but it was too late now. As I walked back to my car I heard Annie's delighted cries as she greeted her mother.

I fried the sirloin in butter, very quickly in a hot pan, and ate it with some canned green beans, delicatessen potato salad, and bread and butter. It was nine o'clock by the time I'd washed the dishes and changed into pajamas and slippers. My head still ached from the bump I'd absorbed in Anthony Kovak's house, and my arms and legs were heavy with fatigue. I stretched on the divan with the day's papers.

The Cleveland Plain Dealer, the *News* and the *Press* all carried blackface headlines over two- and three-column stories on Roger Quinn's killing. *Executive Found Hanging From Factory Flagpole* was a typical heading. All of the stories were brief and one of them described Roger as a *dynamic and popular young executive, the son-in-law of Jesse L. Connors, owner and president of the Connors Electric Company*, and hinted that a disgruntled and possibly deranged employee had perpetrated the deed. All of the papers gave only the barest facts, ending with statements that the police were conducting an extensive investigation. My name was not mentioned in any of the stories, although the guard, Alvin E. Semms, was described as on duty at the time the body was discovered.

The account of Louette's death was in all the papers, too, although in smaller headlines and lower on the front pages. There was no mention of my being with Don when she was found, and the meagerness and evasive nature of all the stories made me wonder what Rockingham and Bronski were up to, and I began to worry.

On the inside of two of the papers, on pages reserved for news from the surrounding communities, there were short accounts of the murder of Melissa Kovak in the Hotel Avalon in East Grange. They repeated what I'd heard on the radio at Helen Quinn's house and stated that the police were searching for the mysterious A. J. Holman, of Detroit, and for the dead woman's husband, Anthony S. Kovak.

After I'd looked through all three papers I dozed off into an uneasy sleep.

The shrill insistent ringing of the telephone awakened me. I floated upward from sleep and clawed myself off the soft divan. I stumbled across the room, grabbed the phone, and said hoarsely, "Hello." I said it three times and the only answer I got was a soft click in my ear.

Cursing under my breath I went back to the divan. Then I changed my mind and moved to the bedroom. I was nicely settled with the sheet pulled up when the phone rang again. I let it ring awhile, but it didn't stop. I couldn't ignore it and I got out of bed and answered it once more.

"Hello," I snapped.

A deep male voice said four words, "Lovers' Lane at eleven," and there was a sharp decisive click as he hung up.

I replaced the phone and for a few minutes I wandered aimlessly around the apartment. Then I looked at my wristwatch. Ten-thirty. I made up my mind, entered the bedroom, and put on flannel slacks, canvas crepe-soled shoes, a light pullover sweater, and a corduroy jacket. Before I left the apartment I took a loaded .32 automatic from a dresser drawer and dropped it into the pocket of the jacket.

Lovers' Lane, to the people I knew, was like all lovers' lanes from Bar Harbor to Catalina, a deserted and lonely spot away from the distractions of the city. Our Lovers' Lane was a jutting promontory along the lake, within the city limits, but between Cleveland proper and the communities extending east. A seldom-used road wound through it from the highway to the lake and ended on a rocky beach. During my last two years in high school we had held numerous wiener roasts there, with Don and Kay usually in the crowd—they had been "going steady" then—while I would be with whatever girl I happened to be dating at the time. It had been a favorite spot for the whole high school—still was, for all I knew. The flat rocks on the beach made ideal benches upon which to sit and look at the moon shining over the lake, and the ridge beyond the beach screened the spot from the highway.

I parked the Ford beside a clump of stunted fir trees and walked down the sandy rutted road, trying to place in my mind the voice of the man who had called me. But I couldn't; it had sounded like no one I knew. It was a dark night and a strong steady wind off the lake smelled damp and cool. When I reached the crest of the ridge I could hear the pounding of the waves on the beach below me, and the lake was a black mass stretching to Canada. I moved cautiously along the ridge, keeping in shadow as much as possible. Every few feet I stopped and listened, but I heard only the sound of the wind and the booming roar of the waves. Nothing moved in the darkness but the lights of a freighter far out on the dark horizon and the tops of the trees blowing in the wind against the murky sky.

I climbed a huge slanting rock, the wind whipping at my hair and jacket. There were several wind-gnarled trees here, leaning high against the sky. I stood beside them and looked back the way I had come. I could see the tiny headlights of cars streaking along the highway for Cleveland in one direction, for Buffalo and points east in the other. I felt very lonely and suddenly I wanted to get away from there.

The wind died down and abruptly it was quiet. I turned my head to look at the dark moving mass of the lake, and the wind came up again. In that instant, above the sound of the wind, I heard a sharp twanging sound from not far away. Something slammed out of the darkness and thudded with a firm sickening sound into the tree beside my head.

I swung my head sharply and my cheek struck a long smooth object which was vibrating thinly. I dropped to the naked rock and I reached for the .32 in my jacket pocket. I had the gun in my hand when I heard the twanging sound again and the *thunk* in the tree above me, lower this time. Holding the gun clear, I rolled over the crest of the ridge and flattened myself on the slope among the rocks. Cautiously I lifted my head. I saw a shadowy movement, a ghostly furtive something in the trees along the edge of the narrow road. I leveled the .32 and fired once. The wind whipped powder smoke past my eyes and I fired again. Then I stood up, scrambled to the top of the ridge, and ran for the road. I couldn't see anything to shoot at but I kept on running. Then I heard the high fast roar of a car motor and the whine of wheels spinning in sand. A dark shape sped through the trees and slowed as it approached the highway; slowed for only a second, and then, with headlights suddenly shining, it merged with the streaming traffic. I lost it among the lights of other cars as it streaked toward Cleveland.

Back at the gnarled trees on the rocky ridge I didn't need a light to tell me what had been aimed at me. Arrows—two of them—long, slim, polished, with feathered ends, one below the other in the trunk of the tree. When I attempted to pull them loose I realized how deeply they were imbedded, and it was easy to picture what they would have done to me had they found their mark. It took me quite a while, using all my strength, to work them loose without breaking the shafts. When I finally got them free, my fingers told me that the heads were of steel, polished and fitted flush with the shafts, and ground to needle points.

I carried them back to my car and drove into town. Up in my apartment I locked the door and inspected the arrows carefully. They were murderous missiles, made from some sturdy polished wood, notched and feathered. There may have been fingerprints on them in addition to mine, but I doubted it. Nevertheless, I wrapped them in a bath towel, laid them beside me on the divan, and thought things over.

The telephone rang, shattering my meditations. Wearily I got up, moved over to the instrument, and said, "Hello."

A female voice said, "Mr. Bennett?"

"Yes."

"This is Rebecca Foster." Her voice sounded queer and hurried.

"Yes," I said again, thinking of Rebecca, of the carrot juice and the athletic body, of the tawny hair and the tanned skin. Rebecca, who didn't smoke or drink or care about men, but whose lips held a surprising warmth and promise—and who owned a dog named Eric. I liked Rebecca, I thought, more than a little, but I didn't like her damned dog.

"I—" she began.

"What's wrong?" I asked sharply.

"Something—just happened. I—I guess I'm still shaking. I wanted to tell you—"

"What happened, Rebecca?" I tried to keep my voice quiet.

"I—I don't know, exactly." She attempted a laugh, but it was weak and tremulous. "I was restless tonight, and bored, I guess, and I decided to take a short drive. Eric likes to ride, and I took him with me. I tied his leash to the steering post. He sat beside me on the front seat. We drove along the lake for a while and when we returned I put the car in the garage and opened the door. I was about to untie Eric when I heard a noise behind me. I—I turned, and I saw somebody behind me, just a shadow close by the wall. It—it jumped toward me, and I screamed. Then Eric lunged past me out of the car, but the leash stopped him, and I heard somebody running, and—"

"Are you all right?" I broke in.

"Yes—just scared," she said weakly.

"You couldn't tell if it was a man or a woman?"

"No. It happened so quickly, and Eric was making such an awful fuss. I thought he would break the leash. He's still growling."

"You should have let him loose," I said grimly.

"I—I didn't think—"

"Good old Eric," I said, thinking that he wasn't such a disagreeable pooch, after all. "Keep him with you, and lock your doors. Do you want me to come over?"

"No, no. I just wanted to tell you about it. Should I call the police?" Her voice sounded stronger.

"You can if you like, but I'm afraid they can't do anything without a description. I'm glad you called me, Rebecca. It fits in with some other things." I remembered the knife wound in Kay's arm, and the arrows aimed at me, and I added, "You're lucky. By the way, do you know any archers?"

"What?"

"Archers. People who shoot arrows from bows."

There was a silence on the wire for maybe a couple of seconds. Then she said, "I guess I'm still a little confused— Archers?"

"Yes." I told her quickly about my visit to Lovers' Lane and what had happened there.

"That's—horrible," she said. "And here I've been bothering you about some prowler I surprised in the garage and who was probably more scared than I was."

"We're both lucky," I said.

She said seriously, "We have an archery club at the plant, but I don't think—"

"How many belong to the club?"

"About twenty, I believe."

"Can you give me their names?"

"Some of them," she said. "The complete record is at the office."

"Name a few—offhand."

"Well, I'm a member, and there's Mr. Connors. He was pretty active in it until he began to have trouble with his heart. But he still takes part occasionally, and he makes excellent target scores."

"You mean the boss?"

"Yes. I told you that he believes very strongly in personal contact with the employees. He's in the plant glee club, too, and he usually attends the Foremen's Association meetings."

"What about Roger Quinn? Was he a member?"

"No—he didn't generally participate in plant activities. But Mrs. Quinn is a member."

"Good for the boss's daughter," I said.

"Yes. I admire her attitude. Mr. Connors has always said that the success of any company is in making the workers feel as if they were all part of a team working together. He believes it's the main incentive that increases production."

"The main incentive is a fat pay check," I said. "Is Mrs. Quinn a good archer?"

"Just average. Of course, she isn't very—very robust, and she uses a bow with a light pull. But she is quite accurate at short range."

I tried to picture frail little Helen Quinn on an archery range. I couldn't, and I asked, "Who else?"

She hesitated, and I said, "I know this is a hell of a time to be pestering you with questions, but it may be important."

"I want to help," she said. "It's just that I guess I'm still a little nervous— Alvin Semms is a member of the club."

"The little guard on the main gate?"

"Yes. And Mr. Canfield belongs, but he doesn't take part very often—he's away so much. But Mrs. Canfield is quite enthusiastic about the sport."

"Kay?" I was surprised.

"She makes very good scores. In fact, she was runner-up in the plant women's championship last year."

"Who won it?"

"A Mrs. Johnson—she works in the plant, on the motor inspection line."

"Where did you finish?"

She laughed. "Fourth place, I think. I prefer the more active sports."

"Can you think of any other members?"

"I'm afraid not. The rest are mostly plant employees. I can get their names from the personnel office."

"Do that, Rebecca, and send the list over to my office in the morning."

"All right."

"Don't forget about locking your doors."

"They're locked."

"And keep Eric with you."

"He's always with me at night. After what happened, I—I think I'll keep him for a while."

"I'll bring him a bone tomorrow night," I said. "Don't forget that we have a dinner date."

"I won't." I liked the sudden warmth in her voice.

We talked a little longer and she assured me that she wasn't frightened anymore; we hung up on a friendly note. I tried to sound more cheerful and unconcerned than I felt, and I wondered privately if Eric Bismarck Von Tonder the Third slept in the same room with her. I decided that he probably slept in the same bed, and that was all right with me. I realized, of course, that I was becoming more than a little attracted to Rebecca Foster, but not so attracted yet that I was jealous of a dog.

As I crawled into bed I thought that Lieutenant Bronski and his collection of crackpot notes to Roger Quinn from peeved and revengeful employees and ex-employees had nothing on me. I was about to receive a list of probable potential killers, with me as an intended corpse. And then I realized that it would be a tremendous task for me to investigate each person on the list. But Bronski, with all the facilities of the police department, could do it, and I decided to give him the list as a gesture of friendship and cooperation. Maybe it would keep him occupied long enough for me to dig a little deeper into the matter of the dead blonde in the Hotel Avalon before Bronski and Rockingham got together and began to sense the connection, as I vaguely did, between the deaths of the blonde and Louette and Roger Quinn. After all, I thought bleakly, if things got really hot, Cornelius Hogmyer could identify me, and Helen Quinn, too, and then there would be hell to pay.

I slept, at last, and I didn't move until the alarm stirred me to life at eight in the morning.

CHAPTER SEVENTEEN

When I arrived in the office a little after nine on Tuesday morning I explained to Sandy Hollis about the list of names of the Connors Electric archery club I expected to receive, and I asked her to make an extra copy. Then I called Lieutenant Bronski to tell him about the list and maybe feel him out a little, but he wasn't at the station. I asked for Rockingham and was told that he hadn't come in yet. I called Rockingham's home and an elderly female told me in broken accents that she was Mrs. Piccutio, that she was staying with the bambinos, that Meester Rockingham he was at the hospital because Theresa, she was not doing so good. I told her I was sorry and expressed the hope that Mrs. Rockingham would improve, and that

I would get in touch with Mr. Rockingham later. I had not known before that his wife was of Italian parentage, or that her name was Theresa.

I was fiddling around with some routine desk work with Sandy at my elbow when the phone rang. It was Jesse L. Connors. "Bennett?" he asked in a rasping, breathless voice.

"Yes."

"Helen—she's gone." I could almost see his head jerking back and forth in tiny quick movements.

"How long?"

"I—I don't know. Her mother and I have been staying with her. We all retired about midnight, and this morning she didn't come down to breakfast. I went to her room. She wasn't there. Her car's gone, too."

"The blue Mercury?"

"Yes. Her bed had been slept in, but God knows when she left. Bennett, we can't have her gallivanting around alone—not at a time like this, and in the mood she's in. You've got to find her."

"Have you told the police?"

"No, no."

"Good."

"Bring her home, Bennett. Bring her home to her mother and me."

"I'll try, sir."

He said something, but I couldn't understand it, something between a sob and a mumble, and the receiver crashed in my ear.

Alec Hammond entered the office. As usual, he was wearing a dark-blue suit, a black knit tie, and sober gray felt hat. He sat in a chair, tilted it against the wall, chewed on a matchstick. "Morning, Jim," he drawled. "So they took our boy to the pokey?"

"Yeah. Listen, Alec, I want you to go out to the home of Roger Quinn. Do you know where that is?"

"I'll find it. You on that, too?"

"Yes, I'm on that, too. Go out there and see what goes on."

"Anybody special?"

"Do you know Jesse Connors?"

"Seen his picture in the papers—his son-in-law's, too. Looked like a lady-killer to me. The old man is a skinny gaffer, gray hair, narrow face, a mean look in his eye."

"That's Jesse," I said. "He and his wife are staying with their daughter. If he leaves, follow him. If he goes to the factory, go back to the house and watch for Mrs. Quinn."

"Wife of the flagpole corpse?"

"Yes. Small woman, thin with brown hair, pale face, well dressed. Drives a new blue Mercury. She's not there now, but if she comes back I want to know about it. Report to Sandy at noon. I'll call her later."

"Right." Alec stood up and called into the adjoining office where Sandy was doing some filing. "Morning, honey."

"Hi, Alec," she called out. "Today's payday. Do you want your check?"

Alec winked at me. "Hold it for me, honey. If I had it, I might go out and get liquored up, and I got a job to do for Jim today."

Sandy laughed and Alec moved to the door. With his hand on the knob, he said, "Jim, I don't usually get nosy, but I keep thinking of that babe who went up to see Canfield yesterday. Who is she?"

"His ex-wife," I said.

He whistled softly. "Why did he let that get away from him?"

I shrugged. "One of those things."

He shook his head sadly and went out.

I stared at the closed door and thought of Kay and Don. It was time to clear things up. It was way past time to clear Don, if he could be cleared, and to find the killer of Louette and the killer of Roger. I lit a cigarette and I thought: *Bennett, this is your work. You're supposed to be an expert. Now, listen, Bennett, who killed Louette? Think hard. Who killed the blonde at the Avalon? Roger Quinn? Maybe, because he was being blackmailed. That's logical. But who killed Roger? Don Canfield, after he caught him with Kay? Helen, the long-suffering wife, the worm who maybe turned at last and went wild in a pent-up burst of jealous rage? Nonsense, Bennett—she isn't strong enough to string a man to a flagpole. Unless somebody helped her. What about Jesse Connors? Would he kill because of what Roger was doing to the life and the gentle spirit of his only daughter? Who else, who else? Some evil stranger who maybe right now was lurking on the fringes of the hubbub and laughing wildly and silently?*

My thoughts went round and round, and none of them connected. I was supposed to be learning things digging up clues, questioning people, closing the trap. But I was just blundering about in a thick darkness and time was running out. And all the while the grimly eager men of the law were swarming over the city and probing about, learning things, maybe really closing the trap.

From a desk drawer I took a Smith and Wesson .38 revolver and checked the cylinder, saw that it was full of bright brass-bound cartridges. I clicked the gun shut and hefted it in my palm. It was a pleasant weight, pleasing to the touch, cold and smooth and deadly, blue steel with a hard-rubber grip, a standard model. The two shots I'd fired from the .32 at Lovers' Lane the night before were the first I'd fired in a long time. A hell of a long time. Too long. I dropped the .38, muzzle down, into my inside coat pocket. Its weight made my coat sag, but I didn't mind. I wanted the gun there.

Sandy came in. She glanced at the open drawer where the gun had been and looked at me with grave worried eyes. I closed the drawer and said to her, "Alec will call you at noon. Don't go to lunch until he does. I'll call you sometime this afternoon." I put on my hat and moved to the door.

"Where are you going now?" she asked.

I started to answer, and then I paused. Where was I going, indeed? I looked at Sandy blankly. "I don't know."

"One of those days, huh?"

"One of those days." I sighed. "Do you know of any nice soft grocery clerk jobs?"

"You'll be all right, Jim. Is there anything I can do?"

I shook my head. There wasn't anything anyone could do, except me. As I went out, Sandy said softly, "Be careful, Jim."

I knew she was thinking of the gun, and as I took the elevator down I thought that at least one person in the world was concerned about my welfare. But the thought gave me little consolation. I was out on a long limb and I had the uneasy feeling that someone was busily sawing away at the other end.

Here it was, a bright Tuesday morning in May. Louette Canfield and Melissa Kovak had died on Sunday. Roger Quinn had died early Monday morning. I had come close to dying on Monday night, last night. My friend Don was in jail for the murder of his wife. The police at this moment were no doubt watching Kay Canfield, waiting to pounce. Rockingham suspected me of obstructing justice. Rebecca Foster unthaws a little with me and right away somebody jumps for her in a dark garage. Helen Quinn had disappeared and Jesse Connors was about due for another heart attack, judging from the way he'd sounded on the phone.

I was doing fine, just fine.

It wasn't until after I'd left the city and was driving through rolling hills that I realized I was heading for the little town of East Grange, Ohio. It was ten-thirty when I drove down the length of the main street and parked before the Hotel Avalon.

Cornelius Hogmyer was tilted back in a chair behind the desk, reading a newspaper. A thin shaft of sunlight shone red on the puckered lump of flesh that had once been his left ear. I leaned my elbows on the desk and looked at him. This was as good a place as any to start, maybe the best place. After a while he became aware of me and peered over the top of the newspaper. The front legs of his chair hit the floor.

"Go away," he said.

"Has she been back here?"

"Who?"

"That woman who paid you the money."

He waved the paper angrily. "All I've had is cops, cops, cops. And now I got you again. I don't know nothing about nothing."

"I thought you were the night clerk."

"On Tuesdays I do a double trick until noon. Then I'm off till Wednesday night, and I work every other Sunday. That okay with you?" His little eyes glinted nastily.

"I asked you a question. Was she here this morning?"

He folded the newspaper and swatted a fly on his bony knee. "You ain't no cop," he sneered. "What're you sticking your nose into it for? I talked to the cops and I ain't talking to nobody else."

"What did you tell them?"

He lifted the newspaper, ignoring me, but his little eyes kept flicking sideways nervously. I took a bill from my pocket and held it so that he could see the big fat 10 in the corner. Then I folded it into a square and snapped it across the desk at him. It hit the floor beside his chair. He picked it up, stuffed it into his shirt pocket along with the pencils and pens, and raised the newspaper once more. "What do you think I told 'em?" he said in a low voice, without looking at me. "I told 'em that he was A. J. Holman, from Detroit, and I showed 'em the register—A. J. Holman and wife. If old A. J. cut his wife's throat, that's no skin off my nose. He's still A. J. Holman, from Detroit."

"Did you tell the police about the woman? The one who paid you the hundred bucks?"

"Hell, no. That's private business between me and her."

"Did you tell her that you kept her name from the police?"

"Sure," he said. "I told her—" He stopped abruptly, realizing that

I'd trapped him.

"How much did it cost her this time?"

He lifted the paper. "I'm busy. You bother me."

"Then she was here this morning?"

He didn't answer.

"Is she still in town? Where is she?"

He didn't answer for a second. Then he said sullenly, "I don't know. Maybe the Grange Bar."

I moved away. At the door I turned. He was watching me furtively from behind the newspaper. When I looked at him, he jerked the paper in front of his face. I went out and walked down to the Grange Bar. As I approached it, I saw something I should have noticed in the first place; Helen Quinn's blue Mercury was parked a block down the street, on the far side.

Except for the big bartender with the butter-bowl haircut, the Grange Bar looked deserted. He was leaning against the beer taps with his back to the bar, reading a gaudy magazine called *Gorgeous Models*, and he was so engrossed in a full-page photo of a billowy brunette lying in the sunlight on the sand, with a towel covering approximately one fourth of her, that he didn't see or hear me enter. I moved past him to the booths in the rear.

Helen Quinn sat huddled in a corner of the last one.

She saw me and for a second I thought she was going to make a run for it; not because of any movement she made, but because of an expression of sudden panic in her eyes. But she managed a tremulous smile as I sat down opposite her. She was wearing a tailored beige gabardine suit and a dark-green blouse. Her soft brown hair was combed neatly and she had made an attempt at applying lipstick to her thin little mouth, but it was too thick and too red, like a gash in her narrow pale face. Delicate spiderwebs of blue veins were visible beneath the waxy skin of her temples. A half-consumed Manhattan cocktail was on the table before her and there was a little pile of red-tipped cigarettes in an ashtray.

Drab little Helen Connors Quinn, the wallflower of the high school prom, sitting all alone in a country town, drinking cocktails and smoking cigarettes. It was too tragic to be incongruous, more pitiful than funny.

"Hello, Helen," I said. "Your dad's worried and he sent me to look for you."

Her eyes met mine for an instant and then she looked away and slowly crushed out a cigarette. "Why did you look for me here?" she asked in a low voice.

Up front, the bartender started back for the booth, but I waved him away.

I said, "Because I thought you might have been wondering what One Ear told the police."

She fingered the stem of her glass. Her hand was small and thin, with unpainted nails. A big diamond and a broad gold wedding band captured and held a small brilliance in the gloomy room. "That's right," she whispered.

"Helen," I said gently, "do you think that Roger killed her?"

She seemed to shrink inside the gabardine suit. "I hope not, Jim. I hope that he wasn't capable—of that."

"You never know what people are capable of," I said.

"I thought, if I could—could save his memory, no matter what he was, or what he did to me— It just isn't because that woman was killed, but because he was with her. I don't want people to know about that—ever."

"There were other women," I said harshly. "Surely you must know that. And Roger is dead. Nothing can hurt him now. How much did it cost you?"

"Five hundred, Jim. He promised he wouldn't tell."

"Cheap," I said.

She looked up at me then, and I saw the grief and the fear in her eyes.

"Did Roger mean so much to you?" I asked.

"Maybe I'm selfish, too," she said. "It wouldn't be nice for me, or for the children, to live the rest of our lives with people knowing that Roger was—was unfaithful, and had maybe—"

"Killed somebody?" I finished for her.

She closed her eyes and nodded silently.

I reached out and touched her hand. "Listen, Helen, don't you realize that when the five hundred is gone he'll want more? And more?"

She opened her eyes. They weren't soft anymore, but hard with a dark, hot light. Her chin came up. "Then I'll give it to him," she said.

I shook my head sadly. "Helen, Helen—"

She began to cry, almost silently, her lips contorted like a child's. Tears squeezed from her tightly closed eyes and she turned away from me and held her thin hands over her thin face, her narrow shoulders quivering.

"Come on, Helen," I said, "I'll take you home." I stood up.

It was then that I saw the man sitting at the bar. He had come in while we were talking. I looked at him closely and then I said to Helen, "Wait here." I left her and walked up to the bar.

The man had a glass of beer before him, but he wasn't drinking it. He just sat staring at the glass. He wore a dirty gray felt hat, a gray work shirt, blue jeans, and heavy grease-stained shoes. He was a dark man, with black hair and heavy shoulders. His face in profile showed a strong unshaven jaw and a broad short nose, with black brows protruding like a ledge over his deep eye sockets. I remembered a photo inside a tiny gold locket and I stepped up beside him.

"Hello, Tony," I said.

CHAPTER EIGHTEEN

He turned his head slowly, looking at me slantwise out of the corners of liquid brown eyes. His hands stayed on the bar, his left relaxed, lying loosely, the right clasped around the glass of beer. The back of the hand was covered with thick coarse hair.

"You've made a mistake, brother," he said. His voice was deep, with a faint rasp.

"What did you hit me with, Tony?" I asked softly. "A crowbar?"

White teeth showed at a corner of his mouth. "Scram."

I leaned on the bar. "Let's talk a little, Tony."

He said to the bartender, "What's he been drinking, Mac? Panther milk?"

The bartender looked around, annoyed. "I wouldn't know," he grunted. His eyes went back to his book and a different photo of a more or less naked blonde on a bearskin rug.

The dark man laughed shortly, took a cigarette from his shirt pocket, and placed it between thin hard lips. His left hand started casually for his hip pocket, as if for a match, but I knew that if you carried cigarettes in a shirt pocket you carried matches there, too, and I stepped quickly behind him and grabbed his wrist. He wiggled like a snake and twisted free, and when he whirled to face me he was off the bar stool and had a knife open in his right hand. He shot a glance over his shoulder, saw that his path to the door was clear, and his dark eyes glittered wetly.

"Stay away, copper," he panted.

I took a slow step toward him. He backed up, holding the knife in front of him. I took another step. His eyes darted from left to right and he backed toward the door. I kept moving forward, crowding him.

Suddenly he lunged for me with a kind of animal cry, a cry of hate and fear. I kicked out hard and my heel caught him on his left side, just above his belt. He grunted and stumbled sideways, turned, and raced for the door. I had plenty of time to clear the .38 and put a bullet through the back of his left leg above the knee. The tendons are there, and it usually stops them. He pitched forward as the sound of the shot hammered against the walls and I jumped for him. I pressed a knee against his writhing back, grabbed his right wrist, and twisted his arm behind him, tight against his shoulder blades. He uttered a hoarse cry of pain and his fingers opened. The knife fell to the floor. I released him and kicked the knife away.

I thought I had him, but I was wrong. He rolled over on his back, lunged upward, and his fist smacked against the underside of my jaw. My teeth clicked shut and I staggered backward, the room swinging around in big looping circles. I hit a bar stool and hung on while it whirled around and banged me against the bar. I clutched the stool, my head down, and I saw the floor very clearly, with its litter of cigarette butts and ashes and burned matches. I clung to the stool and waited for the room to stop looping. From nearby there was a scurry of footsteps, followed by a dull thunk of sound, and then silence.

I took a deep breath, pushed myself clear of the stool, and stood on wobbly legs. The dark man lay quietly on the floor. A thin line of blood was oozing from beneath him. The bartender stood over him with a pick handle in his hand.

"Nobody pulls a knife in my joint," the bartender said.

Feeling my jaw tenderly, I turned and looked back at the booths. Helen Quinn yeas standing far back in the gloom with a hand over her mouth, her eyes wide and frightened. I waggled a couple of fingers at her reassuringly and said to the bartender, "Call the cops."

"You're damned right I'm calling the cops," he said viciously. "You know who the hell he is? I never saw him before."

"Me, neither," I said, which was the truth. I kneeled beside the still form on the floor and from the hip pocket of the blue jeans I pulled out a battered billfold and opened it. It contained six one-dollar bills, an assortment of lodge and labor union cards, a Social Security card, a state driver's license, a truck driver's license, and a photograph, a fuzzy snapshot of a blond girl whom I recognized as Melissa Kovak. All of the cards bore the name and address: *Anthony S. Kovak, 1428 Puxatawny Drive, Columbus, Ohio.* I put the billfold back in his pocket and stood up.

"Go ahead," I said to the bartender. "I'll watch him."

He handed me the pick handle and moved around the bar to a phone at the far end. Kovak opened his eyes. He stared up at me blankly, and then a look of pain crossed his face and he pushed himself slowly to a sitting position.

I touched his shoulder. "Take it easy, Tony. You've got a bullet in your leg."

He brushed my hand away contemptuously. A little fresh blood seeped out from beneath his leg. He stared at the blood, touched it with a finger, and moved the finger over the floor. It left a red streak. "I didn't do it," he said to no one in particular.

"Do what?" I asked. Behind me I heard the bartender talking into the phone.

"Kill her," Kovak said. "I didn't kill Melissa." He looked up at me. "But I shoulda killed you, you bastard, instead of slugging you, when you snuck into my house yesterday. I was getting ready to lam, because I knew they would try and pin it on me. I wanted to take her stuff with me. She didn't leave much when she moved out, but it was all of her I had anymore—" He bent his head, clenching his hands into fists.

The bartender moved up beside me. "The chief's coming," he said, taking the pick handle from me.

I turned and looked back. Helen Quinn still stood by the booth, far back in the shadows. She hadn't moved. I wanted to go to her, to tell her to sit down, to stop standing like that. But I didn't. I turned back to Kovak and gazed down at his dark bent head and his wide heavy shoulders. "Go on, Tony," I said. "Finish it up." He'd have to go through it all again to the police, but I wanted to know now, before I left town, before I talked to Helen again, before I did a number of things.

"All right," he said in a dead voice. "I'm glad it's over, and I'll finish it, and it's the truth." I had to lean down to hear him.

"I been following her lately, trying to get her to come back to me. She wasn't no good, but she was all I ever had. Sunday I was watching the place where she worked, that drive-in. I see her leave with a guy and I follow them to the hotel. I go up the back way, see what room they go in. Then I wait. He wasn't the only guy she had. I don't care about the guys—I just want her back. After a while the guy leaves. I follow him. He buys some sandwiches and goes back up. Then he comes busting out, gets in his car, and barrels out of town fast. I go up the room and I find her, like she was—on the floor—and the blood—" His big shoulders trembled and I heard choked sobs.

"What else?"

"That's all, honest to God. I'm scared as hell, but I can't leave her like that. Maybe it's screwy, but I go down and pick some violets I see behind the hotel. She always liked flowers, see? I lay her out on the bed and I cover her up and put the violets in her hand." He paused and said in a broken, bitter voice, "It's the only funeral she'll ever get." He stopped talking.

"Go on," I said.

"That's all. I go back to Columbus and I have some drinks on the way. At the house I sleep awhile. Then I pack up. You come in and I hide in the kitchen and slug you and get the hell out. I hear on the radio they're hunting for me and I come back here to find that bastard, that guy she was with. If I find him, the cops will lay off me— I can't go to the cops myself— I know what they would do to me. So I come back here to start looking."

"Did you find him, Tony?" I asked gently, thinking of Roger Quinn's body hanging from a flagpole.

He shook his head slowly from side to side. "Not yet, not yet. But I'll know him when I see him, and I'll know his car, a gray Caddy." He rubbed his leg above the knee. "My leg," he whimpered, "it hurts—"

Beside me the bartender breathed, "It's him—he killed that babe at the Avalon."

I turned and it was then that I saw Helen Quinn standing beside me. I don't know how long she'd been standing there. She was staring down at Anthony Kovak and there was something ugly in her eyes, something that should never have been in the eyes of a woman like Helen Quinn.

"He killed Roger." It didn't sound like her voice. The screen door opened then and two men stepped inside. Out on the sidewalk people were beginning to gather. A man in blue overalls with a silver badge pinned to the bib was pushing them away from the door and I heard his plaintive voice, "Now, dammit, folks, stand back, jest stand back. I gotta keep this here door clear. Stand back, jest stand back, please—"

One of the men who had entered was short and thin with a long nose and a visored cap which was too big for his narrow head. He wore blue trousers, a blue blouse, and a black Sam Brown belt supporting a black leather holster with the heavy butt of a revolver protruding from the unsnapped flap. A silver shield pinned to his blouse bore the inscription: *East Grange Police—CHIEF*. The other man, also in blue pants and blouse, was fat and sleepy-looking. The chief looked down at Kovak.

The bartender said excitedly, "That's him, Ed, that woman's husband. I heard him tell it. He's the one you want." He pointed at me. "He pulled a knife on this fella, and I hit him with the pick handle."

The chief looked at me.

"Kovak is his name," I said. "Better get him to the hospital. He's got a bullet in his leg."

The chief looked startled. "My Gawd—Kovak? They got a dragnet over six states for him."

The sleepy-looking cop grasped Kovak's thick black hair and jerked his head upward. "It's him, Ed," he said triumphantly. "Just like his pitcher." He pushed Kovak's head away viciously.

Kovak slumped sideways, supporting himself in a half sitting position with his elbows, and he muttered in a desperate hopeless voice, "I didn't do it, I didn't do it."

I was the only one who heard him.

"Call the ambulance, Virgil," the chief snapped. "We don't want him to bleed to death before we get credit for him."

Virgil lumbered for the phone. The chief fixed me with a steely gaze.

"Who are you? And how come you carry a gun?"

"My name's Bennett," I said wearily. "Let's get it over with."

I went through the tired routine of explanation and identification. I told him that I was passing through on my way to Cleveland, stopped at the Grange Bar for a beer, met a friend there, and talked to her for a short time. From photos in the newspapers (I really hadn't seen any) I recognized Kovak at the bar and spoke to him. He pulled a knife and tried to run out. I shot him in the leg and the bartender hit him with a pick handle. Then the bartender called the police.

"That's right, Ed," the bartender said eagerly. "He told it just like it was. Him and the lady was minding their own business, and this fella just speaks to Kovak very politely. I ain't paying much attention and the next thing I know Kovak's got a knife out."

"All right," the chief said importantly. "I might want you all as witnesses." He wrote my name and address in a notebook, and Helen Quinn's. Apparently, neither of our names meant anything to him, and I was glad of that. He wasn't interested in us. We might detract from his personal glory in capturing a killer named Anthony Kovak.

The siren of an ambulance wailed and died at the curb. The crowd outside, at the pleading of the man in overalls, parted and made a path. The fat cop named Virgil opened the screen door. Anthony Kovak sat quietly on the floor, his head on his chest, supporting himself by his elbows. It was an awkward position, but that was the way he'd been for the past ten minutes. More blood had run out from beneath his leg. Suddenly I felt sorry for Anthony Kovak. As I guided Helen Quinn past him, I paused and placed a hand on his shoulder.

"Good luck, Tony," I said softly.

He didn't move or make any sign that he had heard me, and I thought with a faint sadness of the violets in the cold dead hands of his wife.

I guided Helen Quinn through the curious gawking crowd and held her arm until we reached her car parked across the street. She got in behind the wheel and sat with her hands in her lap. I closed the door and leaned in at the window. "I'll follow you home," I said.

She nodded without looking at me.

"Do you feel okay?"

She gave me a wan smile. "I'm fine." She was not a pretty girl; she had never been a pretty girl, but there was a kind of frail haunting beauty about her, and a quiet dignity. Maybe it was her eyes, soft and brown, full of sadness and pain. And then I remembered the ugly look in them as she had stared down at Anthony Kovak. I walked away quickly.

As I got into the Ford in front of the Hotel Avalon, I saw Cornelius Hogmyer standing in the doorway, staring down at the crowd in front of the Grange Bar. They had Kovak on a stretcher and were shoving him into the rear of the ambulance. Cornelius Hogmyer didn't look at me, but I was certain that he'd seen me. I backed out of the parking place and a block down the street I stopped at a traffic light behind Helen Quinn's blue Mercury. The light changed to green and I followed her out of East Grange and into the sunlit countryside.

It was twenty minutes until one o'clock in the afternoon.

She drove fast and we reached her home a little after one o'clock. As I parked behind her in the drive, I noticed that Jesse Connors's Buick was not in the garage and that the agency Ford which Alec Hammond was driving was not in sight. That meant that he was following Connors somewhere. I walked with Helen Quinn to the front door.

She said, "Would you like to have lunch with me, Jim?"

"No, thanks. I've got to get back to the office."

"I—I can't forget that man. Do you think he really killed her—that woman in the hotel?"

"He was her husband," I said, "and he had a good reason to kill her."

She sighed. "I'm sorry I caused you so much trouble, but Daddy shouldn't have called you."

"He was worried, and I'm working for him."

"The funeral is tomorrow," she said. "You're coming, aren't you?"

I hadn't thought about Roger Quinn's funeral. But he was dead and he had to be buried. It meant that Bronski had released the body, that the coroner was finished with it and the lab men, and I wondered once more what Bronski knew that I did not.

I said, "Where is it to be held?"

"The Evergreen Funeral Home at two-thirty."

"I'll be there."

"Will I see you, Jim? Afterward, I mean?"

"Of course, Helen."

"I'm alone now. We'll always be friends, won't we?"

"Yes, Helen." I was a little uncomfortable. "I—"

The screen door opened and Mrs. Connors stepped out. "I thought I heard somebody drive in," she said. She placed a hand on her daughter's arm. "Helen, honey, I'm glad you're back. Your father was so worried."

"I'm sorry," she said in a choked voice. She slipped away from her mother's arm and quickly entered the house.

Mrs. Connors looked at me and shook her head. "That poor girl. It's an awful thing to say, but I just can't feel too badly about Roger, and neither can Jesse. When we think of the misery and the heartaches he's caused her—" She shook her head again and sighed deeply. "Jesse is all upset over this, and he shouldn't be, because it's bad for his heart. Thank you for bringing her home, James."

"You're welcome," I said, thinking it odd that she hadn't asked me where I'd found Helen. I had a fake answer all ready.

"The funeral will be an ordeal for her," she said, "but afterward I think Jesse and I will take her away for a while—maybe to California. I have a brother out there, in Oakland. We'll leave the children with my sister here, and make a real holiday of it." She paused and peered at me, her glasses and her gray hair glinting in the sun. "The police were here this morning, that Lieutenant Bronski and another officer—I believe his name was Rockwood, or something like that. They talked to Jesse for a long time, but he didn't tell me what they said, and he went right out to the plant. James, do you think one of the workers did it—to Roger?"

"I don't know, Mrs. Connors," I said, thinking dismally that Bronski and Rockingham had at last gotten together, and I wondered what facts or circumstances had prompted the alliance.

"Well," Mrs. Connors said, "it's a matter for the police, and it can't be helped now. It was a horrible way for Roger to die, but I console myself by thinking that it was a just payment for a life of sin. Our Maker decides such things and only He can redeem Roger. I only hope that in his last minutes alive he repented for what he has done to poor Helen. Don't you feel that way, James?"

"Yes, ma'am," I said, edging away.

"Come and see us," she invited. "Helen always spoke so well of you, always liked you, and she'll be lonely." There were tears on her soft plump cheeks.

"I will," I promised. "Goodbye."

"Goodbye, James."

She waved to me as I backed the Ford and drove away.

CHAPTER NINETEEN

I called the office from a drugstore phone booth. Sandy told me that Alec Hammond hadn't called in yet. That wasn't like Alec and it puzzled me. I told Sandy to have her lunch sent in and to wait for Alec's call. Then I called Lieutenant Bronski. He was in his office.

"George, this is Jim Bennett. Anything new on that Quinn killing?"

"Not much," he said shortly.

I didn't like the tone of his voice, but I proceeded to tell him quickly about the arrows slamming out of the night at me in Lovers' Lane, and about my list of archery club members. I didn't mention Rebecca Foster's would-be attacker. "I had a copy of the list made for you, George," I said. "All I ask is that if you uncover anything to let me know."

"That's very interesting, Jim." His voice was a little more cordial. "It ties in. I've thought all along that somebody from the factory killed Quinn, and I still think so." He paused, and then said, "If it isn't too personal, what were you doing at Lovers' Lane?"

"A man called me. All he said was, 'Lovers' Lane at eleven,' and I went out there."

"Hmmm," he said, "a trap, and you fell for it. What have you been doing to get somebody so scared that they tried to eliminate you? You holding out on me?"

"Nope." I hoped that I sounded sincere.

"All right, Jim. I appreciate your cooperation." He hung up abruptly.

I should have tried to get in touch with Rockingham, too, but I wasn't in the mood to talk to him. I stopped and had one dry Martini, two hot ham sandwiches, and a glass of milk. Then I drove across town. It was after two o'clock by the time I'd found a parking lot close to the station where Rockingham had taken Don Canfield. I knew the cop on the desk and he let me into the cell block. I talked to Don through the bars.

"Need anything, Don?"

"No."

"Has Kay been to see you?"

"No."

"That's smart. The farther she stays away from you the better—until this is cleared up." I hesitated and then I said, "But you should have told me about you and Kay planning to remarry."

"To hell with it," he said.

"I'm trying to help you, Don."

"You've helped enough. I've caused you enough trouble—and Kay, too."

"Is there anything you haven't told me?"

"No—and I didn't kill Louette."

"Listen, Don. Think hard about Sunday afternoon at the park. Isn't there anything I can work on, anything at all that might place you there at the time Louette was killed?"

"Just Annie," he said in a dull voice. "She knows that I was there all afternoon."

"That witness Rockingham has, the blonde, she's lying about seeing you leaving the apartment at three o'clock."

"I know it," he said bitterly. "I wasn't there at three o'clock." He lit a cigarette with a hand that trembled. "I know you mean well, Jim, but forget it. I've got a lawyer now."

"Who?"

"Owen Harris."

"He's a good one. Well, so long, Don."

"Thanks for coming, Jim."

"Anything you want me to tell Kay for you?"

He shook his head.

As I went out, the cop on the desk said cheerfully, "How's every little thing, Jim?"

"Terrible."

His loud laugh followed me out the door.

I ransomed the Ford from the parking lot and headed west on Route 20 to Elyria where I had the loose ends of a minor job to tie up. It was after five o'clock by the time I'd wound up my business and was heading out of Elyria on Cleveland Street in the thick traffic. In a pay phone beyond Ridgeville I called the office. Sandy was still there. She told me that Alec had called in at two o'clock, and that he hadn't called sooner because he had been following Jesse Connors to East Grange and back.

"East Grange?"

"That's what Alec said. He called in again at four-thirty and said that Connors was at your apartment waiting for you. Alec is camped outside."

"Okay. What else?"

"A young man from the Connors Electric Company brought your list. I made a copy and a policeman picked it up for Lieutenant Bronski. And Mr. Connors has called four times for you."

"Did he say what he wanted?"

"No, but he sounded awfully impatient."

"All right, Sandy, thanks. I'll see you in the morning."

I remembered my dinner date with Rebecca Foster and regretfully I called her apartment. She answered right away. I said, "This is Jim."

"Hello." Her voice was soft and warm.

"Rebecca, I'm twenty miles out of town and it looks like I'll be tied up for a while. Can I have a rain check on our date?"

She hesitated, and then said, "Yes, Jim ... but I'm sorry."

"I'm sorry, too. Can I call you tomorrow?"

"Of course." She sounded friendly, and I left it at that.

At six-thirty I pulled into the drive of Kay Canfield's house. Mrs. Mahoney told me that Kay had taken Annie out to dinner, and that Kay's injured arm apparently was not causing her much trouble. She expected them back by eight o'clock. I didn't know where I'd be at eight o'clock, or what I'd be doing, and I asked her where they'd gone to dinner. Mrs. Mahoney didn't really know—probably to one of the tearooms in the neighborhood, or maybe a downtown restaurant. That didn't help much. I thanked her and drove away.

I was hungry, but I didn't take time to eat. Instead, I drove to my apartment as fast as the traffic would allow. I parked a block away and moved along the sidewalk until I spotted Alec's lean figure loitering on the curb. He saw me coming and walked to meet me.

"Where is he?" I asked.

He jerked his thumb toward the apartment building. "Still inside, on a chair. He looks mean."

"He gave you a chase, huh?"

"Yeah—that's why I couldn't report in at noon. Just as I got set at the Quinn place this morning, two cops drive up—Bronski and Rockingham. They go in and stay maybe forty-five minutes. Then they leave. Then Connors drives to his factory. At a quarter of twelve he comes out and I follow him to East Grange. He parks by a jerkwater hotel called the Avalon and talks to a kid on the desk; then he goes upstairs. I'm right behind him. He knocks on a door at the end of the hall, no number on it. An old guy lets him in. I go back down, ask the kid who is in the room, and he tells me it belongs to a man named Hogmyer, the night clerk. In twenty minutes Connors comes down, drives back to Cleveland, to his factory. I call Sandy and wait. At four o'clock he drives here. I call Sandy again, and here we still are."

"Nice work, Alec. Stick around."

"Right, boss."

The apartment building where I live has a small foyer containing three leather chairs, a potted palm, a telephone booth, and a row of mailboxes on the wall beside the elevator. Jesse Connors was sitting in one of the chairs with his hands resting on the arms and his head against the back. His eyes were closed and his thin gray face was in repose. I guessed that he was past seventy years old, but he looked about eighty. He heard me come in and opened his eyes. They were clear and alert.

"Bennett," he said sharply, "I called your office four times and I've been waiting over two hours. Where in tarnation have you been?"

"Looking for your daughter—among other things."

"You brought her home at noon," he said impatiently. "I called Mrs. Connors and she told me."

"I've been busy since then," I said. "What did you want?"

He picked up his hat from the floor beside the chair, placed it carefully on his narrow head, and stood up. "We can talk outside," he said.

I followed him down the street to where his Buick was parked. He placed one thin veined hand on the door handle and turned to face me. His head began its tiny quick jerking. "I won't require your services any longer," he said. "I'll mail you a check for five hundred dollars for your efforts and time to date. Will that be satisfactory?"

"It's too much. May I ask your reason for dismissing me?"

"I no longer feel that your services are necessary. I have decided to let the police handle it." He paused, and added, "Entirely."

"All right, but don't you want to know where I found Helen?"

"I know where you found her," he said coldly. "Her mother told me—right after I called you this morning. The two of them had been keeping it from me—about Helen knowing of Roger's sordid affair with that woman in East Grange."

His head was shaking more violently now. I placed a hand on his arm. "Are you all right, Mr. Connors?"

He brushed my hand away. "Certainly I'm all right."

"Why did Helen tell her mother?"

"Mrs. Connors inadvertently found the note that man had written her. When she asked Helen about it, she broke down and told her."

"All of it?"

He nodded grimly. "The whole story—about her dealings with that man in East Grange. They kept it from me, not knowing that you had told me the beginning of it, about Roger and the woman. Mrs. Connors knew where Helen had gone, but she didn't tell me until after I'd asked you to find her." He fixed me with his cold eyes. "She also told me that you knew about Helen paying money to that man. You should have told me that, Bennett."

"I intended to."

He made a snorting sound. "Like you intended to tell me about the trouble Don Canfield is in? Don't tell me you didn't know about that?"

"I knew about it," I admitted.

"I had to find it out from the afternoon papers," he said bitterly.

"Do you think he killed his wife?"

"I don't give a damn," he snapped. "If he did, he had a good reason. Don is one of my best men. When they release him, the general manager's job is his. He should have had it in the beginning. I shouldn't have let my feelings for Helen influence me."

"They may not release him," I said.

"Like hell they won't! I'll hire the best lawyer in town, in the country, for him. I need men like him. If Helen had only married a man like Don, she—" He stopped abruptly and said in a quieter tone, "Have you reported any of your findings to the police?"

"Not my East Grange findings, not yet. But I may be forced to."

"That's why I want you to drop it, Bennett. Then you will be under no obligation to tell the police anything. It would serve no good purpose and would only excite unpleasant publicity for Helen. Nothing can help Roger now, or that woman. You just drop the matter. Understand?"

"When I start something, I like to finish it."

He gazed at me as steadily as the jerking of his head would permit. "A thousand dollars, Bennett, for you personally, to drop it."

"Do you think that Roger killed that woman at East Grange?" I asked.

"It doesn't matter," he snapped. "I am only trying to protect my daughter. I am thinking of her, of Mrs. Connors, and our grandchildren."

"Do you know that Helen paid Hogmyer five hundred more dollars this morning?"

"Yes." His face seemed grayer than ever.

"He'll want more," I said softly. "More than you gave him today. He'll always want more—to keep a secret like that."

His thin jaw sagged. "You know—"

"Of course," I said gently. "I know you went to Hogmyer. You think a lot of your daughter, don't you?"

His whole body began to shake and he shouted at me in a high shrill voice. "Yes, I do! I won't have her name dragged through filth because of a cheap, fortune-hunting, woman-chasing, no-good son of a bitch like Roger Quinn, a miserable bastard who married my only daughter and grew fat on my money and antagonized my employees, and—" He leaned against the Buick, his head down, his thin lips working convulsively.

I put an arm around him to keep him from falling. There was sweat on his face and I heard the rasping whistle of his breathing. "Take it easy," I said.

He pushed me violently away and I was amazed at the strength in his thin arms. "Five thousand," he said thickly. "You'd better take it." He opened the car door and crawled in behind the wheel. With a trembling hand he started the motor and he gazed at me with bleak cold eyes in his rapidly shaking head.

"No, thank you," I said.

"You're a fool, Bennett."

"Probably."

From his coat pocket he took the small glass vial, shook out two of the black pellets, and swallowed them. Then he leaned back against the seat. "Bennett," he said in a tired voice, "I assume that when a client stops paying, you stop working for him?"

"Usually."

"I've stopped paying."

"Very good. Would you let me drive you home, sir?"

"I'm perfectly capable of driving myself." The Buick's motor raced. I stepped back.

Without looking at me or speaking again he drove slowly and carefully away from the curb. I watched him until he reached the corner, and I hoped that he would make it safely home.

CHAPTER TWENTY

I glanced down the sidewalk at Alec Hammond. He was watching me intently, poised, like a track runner waiting for the starting gun. I shook my head at him, indicating that he was not to follow Jesse Connors. He relaxed and leaned against the apartment building wall. I walked down to him, said, "Let him go, Alec. He just fired me."

"Too bad, boss."

"Alec," I said, "I've had a hard day. I'm tired and discouraged and confused. I don't know what the hell is going on or why, and I've arrived at the point where I don't give a damn. Come on—I'll buy a drink."

We started back up the street toward a bar on the corner. As we passed the entrance to the apartment building a girl came down the steps and I saw that it was Francine, the little French number with the yellowish eyes and the straw-colored hair. She looked a little bedraggled; her hair needed combing and her tight black dress looked soiled and wrinkled. There were dark hollows beneath her eyes and she needed fresh lipstick. She saw me at once and came swiftly across the sidewalk and stood before me. Her eyes narrowed and her small high breasts moved with her quick breathing. She tapped a finger against my chest.

"Hah!" she cried. "I find you at last! Where is my Paul? What have you done to him?"

"What?" I said. "Who?"

"My Paul, my lover. You are of the police. Where is he?"

"I don't know."

"You do, you do!" She stamped a heel on the sidewalk. "You are lying to Francine. You have taken my Paul away. You are torturing him. You are giving him the—the third degree. Poor, poor Paul. He did not kill Louette. He would not harm a mouse. And now he is gone. I cannot find him. The other police, they lie to me. And now you lie to me." Once more she stamped her foot and hissed at me, "*Where is he?*" Tears ran down her cheeks and her mouth trembled.

"I don't know," I said again, beginning to wonder myself where her Paul had gone and what he was up to. Paul Reynard, the legal husband of Louette, with the black-market francs in a joint account in a Paris bank. I glanced at Alec. He was watching Francine with an interested expression.

"You are lying!" Francine cried.

"Francine," I said, "in America there is a law against telling a lie under oath. It is called perjury. You did not see Mr. Canfield leave his apartment on Sunday afternoon. You are trying to protect Paul Reynard. Why don't you go to the police and tell them that you lied?"

She spat something at me, something French and nasty, and she turned abruptly and flounced away. Her pale hair tossed over her shoulders with the jounce of her body and her high heels went *click, click, click*. I watched her cross the street a half block away and get into a battered 1937 Chevrolet sedan. But she didn't drive away; she sat behind the wheel and made passes at her face with what I guessed were a lipstick and powder puff.

Alec gave me a sidelong glance, his eyebrows raised. "Hmmmm," he said.

"She kills rats with hammers," I told him, "and she's your new assignment. Guess we'll have to postpone that drink. Feel like working a double trick?"

"Sure," he said, grinning. "It's time and a half, ain't it?"

"That's right. Have you had anything to eat?"

"Yeah—while Connors was parked inside."

"Good. Stick with the blonde tonight and call me when you get a chance."

Alec said, "I thought Connors fired you. You still got clients?"

"Too many," I said, "but this'll be charged to Connors. He has to pay for today anyway and he may as well get his money's worth."

Alec grinned and jerked his head at the Chevrolet. "Does she have anything to do with Connors's problems?"

I shrugged. "Who knows?"

He gave me a two-fingered salute and crossed the street to the agency Ford. It was parked in the same direction as the Chevrolet. Alec got behind the wheel of the Ford, looked across the street at me, and grinned.

I walked down to the corner bar, intending to call Rockingham and ask him what the score was on Paul Reynard. But he wasn't at the station. I tried his home and Mrs. Piccutio, his mother-in-law, told me that Meester Rockingham had just left for the hospital and that Theresa, praise the saints, was much better. I thanked her and hung up, deciding against calling Rockingham at the hospital. Even a homicide cop has a right to a little private life.

When I came out of the bar the street was quiet and there wasn't much traffic. The sun was down and the sky over the tops of the buildings was red with the evening glow. I knew that for a brief time there would be empty parking spaces along the curbs, and then suddenly, with the beginning of darkness, the street would fill with cars and the drivers would cruise endlessly and hopelessly, looking for a place to park while they attended the nearby movie houses, the bars, and the nightclubs. The Chevrolet was gone, I noticed, and so was the agency Ford, and I wondered where the blond Francine was leading Alec.

At a restaurant three blocks down the street I had two Martinis followed by a medium-rare tenderloin, a baked potato, and a head lettuce salad. I was drinking my coffee when Oswald McKinney came in and insisted upon buying me a brandy. Oswald lived across the hall from me. He was a special investigator for the United States Treasury Department and he spent his time hounding people who owed income taxes which the Bureau of Internal Revenue had been unable to collect in the usual manner. Oswald McKinney was the tax delinquent's last chance. If they didn't pay him he smacked attachments on their property, if any, and their income. It was a hell of a job, I thought, but he seemed to like it. Anyhow, he was always cheerful.

I said, "How many poor old widows did you foreclose today, Oswald?"

"Now, Jim, all the government wants is its just taxes, and not a penny more." He was a fat, pink-cheeked man, addicted to dazzling neckties.

"Plus a little blood and maybe an arm or a leg," I said.

He laughed loudly. Nothing bothered Oswald. We finished our brandy, and then it was my turn to buy one, and then his again. Three hours and six brandies later we left the restaurant. Oswald walked back to the apartment with me and we said good night in the hall. He remarked that he wanted to get a good night's sleep because in the morning he was filing wage attachments against ten reluctant taxpayers.

"But I warned 'em," he said. "They had their chance."

"Shylock," I sneered.

His jolly laugh followed me as I entered my apartment. As I closed the door my glance fell on the divan. Something was missing. And then I realized that the arrows, which I'd left there wrapped in the towel, were gone.

It was almost midnight by the time I'd smoked a couple of cigarettes and read the evening papers. The murder of Roger Quinn was still on the front pages, but in smaller type, and no new information was given, except that the funeral was the next day. The killing of Louette was still worth a quarter column on page three, but was a rehash of the first story, and I wondered once more how much Bronski end Rockingham were holding back.

All of the papers carried the news of the capture by East Grange police of Anthony Kovak, fugitive husband of the murdered Melissa. As I had hoped and expected, neither my name nor Helen Quinn's was mentioned, although the name of Edward H. Cory, chief of the East Grange police, appeared prominently as the arresting officer. All stories ended with the statement that Chief Cory expected a signed confession momentarily.

I let the papers fall to the floor and I gazed at the ceiling. Once more people and events began to crowd my brain; names and places and snatches of conversation, beginning on a night in September. But I thought mostly of the people, and the things that people do and their reasons for doing them. Somewhere there was a person, maybe more than one person, who had killed Louette and Melissa and Roger Quinn. But still the thought stuck with me that the blood of three people was on the hands of one person, someone who wanted three people to die. Maybe this person had a reason, or maybe no reason; a killer on a spree for just the killing is the most difficult to catch. But Louette and Melissa and Roger had all been flirting with the outer reaches of convention, away from the norm; and then in the space of a day and a night they had been taken into the big darkness.

Kay and Don Canfield, Helen and Roger Quinn, Louette and Francine and Paul Reynard, Rebecca Foster and Anthony Kovak, a sly one-eared old man named Cornelius Hogmyer, Chief Edward H. Cory and Lieutenant George Bronski and Sergeant Dennis Rockingham, Jesse Connors and his plump wife, a skinny factory guard named Alvin E. Semms, and a little girl named Annie—all of these people, and more, had crossed my path in the last three days and here I sat at midnight—

A brunette corpse on a divan, a blond corpse on a bed, a black-haired male corpse dangling from a flagpole. A knife, a rope, arrows winging out of the night, a strange male voice on the telephone, a Martini cocktail, Scotch and bourbon and rye, beer and brandy and carrot juice; black-market francs and rats in a love nest in Paris; a hamburger drive-in and a cowgirl rolling Bull Durham; a shabby house on Puxatawny Street and a pitiful little pile of letters and discarded clothing; a man bleeding on a barroom floor and a little girl riding a green horse with golden eyes—

And from somewhere out of the blackness of memory came a picture of an old white-whiskered man standing in late-afternoon sunlight dropping a penny into a slot.

Above me was an old-fashioned chandelier. The bulbs in it were all burned out and as far as the cleaning women were concerned it was a dust-catching monstrosity from another era which did not exist. Around its edge, above the dangling glass pendants, was a parade of prancing bronze horses, green with age and fuzzy with dust. They reminded me of the merry-go-round and I drifted backward three days in time to Sunday afternoon when I had sat on a bench with Don Canfield, and once more I was hearing Annie's piping voice.

More tickets, Daddy. I gave the man our red fortune tickets, but he said I need the yellow tickets for the merry-go-round ride.

I sat quietly for a while, knowing what I was going to do, but still waiting, thinking it over. At last I stood up and put on my coat. It felt heavy, and I remembered the gun I'd placed in the pocket at the office that morning. The weight felt good against my ribs.

I had left the Ford down on the street. Before I drove away I made certain that there was a flashlight in the dash compartment, and that it was working. I headed west across town, but I made the mistake of taking the lake boulevard—I had forgotten that the Indians were playing Detroit. It must have been an extra-inning game, because as I approached the stadium, cars loaded with ball fans were spewing up to the boulevard in an idiotic confusion of juvenile horn-blowing. Then I was caught, trapped in a line of cars, bumper to bumper. From the whistling and shrill shrieks around me I guessed that the Indians had beaten the Tigers, and I was properly and loyally pleased, but in my haste to get where I wanted to go I thought wryly that there was no one more enthusiastic, to the point of nausea, than the American baseball fan.

It took me over an hour, moving a few feet at a time in the packed line of cars, to reach Rocky River, and another twenty minutes to battle my way through the now thinning baseball crowd to the highway leading to the Lake Shore Amusement Park. It was one-thirty in the morning before I pulled up at the entrance. The park closed at midnight and now it was a silent place of moonlight and deep shadows, with only the memory of the voices of kids and the sound of music and the chatter of people on a holiday.

I parked outside the gate beneath the looming dark skeleton of the roller coaster. Taking the flashlight, but not turning it on, I walked along a gravel path past the dark and locked-up concessions, the picnic pavilions, the towering Ferris wheel, the scooter rides, the pony corral, the miniature railroad, and I came at last to the merry-go-round. It squatted huge and round and flat in the moonlight. A heavy canvas hung from the circular roof and hid the green horse with the golden eyes and the other assorted wooden animals. I passed the bench where I'd talked with Don Canfield, moved to the merry-go-round, lifted the canvas, and stepped to the wooden platform.

When the canvas fell behind me I turned on the flashlight. The yellow pig was beside me and the zebra's prancing gilt hoofs hung poised in the yellow beam. I swung the light on the clumsy gasoline motor with its greasy gears, wheels, and belts. Beside the motor was a record playing device connected to a loudspeaker and beside the speaker was what I was looking for.

It was still there, the tall metal can into which I had seen the operator drop the tickets after he'd torn them in two—the yellow tickets collected from hundreds of kids for countless merry-go-round rides. The can was large enough to hold thousands of tickets, days and days of rides, if they didn't dump them after each day. I held my breath as I tipped the flashlight into the can. It was almost half full of torn yellow pieces of cardboard. More, surely, than would be collected in a day. Two days? Three days, perhaps? Back to Sunday? My hand trembled a little as I thrust it down into the mass of tickets. I dug deep, lifting my hand, the pieces falling between my fingers. All yellow, just pieces of yellow tickets; no glint of red in the cascade of tumbling yellow.

I wedged the light between the gears of the motor and upended the can, dumping the contents on the smooth bare earth. My fingers raked through the yellow pile. Yellow, yellow, yellow. Then I uncovered the first piece of red cardboard! And another. I rooted desperately and found them all. They stood out like blood in the strewn yellow heap. Four little pieces of cardboard, two tickets torn in half. I laid them on the platform and fitted them together. It was like a simple jigsaw puzzle, and when I had them arranged before me I knew I had what I wanted.

Little red tickets with fortune-telling lingo printed in fine type on one side. I read: *You are headstrong and stubborn, but your instinctive knowledge of right and wrong will win for you in the end. Stick to your ideals!* That was Don Canfield's ticket. I knew it was his because on the reverse side was the printed date of the Sunday three days before followed by, *186 lbs., 3:04 p.m.* On the other ticket was the same date and: *45 lbs., 3:03 p.m.* That was Annie's. I didn't bother to read her fortune.

I stood up, placed the four bits of cardboard in my pocket, and smiled to myself. If Rockingham was so hell-bent on using Annie's testimony against Don, he would have to recognize the fortune cards as evidence in Don's savor. They placed Don and Annie in the park shortly after three o'clock in the afternoon, over an hour's drive from the spot where Louette had been killed. Almost conclusive evidence—if Don weighed a hundred and eighty-six pounds and Annie weighed forty-five, but I had no doubts about that.

As I picked up the flash and turned I saw a pale oblong of moonlight across from me, low down, between the wooden animals, and I heard a soft scratching sound. I turned off the flash and crouched down. The space of moonlight disappeared as the canvas fell with a rustling sound and I heard running feet crunching over the stones. In deep darkness I scrambled across the circular platform, feeling my way between the animals, and lifted the canvas. In the bright moonlight I saw the figure of a woman running for the trees beyond a picnic pavilion.

"Stop!" I yelled, like a character in a TV mystery, and I jerked at the gun in my coat pocket. The hammer caught on the silk of the lining and for an instant I grudgingly conceded that maybe the shoulder holster boys had something. Then the gun was clear. The figure was still in the moonlight, running knock-kneed, like a woman runs, for the black shadows of the trees. I cried, "Stop!" once more and fired twice into the ground. I was appalled at the sudden brutal noise in the peaceful park. But she didn't stop running. I jumped from the merry-go-round and ran after her.

Something moved in the shadows by the pavilion. A voice cried out and I saw a bright orange flash of flame. The running figure faltered, stumbled forward to hands and knees, and then sank slowly to the ground at the edge of the shadow cast by the trees.

I moved slowly forward, holding the gun out in front. A man stepped out from the shadow of the pavilion and stood over the fallen form of the woman.

I moved closer and saw the man very clearly in the moonlight.

"You didn't shoot to hit her?" I said to Alec Hammond.

"Hell, no, Jim." He sounded annoyed. "Like you, I figured to scare her." He nudged the form of the woman with a toe. "Come on, honey, get up. You ain't shot."

I leaned down, placed a hand on a round shoulder, and turned the woman over. In the moonlight her tumbled hair was like bright silver. She stared up at the night sky and her lips worked soundlessly. Then she whispered, "Tell my mother—in Bordeaux. Tell her I was hit by a—a streetcar in America. Do not tell her that I died trying to help my Paul, or that he was unfaithful to me. Tell my mother that everything was fine until the streetcar came along."

Her yellowish eyes rolled, glinting like gold in the moonlight, and she smiled a faint, sad smile. "The sound of the guns," she said softly, "it was like the liberation, so long ago." Her eyes shifted to me. "James T. Bennett, I remember your name. You are of the police, doing your duty. Please do not grieve for Francine. I lied to you—about the photo. I did not see Mr. Canfield leave his apartment. I make it up, to protect my Paul. Where is he? What have you done with him?"

"Did Paul kill Louette?" I asked.

"Let me die," she breathed. "For Paul."

I looked at Alec Hammond.

He spread his arms. "I tail her. She don't move. Then pretty soon she takes the Chevvy to a spot down the street where she can watch your apartment and you can't see her. I move the Ford. We wait. You come up the street with a fat guy and go inside. We still wait. I want to call you, but I see she's fidgety and I hate to leave her. After a long while you come out and drive away. She zooms after you. I'm on her tail and here we are. Wasn't that ball game crowd a mess?"

"Sure was."

"The Indians won," he said.

"Goody," I said. "Hurrah for our boys." I looked down at Francine. "Come on, get up. You're not hurt."

"Not—shot?"

"No, no," I said impatiently. "I want you to tell the police what you told us—that you did not see Mr. Canfield leaving his apartment on Sunday afternoon."

"I will tell them—but where is my Paul?"

"We'll see." I leaned down and pulled her to a sitting position.

"My ankle," she moaned. "It is twisted. Please—" With a swift motion Alec leaned over and picked her up. "Ups-a-daisy, honey." He moved away with her. Her pale hair was like a waterfall in the moonlight. At the gate a thin little watchman with a leather-covered time clock slung over his shoulder came running up to us. "What's going on here?" he cried in a quavering voice.

I flashed the light on him. He blinked like a scared animal. "Police," I growled.

He backed away into the shadows and I didn't see him anymore.

We left Francine's battered Chevrolet at the park gate and I led the way in my car through the early morning to the police station in Rockingham's precinct. I hated to telephone him at four o'clock in the morning, but I did. He came down.

Francine, rubbing a slim ankle, told him in a hesitant voice that she had lied about her identification of Don Canfield, that she had merely been attempting to protect her lover, Paul Reynard, who would not harm a mouse. "Where is he?" she pleaded. "He needs me. Where is my Paul?"

Rockingham, unshaven and tieless, his eyes bleary from lack of sleep, pointed a stern finger at her. "You swore under oath that you saw Canfield leaving that apartment at three o'clock."

"I lied," she moaned. "Francine confesses it. I lied for love of my Paul. I was afraid you would suspect him. Do what you want with me—I do not care. Just tell me that my Paul is safe, where I can find him."

"Did Paul kill her?" Rockingham asked harshly.

"*Non, non!*" she cried. "I feel it here." She pressed a hand beneath her left breast. "He would not harm a—a—"

"Mouse," I finished for her.

"Did you kill her?" Rockingham barked.

"*Non!* I hated her, but I would not kill her."

Rockingham looked at me helplessly.

I jerked my head at him and he followed me into an adjoining office.

"Listen, Jim," he snarled, "we've been watching her damned Paul. Right now he's shacked up with a chunky brunette in a room on Chester Avenue. He's scared to go to the john by himself, and I've just about crossed him off my list." He nodded at the outer room. "Her, I don't know."

I handed him the four pieces of cardboard. He peered at them carefully, scowling. I pointed out the dates and the time of day on them and explained how I'd gotten them. I told him about the machine by the merry-go-round which for a penny spewed a ticket, giving the date, the time of day, your weight, and your fortune.

He caressed his red mustache with a little finger and gazed intently at the tickets.

"To cinch it," I said, "you can put Don Canfield on the scales, and the kid, too, to see if their weights jibe with the tickets."

He died hard.

"Canfield could have rigged it," he said, "by sending someone who weighed the same as he does over to the park with the kid at three o'clock."

"My God, Rock. If he rigged it for an alibi, do you suppose he'd give the tickets to his daughter for her to give to the merry-go-round guy—for him to tear up and throw away? I was lucky to find them still in the can."

He pulled a hand down over his stubbled cheeks. "All right, Jim," he said wearily. "I'll accept it as evidence that he was not at his apartment at the time his wife was killed. And that blonde going back on her identification seems to put Canfield in the clear—as far as his wife's death is concerned. That's what you want, isn't it?"

"It's part of what I want," I said.

"I know," he said. "You're working on the Quinn killing, too."

"Yes." A little warning signal flashed in my brain.

"I'll tell you something, Jim. It might interest you. We found Quinn's fingerprints all over Canfield's apartment. The lab men took his in the morgue as a matter of routine, and when they got to cross-checking they found that they matched prints found in the apartment." He looked at me narrowly.

"Quinn's prints were on the knife, too, I suppose?" I said mockingly.

"No," he said quietly, "the knife was clean."

"Why shouldn't Roger's prints be in the apartment?" I asked. "He visited there."

"Just an old family friend? Like you?"

"Sure."

"Anything you should tell me, Jim?" he asked softly.

"No." If I'd been telling the truth I couldn't have looked him in the eye any steadier.

"All right," he said, "I'll lay it out for you. We're not getting anywhere on Quinn, not even with that damned list of bow-and-arrow shooters you gave Bronski. Since we found Quinn's prints in Canfield's apartment, we've been working together. This morning we had a talk with Jesse Connors. We figure there's a connection between the two killings. So Quinn was a pal of Canfield and his wife?"

"More or less. Don met her through Roger."

"Oh?" He raised his eyebrows.

"Bronski told you about the arrow ambush?" I asked.

"Yeah. The arrows that were shot at you belonged to the company archery club, but there's twenty-four people in the club and so far Bronski has found only six with airtight alibis. The rest say they were at the movies, out for a ride, taking a walk, watching television, in bed—you know how it goes; they can't prove they were, and we can't prove they weren't. But George is still checking. Maybe the man who lured you to Lovers' Lane has something to do with the killings—and maybe he just doesn't like you." He grinned at me. "You got any enemies, Jim?"

"Millions. Say, Rock, how did Bronski get those arrows?"

"He couldn't locate you, so he sent a man to your apartment for 'em."

"I see," I said. "Tell me more."

"Quinn was a chaser, a lady's man. We know that now. And he was sneaking around to see Canfield's wife and—"

"Which one?" I asked, and instantly I swore bad words at myself. The last thing I wanted was to bring Kay into it, and I decided that my nerves were getting frazzled. But from the quick, calculating look in Rockingham's eyes I knew that the damage was done.

"I mean the wife that's dead," he said softly. "The one called Louette." He paused. "You know, Jim, I've been thinking about the other one, too—ever since I found her at his place yesterday. Damned pretty woman."

"Yes," I said hopelessly. He wouldn't drop it now, and if he learned that Roger had been seeing Kay, and that Don had caught him with her

He watched me silently for a moment, and then he laughed. It was not a pleasant laugh, but I knew that he'd decided to drop it, at least for now, to keep me squirming on the hook.

"In addition to Quinn's fingerprints," he said, "we found butts of fancy cigarettes in Canfield's apartment—the kind that Quinn smoked. And we know that Quinn was there one night last week—when Canfield was out of town. He was seen entering and leaving. They have nosy neighbors, you know. Your pal, Canfield, may be out of the woods on one count, thanks to you, but he sure as hell had a swell reason for killing Quinn."

I didn't trust myself to say anything. I'd said too much already.

"Listen," Rockingham said, "I let Canfield loose late Sunday night. Quinn was killed early Monday morning. The guard at the Connors plant who was on duty—Semms is his name—admitted under questioning that he left the gate for about twenty minutes to have some coffee with the fireman in the boiler room. And during that time Quinn was strung to the flagpole." He looked at me with a gleam of triumph in his eyes. "And we're still digging, Bronski and me."

I tried to smile at him, thinking dismally of the things they were learning, and of the things they were still to learn. I changed the subject. "What about that blonde?" I asked, motioning toward the outer room. "She's worried about her Paul."

"I'll tell her where her Paul is," he said savagely. "I'll tell her good. I'll let her surprise him with that brunette." He looked at me and his eyes grew bright. "It would serve her right for lying about seeing Canfield."

"Yeah," I said, "but it's a dirty trick."

He turned abruptly and strode out. I stared out of a dusty window and watched the daylight creep over the city. Presently I heard Rockingham's footsteps. He grinned maliciously. "I told her where she would find her Paul, and she took off. Riggio's on her tail. Nothing like stirring things up a little."

"Rock, Rock," I sighed, "to what depths won't you sink?"

He began to hum a little tune. "Want to stick around, Jim? She'll catch her Paul in bed with the brunette." He resumed his humming.

"No," I said. "I'm not that depraved yet."

He stopped his humming long enough to say in mincing tones, "Dear me."

I moved to the door and said to him, "Why don't you go over there, too? You and Riggio could take turns at the keyhole."

"Say," he said, "that's a charming idea." He went past me out the door, still humming.

Alec Hammond was sleeping on a bench with his long legs drawn up to his chin. I shook him gently and he awoke with a start. I told him to drive the agency Ford home and to take the day off. As we went out to the street, some of the cruise cars from the dawn patrol were rolling up the ramp to the garages in the rear. It was full daylight now and the sun was red behind the Terminal Tower. Alec and I drove away and I followed him until he swung south at East 93rd Street. It was five-thirty when I reached my apartment.

As I opened the door, I heard the phone ringing.

CHAPTER TWENTY-ONE

It was Rockingham and he was laughing.

"It worked, Jim," he said, "damned if it didn't. Riggio and I listened outside the door. Reynard and the brunette were there and the blonde was working over the brunette. Sounded like a couple of cats in an alley. Not a peep out of Reynard. We let 'em mix it for a while, and pretty soon the blonde spills it. Everybody in the whole building could hear her." He paused and laughed some more.

"Go on," I told him. "I can hardly wait."

"This is good, Jim. The blonde screams that she knows Reynard killed Canfield's wife, Louette, because she wouldn't sign off for some money in a joint bank account in Paris so that he could get it. She said she had been trying to protect him because she loved him, but that now she was finished with him for good and she was going straight to the police. Then she calls them both a lot of bad French names and starts in on Reynard all over again. That was when Riggio and I busted in. She was pulling Reynard's hair and scratching and slapping him. His face looked like hamburger. We pulled her off him, and he scooted under the bed. Both he and the brunette were naked as a couple of eggs. The brunette just laid on the bed and moaned. God, what a show. You shoulda come along."

"So Reynard killed Louette?" I asked.

"Yeah. I held the blonde while Riggio dragged Reynard from under the bed and got some clothes on him. We took 'em both to the station. The blonde signed a statement saying that Reynard told her he killed Louette."

"Reynard talk yet?"

"Hell, no. He's still shaking. He's too scared to talk, but he will, he will."

"Nice work," I said. "One down and one to go, huh?"

"You mean Quinn's murder? Hell, we'll wind that up." He was riding high. "We still got Canfield. Remember?"

"I remember," I said. "Well, Rock, thanks for calling me."

"I just thought you'd like to know," he said modestly, "seeing as how you're an interested party, and all."

"Goodbye. Me for bed."

"Bed? What's that?" He hung up laughing.

I leaned back in the chair by the phone. The sun shone through the bars of the Venetian blinds and filled the room with a soft mellow light. I bent over and untied my shoelaces, thinking of my bed as a lover thinks of his sweetheart. I leaned back in the chair, intending to move presently into the bedroom. But I never made it. I went to sleep in the chair.

The shrill ringing of a bell was like the blast of doom in my ears. I jerked awake, groped blindly for the phone, almost dropped it, and mumbled something, probably hello.

A female voice said, "James?"

"Yes, ma'am," I answered, rubbing my eyes. Any female who addressed me as James deserved the "ma'am." I brought my left wrist around in front of my face. Eight o'clock.

"James, this is Mrs. Connors."

"Pardon?"

"Helen's mother."

"Oh, yes." I smothered a yawn.

"I wanted to catch you before you left for your office."

"You caught me," I muttered.

"What, James?"

"How are you this morning, Mrs. Connors?"

I heard her sigh. "As well as could be expected, I guess. James, would you be one of the pallbearers this afternoon? Owen Harris was called out of town. Mr. Fortney suggested one of the men from the plant as a substitute, but, well, under the circumstances, Jesse and I thought it would not be—advisable. You understand, don't you?"

"I understand," I said, thinking of Roger Quinn's unpopularity with the thousand employees at Connors Electric.

"Of course," she said, "Mr. Fortney can supply a pallbearer, but it would be someone who did not know Roger, not one of his friends, and Helen asked me to call you. Would you, please?"

I wondered dismally if when I died there would be trouble in finding six friends to carry my coffin, and I said, "I'll be glad to. The funeral is at two-thirty, isn't it?"

"Yes, but Mr. Fortney would like the pallbearers to be there a little earlier. Something about the seating."

"All right. How's Helen holding up?"

"Oh, that poor girl. She just stays in her room and grieves. It's been a terrible ordeal for her, just terrible. And the worst is to come. At the grave is the worst. I guess she loved him, poor child, no matter what he was—" Her voice trailed off and she sighed again.

I thought of Helen Connors sobbing to her mother the confession of money paid to a one-eared old man in East Grange, and of her resolution to pay him more money if need be, and of Jesse Connors's trip to see the one-eared man personally about the matter of a dead woman in the Hotel Avalon, and about the matter of a wayward son-in-law and a blackmailed daughter. And I thought, too, of Jesse

Connors firing me, and of his offer to pay me to drop my investigations.

Mrs. Connors said briskly, "Well, thank you, James. I'll tell Helen that she can count on you."

I replaced the phone, settled back in the chair, and closed my eyes. But not for long.

This was the morning for my phone to ring. It began again. I couldn't ignore it—it was too loud and too close to my ear. I pushed myself up in the chair, lifted the phone to my ear.

"Yes," I said wearily, "yes, yes."

George Bronski's quiet voice said, "Jim, you sound irritated."

"I was trying to get some sleep. I was up all night."

"Rock told me. Nice piece of work you did—but I'm afraid it won't help your friend, Canfield, much."

"Why the hell not? It cleared him of a murder rap, didn't it?"

"One murder, maybe," Bronski said softly. "Listen, Jim, Rock and I have just come from Mrs. Canfield's house—"

"You mean Kay?"

"I believe that is her name. The *first* Mrs. Canfield. She wasn't there. The housekeeper said she'd left for Akron around seven-thirty, to go to a dress shop there, a branch store owned by the outfit she works for here. She drove down and she took the little girl with her. The housekeeper said she expects to be back in time to attend Quinn's funeral this afternoon. Incidentally, we asked the housekeeper a few questions and we learned some rather interesting things."

"Like what?" I was sitting up straight in the chair.

"Oh," he said casually, "things like Quinn coming to see Mrs. Canfield—the first Mrs. Canfield—and about the fight Don Canfield had with Quinn one night last week. Seems he was visiting his ex-wife, too."

Here it was. Rockingham hadn't waited long to get more ideas and to share them with Bronski. "What of it?" I asked.

"It keeps adding up, Jim. Right now we want to talk with Mrs. Canfield. In fact, I've called the Akron police to pick her up and I've sent a car down there. Rockingham went with the car."

"An arrest?"

"A routine questioning, let us say." He coughed delicately and added, "Jim, could you come over to the station—in about an hour, say?"

"What for?" I felt a sudden cold sweat on my face.

"There are a few little items I'd like to discuss with you."

"All right, George. But you're making a mistake about Mrs. Canfield."

"I have made many mistakes," he said sadly. "But not this time."

"You sound pretty certain."

"I am, Jim."

"So certain that you can't wait until she returns from Akron?"

He said carefully, "I have only the housekeeper's word that she has gone to Akron. If she hasn't, I want to know it as soon as possible. Frankly, Jim, it appears that she has withheld important information about her relationship with her ex-husband."

I thought of the information I was withholding and I tried to make my voice casual. "By the way, George, Mrs. Canfield's arm was injured. She shouldn't be driving a car."

"The housekeeper told us about it. Quite an odd occurrence; burglars don't usually swing a knife when surprised—they just run. However, the housekeeper said that Mrs. Canfield assured her that she could drive without any trouble."

I couldn't think of anything to say, and he said, "See you in an hour, Jim?"

"All right."

I sat staring at the cradled phone for maybe two minutes. Then I placed a call to the Akron branch of Kay's Cleveland store. When it came through a crisp feminine voice told me in response to my query that Mrs. Canfield had arrived, but at the moment she was busy. Could she take a message for Mrs. Canfield? The voice was trying very hard to be efficient and career-womanish. I told her no, I wanted to speak with her personally. Mrs. Canfield was very busy. The store would be opening in a short time for the big sale of the Kay Canfield models, and right this minute she was talking to these—these men. Could I call back? No, I couldn't call back, and would she please ask Mrs. Canfield to come to the phone immediately?

"Well—I'll see, sir."

I waited a good three minutes. Then the crisp voice, not quite so crisp now, said, "I'm sorry, sir, but Mrs. Canfield and her daughter just stepped out of the store and—"

"With those men?"

"Yes. It seems that something has come up—"

I knew what had come up; the men were Akron cops. I said, "So Mrs. Canfield's daughter is with her?"

"Oh, yes. In the sale this morning we are also featuring preschool frocks designed by Mrs. Canfield. Her little daughter is going to model them. If you will give me your name, sir, I will ask Mrs. Canfield to call you."

"Never mind." I hung up, thinking that the branch store in Akron was going to have to struggle through the big sale of dresses bearing the Kay Canfield label without the personal appearance of Kay Canfield, and without little Annie's modeling of the preschool frocks.

There was nothing I could do now. Bronski and Rockingham were closing in on me. I looked at my wristwatch. Eight-thirty. Akron was about an hour's drive from Cleveland. Bronski expected me in an hour, which would be approximately the time Rockingham would be arriving with Kay. Suddenly I was glad, in a perverse way, that Bronski wanted me on hand. I would get it over with and tell them of my activities in East Grange, of my conviction that somewhere there was a connecting link between the attack on Kay and the deaths of Louette, Melissa, and Roger Quinn. And then there was Helen Quinn, and her father, Jesse Connors. What would I tell Bronski and Rockingham about them?

But no matter what I told them, it would mean bad trouble for me, and I tried not to think of two pairs of cold outraged eyes, Rockingham's and Bronski's.

There was no time for any more sleep, not this day, the day of Roger Quinn's funeral. I wanted to be shaved and showered, dressed in clean fresh clothes, looking bright and cheerful and alert when I faced Bronski and Rockingham with my confession. As I walked slowly to the bathroom I remembered, after all the years, the voice of the old man in New York on the day I'd graduated from the agency training school. It was a sort of oath he'd made us take and then memorize, and framed copies of it hung in every agency office all over the world.

Always play fair with the police. If they trust you, they will help you. Do not ever withhold evidence from them, or anything which they might use. Do not ever forget that the police can help you far more than you can ever help them. You are now part of a vast, respected organization, an organization only second to the Federal Bureau of Investigation. It is your sworn duty to uphold the honor and the integrity—

As I laid out my razor and shaving cream the words rang clear and loud in my memory.

Your responsibility to your client is no greater than your responsibility to the legally appointed officers of law enforcement. No man and no woman in this organization must ever consider that he or she is beyond the law, or that the interest of a client comes first. If a client is involved in a violation of any federal, state, or local statute, then it is your sworn duty to—

And the telephone rang once more.

When I answered it, a breathless voice said, "This is Rebecca. Can—can you come over right away?"

"What's wrong, Rebecca?"

"I—I can't tell you now. But please, please hurry."

"Where are you? At the office?"

"No, no—at home. The plant is closed today because of Mr. Quinn's funeral. It—it's about Mrs. Canfield. She—"

"Kay?" I asked sharply. "What about her?"

"I—I can't talk now. Please understand. But hurry."

"All right. I'm leaving now."

The receiver clicked in my ear.

I needed a shave, my shirt was wilted, my gray tweed suit was wrinkled in the wrong places, and my shoes still needed polishing. I had a drawn, hollow-eyed, sleepless feeling and when I bent over to tie my shoelaces my back hurt from sleeping in the chair. I returned to the bathroom, washed my face quickly with cold water, feeling the stiff stubble of beard beneath my fingers. As I ran a comb through my hair and hastily straightened the knot in my tie I saw that my image in the mirror was not attractive; black hair, parted on the side and long over the ears because I was past due at the barber's; blue eyes, slightly bloodshot, with blue pouches beneath them; black whiskers, gray-tinged in spots. I was pushing forty, but there was no gray in my hair, just in my beard.

I wished I at least had time to shave before I faced Bronski and Rockingham, but time was running out for me. I put on my hat and coat and went out swiftly before the damned phone could ring again.

CHAPTER TWENTY-TWO

The hallway outside Rebecca Foster's door was bright with sunshine. At the far end beside an open door two women chattered brightly about what a nice day it was to take the children over to the park. They stopped talking and looked at me as I knocked on Rebecca's door. I. smiled at them and tipped my hat. They looked quickly away and resumed their chatter in subdued tones.

The door opened.

"Come in," Rebecca Foster said soberly.

I stepped inside and turned to face her. She closed the door, locked it, and removed the key. She held the key and gazed about the room, apparently looking for a place to put it. Her strong white teeth gnawed at her plump lower lip.

"Stick it back in the lock," I said.

She didn't answer and her gaze continued to dart about. She looked quite feminine and alluring in a transparent blue silk robe over a pale-blue nightgown. Her feet were bare and her tawny hair, streaked with light sun-bleached lanes, hung in soft folds over her shoulders. The blue robe hung open, revealing the low neckline of the nightgown and I was faintly embarrassed. The gown was extremely sheer and the robe should have been belted around her.

I looked about. I didn't see Eric Bismarck Von Tonder the Third, and I wondered if she had him chained to a clothesline in the back yard.

Her quick-darting eyes came to rest on me. There were tiny beads of sweat on her upper lip and a queer smoky look in her gray eyes. And then I saw that her big rounded body was trembling. I took a step forward and touched her shoulder. Her skin felt hot beneath the silk.

"Take it easy," I said.

She turned her body slightly away from me and lowered her head in a half-shy gesture. I could see the clean whiteness of her scalp where she had parted the honey-and-cream-streaked hair. Behind her on the mantel was the glittering row of trophies—golf, tennis, swimming, bowling, archery, softball, and some I didn't recognize. Soccer and wrestling, no doubt, I thought, and maybe hockey and football.

"What about Kay Canfield?" I asked. "Have you seen her?"

Abruptly she stopped trembling and looked directly at me. "Yes. She was here."

"When?"

"This morning, just before I called you—about eight-thirty."

"Oh," I said.

She took two steps toward the doorway leading to the kitchen. Then she stopped and smiled at me over a round firm shoulder. "Would you like a drink, Mr. Bennett?"

"Call me Jim," I said. "Listen—"

"Jim," she said, "would you like a drink? Or is it too early in the morning?"

"A little early," I said. "Rebecca—"

"I have some coffee," she said quickly. "Please sit down." She left the room swiftly, the blue robe billowing behind her.

I was glad to sit down. I sat with my hands on my knees and gazed at the display of trophies. What the hell was the matter with her? As I listened to her making noises in the kitchen, thoughts formed and curdled in my tired brain. They jumped from the Hotel Avalon to Don's apartment, to a flagpole in the dawn and back to the Avalon. Once again I was hearing Cornelius Hogmyer's words as he described Roger Quinn's assortment of women. What had he said? And what about Kay's early visit to Rebecca Foster this morning? What about that?

Rebecca returned, carrying a cup and saucer. She placed them on a low table beside me. "Cream? Sugar?" she asked.

"Neither." I sipped at the coffee. It was hot and strong, but it had a bitter taste, as if it had stood in the pot too long.

She stood gazing down at me, an odd dreamy expression in her eyes. My eyes met hers and she seemed to start slightly, like a person awakening from a deep sleep. Then she turned slowly away, entered the kitchen, and came back with a tall glass in her hand. The glass was filled with a thick red liquid and I wondered if she had forsaken her carrot juice. She stood in the center of the room and her gaze skittered away from mine. Her big full breasts began to rise and fall rapidly beneath the thin nightgown.

"Rebecca," I said gently, "Kay Canfield was not here. It eight-thirty this morning. She was in Akron."

She drank some of the red liquid and gazed at me languidly over the rim of the glass. "Of course not," she said, "but I had to be sure that you would come."

"I would have come just for you, Rebecca," I said sadly. "Why did you have to lie to me?"

She tossed a loop of her oddly streaked hair back from her face and smiled at me.

I nodded at her glass. "What's that? Blood?"

"Tomato juice," she murmured.

"It looks like blood to me," I said.

"It could be blood."

She watched me dreamily.

I had it, all I needed to know. I couldn't prove it, not yet, but I had it. I thought of Louette, dead on a divan; of Melissa Kovak, slaughtered like a pig in a packing house; of Roger Quinn, kicking out his life on a flagpole. I thought of a knife striking at Kay in the darkness; and of drab little Helen Quinn, grieving for a faithless husband and trying pitifully to protect his memory, and of Jesse Connors doing what he thought best for his only child. I remembered the blind misery in Anthony Kovak's eyes, and I suddenly knew that Paul Reynard had not killed Louette, no matter if the blond Francine, in her jealous rage, swore that he had. Probably even now she had repented and was pleading for her Paul. I had it, the link in a chain of murder, the link I had been looking for since early Monday morning.

I finished the coffee and placed the cup in the saucer. It made a clear clinking sound in the quiet room.

"More?" Rebecca asked.

I shook my head. "Rebecca, you tricked me into coming here by mentioning Kay; the door is locked and the key is God knows where. Now what?"

She smiled tenderly.

"You killed them all," I said, "and you tried to kill Kay and me, too."

"Yes," she whispered. "Yes, yes, yes."

"Once you slipped and called him Roger," I said "Only once, but I wondered about it. You're just a weak woman, after all."

"Yes, yes."

"You wanted kids and a cottage and a television set, but you pretended that all you cared about was the wonderful world of sports. You didn't have a man like the other girls, and so you tried to triumph over the man-girls by being a champion swimmer, a golfer, or softball player—or an archer."

"Yes," she said.

"But when a man came along at last you were denied the fun and the pride of parading him before the other girls because your man was married. Your love affair had to be secret, but it was a love affair, and you wanted to keep it. You couldn't bear to share him with any other woman. He was the only man in your life, the first real man you ever had, and you had to be first with him as you are in everything else." I paused.

She watched me silently, a smile on her lips.

"But you learned you were not the only one," I said, "and if you couldn't be first you did not want to play. You found out about Louette and Melissa, and you killed them. You tried to kill Kay because you thought she was one of Roger's women, and you tried to kill me because you feared me. Isn't that it, Rebecca?"

She said it again, the one word. "Yes."

I pushed myself slowly up from the chair. She laughed softly, deep in her throat and backed away. Then she lifted the glass and tilted it until the tomato juice poured out onto the rug. It made an ugly, thick, splattering sound. When the glass was empty she tossed it into a corner, where it shattered very completely, and she looked at me with half-lidded eyes.

"You came here this morning," she said in a kind of high singsong voice. "You made advances. I struggled with you." She placed a hand in the neck of the nightgown, grasped it firmly with her strong brown fingers, and slowly tore the gown downward to her navel. "See? You tore my nightgown." With a lithe movement she slipped the robe and gown down over one smooth, strong shoulder and dug her fingernails into the flesh until I saw the drops of blood oozing out.

"You scratched me," she said from between her teeth. "You were brutal."

"I'm sorry as hell," I said, and took a step toward her. She smiled and backed away.

"But Eric saved me," she said.

I stood still.

She leaned slightly forward, her eyes bright. "Eric is waiting," she said softly. "He is just inside the kitchen door. I told him to wait there. When I call him, he will come. Then I'll start screaming—and when the people arrive they will find Eric crouching over you. He is a watchdog. Everyone in the building knows that. He was only defending his mistress."

I felt suddenly cold. "So that's why you got me here?"

"Of course. I must finish what I tried to do at Lovers' Lane last night. I did not plan on missing you, but the wind was stronger than I thought. But I was afraid the arrows had given me away, and that is why I called you when I returned home and told you that someone had attempted to harm me—I wanted to throw you off the track, to make you think that I was in danger, too—like Kay Canfield and yourself. I lied, of course, and then when you questioned me about the archers I knew that I must try once more, and not fail. I wasn't worried about the police, but I was afraid that you already knew too much, and that you would learn more."

She smiled at me, but something ugly was building up behind her eyes.

I said, "It was a *man* who called me about Lovers' Lane."

"Did that confuse you?"

"Yes."

"*I* couldn't call you," she said. "Could I? I went to a downtown hotel and telephoned your apartment to make certain that you were there. When you answered, I hung up. Then I paid a bellboy five dollars to call you for me. I told him it was a joke—the Lovers' Lane part. Wasn't that clever of me?"

"Very."

She gazed thoughtfully at the kitchen door.

I said quickly, "You shouldn't have tried to kill Kay. Roger meant nothing to her."

She turned her head slowly and looked at me, but I knew that her thoughts were now of the dog. "I only knew that Roger was going to see her," she said simply. "That was all that mattered to me."

"You must have been quite busy from Sunday afternoon until Monday morning," I said. I was also thinking of the dog, but thinking, too, of what I wanted to know.

"Yes," she said, smiling again, as if she were remembering a pleasant interlude. "It was very—exciting." She frowned and lifted a finger, like a teacher explaining a simple fact to a dull pupil. "You see, I warned Roger about his women. I didn't care about his wife. She meant nothing to him—he married her because of the Connors money. But I warned him about the others. He laughed at me. Then he stopped coming here to see me, and he was cool to me at the office. I—I couldn't stand it. I began to follow him. I learned that he was seeing Louette, and I saw him take that other woman, the blonde, to the hotel in East Grange, and I knew that he was seeing Kay Canfield. I told him what I knew. We quarreled, very bitterly. Then he kissed me and made promises. He—" Once more her eyes strayed to the kitchen door.

"And you believed his promises?" I said.

She looked at me, surprise in her eyes. "Of course. I wanted to believe him. He was all I had, my only love. Don't you see?"

"Yes," I said, "and so you killed him."

She nodded gloomily. "I had to. There was nothing left for me to do—after he broke his promise. Last Friday he went to Detroit to a manufacturers' convention, expecting, he said, to be gone until Monday or Tuesday. But he promised to come back Saturday night to see me, for dinner, here in my apartment. I was happy. I prepared everything he liked, and I waited for him. He never came. At one o'clock in the morning he phoned me. He was drunk, and I heard a woman laugh, some woman standing close to him. And there was music, and people laughing. He said he had been detained, unavoidably, and he could hardly keep from laughing as he said it—"

Her lips quivered and tears filled her eyes and I saw the bitter heartbreak in them.

"Never mind, Rebecca," I said gently. "Then what?"

"The—the woman, the one beside him, she said, 'Roger and I are terribly sorry, darling. Will you forgive us?' Then I heard them both laugh, and I—I hung up." She swung her head toward me and I saw that the heartbreak was still in her eyes, but a black rage was there, too. "Do you know what I felt then?"

"Yes," I said.

"I wish I drank," she said. "Maybe it would help."

"It wouldn't."

"I swore to him that I would kill them—the women—and then I would kill him."

"And Louette was first?"

She nodded. "It was all I had left—my promise to him."

"Do you want to tell me about it?"

"Yes, very much, but I don't want to bore you."

"You won't bore me," I said, thinking of Eric crouching inside the kitchen door.

She said, "I went to her apartment at three o'clock Sunday afternoon intending at first to talk to her and perhaps tell Don, her husband, what she was doing. But she was alone, packing her clothes, and I knew that I would do it then. I went to the kitchen and got a knife and—I did it. She was cheap—she deserved to die. Then I telephoned Detroit. I wanted to tell Roger what I had done, what I still intended to do. But the hotel told me that he had checked out at noon. I suspected that he wouldn't be coming home, not when he wasn't expected until Monday or Tuesday—oh, I knew my Roger. So I got another knife from the kitchen and left."

"And Melissa was next?"

"No, no. I went to Kay Canfield's house. *She* was to be next. But she was not at home. Her housekeeper told me that she expected her back around dinnertime. I parked across the street and waited. After a while Don and the little girl drove up, followed by you. I left. I remembered Roger's visits to the hotel in East Grange, and I drove there. I saw his car parked near the hotel. I waited a long time. I wanted the woman alone and I wanted Roger alone. At ten o'clock he came out of the hotel and walked away. I went inside. An old man was asleep at the desk. I looked at the register. The last signature was in Roger's handwriting. I don't remember the name he signed—"

"A. J. Holman and wife, Detroit," I said.

She raised her eyebrows. "Really? Holman was my mother's maiden name. I told Roger one time— You know quite a lot, don't you?"

"Quite a lot."

She smiled a secret smile. "But all I saw was the room number— Two-O-Six. It was very easy. Much easier than Louette. She had struggled a little. But Roger's blonde—such a puny, miserable creature." Her lip curled in contempt. "She just stared at me dumbly and watched the knife." She stopped talking and appeared to be lost in reverie.

I prodded her. "And then Roger?"

She started. "What?"

"Roger was next?"

"That was the hardest part, really," she said, her voice breaking a little. "And yet, it was—wonderful. I felt close to Roger then, closer than I ever felt before. There were just the two of us in the dawn, and I knew that no other woman would ever have him, not ever again. He was my Roger then, all mine, for the very first time." She began to cry silently. Her mouth worked and the tears crawled slowly down her face.

"Tell me," I said softly.

"I—I waited in the car. I made my plans. Then I got a tow rope from the trunk compartment of my car, and the handle of a jack. I put them on the seat beside me. Roger came back, carrying a paper sack, and went into the hotel. Almost immediately he came running out and I smiled to myself. I followed him to Cleveland, to your place, and I followed both of you back to East Grange, and then to Cleveland again. Then, when Roger left you, I drove behind him to his home. He left his car in the garage and when he came out he saw my car. I called to him. He got in beside me and laid his head on my lap. He cried like a little boy. He said, 'Help me, Rebecca, I'm in a terrible jam—'"

"And you helped him," I said grimly.

"I kissed him first," she said.

"Then what?"

"I struck him on the head with the jack handle. I—I thought he was dead. I drove out to the plant with the hazy idea of leaving him there, maybe on the front lawn, where everyone could see him. I—"

I said quickly, "You wanted it to appear that some Connors Electric employee had killed him? You knew he wasn't popular, that he had received threats. Is that it?"

"No, no," she said. "Not at all. I didn't think of that. I just wanted him to be seen, so that people, women, would know that he was not for them, ever. I wanted the world to know that Roger was mine at last. I couldn't tell people, of course, but *I* would know. It—it was something like winning a trophy. Roger's body was my trophy. I had won it, and no one else could have it."

"I see," I said.

"Oh, no, you don't," she said quickly. "There's more. As I drove past the plant gate I saw that the guard was not on duty, and I had a better idea. A lovely idea. I drove back to the corner of the plant where the flagpole is. I tied Roger's hands and feet and knotted the flagpole rope around his throat and I pulled him up very gently." She smiled at me. "I'm quite strong, you know."

"I know," I said. "And so you put your trophy up where everyone could see it—like the ones on your mantel?"

"Yes," she breathed. "That's what I wanted." She paused, and then said mockingly, "I suppose there is a name for it—the psychologists would probably say that it was exhibitionism, resulting from inferiority and frustration. Do you think so?"

"Yes, Rebecca," I said soberly.

She laughed softly. "They're wrong, you know. I knew what I was doing. I wanted to do it."

I said, "Then why didn't you just use the knife on Roger—like the others?"

She shuddered. "Oh, no. Not a knife, not for Roger. I didn't mind with the others, but for Roger it would have been—horrible. Besides, I threw the knife away outside of East Grange." She paused, and her eyes grew pensive. "But there was something I hated," she said sadly. "I thought he was dead, but he wasn't. He began to jerk on the rope. I looked up at him and I tried to talk to him. I tried to make it easier by telling him that I loved him, that I would always love him, that there would never be another man for me. And I told Roger that I was sorry, but I reminded him of my warning—"

She clasped her hands before her and gazed at some dream spot behind me. "I was very happy and I whispered to Roger to go to sleep and that someday I would be with him again. I think he heard me, because presently he stopped jerking and was quiet. I drove away then, past the gatehouse. The guard was still absent. At the corner I looked back, but it was too dark to see Roger. I loved him, but I am glad that he is dead. He is all mine now, sleeping, waiting for me." Her eyes grew tender and dreamy with love.

I heard my voice say, "I'm sorry, Rebecca. I'm sorry for you, and for Roger, and for Roger's wife."

She turned her head slowly to gaze at me. Her eyes were suddenly clear and calm and sane, and her mouth trembled. "I am sorry, too," she said brokenly. "In the morning, with the sun shining, I thought it had been a dream, a—a nightmare, and I—I—"

I winced at the naked fear and grief in her eyes.

"Did I do it?" she whispered. "*Did I?*"

"Yes," I said. "After Louette, the others were easy, weren't they?"

She nodded dumbly, her eyes wide with horror.

I held out a hand. "Come with me, Rebecca."

She took a step toward me. "Help me, Jim," she whispered.

The dog growled.

The horror and the fear end the grief died in Rebecca's eyes, and the murky ugliness was there once more. "Listen," she whispered, holding up a finger. "Eric is becoming impatient." She smiled at me, a cold, bright smile. "It was the arrows that gave me away?"

"No. Nothing gave you away until you told me that you had seen Kay at eight-thirty this morning—and until I remembered at last that an old man at the Hotel Avalon had told me that one of Roger's women was a 'big mixed blonde.' That fits only you. So Roger took you to the Avalon, too?"

"Twice," she said proudly, "on Sunday afternoons, when his wife thought he was playing golf." She ran a hand through her streaked hair. "If I were a cat, they'd call me calico. The sun does it."

Her gaze strayed slyly to the kitchen door. I saw the glint of madness in her eyes. "Do you have a gun?" she whispered.

"Yes."

"It won't help you. Eric is too quick."

I heard the dog's paws scratching the floor.

Rebecca said poutingly, "Don't you want to kiss me first?"

"No."

"Didn't you like it—the other time?"

"Very much."

"I haven't kissed many men," she said sadly. "Only Roger—and you."

"I'm grateful, Rebecca."

"Goodbye—Jim."

I started to speak, hoping to keep her talking, but it happened then, sooner than I'd expected.

She swung away from me screaming, "Eric! Eric!"

The dog leaped instantly into the room. I had a glimpse of a mass of gray-and-black fur covering a powerful wolf's body and I saw a pair of yellow eyes intent upon my throat. I jumped behind a chair, pushed it violently away from me. It toppled against the charging dog and he slithered sideways, his teeth bared. I clawed for the gun in my pocket, jerked it free as the dog leaped upward over the chair, and I fired two quick shots before he struck me.

I went down behind the chair, feeling the furry weight upon me and the digging of hind paws into my stomach. I heard the snapping click of his jaws and something hot and wet dripped over my face. I felt a cold nose snuffling eagerly and nuzzling for my throat. I jammed the barrel of the .38 against fur and I kept pulling the trigger until the muffled explosions were ended and there was only the *click, click, click* on empty shells. There was fur in my mouth and eyes and a snarling liquid gurgling in my ears. The hot wetness ran across my chin and I smelled gunpowder and burned hair as I rolled clear of the kicking and snapping mass of fur and blood.

Above me a voice kept screaming madly, "Kill him, Eric! Kill him!"

I kept on rolling until I hit the wall and I pushed myself to my feet. There was blood in my eyes and the room was a swirling red haze. Then a soft billowing cloud enveloped me and I felt silk and warm flesh beneath my hands and fingernails dug viciously at my face.

I lifted my arm and chopped the .38 down in a short arc. There was a soft thudding sound and Rebecca fell away from me, turning as she fell, the robe floating like a blue cloud around her. She hit the floor, limp and sprawling beneath the pale silk, and she lay still beside the feebly kicking body of the dog.

Somebody began to pound upon the door.

THE END

Crime classics from the master of hard-boiled fiction...

Peter Rabe

The Box / Journey Into Terror $19.95
"Few writers are Rabe's equal in the field of the hardboiled gangster story." —Bill Crider

Murder Me for Nickels / Benny Muscles In $19.95
"When he was rolling, crime fiction just didn't get any better."
—Ed Gorman, *Mystery Scene*

Blood on the Desert / A House in Naples $19.95
"He had few peers among noir writers of the 50s and 60s; he has few peers today."
—Bill Pronzini

My Lovely Executioner / Agreement to Kill $19.95
"Rabe can pack more into 10 words than most writers can do with a page."
—Keir Graff, *Booklist*

Anatomy of a Killer / A Shroud for Jesso $14.95
"*Anatomy of a Killer*...as cold and clean as a knife...a terrific book."
—Donald E. Westlake

The Silent Wall / The Return of Marvin Palaver $19.95
"A very worthy addition to Rabe's diverse and fascinating corpus."—*Booklist*

Kill the Boss Good-by / Mission for Vengeance $19.95
"*Kill the Boss Goodbye* is certainly one of my favorites." —Peter Rabe in an interview with George Tuttle

Dig My Grave Deep / The Out is Death / It's My Funeral $21.95
"It's Rabe's feel for the characters, even the minor ones, that lifts this out of the ordinary." —Dan Stumpf, *Mystery*File*

The Cut of the Whip / Bring Me Another Corpse / Time Enough to Die $21.95
"These books offer realistic psychology ... and delightfully deadpan humor."
—Keir Graff, *Booklist*

Girl in a Big Brass Bed / The Spy Who Was 3 Feet Tall / Code Name Gadget $21.95
"Decidedly different from other works of spy or espionage fiction."
—Alan Cranis, *Bookgasm*

War of the Dons / Black Mafia $19.95
"Treachery, double-crosses, and sudden violence crackles across the pages..."
—George Kelley

New Man in the House / Her High-School Lover $19.95
"Reads like a Machiavellian *Lolita*-esque story..."—Rick Ollerman

Stop This Man! / Tobruk $19.95
"There are shootouts, heists, bare knuckle brawls, double crosses, and a shining romance..."—Dave Wilde

In trade paperback from:
STARK HOUSE PRESS
1315 H Street, Eureka, CA 95501
griffinskye3@sbcglobal.net www.StarkHousePress.com

Available from your local bookstore, or order direct with a check or via our website.

www.ingramcontent.com/pod-product-compliance
Lightning Source LLC
LaVergne TN
LVHW021232080526
838199LV00088B/4315